SUPERSTITION

SUPERSTITION

KAREN ROBARDS

G. P. PUTNAM'S SONS

New York

||P

G. P. PUTNAM'S SONS
Publishers Since 1838
Published by the Penguin Group
Penguin Group (USA) Inc., 375 Hudson Street, New York, New York 10014, USA •
Penguin Group (Canada), 10 Alcorn Avenue, Toronto, Ontario M4V 3B2, Canada (a division
of Pearson Penguin Canada Inc.) • Penguin Books Ltd, 80 Strand, London WC2R 0RL,
England • Penguin Ireland, 25 St Stephen's Green, Dublin 2, Ireland (a division of Penguin
Books Ltd) • Penguin Group (Australia), 250 Camberwell Road, Camberwell, Victoria 3124,
Australia (a division of Pearson Australia Group Pty Ltd) • Penguin Books India Pvt Ltd,
11 Community Centre, Panchsheel Park, New Delhi–110 017, India • Penguin Group (NZ),
Cnr Airborne and Rosedale Roads, Albany, Auckland 1310, New Zealand (a division of Pearson
New Zealand Ltd) • Penguin Books (South Africa) (Pty) Ltd, 24 Sturdee Avenue,
Rosebank, Johannesburg 2196, South Africa

Penguin Books Ltd, Registered Offices:
80 Strand, London WC2R 0RL, England

ISBN 0-399-15280-6

Printed in the United States of America

This is a work of fiction. Names, characters, places, and incidents either are
the product of the author's imagination or are used fictitiously, and any
resemblance to actual persons, living or dead, businesses, companies,
events, or locales is entirely coincidental.

This book is for Jack, who is always so good,
with lots and lots of love.

ACKNOWLEDGMENTS

———

MANY THANKS TO ALL who made this book possible: Peter Robards, for indefatigable technical support, without which, frankly, I would be stumped more often than I care to admit; Christopher Robards, for invaluable critiques of my plot points and/or humor; Jack Robards, for always seeing the sunny side of everything; Doug Robards, who holds down the fort while I'm lost in my writing; Peggy Kennady, for research assistance and for always being there; Robert Gottlieb, agent extraordinaire; Christine Pepe, who is an absolutely wonderful editor; Lily Chin, for keeping track of everything; Stephanie Sorensen, for doing such a good job with publicity; Dan Harvey, who gave so unstintingly of his time while I was in New York; Sharon Gamboa and Paul Deykerhoff, for working so hard to sell my books; Leslie Gelbman, Kara Welsh, Claire Zion, and the entire Berkley group; and, of course, Carole Baron, with many thanks and much appreciation for her kind words and support.

SUPERSTITION

1

———

"GET AWAY FROM ME! Oh, God, somebody help me!" Tara Mitchell screamed, glancing over her shoulder as she fled through the dark house, her widened eyes seeking the blurry figure of the man chasing her.

She was slim. Tanned. Blonde. Seventeen years old. Blue jeans, T-shirt and long, straight hair: In other words, she pretty much had the average-American-teen thing going on. If it hadn't been for the terror contorting her face, she would have been more attractive than most. Beautiful, even.

"Lauren! Becky! Where are you?" Her cry was shrill with fear. It echoed off the walls, hung shivering in the air. No answer—except for a grunt from her pursuer. He was closing in on her now, narrowing the gap between them as she fled across the living room, the knife in his hand glinting ominously in the moonlight that filtered in through the sheer curtains that covered the French doors at the far end of the room. Tara reached the doors and yanked frantically at the handle. Nothing happened. They were locked.

"Help!" Glancing desperately behind her, she clawed at the dead bolt, her nails scraping audibly over the wood surrounding it. *"Somebody help me!"*

The doors didn't budge. Giving up, Tara whirled. Her face looked ashen in the gloom. A dark stain—blood?—spread like a slowly opening flower across the pale sleeve of her T-shirt. Her back flattened against the French doors as her eyes fixed fearfully on the man stalking her. He was no longer running. Instead, having cornered his prey, he was slowly closing in on her. The sharp pant of her breathing turned loud and harsh as she seemed to realize that she was out of options. Besides the locked doors at her back, the only way out of that room was through the pocket doors that led into the hall—the doors through which she had run moments earlier. They were ajar, admitting just enough light from some distant part of the house to enable her to see the outline of shapes—and to backlight her pursuer.

Big and menacing, he stood between her and the door. It was obvious to the most casual observer that she had no chance of getting past him. He clearly realized it, too, and savored the knowledge that he had her trapped. Murmuring under his breath, the words not quite audible, he talked to her. The knife waved slowly back and forth in front of him as if to leave her in no doubt about what was coming.

For the space of a couple heartbeats, her fear shimmered almost tangibly between them. Then Tara broke. Screaming, she bolted for the door, trying to dodge the man. He was too fast for her, jumping toward her, blocking her exit, catching her. His hand clamped around her arm, yanking her toward him. She screamed again, the sound an explosion of terror and despair.

The knife rose, sliced down . . .

Watching from the couch, where he had sat bolt upright after having been awakened by who-knew-what from what must have been his third involuntary catnap of the day, Joe Franconi broke out in a cold sweat.

"Like I told you before, pal, you're losing it," Brian Sawyer observed wryly from behind him. Brian was thirty-five years old, six feet tall, blond, and good looking. He was also dead. That being the case, Joe ignored his comment in favor of listening to the TV reporter, who was now alone on the screen. Violence, even televised violence, was no longer his thing. True crime might be the TV flavor of the month, but to someone like himself, who had seen way more than his fair share of crime in real life, it didn't qualify as entertainment. Didn't even come close.

So why was he still watching?

Good question.

Was it the reporter? She was maybe in her mid-twenties, a slim, good-looking redhead with big brown eyes and a cool, matter-of-fact manner. High cheekbones. Porcelain skin. Full, pouty red lips. Okay, she was hot. In his previous life, though, he'd never once felt the slightest stirring of interest in a talking head, no matter how attractive, and after considering the matter, he was glad to realize that his apathy toward media types remained unchanged.

It wasn't the reporter. But there was something—something . . .

Trying to figure out what that something was, Joe frowned and focused on what she was saying.

"Fifteen years ago this month, seventeen-year-old Tara Mitchell was brutally murdered in this house," the woman said. A shot of a white antebellum mansion, once grand, now sagging and neglected, filled the screen. Three stories, double porches, fluted pillars, overhung by huge live oaks, branches bearded with Spanish moss, leaves the delicate new green that meant spring. Since this was early May, the shot was recent. Or maybe it had been taken in another, past, spring. Whenever, something about the house nagged at him. Joe squinted at the screen, trying to figure out what it was. The shadows that had become an inescapable part of his life kept shifting in and out of the edges of his peripheral vision, which didn't help his concentration any. He ignored them. He was getting pretty good at that, just like he was getting good at ignoring Brian.

The redhead on TV was still talking: "Rebecca Iverson and Lauren Schultz vanished. No trace of them has ever been found. What you just saw was a reenactment of what authorities think may have occurred in the final few minutes of Tara's life, based on the evidence in the house. Earlier that night, Lauren's parents had taken the girls out to dinner to celebrate Lauren's seventeenth birthday, which was the following day. Becky, who was sixteen, and Tara were planning to sleep over at Lauren's house. Lauren's parents dropped them off at the house at around ten-fifteen that night, then went to check on Lauren's grandmother, who lived less than half a mile away. When they returned, it was twenty minutes until midnight. Andrea Schultz, Lauren's mother, describes what they found."

Another woman, mid-fifties maybe, with short, blond hair, faded blue eyes, and a face that had been deeply etched by time or grief, or some combination of the two, appeared on the screen. She was sitting on a deep gold couch in what appeared to be an upscale living room. A man of approximately the same age was sitting beside her. Gray-haired, a little paunchy, with the look of a solid citizen about him, he was holding her hand.

Mrs. Schultz spoke directly into the camera. "We noticed coming up the driveway that the only light on in the house was in the downstairs bathroom, but that didn't really strike us as odd. We just thought the girls had gone to bed a whole lot earlier than we had expected. We came in through the kitchen door. Mike—my husband—put away the doughnuts and milk we'd picked up for their breakfast, and I went on out into the center hall. When I turned on the light"—her voice shook—"I saw blood on the floor of the hall. Not a lot. A few drops about the size of quarters leading toward the living room. My first thought was that one of the girls had cut herself. I started calling Lauren, and I went into the living room and turned on the light. Tara was there on the couch. She was d-dead."

Mrs. Schultz stumbled over the last word, then stopped, her eyes filling with tears, her composure crumpling. The man—Joe assumed he was her husband—put his arm around her. Then they were gone, and the reporter was back on-screen, looking coolly out at him as she continued.

"Tara was stabbed twenty-seven times that night, with such violence that the knife went all the way through her body to penetrate the couch in at least a dozen places. Her hair had been hacked off to within an inch of her scalp. And her face had been damaged to the point where it was almost unrecognizable."

"Shit," Joe said, suddenly transfixed. He'd just figured out what had been nagging at him. That morning, he'd seen a photo of the murder house, which had been in the file he'd been reading through. The file on this case. The details were unforgettable.

"Thought you'd want to see this." Brian sounded smug. "You would have slept through it, too, if I hadn't dropped the remote on your lap. You can thank me anytime."

Joe couldn't help it. He glanced down and, sure enough, there was the remote, nestled between his jean-clad thighs, where it would have landed if it had been on his lap when he'd jarred awake. Had it been on his lap when he'd fallen asleep? Christ, he couldn't remember.

"Dave!" he yelled, at the same time doing his best to keep his focus on the screen. Dwelling on the state of his mental health was a good way to drive himself nuts—always supposing he wasn't there already. "Get in here! Stat!"

The program went to a commercial.

"Jeez, Joe, you might want to keep it down. You'll wake the kid," Dave O'Neil said as he appeared in the doorway between the kitchen and living room, his slow Southern drawl effectively robbing the words of any urgency that they might have been meant to impart. He'd attended his church's five P.M. Sunday service—almost all the local churches had one—but his church jacket and tie were long gone now. The sleeves of his white dress shirt were rolled up past his elbows, there was a blue-checked apron tied over his neat gray slacks, and he held a long-tined meat fork in one hand. Thirty-two years old, he was about five-eight, pudgy, and balding, with what was left of his dark brown hair grown long and slicked back in a mostly futile attempt to cover his scalp. Sweat beaded his forehead, and his round cheeks and the tip of his pug nose were rosy, making Joe think he'd just straightened up from checking on the progress of the roast chicken that at some time tonight was supposed to be dinner.

In an unfortunate triumph of hormones over common sense, Dave was infatuated with a high-maintenance divorcée whom he'd recently allowed to move into his house with him—the house he and Joe were currently in—along with her three bratty kids, two of whom thankfully had not yet been returned by their father, who had them for the weekend. The third, a toddler, had fallen asleep shortly after Joe had arrived as agreed at seven for Sunday-night dinner, which was still cooking, although it was now just after eight-fifteen. Amy Martinez, Dave's girlfriend and the children's mother, had run to the corner store for some forgotten essentials a good twenty minutes before, leaving Dave to hold down the fort. Not that Dave had a problem with that. In fact, since Joe had known him, Dave had never to his knowledge had a problem with anything. When Joe had been hired as Chief of Police of tiny Pawleys Island, South Carolina, five months earlier, Dave was already the Assistant Chief of the twelve-man force. Joe's first impression of him had been that he was a slow-moving, slow-talking, slow-thinking bumbler, but he'd kept him on, kept everyone on, just like he'd resisted making any but the most minor of changes in the way things had always been done, whether he'd found them irksome or not. The truth was, he'd needed the job too badly to risk making waves in those first few weeks, and now he found the Southern-fried culture of his department—in fact, the whole island—more soothing than crazy-making. And he'd developed a real fondness for Dave, who had done his best to make his new boss feel at home in what was, for the Jersey vice cop Joe had once been, an environment as alien as Mars.

"I forgot about the kid." Remembering the two-year-old's pre-bedtime antics, Joe was truly remorseful. Keeping his voice down, he pointed to the TV. "Listen to this."

The redhead was on again. She was standing in front of the house in which the crime had been committed, the Old Taylor Place, as it was called, if his memory served him correctly. The case she was profiling was the only unsolved homicide in the island's recorded history, and it had come to his attention for just that reason: The file had been the only one in its section. This time Joe didn't miss the signs that she was operating in what was now his territory: The pink and white of the overgrown oleanders that crowded around the wide front porch, the head-high clump of sweetgrass off to the reporter's left, the hot, bright blaze of the sun, and, underlying it all, the faint gurgle of the ocean that he had learned was the never-ending backdrop to life on Pawleys Island.

"The police investigated," she said, "but the crime has never been solved. Over the years, evidence has been lost or has deteriorated, witnesses' memories have blurred, and the detectives on the case have long since moved on to other, more urgent priorities. But the girls' families haven't forgotten. Their friends and neighbors haven't forgotten. They continue to wait for justice to be done. And some say that the girls are waiting for justice, too. They say that their spirits still linger here in the place where they were last seen alive—this once majestic Southern mansion at the heart of Pawleys Island."

A panoramic shot of the island taken from the air filled the screen. It was all there, the ingredients that made Pawleys Island a picture-perfect mini-paradise: the sapphire ocean, the sugar-white beaches, the swooping gulls and egrets wheeling through a cloudless azure sky, the deep green of near-tropical vegetation, the small, pastel bungalows clustered near the center of the island like sprinkles on a cupcake, the more imposing, multistoried summer "cottages" that predated air-conditioning—and, in many cases, the Civil War—hugging the outer edges along the waterfront. The best way to describe it, Joe had decided not long after taking up residence here, was as the place that time forgot.

As proof of what the island lifestyle did to a person, he had to remind himself less and less often lately that there wasn't anything wrong with that.

The redhead was still talking. "The Schultz family sold the property two years after Tara's murder and Lauren and Becky's disappearance. Since then, four other families have moved in—and moved out. None has stayed longer than six months. For the last three years, the house has been on the market. So far, no takers. Why? Because local folks say the house is haunted by the ghost of Tara Mitchell and, though their bodies have never been found and their families still cling to a last faint hope that they are alive and maybe one day they will come home, by the ghosts of Lauren Schultz and Rebecca Iverson, too."

The shot cut to a gleaming white kitchen. A fortyish man and woman and a pair of teenagers were sitting around a table in the middle of the room, looking earnestly out at the TV audience.

The redhead was standing beside the table, talking into the camera. "I'm here with Paul and Susan Cook and their children Ben, twelve, and Elizabeth, fourteen. The Cooks bought the house four years ago, and were the last family to live in it." She turned to the Cooks. "You only stayed in the house for six weeks, isn't that right? Can you tell us why you moved out?"

"It was Elizabeth," Paul Cook said. The camera zoomed in on the girl. She was petite, cute rather than pretty, with dark hair, a freckled nose, and braces. Her hair was pulled back off her face in a low ponytail, and she wore a white button-down blouse.

"They came into my bedroom at night," Elizabeth said in a small voice. "I know it was them now—those three girls. Back then, when it was happening, I didn't have a clue what was going on. See, I would be asleep, and then I would wake up and the room would be cold as ice and I knew I wasn't alone. At first I just kind of heard them, like their footsteps, like they were walking across the floor. And . . . and sometimes the closet door would open and close again, even though I always checked to make sure it was shut when I went to bed. A couple of times I heard them giggling. Once it felt like one of them sat down on the edge of the bed. I felt the mattress sink and kind of jiggle like a weight was on it, and this . . . *presence*." Elizabeth shuddered. "I kept telling my mom, but she said it was bad dreams and I should just close my eyes and go back to sleep. Then . . . then I saw them. All three of them. It was the middle of the night, and I heard them and opened my eyes, and they were standing around my bed, looking at me. Just these three kind of shapes, you know, like girls, only—not solid. They were real pale, with like these black holes where their faces should have been."

She stopped and took a deep breath, and as the camera pulled back, her mother could be seen reaching for her hand across the table.

"Elizabeth was afraid from our first night in that house," her mother said. Susan Cook was petite like her daughter, attractive, with dark-brown hair cut short and shaggy, and light-blue eyes. She was wearing a blue button-down shirt. "It got so bad that I had to lie down with her before she would go to sleep. We moved to Pawleys Island from Ohio, and when we bought the house, we didn't know anything about what had happened there. Later, we found out that Elizabeth's bedroom had once been Lauren Schultz's. But I didn't know that then, and when Elizabeth started telling me all that stuff about there being ghosts in her bedroom, I just thought she was being over-imaginative. The last night we spent in the house, it was about two o'clock in the morning and Elizabeth just started screaming. Paul and Ben were gone on a Boy Scout camping trip, so it was just Elizabeth and me. I jumped up and ran into her room to see what on earth was going on. She was still lying in her bed, just hysterical. I thought she'd had a bad dream, and I got in bed with her to calm her down—and then it started."

"What started?" the redhead asked.

"The bed started shaking," Mrs. Cook said. Her hand was still entwined with her daughter's. It was obvious from the whiteness of both their knuckles that they were gripping each other hard. "Elizabeth and I were both lying on her bed, and it just started shaking like there was an earthquake. It shook so hard that the mirror over the dresser rattled against the wall. And then the bed rose a couple of inches off the floor. It just *levitated*."

"And then we heard her scream," Elizabeth added.

"Heard who scream?" the redhead asked.

"Tara Mitchell," Elizabeth said with a shudder. "I know that's who it was. At least, I know now. She sounded like she was being stabbed to death right there and then."

Her mother shook her head. "We don't *know* it was Tara Mitchell. We don't know who screamed. Not really. All we know for sure is that it sounded like a young girl, and it was blood-curdling. And . . . and it seemed to come from the first floor of the house, right beneath Elizabeth's bedroom."

"Where Tara Mitchell was killed," Elizabeth said. She was wide-eyed and pale as she glanced at her mother, who squeezed her hand.

"We called the police," Mrs. Cook said. "They came. They searched the house. They didn't find anything. They were the first ones to tell us about what had happened there. They said we weren't the only ones to experience what we did. Apparently, everybody who'd lived in the house since the Schultzes had seen things. And heard the screams."

She broke off and took a deep breath.

"Anyway, that was it," Mr. Cook said. "They wouldn't stay in the house another night, either of them. We had to move out. They wouldn't even stay on the island, so we ended up in Charleston. We finally managed to sell the house, but we took a bath on it."

"I don't care," Mrs. Cook said. "There's no way we were spending another night in that house. I've never been so scared in my life. The place is haunted. There is just no other explanation I can come up with."

The redhead was back alone on the screen. "As you heard, the Cooks aren't the only people who have witnessed something unusual at the house."

The camera angle widened to show that she was once again outdoors, in front of a backdrop of what looked like old white clapboard siding. A pimply teenager in a baseball cap and a green T-shirt that read "Pro-Lawn" stood beside her.

"I have with me now Thomas Bell, who works for the lawn-care service responsible for keeping the grass cut." She moved the microphone she was holding in front of the kid's face. "Tom, would you tell us what you experienced here?"

The boy swallowed as the camera zeroed in for a close-up of his face. "Well, see, it was last August, a Thursday, and I was working later than usual so I could get all my lawns done because I wanted to take off early Friday. I got to the house, oh, about nine P.M. It was just starting to get dark out. This here's a good-sized property, about two acres with lots of trees, but I was working fast, so it only took me about forty-five minutes to get done. There wasn't a lot of light left by the time I was finishing up, but I could still see some, and I was just getting around the front of the garage with my Weed Eater when I saw somebody walking up the driveway toward me."

The camera pulled back so that the audience could see that the white clapboard wall was actually the front of a detached three-car garage. It looked old and rickety, and its closed gray auto doors seemed to sag.

"At first I couldn't see anything except, you know, that there was just somebody coming. The house was empty—it's been empty since I started cutting the grass—so I thought it was kind of funny that somebody would be walking up the driveway." The camera moved, panning down a narrow blacktop driveway that curled through a stand of shaggy pines toward the street in front of the house. "Then I saw that it was a girl, a teenager, with long, blond hair, wearing blue jeans and some kind of light shirt. She was walking toward me, just normal, you know, and I shut off the Weed Eater in case she wanted to say something to me and I wouldn't be able to hear her. She was real close when I did that, like right there beside that big pine."

He pointed to a towering evergreen about thirty feet from the garage.

"I swear, she seemed to look right at me. Then, while I was still looking at her, she just kind of . . . vanished. Like she dissolved into thin air or something." He swallowed. "It was weird."

The redhead asked, "Then what did you do, Tom?"

The kid gave a sheepish half-smile and dug his hands into his pockets. "I let out this big ole yell and threw my Weed Eater down and ran like my pants was on fire. I never did go back here, either. Not before today. Harvey—that's my boss—he had to send somebody to pick up my stuff."

"What do you think you saw, Tom?"

"There's no 'think' about it," the kid said. "People can laugh all they want—some of my friends think it's the funniest thing ever—but what I saw was a ghost. And I saw it as plain as I'm seeing you right now."

The redhead was suddenly in close-up again. She spoke directly into the camera.

"We asked Tom to look at six dozen photographs we put together of young, long-haired blonde girls, some of whom live in the vicinity of the Old Taylor Place now, to see if he could find the girl he saw, and he was indeed able to pick one out." The camera pulled back so that Tom Bell was once again sharing the screen with the redhead. They were still standing in front of the garage, and the kid was holding what looked like a 5x7 photo. "Is that picture you're holding of the girl you saw, Tom?"

"Yes, ma'am, it is," he said.

"You sure?" she asked.

"Sure as I am that I'm standing here talking to you."

"That's pretty sure," she said with a slight smile. The camera zoomed in on the photograph. The image of a pretty, smiling blonde teenager filled the screen. Joe remembered that picture from the case file, too. He felt a twinge of something—pity? Sorrow, maybe?—for the girl, who had no idea when that picture was taken that her life was getting ready to end shortly thereafter in a burst of horrifying violence.

"This is a picture of Tara Mitchell," the redhead said, as the camera continued to focus on the photograph. "It was taken just a week before she died."

A door slammed in the kitchen behind them, making both Joe and Dave jump and look around.

"I'm back," Amy called. The rattle of grocery bags underlined her words.

"Be with you in a minute, sweetie," Dave called back as the phone began to ring. There was an extension on the end table by the couch, and Joe grimaced as the shrill peal at his elbow momentarily drowned out the sound of the TV.

"Can somebody get that?" Amy yelled. "My hands are full."

"Yeah." Dave reached for the phone. "Hello?"

Joe tried to ignore the distractions as he concentrated on the program. The redhead was alone on-screen again, once more standing in front of the house.

"Tonight, we here at *Twenty-four Hours Investigates* are going to do our best to solve the mystery of what happened to those three innocent girls," she said.

"It's for you, Joe. The mayor." Dave handed him the phone.

Joe swallowed his exasperation.

"Hey, Vince," he said into the phone. "Vince" was Vincent Capra, like himself a former Jersey vice cop who had found unlikely sanctuary on this sweltering finger of sun-drenched sand. Vince had retired seven years before at age fifty-five, moving with his wife, Ann, into what had been their yearly vacation rental on the island. But the man's restless Jersey spirit had resisted being acclimated. Apparently congenitally immune to the "do it tomorrow, take it easy today" spirit of the island, Vince had bought up more cottages, which he rented out, stirred up the locals (well, as much as anyone could) to fight off a big hotel chain that had tried to move in, built his own exclusively low-key beach resort, and somehow, in the process, wound up mayor. When, in the aftermath of the disaster that had shattered his life, Joe had needed a place to lick his wounds, a couple of guys in the department had contacted Vince. And the rest, as the saying went, was history.

"You watching TV?" Vince bawled in his ear. Even after all this time, Joe noted absently, the man hadn't lost his Jersey accent.

"Yeah," Joe answered, his eyes on the screen.

"Channel eight? That crappy crime show?"

"Yeah."

The redhead was still talking. "The police investigation has stalled. Modern forensics applied to what little surviving evidence remains has failed to turn up any leads. This is the coldest of cold cases."

"That's us," Vince said, sounding outraged. "She's talking about us. That's the Old Taylor Place she's standing in front of there."

"Yeah, I know."

"I don't fucking believe this."

The woman kept talking: "But as those of you who are regular viewers know, we here at *Twenty-four Hours Investigates* never give up. Tonight we are going to go further than any investigator has ever gone before, beyond the realm of science, to seek the truth from the victims themselves." She took a deep breath, and seemed to swell with the importance of what she would say next. "We have enlisted famed psychic medium Leonora James to reach into the Great Beyond to try to contact Tara and Lauren and Becky themselves. At nine this evening, on this channel, Leonora James will conduct a séance, which we will televise live, right here inside this house where Tara was murdered and Lauren and Becky were last seen alive."

"Can they do that?" Vince asked. "Don't they need a permit or something?"

"Beats me," Joe replied. "You're the mayor."

"So that means I'm supposed to know everything?" Then, speaking to someone who was obviously in the room with him—Joe guessed it was Ann—Vince added in slightly muffled tones, "Get Lonnie Meltzer"—Meltzer was the city attorney—"on the phone, would you? Check if they need a permit."

"This is the first time that a séance has ever been conducted live on TV to try to contact the actual victims of a homicide to give them a chance to tell the living what happened and who did it," the redhead continued. "Our viewers at home will get the answers right along with us. Tonight, at nine P.M., just half an hour after the end of this program, we invite you to join us as Leonora James uses her psychic talents to try to finally solve this horrendous crime." The redhead gave a tight little smile. "I'm Nicole Sullivan, and I'll see you at nine tonight on this very special live edition of *Twenty-four Hours Investigates.*"

A commercial came on.

"Shit," Vince said. "This kind of publicity we do not need. A goddamn triple murder! With the high season coming up! What I want to know is, did they contact anybody? Did anybody know about this?"

The unspoken subtext was that if anybody did, they were toast.

"If it's going to be live at nine," Joe said, ignoring the thrust of Vince's questions as his still-not-quite-up-to-speed brain synapses finally made all the right connections, "they're here on the island. Right now."

It was eight-twenty-seven P.M.

"Jesus, Mary, and Joseph," Vince groaned. "Who needs this crap? Meet me over there. Ten minutes."

"Yeah."

Joe hung up and got to his feet. The remote control, forgotten, hit the hardwood floor with a clatter. Thus reminded of his other, larger, problem, he retrieved it, glancing cautiously around as he set it down by the phone. No sign of Brian. That was good. A good thing. He found himself looking at his reflection in the mirror that hung on the wall behind the couch. He was thirty-six now, still six-two, with thick, wavy black hair, but he was thin, thinner than he'd ever been, so thin that he was all muscle and bone and wearing jeans that were two waist sizes smaller than he'd once been accustomed to buying. His shoulders were still wide, but he was conscious of the jut of his collarbones against the soft cotton of the old Nets T-shirt he had on. His features were the same—thick, black brows above hazel eyes; long, straight nose; normal guy mouth—and he was even tan again, thanks to the island's near-constant sunshine. Tan enough so that the two jagged scars above his left temple were no longer so glaringly obvious. But his jaw was leaner, his cheekbones sharper. His eyes were deeper set, shadowed. He looked like an older, harder version of the self he remembered.

He looked haunted.

Hell, he thought with a grimace, he *was* haunted. Or something.

"So us being on TV's not popular with the mayor?" Dave asked, providing a welcome distraction.

"He seems to think it's bad for business. Come on, we better get over there." Joe turned away from the mirror and started moving toward the door. "Did anybody know about this?"

"Not me." Dave was moving right along with him.

"Supper'll be on the table in five minutes," Amy said, appearing in the doorway between the kitchen and the living room. She took in the situation at a glance and planted both fists on her hips. A slim, suspiciously buxom bottle blonde with some obvious mileage on her, she was wearing Daisy Dukes with a blue-checked shirt tied at her waist and high-heeled white mules. Deeply tanned and reasonably attractive, she narrowed her carefully made-up blue eyes at them. Given the fact that they were at that moment making tracks for the front door, which opened directly out of the living room, with the obvious intent of bypassing the kitchen, where she had until that moment been, Joe couldn't exactly blame her.

"You guys aren't taking off, are you?" she asked suspiciously.

Still some three feet shy of the door, Dave cast her a hunted look.

"Work," he said in a strangled tone.

"An emergency's just come up," Joe explained. With Amy's gaze drilling into him, Dave froze in that spot like a rabbit when a dog catches sight of it. Joe pushed him toward the door, then reached around him to open it.

"But what about supper?" Amy demanded.

"We'll be back," Dave called desperately over his shoulder as Joe shoved him out the screen door onto the small concrete stoop. "Thirty minutes, max. Keep it hot."

The screen door banged shut. Somewhere in the depths of the house, the kid started to wail.

"Like hell I will," Amy yelled after them. "You . . ."

Dave hunched his shoulders as her insults followed them to the street. It wasn't full dark yet, and there were still quite a few people out and about in this neighborhood of neat, close together ranch-style houses that had been constructed just after the conclusion of World War II. The kids running around the yard next door shooting each other with squirt guns appeared oblivious to Amy's X-rated suggestions as to what Dave could do to himself. But the older couple sitting in lawn chairs in the yard on the other side looked startled, and the woman bicycling with her little girl down the street threw Dave's house an outraged glance.

"Oh, man," Dave said, as the furious slam of his own front door cut off the tirade just as they reached Joe's cruiser, which was parked along the street out front. Having waved feebly at his lawn-sitting neighbors and grimaced an apology at the bicycling woman, Dave looked like a turtle doing its level best to withdraw into its shell as he walked around to the passenger-side door. Meeting Joe's gaze over the top of the car, he made a face. "Women. What're you gonna do?" Then, on a more glum note, he added, "You can bet your fanny she's going to make me pay through the nose for this."

Joe thought about telling his Number Two just how, in his opinion, his love life could be better managed, but he remembered in the nick of time that he was not in the doling-out-advice business. He didn't have the energy, for one thing, and anyway, it was easier just not to get involved. Dave was a big boy. He could figure it out for himself—or not.

Either way, as long as it didn't affect Dave's performance on the job, it was no concern of Joe's.

Then he noticed what his second-in-command was still wearing.

"Take off that damned apron, would you?" Joe growled as he opened his door. "And get in. We've got work to do."

Casting a quick look down at himself, Dave flushed and fumbled with the lopsided bow behind his back for a minute before finally managing to get the apron off. Crumpling it in one hand, he slid into the car. Joe was already inside. He had the car started and was staring out through the windshield grimly. As soon as Dave's butt hit the seat, Joe put the car in gear and took off, pulling out into the street and heading west.

With a quick glance over his shoulder, Dave tossed the apron into the backseat and reached for his seat belt. Clearly, he had no inkling that the despised garment landed right beside Brian, who was grinning broadly as he made himself at home in the backseat.

2

"BAD NEWS, NICK. Mama says she can't do it," Livvy said casually, as though she could conceive of no earthly reason why this should be a problem.

Having just burst in through the back screen door of her mother's rambling "cottage" on Pawleys Island, Nicole Sullivan stopped dead and stared at her older sister. Spoon in hand, Livvy was sitting at the rectangular oak table in the typically messy kitchen, digging into a quart of her favorite rocky road ice cream. The old paddle fan turned lazily overhead, adding a rhythmic *fwump-fwump* to the sounds of the TV show that Livvy was watching. The color scheme, the product of a 1960s-era redo, was harvest gold and avocado, with Formica countertops and linoleum flooring. Fluorescent tubes glowing through two frosted panels in the ceiling were designed to illuminate the cooking area, not to flatter. In other words, nobody ever looked like a beauty queen in this particular kitchen, but her sister's appearance was still enough to make Nicky do a double-take. Livvy's normally tan and slender face was as pale and round as a full moon. Usually a meticulously kept blond pageboy, her hair was twisted into a haphazard knot on top of her head and—unheard of in Nicky's experience with her sister—was showing at least two inches of dark roots. Beneath her hot-pink maternity top, Livvy's previously perky B-cups had engorged until they resembled twin Matterhorns. The table hid the rest of her, but Nicky had seen enough to realize that their mother hadn't exaggerated when she'd reported that Livvy, now seven months along and in the process of divorcing the scumbag who'd left her for another woman, looked like hell.

"What do you mean, she says she can't do it?" Nicky resumed her race toward the master bedroom, which was the only one on the ground floor. Livvy was a problem that could be dealt with later. Her quest for her mother, on the other hand, was urgent. "She *has* to do it. She's on live TV in *twenty-five minutes*."

"Nicky, thank God you're here." Karen Wise, one of *Twenty-four Hours Investigates*'s hapless production assistants, emerged from the adjacent den, where Nicky assumed she'd been holed up making more desperate phone calls of the "what do I do now?" variety, like the one with which she had summoned Nicky, who as a result had made a ninety-mile-per-hour detour on her way to the Old Taylor Place. Karen was twenty-two, with shiny black hair razored into one of those chic nape-length 'dos that required minimal styling, near black eyes, clear olive skin, and a slender, petite build that made her look like a teenager. Along with Mario García (hair and makeup), Karen had been sent to Twybee Cottage—all the old houses on Pawleys Island had names, and Nicky's mother's was called Twybee Cottage—to prep tonight's guest star for her upcoming appearance and then accompany her to the site. "She says she's changed her mind. She flat-out won't go."

"Oh, yes, she will," Nicky promised, sweeping past. *Difficult* and her mother were practically synonyms. Fortunately, over the years—her entire twenty-nine years of life, to be precise—she'd learned to cope.

"Ni*cole*! Sweetie! Oh, you look so *good*." Having obviously heard her coming, a man rushed out of her mother's bedroom, arms extended in welcome, a huge smile on his face as he blocked the hall under the pretext of greeting her. About five-ten, he was stoop-shouldered and thin except for a slight tendency toward a potbelly. Thanks to a lifetime's worth of careful sunscreen use—a must, as he'd reminded Nicky countless times, for fair-skinned people like themselves—his face was, at fifty-seven, as pale and unwrinkled as a baby's. He had thinning reddish hair; bright hazel eyes; an aquiline nose; big, puffy fish lips that he hated; and a soft, slightly receding jawline that he hated even more. He was meticulously dressed—for Pawley's Island—in madras Bermudas and a grass-green polo shirt, tucked in and belted. Which told Nicky that whatever position her mother was taking now, she had, at some time in the recent past, at least planned to show up for the gig that her daughter had put her less-than-stellar career as a TV journalist on *Twenty-four Hours Investigates* on the line to get for her.

"Get out of my way, Uncle Ham," Nicky said grimly, shouldering past her mother's brother—otherwise known as Hamilton Harrison James III—as he attempted to wrap her in a delaying bear hug. His face fell. "I know she's in there."

"But Nicky, she says she can't . . ."

The rest of Uncle Ham's protest was lost as Nicky reached her mother's bedroom and threw open the door. It was a large room, done in soft, feminine turquoises and creams, with a queen-sized four-poster bed nestled against the wall to the left of the door, and a big window that looked out over the ocean at the far end—the end Nicky was looking at as she came through the door. The turquoise silk curtains were closed against the encroaching night, making a nice backdrop for her plump, flame-haired mother, who was sitting in one of the two cream velvet tub chairs in front of the window, puffing into a brown paper lunch bag that Nicky's Uncle John—John Carter Nash, Uncle Ham's longtime partner—was holding over her mouth and nose.

"Mother!" Nicky glared at the pair of them. Not that Uncle John deserved the look particularly. It was obvious even without knowing any details where the problem lay.

"Nicky!" Her mother and Uncle John gasped in almost perfect unison as they jumped, dislodging the bag, and looked at her nervously.

"Your mother—she can't go on. Look at her—the very thought of it is giving her so much stress, she's hyperventilating," Uncle John said. Except for being just about the same age, he was Uncle Ham's polar opposite—bristly blond crew cut, deep tan complete with canyon-deep character lines, and the toned, muscular body of the fitness fanatic he was. He, too, was dressed as if he'd planned to go somewhere, in a snug black T-shirt and khaki slacks.

"She has to go on," Nicky said ruthlessly, pinning her mother with her eyes as she bore down on her.

Her mother—otherwise known as Leonora James, famed psychic medium, once star of her own short-lived television show, author of countless books on communicating with the Other Side, prized consultant to police departments and private clients, recipient of dozens of fan letters a month—gave a despairing wave of her perfectly manicured hands.

"Oh, Nicky, I think I have . . . I have psychic's block!" she wailed, her heavily mascaraed lashes batting like hummingbird wings as Nicky reached her side.

"What?" Nicky stared down at her mother, momentarily dumbfounded. This was new. Creative, even. Not that she had time to appreciate her mother's ingenuity. The clock was ticking, and this time it was her career that was on the line. Her eyes narrowed dangerously. "That is the most ridiculous thing I've ever heard. There is no such thing as psychic's block, and you know it! Anyway, even if there is such a thing and you do have it, I don't care. You have to be on the air in"—she glanced at her watch—"twenty-two minutes. So *deal with it*. We've got to go."

Nicky curled a hand around her mother's elbow, urging her—not all that gently—to her feet.

"You don't understand," Leonora wailed, resisting. Still clutching the paper bag, Uncle John made a distressed sound and fell back. With her peripheral vision, Nicky saw Uncle Ham watching from the bedroom doorway. Behind him, Karen and small, wiry Mario hovered, looking equal parts fascinated and worried.

Great, Nicky thought. She got to deal with her mother in front of an audience.

"I do understand," Nicky said, doing her best to keep her voice, expression, and body language within the realm of acceptable loving-daughter behavior as she once again asserted steady upward pressure on her mother's elbow in a futile effort to lift her from her chair. "You have stage fright. You'll get over it as soon as you're in front of the cameras."

Just as Nicky had expected, Leonora swelled with indignation even as she settled her backside deeper into the seat cushion.

"I do *not* have stage fright. I've never had stage fright in my life. I'm telling you, I have psychic's block."

Nicky repressed an urge to give vent to a few choice words. This was vintage Leonora; she should have expected it. It was clear that her mother had at one point intended to go on: She was dressed in her official psychic's garb of sparkly purple caftan, tons of gold jewelry, and enough black eyeliner and red lipstick to do Kelly Osbourne proud. But for some reason, the tide had turned: Despite Nicky's best efforts at heavy lifting, her mother was sticking to her chair as stubbornly as if she'd been glued to it. If there had been time, Nicky would have kicked herself. She should have known better than to mix family and job; the two were like oil and water. In fact, she had known better. But . . .

"Mother." Taking a deep breath, Nicky fought to stay calm. Her fingers did *not* tighten on her mother's arm. Her teeth did *not* clench. But there didn't seem to be anything she could do to keep the edge out of her voice. "If you don't show up, the show won't pay you. If the show doesn't pay you, you won't have the money to go in with Uncle Ham and open a restaurant. That's what you wanted, remember? When you called me and asked if I could get you just one quick little TV gig? Also, if you don't show up, I'll probably get fired, because using you was my suggestion. Then I'll move back to Pawleys Island and we can all live here, together, unemployed, drawing on our savings, until we all run out of money and the bank repossesses the house and we're out on the streets and we *starve*."

A beat passed in which two pairs of nearly identical brown eyes stared measuringly into each other.

"Don't exaggerate, Nicky. You've always had a tendency to exaggerate," her mother said at last.

This from the drama queen of the Western world. Nicky barely managed to keep herself from rolling her eyes, which, as she knew from bitter experience, would prove fatal to her chances of getting her mother to do anything at all except pitch a royal hissy fit.

"We have to *go*, Mama," Nicky said, tugging.

"I tell you, I can't do it." Leonora nevertheless allowed herself to be pulled to her feet at last. Underneath the drama queen was a pragmatist, after all. It had been eight years since Leonora's TV show had aired—and been cancelled. Her fame had been at its peak; since then, it had dwindled. With the stock market in the shape it was in and her book royalties having steadily decreased until they amounted to maybe a couple thousand dollars a year at best, Leonora's income was at its lowest tide ever. Luckily for the success of Nicky's efforts at mother-moving, even famous psychic mediums had to eat—and pay the bills. "Ever since I saw Harry"—Harry Stuyvescent was her third husband, a sensible man who was in all likelihood at that moment watching ESPN in the detached garage, well removed from all the hullabaloo—"walking toward me all covered in blood, I haven't been able to see a thing."

By "seeing" Harry, her mother meant that she'd had a vision of him, something that psychics were—fortunately or unfortunately, depending on the circumstances—prone to. Nicky remembered full well the semi-hysterical phone call she'd gotten just before Easter, during which her mother had insisted that her beloved Harry must be going to die in some horrible, tragic fashion in the near future, because she'd "seen" him all bloody.

Okay, so Leonora had "seen" her first husband—Neal Sullivan, Nicky and Livvy's dad—lying in their bed, soaking wet, in the weeks before he'd drowned in a boating accident. And she'd "seen" her second husband, Charlie Hill, on a beach in the Bahamas when he was supposed to be in New York on business—a little vacation he'd taken with his secretary that had ended up costing him his marriage to Leonora. Those visions did, perhaps, argue in favor of Leonora's ability to predict husband-related calamity. But . . .

"Harry got hit in the head with a golf ball two days later, Mother." Now she was talking through her teeth. Nicky deliberately tried to relax her jaw muscles, without success. "It wasn't even a bad injury. It was just a little bitty scalp wound that bled a lot. He didn't even need stitches. He walked home from the golf course and put a wet washrag on his head, and that was that. Remember, you called me that night and told me all about it. You were so relieved. You said it yourself: *That* was why you saw him covered in blood."

"But the *trauma*," Leonora wailed. "You don't understand how visions like that affect me. You've always been so insensitive, Nicky. If I hadn't watched you being born and you didn't look just like me, I'd say you couldn't possibly be my child."

This all-too-frequently-heard refrain of her childhood started pushing buttons Nicky had almost forgotten were there.

"I don't have time for this," Nicky muttered, exasperated, and began physically hauling her mother toward the door. Leonora outweighed her by a good fifty pounds and was perfectly capable of planting her feet and refusing to go if she truly didn't want to. That her mother allowed herself to be pulled along, with whatever degree of apparent reluctance, reaffirmed what Nicky had suspected all along. Her mother had never actually intended not to show up. Ever the diva, she'd just needed to feel as though all eyes were on her first. In other words, this was just another big scene in the ongoing star vehicle that was Leonora James's life.

"I can't just turn the gift on and off like it has a switch, you know," Leonora protested, even as Uncle Ham and Karen and Mario fell back out of their way. The hall was long and narrow, white-painted beadboard with a hardwood floor. Nicky, with Leonora in tow and John following, charged up it like the little engine that could. The others had to practically run to stay ahead of them, and as a result, they all popped out into the kitchen like spray shooting out of a shaken-up soda bottle.

"I know that, Mother."

Hanging on to her patience with grim determination, Nicky pulled Leonora across the kitchen while at the same time giving Livvy, who had paused with a heaping spoonful of Rocky Road halfway to her mouth to watch, a dagger look that dared her to say or do anything to further complicate the situation.

"The connection happens when it happens. I have to *feel* it. And I'm not—definitely not—feeling it tonight," Leonora continued.

This time Nicky couldn't stop herself: Her eyes rolled practically of their own accord. Her mother, fortunately, didn't see.

"So fake it, Mother," she said through her teeth.

The hissing sound that filled the sudden silence, Nicky realized, was Livvy sucking in air.

"Now you've done it," her sister said.

Even without looking at her mother, Nicky knew it was true: She could almost feel Leonora swelling. Her own shoulders tensed in anticipation.

"I . . . *never* . . . fake it," Leonora said awfully.

"Was that ever the wrong thing to say." Livvy sounded almost gleeful.

"Oh, finish your ice cream," Nicky snapped, shooting her sister a shut-up-or-die look. She was already regretting her words. Occasionally, on her mother's defunct TV show, the producers had used certain special effects to, as they put it, "enhance" the experience for the audience. It was still a sore spot with Leonora.

"I don't need to *fake it*. I would scorn to *fake it*. Only charlatans ever *fake it*."

"I know, Mother. I'm sorry, Mother. You know I didn't mean fake it as in *fake it*."

Nicky verbally backtracked as fast as she could while towing her sputtering mother out through the screen door, which banged shut behind them, and across the narrow covered porch that ran the length of the back of the house. Twybee Cottage was a beach house, and just like all the other oceanfront houses on Pawleys Island, it was situated so that its back faced the street, while its front looked out over the dunes and sea oats and sand toward the ever-changing sea. It was full dark now, and all she could see of the ocean was a glimmer of shiny black between the end of the crepe myrtle hedge that lined the driveway and the side of the house. The murmur of the waves was almost drowned out by tree frogs and crickets and other assorted nocturnal noise makers as they engaged in their nightly sing-along. The moon was a pale disk floating low in the inky black sky. It gave off just enough light to outline the pea gravel driveway in barely-there silver. The night was warm as it nearly always was on the island when it wasn't downright hot, but a sudden gust of cooler wind blew in just then from the ocean, smelling of seawater and heavy with the promise of rain. It rustled the glossy leaves of the giant magnolia that shaded the porch and parking area, and lifted Nicky's hair away from her face and neck. Her skin was damp with perspiration, and the quick rush of air felt wonderful. She lifted her face to it in automatic appreciation as the words *I'm home* flashed through her mind. In many ways, she loved this island better than any place on earth. Until she came back to it, she always forgot how deeply the sights and sounds and smells of her childhood were ingrained in her soul.

"Just what *did* you mean then, Nicole?"

When her mother called her Nicole in that tone, Nicky knew she was in deep doo-doo, which she had to admit that this time she deserved. Suggesting that anything about what Leonora did was faked was the verbal equivalent of waving a red flag in front of a bull. She *knew* that. The only explanation was that stress was disordering her senses. Fortunately, her rented black Honda Accord was parked right at the base of the porch steps. She was able to reach it and yank open the passenger-side door before Leonora got worked up enough to balk again.

"I meant just do what you usually do and don't worry about the outcome. Whatever happens happens. If you make contact, good. If you don't, well, that's the way it goes."

Leonora stopped dead to glare at her. "So then your program runs a solid hour of me just wandering around empty rooms, saying things like, 'Nope, nothing here,' 'Sorry, nothing's coming through,' 'I'm drawing a blank, folks, the ghosts seem to have better things to do than talk to me tonight'?"

Nicky had forgotten how well her mother did sarcasm.

"Come *on*, Mama." A tug got her mother moving again.

"You think I *want* to look like a fool on live TV?"

"You aren't going to look like a fool on live TV." Doing her best to stay in soothing mode, Nicky bundled her mother into the passenger seat, even bending to lift her feet from the ground and tuck them safely inside the footwell. "*If* nothing comes through tonight—and that's a very big if, and you know it—you'll look like the legitimate psychic you are, who tried and simply was unable to make contact with the Other Side." Nicky tried not to contemplate the prospect of televising a live séance at which not a single ghost showed up. Heads would roll. No, correction, *a* head would roll: hers. "Anyway, how many séances have you done? You could probably do one in your sleep. And you always get *something.*"

"Hundreds, probably," Leonora replied gloomily as Nicky pulled her seat belt around her, fastening it less as the loving gesture it looked like and more as a precaution against her mother attempting a quick exit. "People always ask for séances. They don't realize you don't need to do that to get in touch with those who've crossed over. Séances are basically just entertainment. At least, the kind people always picture—where a group sits around a table, holding hands with their eyes closed—is." Leonora sniffed dismissively. "That's not how I work."

"I know. So just do what you do and don't worry about it."

Closing the door on her mother, she rushed around to the driver's side before it could occur to Leonora that she could, theoretically, get back out again. Nicky was curling a hand around her door handle when the banging of the screen door caused her to glance up. Karen, cell phone to ear, was running down the back steps with Mario behind her, heading toward their own car, a rented blue Neon parked in front of the garage. Karen gave her a thumbs-up as she went past, which Nicky surreptitiously returned, knowing that if her mother saw her, there would be hell to pay. Another bang of the screen heralded the appearance on the porch of Uncle Ham and Uncle John, who also hurried down the steps toward, Nicky presumed, their car, which she also presumed was parked in its usual spot behind the long, low frame building that was the three-car garage, which was situated between the house and the street and went a long way toward making the back porch and the parking area totally private. Having been converted into an office/hangout spot for Harry, the garage hadn't housed cars for years. A third bang, and there was Livvy. The single quick glance that she spared her sister was enough to tell Nicky that the table had been kind. The boobs were nothing. Livvy's belly was so big that she looked like she'd swallowed the Goodyear Blimp. Whole.

"Nick! Nicky! I want to come. Wait for me," Livvy called, waving. She hurried along the porch, flip-flops smacking the wood floor.

On the verge of pretending she hadn't heard, Nicky had an inconvenient attack of conscience and glanced up again in time to watch as Livvy, in unflattering white stretch shorts that she wouldn't have been caught dead in seven months before, practically waddled down the steps. Once widely acclaimed as the prettiest girl on the island, her mother's perfect daughter with the perfect husband and the perfect life, Livvy had fallen far. No matter how urgent the circumstances and how sure she was that Livvy's presence could do nothing but complicate an already fraught situation, Nicky discovered that it just wasn't in her to hop in her car and leave her sister behind.

"Hurry up," Nicky growled in her sister's direction as the Neon sped past them down the driveway. She was still watching the flying pea gravel that was stirred up in the other car's wake when she was distracted by Uncle John and Uncle Ham, who appeared on either side of the Honda, opened the back doors, jumped inside, and slammed the doors shut again.

Just like that. Nicky was left with nothing to do but blink in surprised dismay at the closed door nearest her.

Life on the island: It always had been, and evidently always would be, a never-ending three-ring circus. How could she have forgotten what it was like? The constant commotion was the reason—one of the reasons—she rarely came home anymore. Unlike her nearest and dearest, she liked things calm and well organized and predictable.

"Wait a minute," she protested, sliding into the driver's seat and slewing around to look at her uninvited male relatives. Not that she didn't love and appreciate them, of course, but keeping tonight's chaos level as low as possible seemed the wise thing to do. Leonora all by herself was more turmoil than a full-blown hurricane. Add in her sister, and . . . "Livvy's coming. There's not going to be room."

The left rear door opened, cutting Nicky off.

"I'll scoot over." Uncle Ham suited the action to the words. Livvy plopped into the backseat in the spot he had vacated and closed the door. Given Livvy's bulk, the three of them were wedged in tighter than tennis balls in a vacuum-packed can, but they looked perfectly happy. Anyway, Nicky was out of time to argue.

They were due to be on the air, live, in eighteen minutes. Hopefully somebody—"Where's Marisa?" Nicky asked as she started the car—was setting up. Leonora liked things done in a certain way, and, as their family mantra put it, "If Leonora ain't happy, ain't nobody gonna be happy."

"She left," Leonora said coldly. As Marisa was her mother's longtime assistant and faithful friend who knew just how Leonora liked things done, such coldness could only mean that Marisa had failed to take Leonora's latest attack of diva-ism seriously enough.

"She went on over to the Old Taylor Place to start getting things ready," Uncle Ham explained. "We were supposed to bring Leonora with us."

Good job, guys, Nicky wanted to say as she threw the car into drive, but she didn't. Leonora, in her queen-of-the-universe mode, was more than a match for Uncle Ham—indeed, more than a match for most people.

"Seat belts."

Nicky threw the reminder over her shoulder as she swung around in a tight circle that barely missed clipping her mother's husband, who'd stepped outside the garage just at that moment, probably drawn by all the commotion. The doorway behind him backlit his tall, well-built form and thick, white hair. Sixty-seven years old, he had the calmest disposition of anyone Nicky had ever met. Which, she supposed, was how he had survived six years of marriage to her mother without going totally bonkers.

She waved at him through her window. As her front bumper whizzed by, a scant few inches from the knees of his dark-blue slacks, he simply smiled and waved back at her. Then he was out of sight, and Nicky sent the Honda rocketing down the driveway so fast that churned-up pea gravel peppered the closed windows.

"Whoa," Uncle John said, grabbing the back of her seat. "You might want to slow down a little, Nicky dear."

Nicky did, just long enough to turn left out of the driveway onto Atlantic Avenue, which was a straight stretch and practically deserted, and which she knew like the back of her hand—certainly well enough, under the circumstances, to speed as necessary. And it was necessary. She, personally, was sweaty and flush-faced and about as camera-ready as Livvy. And her mother still had to be powdered, pacified, and put into position. And . . .

She wasn't even going to let herself think about any more "ands" until she got there.

"She drives just like you," Uncle John said to Uncle Ham, in a tone that didn't make it sound like a compliment. "Like Leonora, too. It's that red hair. Does something to the brain, I'm convinced. Reckless as hell, the lot of you."

"Are not," Uncle Ham replied, verbally bristling. Nicky gritted her teeth. Like many couples who had been together a long time, these two had a tendency to bicker. And tonight, of all nights, she was not in the mood to listen.

"Quick-tempered, too," Uncle John continued, undeterred, as Nicky hung a quick left onto South Causeway Road. The headlights sliced through the darkness as she turned, flashing past an expanse of knee-high scrub grass, a stand of bristly palmettos, and a pair of glow-in-the-dark eyes of what was possibly either a possum or a raccoon. The Old Taylor Place was nestled on a high point on the bank of Salt Marsh Creek, facing the mainland. It was, perhaps, a ten-minute drive from Twybee Cottage—*if* she kept to the speed limit, which she had no intention, under the circumstances, of doing. The only thing worse than having no ghosts at the séance would be having the program start with endless seconds of dead air because both the host—that would be her—and the star—that would be her mother—were late. The mere thought made her shudder and stomp the gas. The houses that whizzed past as she accelerated were newer, cheaper construction that had been clustered in the middle of the island, away from the now ruinously expensive waterfront. Lights were on inside most of them, giving this area the look of a miniature Christmas village.

"Red hair's a genetic marker. For all kinds of things," Uncle John said. "Like decreased pain tolerance. I showed you that study. And—"

"That study was a load of crap." Uncle Ham's voice was tight. "All having red hair means is you've got red hair. Anyway, at least *our* hair color is natural."

"Are you saying mine isn't?"

"All I'm saying is this: Clairol's Summer Blonde."

"That package wasn't mine, and you know it."

Livvy, meanwhile, had apparently been struggling with her seat belt the entire time they'd been in the car.

"Ohmigod, it won't fasten." She let her breath out with a *whoosh* as though she'd been holding it. The sound was accompanied by the slither of the abandoned seat belt as it slid back into its moorings. "It doesn't fit. I'm a cow—a *whale*. I could just *die*."

Startled out of her preoccupation by the very real pain in Livvy's voice, Nicky glanced at her sister through the rearview mirror.

"For God's sake, Liv," she said. "You're seven months pregnant. You can't expect to be a size six."

"That . . . that *bitch* looks like she's about a size two," Livvy wailed.

"That bitch" was understood by everyone in the car to be the woman Livvy's husband had left her for.

"You're prettier than she is," Uncle Ham said, wrapping a comforting arm around her shoulders. "Even . . ."

He broke off, apparently realizing the infelicitousness of what he'd been about to say. Livvy, no fool despite being supersized, supersensitive, and supercharged with hormones at present, didn't seem to have any trouble filling in the blank.

"Even if I'm *huge?*" she guessed, on a note of quivering despair.

"You're not huge," Uncle Ham, Uncle John, and Nicky all said in instant, loyal unison.

"I am, *I am.*" Livvy burst into noisy tears. "I'm big as a damned *stadium,* and you all know it."

A stop sign emerged out of the darkness. Nicky saw it, and the car proceeding through the crossroad it heralded just in time. She hit the brakes. The Honda screeched to a shuddering stop.

"We want to find ghosts, not be them," Uncle John said after the briefest of moments, raising his voice to be heard over the sound of Livvy's sobs. Ignoring him, and her sister, and everything except the necessity of making it to their destination in time, Nicky waited for the intersection to clear and then hung a left. They were almost there. . . .

"I don't know how I let you talk me into this," Leonora moaned to Nicky, seemingly oblivious to the hubbub in the backseat. "I can't do a séance if I can't *connect.*"

Her hands were sliding up and down her arms as if she was cold. Recognizing this from experience as a bad sign, Nicky started to feel the first real stirrings of alarm. Maybe there was more to her mother's reluctance than sheer bloody-mindedness. Maybe she *would* get on camera and freeze. . . .

"You can do this, Mama. You have a true gift, remember?" Nicky did her best to stifle her own budding panic and keep her voice calm and reassuring—which wasn't exactly easy, given the fact that her sister was having a meltdown in the backseat, her uncles were arguing about which one of them was most to blame for upsetting her, and her mother was giving every indication that she was going to unbuckle her seat belt and bolt at the next stop sign.

Not that Nicky meant to stop for it unless she absolutely had to. Number one, *they were so late.* Number two, she'd dealt with her mother's histrionics before, and she was perfectly well aware of the lengths to which Leonora was willing to go.

If these *were* just histrionics. Which, if she was really, really lucky, they were. Once a camera was on her, Leonora would be fine. Nicky knew how her mother worked—and, knowing she deserved every bit of what she was getting, she reflected dismally. She'd been a fool to let her mother anywhere near anything that involved her career. But *Twenty-four Hours Investigates* had been tanking in the ratings, the producers had been desperately casting about for some way to provide a big boost in the numbers for the May sweeps, and her mother had called to ask Nicky if she could use her influence ("What influence?" Nicky had wanted to snort; Nicky's show was about a one-point drop in the ratings from being cancelled, and she herself was one of three not all that highly regarded on-air reporters) to get her mother a well-paying, short-lived TV gig. The timing of these three occurrences had been close, so close that Nicky had had a eureka moment and connected them.

At the time, it had seemed like fate.

Now she recognized it as the recipe for disaster that it was.

Too damned late.

"Nicky. I haven't even had a visit from Dorothy. Not in ages," Leonora confided in a hushed tone that riveted Nicky's attention faster than a shout would have done.

The glance she gave her mother was truly alarmed. Dorothy was Leonora's Spirit Guide, and for as long as Nicky had been on this earth, Dorothy had been as constant a presence in her mother's life as Nicky herself and Livvy and Uncle Ham.

"Mother. Are you telling me the truth?"

"Pinky swear."

Ohmigod. Pinky swear, that precious holdover from childhood. The pledge of truth that she, Livvy, and Leonora never violated. Pinky swears were never taken lightly. From one James woman to another, it meant that whoever said it was telling the absolute, total truth.

"Don't panic," Nicky said aloud, as much to herself as to her mother, as visions of Geraldo Rivera and Al Capone's empty vault danced in her brain. Leonora, naturally, took that as a cue to panic. Digging her nails into her wrists so deeply that dark crescents formed around them, she dropped her head back against the seat and started panting like a very large dog in a very hot place.

Like hell? The way she was feeling right now, Nicky wouldn't take any bets against it. She should have flown in from Chicago days ago, should've known that trusting an airline to get her to her destination within any reasonable definition of "on time" was trusting too much, especially when she *really had to be there,* should've anticipated the bad weather that had caused the delay that had caused her and her crew to have to rent cars and drive from Atlanta, which had gotten them to their hotel on the mainland less than two hours ago—just in time to catch part of the regularly scheduled *Twenty-four Hours Investigates* for which Nicky had done the big (taped) setup for tonight's special.

Live at nine—or not.

Nicky shuddered.

"Leonora, you're going to hyperventilate." Having apparently been monitoring the action in the front seat at the same time as he'd been contributing to the turbulence in the back, Uncle John leaned forward and passed Leonora a small paper bag. If it wasn't the one he'd been holding over her mouth and nose in the house, it was its twin.

"Remember," he said. "Just put it over your nose and mouth and breathe normally. Like I showed you in the house."

Leonora grabbed it, pressed it to her face, and started breathing into it.

"Inhale. Exhale. Inhale. Exhale . . ." John encouraged her.

"Oh, God, I can't let anybody see me like this," Livvy wailed. "I look like Moby Dick. I know I wanted to come, but . . . Nick, you've got to take me home."

Nicky was willing to bet that working for *60 Minutes* was never like this.

"Livvy—" Nicky broke off as the car crested a rise and the Old Taylor Place came into view. To her left, the western fringe of the island was swampy near-jungle. Tall marsh grass crowded close to the road, and the still waters of the creek beyond it gleamed faintly in the moonlight. To her right, the higher ground on which the houses were built was shaded by a thick canopy of live oaks, pines, and cypress. Unlike the pretty pastel bungalows in the center of the island where the year-round residents tended to live, the houses along Salt Marsh Creek were mostly big, older ones that predated the turn of the century. At present, most of them were still empty, awaiting their summer residents. In other words, except for the Honda's headlights, the area should have been as dark as the inside of a cave.

But it wasn't. The Old Taylor Place was lit up like the Washington Monument. Every light inside the house seemed to be turned on. Bright klieg lights illuminated the exterior. Half a dozen vehicles were parked in the driveway.

Nicky felt a small lessening of tension as she realized that everything looked just as it should for the upcoming broadcast—until she noticed the pair of police cars, blue lights flashing, that were parked on the shoulder in front of the house.

She was just frowning at them when her cell phone, which she had stowed in the console between the seats, started to ring.

"Yes?" she said into it, shooting an encouraging smile at her mother, who had lowered the paper bag and was now, with a cautious expression on her face, seemingly trying to breathe without it.

"Nicky, you're not going to believe this," Karen whispered over the phone. "They're shutting us down."

3

B RIAN WAS GONE BY the time they got to the Old Taylor Place. That
made Joe feel marginally—but not a whole hell of a lot—better. It had
been almost two years now. He was beginning to think—fear—that Brian
might be a permanent part of his existence.

The ramifications of which he didn't even want to think about.

"They don't have a permit. I told 'em to pack it up." Vince greeted Joe
and Dave on the porch with that information, one hand in his pocket jingling
his keys, his shrewd little black eyes snapping with satisfaction. A massive
man, he was about six-four and nearly as wide, with huge shoulders, chest,
and belly atop oddly short legs. He had a thick head of salt-and-pepper hair,
pugnacious features, and a lot of trouble just being still. Even after years
spent in this motivation-sapping climate, he still brimmed with the kind of
raw vigor and nervous energy that was as foreign to South Carolina as kudzu
was to the North. At the moment, he was wearing a coat and tie and dress
slacks, which made Joe think that—devout Catholic that Vince was—he'd
been on his way to or from Mass. Or maybe not. Vince wasn't a big believer
in the island's casual dress code under any circumstance.

Which was one reason Joe had pulled on the spare uniform shirt he always
kept in his trunk before heading up the yard to the porch. Anyway, he kind of

liked that uniform shirt: short sleeves, gray, with a big, shiny silver badge pinned to the breast pocket. In it, he felt like Andy Griffith.

"So they did need one?" Joe asked without much real concern. On the way over, it had occurred to him that the botched investigation, if indeed the investigation had been botched, hadn't happened on his watch. What had or had not been done fifteen years ago was not his problem. Therefore, whether the program was broadcast or not didn't particularly matter to him; he was simply on board with whatever Vince wanted. It was easier that way. Getting all worked up over things that didn't really matter used to be part of his personality, but it wasn't any longer. He'd left that part of himself, along with lots of other things, behind in Jersey.

"Hey, I'm the mayor. If I say they need a permit, they need a permit," Vince said, his keys jangling harder.

Joe took that to mean that nobody Vince had been able to reach actually knew whether or not a permit was needed for this type of thing.

"Works for me," Joe said.

The last vestige of twilight had faded away long since. Beyond the perimeter of the brightly lit house, the night was dark and quiet. A breeze blew in from the ocean; it smelled of the sea, of course, and also just faintly of flowers. The front door of the Old Taylor Place stood open, although the screen door was shut. Through the faint blur of its mesh, he could see into the wide entry hall all the way back to the curving staircase and into part of what he took to be the living room. Twelve-foot ceilings, dark wood paneling extending three-quarters of the way up the walls, gloomy shadows everywhere. Except for a few folding chairs and the TV crew's equipment, as much of the house as he could see was bare of furniture. A bright light had been set up in a corner of the living room behind some kind of translucent white screen that was intended, he guessed, to diffuse its intensity. A group of people—not locals, as he could tell from their clothes, which, being mostly black and mostly business-friendly, were about as far from island mufti as it was possible to get—huddled together not far from the light. He could see only about a third of them, but it was obvious that they were conferring frantically about something, although in hushed words that he couldn't actually overhear.

Three guesses as to what it was. They weren't likely to be pleased about having the plug pulled on their program.

"Uh-oh, we got one on the move," Dave warned under his breath.

A young woman with short, black hair had just detached herself from the group in the living room to move into the hall. She was frowning as she talked into a cell phone. Automatically, Joe registered that she was attractive, bone-thin in a white blouse, black skirt, and flat shoes, and not really his type. She was also headed their way.

"O'Neil. Go see what they're up to in there." Vince was charting the young woman's progress, too. He glanced at Dave and jerked his head toward the house. "They're supposed to be shutting things down."

Dave nodded and headed into the house. The young woman, still talking on her cell phone, reached the screen door at the same time he did. Ever the gentleman, Dave ended up holding the door open for her. She shot him a sidelong glance rife with disdain as she passed through it onto the porch.

No gratitude there.

Just then, the sound of quick footsteps on the porch stairs made Joe glance around. His eyes widened slightly as he beheld the redheaded TV reporter ascending them two at a time. A motley collection of newcomers straggled across the lawn in her wake, all clearly headed toward the house. Behind them was the trio of klieg lights that had been set up about thirty feet from the house to light the exterior, causing their shadows to elongate until they stretched across the overgrown grass, almost all the way to the thicket of oleanders that hugged the porch. Joe beheld an older woman, redheaded like the reporter, in a long, flowing purple dress, leaning heavily on the arm of a short but muscular blond guy. A little behind them, another man, less bulky but also less toned, had his hand around the elbow of a heavily pregnant lady who seemed to be huffing and puffing with every step. But it was the reporter who was nearest—and closing fast, he discovered as his gaze snapped back to her. She was pencil-slim—slimmer than she had looked on TV—in a figure-hugging black skirt suit that made her absolutely killer legs look about two miles long, and tall heels that clicked loudly on the wood. Her shoulder-length hair looked dark in the shadows at the top of the steps, but then she gained the porch and strode into the glow of the klieg lights. He saw that her hair was indeed the true deep red it had appeared on TV. Earlier, though, it had hung straight to her shoulders, all smooth and shiny like a shampoo ad. Now it was disheveled, with one side pushed behind an ear and bangs straggling over her forehead. Her cheeks had acquired a hectic flush, and her previously luscious mouth appeared hard and tight. Her eyes narrowed as they focused on him and Vince, her lips pursed until they were downright thin, and she said something into the cell phone that she had pressed to her face.

She must have felt him looking at her, because she glanced up just then and their gazes collided. Joe felt a stirring of slightly bemused interest as it occurred to him that she *was* his type—hell, hot-looking redheads were probably everybody's type—except for the fact that at the moment, she was clearly royally ticked off and itching to take it out on some poor, unfortunate soul. Like him? Probably. It had been one of those days.

Reaching them, she snapped her cell phone shut. An echoing snap to his left made him glance in that direction. The black-haired woman was about ten feet away and on the move toward them, her now-closed cell phone in hand.

It was obvious that the two had been talking, and it wasn't much of a stretch to guess what they'd been talking about.

Good thing for Vince they weren't holding any popularity contests out at the Old Taylor Place tonight.

"Nicky." The black-haired woman greeted the reporter with obvious relief, scooting past Joe and Vince and shooting them a venomous look in the process.

"Got it covered." Nicky dropped her cell phone into a side pocket of the purse slung over her shoulder as her gaze slid between him and Vince.

"Mayor Capra?" she asked crisply.

"That's me," Vince said, squaring up to her. Her eyes zeroed in on him, narrowed still more.

Right, Joe reminded himself. This was Vince's call. Vince's problem. *You go, Vince,* he thought, and took a small sideways step out of the line of fire.

If he was any judge of human nature—and, once upon a time, he had prided himself on that—this was going to be something like the clash of the Titans.

"Nicole Sullivan." Her tone was brusque. She stuck out her hand and shook Vince's. Joe wasn't exactly sure whether Vince had cooperated, but whether he had or not, the result was the same: handshake accomplished. The woman was obviously a go-getter, and what she was used to getting was her own way. *"Twenty-four Hours Investigates.* I understand there's some question about whether or not we have the necessary permission to film here?"

"Yes, ma'am," Vince said, going for polite but firm. "Or rather, no, ma'am, there's no question. You can't film here. You don't have a permit."

Nicky smiled. Or more accurately, Joe thought with a bystander's objective appreciation, bared her teeth. Very nice, straight, white teeth they were, too.

"Actually, we don't need a permit. All we need is the permission of the homeowner, which we have, in writing. Would you care to see it?" She unslung her purse from her shoulder.

"No, ma'am, I wouldn't. The bottom line is, you don't have a permit. That being the case, I'm going to have to ask you and your people here to leave." Vince held his ground as she unzipped her purse and plunged a hand inside.

"Here." Nicky thrust a piece of paper at him. "Written permission from the homeowner. We checked, believe me, and that's all we need."

Vince took the paper and scowled down at it.

"Hey, Vince," the blond guy called by way of a casual greeting as he and the older woman reached the top of the porch stairs and started toward them.

Vince—who knew everyone on the island while, so far, Joe was basically acquainted with the guys in his department, their families, the city council, and various assorted lawbreakers—looked up. Joe watched him focus and frown.

"John. Mrs. Stuyvescent." Vince nodded at the newcomers perfunctorily. "I hate to tell you to turn right back around, but I'm going to have to ask you to leave."

"Nobody's leaving," Nicky said through her teeth, snatching the paper from Vince and thrusting it back into the depths of her purse. "We're on the air, live, in"—she glanced down at her watch—"oh, God, eight minutes."

"Without a permit . . ." Vince began, shaking his head in pseudo-sorrow.

"Stuff the permit." Nicky's eyes shot sparks at him. "We don't need one."

"You cuttin' it close, girl." The chiding voice, a woman's, interrupted before the exchange could grow truly heated. It came from behind Joe. Three people—clearly, they'd come from inside the house—rushed past him. A small, wiry, Hispanic-looking man, a tall black woman with close-cropped hair, and a tiny little blonde with a waist-length ponytail and huge platform shoes surrounded Nicky. They wielded, respectively, a hairbrush, lipstick, and a giant pink powder puff. The blonde had what looked like a translucent overnight case hanging from her arm; it was full of makeup. Joe watched with surprised interest as the trio swooped around Nicky like hyperactive fairy godmothers, everybody working on her at once.

"I know," Nicky replied. "I had to . . ."

"Quit talking and purse your lips."

Nicky pursed. A thin brush—lipstick—was whisked over her mouth. Joe watched in fascination as the full, pouty contours he had admired on the screen earlier were restored.

"Hold on there." Vince raised his voice to be heard over the hubbub. His face, Joe noted with interest, was becoming flushed. "There's no point in all this, because there's not going to be any TV show. Not here, not tonight."

If anybody was listening, they could have fooled Joe. Even as the guy used his brush to flip up the ends of her hair, Nicky pulled Mrs. Stuyvescent, who released John with seeming reluctance and murmured something that sounded like a panicky *Nicky, no* into the circle.

"Guys, I think a little powder here," Nicky said. "And . . . should we touch up the lipstick?"

"Oh, definitely."

Mrs. Stuyvescent was attacked by the same giant puff that had just dusted Nicky's face as the fairy godmothers went to feverish work on her, too.

"The show is cancelled," Vince announced loudly, to no visible effect. "*Cancelled,* do you hear?"

"If I were you, Vince, I'd give up on trying to interfere with Leonora's big TV comeback," John said, his eyes, like everyone else's, on the women. "You can't stop a runaway train. Anyway, why would you want to?"

Leonora? Leonora James? For Joe, the other shoe dropped as he figured out that Mrs. Stuyvescent, who was at that moment cringing in the midst of the makeover frenzy, must be the famous psychic who was supposed to conduct the séance that was supposed to air live on Channel 8 in just a few minutes.

"We don't need to have the whole country thinking about us in terms of a triple murder, especially with the high season coming up," Vince growled. "It's bad publicity."

"There's no such thing as bad publicity," John said.

"Hold your breath!" This hardly adequate warning came from one of the fairy godmothers, and it was followed almost immediately by a hissing sound as an aerosol can discharged its contents over the two women at the epicenter of all the activity. To his horror, Joe found himself engulfed in a drifting cloud of hair spray. He accidentally breathed in, choked, and started coughing even as he backed up out of the way.

"Stop . . . this." Vince was coughing too, and waving his hand to clear the vapors. "Damn it, how many times do I have to say it: There's not going to be any TV show broadcast from here tonight."

"Choo-choo," John murmured.

Vince's face turned an interesting shade of magenta. He shot John a fulminating look. "Folks, *it ain't happening.*"

For all the reaction that got, he might as well have been talking to himself. The screen door opened. A short, chubby, sixtysomething woman with gray hair curled close to her head hurried through it. As she bustled toward the party, Joe saw that she was wearing an ankle-length flowery skirt and a pale pink sweater set and looked like somebody's nice old granny. Behind her, carefully holding the door so it wouldn't bang shut, came Dave.

"Oh, thank goodness, Marisa," Nicky greeted the newcomer. Meanwhile, Joe lifted a questioning eyebrow at Dave. He shrugged, looking sheepish. Joe took that to mean that he'd had about as much luck as Vince. Having apparently come to the same conclusion, Vince, who was also looking at Dave, audibly ground his teeth.

"Everything's all set," Marisa said to Nicky with a quick smile. Then she switched her attention to Leonora and her voice turned brisk. "All right, let's get you hooked up. I've got good feelings about tonight."

"You don't have a permit to film here," Vince roared. With his face red and his eyes bulging, he looked like a balloon that was about to pop.

Other than glancing his way for the briefest of seconds, none of the TV crowd paid him any attention whatsoever. Their focus was on Leonora—a fluff of her hair, a flick of lipstick, a tug to straighten her dress. Marisa curled a hand around her arm. Leonora clutched at Nicky's hand with seeming desperation.

"I just don't think I can do it," Leonora moaned.

"She'll be fine," Marisa said to Nicky in a comforting tone. For her part, Nicky looked less than reassured. "Nothing but preshow nerves."

"I'm not feeling a connection." Leonora looked wildly around the group. "Does *no one* understand?" Her lips parted, and she started breathing hard through them. "I'm blocked. I'm *blocked.*"

"Leonora. Here." John stepped forward, produced another folded brown paper lunch bag from his pocket, snapped it open, and pressed it into Leonora's hand. She glanced down, seemed to register what it was, then clapped it over her mouth and nose without relinquishing her grip on Nicky's hand.

"Just do your best," Nicky said, as calmly as though there was nothing at all surprising about this really weird behavior. If her hands hadn't curled into fists at her sides as she spoke, Joe might have believed that she actually *was* calm.

Leonora's reply was incomprehensible through the bag, the sides of which were expanding and contracting as she breathed into it. Marisa tugged on her arm. She didn't budge.

Nicky continued in the same soothing tone: "Remember when you found that little girl who was lost in the woods? Remember when you saw that there were survivors after that boat capsized? They were saved because of you. This is nothing compared to that. Just one more day at the office."

Leonora shuddered and shook her head.

"All right, you're gonna make me do something I don't want to do," Vince threatened loudly.

"Is there somewhere I can sit down?" The pregnant lady—she was blonde, thirtyish, and hugely, scarily with child—trudged along the porch toward them. Flip-flops flapping, wearing micro-sized white shorts and a crotch-length pink tent, she was leaning heavily on the supporting arm of the other guy, whom Joe saw also had red hair. She was breathing hard, perspiring. Her face was flushed and blotchy, and her eyes looked all red and puffy, like she had bad allergies or something.

"You okay?" Nicky asked as she reached them, her voice sounding strained for the first time.

"Fine," the pregnant woman answered, pressing a hand to her belly. "For an *elephant.*"

Then her mouth trembled, her eyes welled over with tears, and she clapped both hands to her face. Joe realized, to his horror, that she was crying.

For the first time that night, he felt a stab of real alarm. Weeping pregnant women were *way* outside his comfort zone. If he hadn't already been backed up all the way to the porch rail, he would have retreated. As it was, he was stuck. Beside him, Dave and Vince looked as horrified as he felt.

"Don't cry, Liv," Nicky said, patting the pregnant woman awkwardly on the arm. "He's not worth it."

"I *know.*" The pregnant lady—Liv—sobbed through her fingers. "I c-can't help it."

"It's the hormones," Leonora said, lowering the bag and sounding surprisingly normal. "I was exactly the same when I was pregnant."

"Three minutes," a voice called from inside the house.

"Don't worry, Nicky, I'll take care of Livvy," the red-haired man said, pulling her away.

"Hold *sti-ill,*" the fairy godmothers chorused.

A hiss heralded the release of another toxic cloud of hair spray.

"I'm gonna have to . . ." Vince began, only to be interrupted by a coughing fit as the fumes engulfed him. Dave, caught by surprise, succumbed, too. Having retained the presence of mind to remember what the warning presaged and hold his breath, Joe had to smile. Folding his arms over his chest, resting a hip against the porch rail as he settled himself more comfortably, he discovered that for the first time in a long time, he was actually starting to enjoy himself.

"Nicky . . ." Leonora gasped over her shoulder as Marisa, with John's help, finally succeeded in moving her.

"*You can do it,*" Nicky said. "There's nothing different about this one. Karen, help them with her, would you please? " The black-haired woman nodded, then moved away to join Leonora and company. Seconds later, Nicky called after them in a sharper tone: "Don't let her go inside until we're ready to start. We want to get her reactions to the house from the very beginning. And one of you, for goodness' sake, *take that paper bag away from her.*"

"Two minutes, Nicky. We need to get you miked," a man called urgently through the screen. Glancing that way, Joe noticed that a TV camera inside the house was now visible. The cameraman appeared to be positioning it so that it captured anyone entering through the front door.

"Coming," Nicky responded, and suited the action to the words. Swinging hair, spine straight as a poker, nice ass with a provocative sway to it, long-legged strides: Yep, no doubt about it, she was walking away.

Mark that down as a whiff for the home team.

"See what trying to be nice gets you? Ignored." Openly seething, Vince stared after her, then glanced sideways at Joe. "You're the damned Chief of Police. You handle it. They don't want to leave, fine. Arrest them."

Joe shot him a disbelieving look. "You've got to be kidding me."

"Hell, no, I'm not kidding you. What do you think we're paying you for? Do your job."

"Shit," Joe said, catching Dave's eye. His Number Two looked as dubious as he felt, but, hell, it was Vince's call. With Dave following and Vince bringing up the rear, he headed semi-reluctantly toward where Nicky was now standing in the middle of a huddle in front of the screen door. A few feet away, in the middle of her own huddle, Leonora was once again breathing into the paper bag.

"Testing, one, two, three . . ." Nicky was saying into a small black microphone that had just been attached to her lapel.

"Great. We're good to go," a man called from inside the house.

"Not quite," Joe said in his best authoritative tone. Nicky looked around at him. Her hair shimmered with ruby highlights as she turned her head and her hair swung away from her face. Pretty. Too bad he was getting ready to sink right to the bottom of her favorite-people list. "Like the mayor said, no permit, no TV show. I'm going to have to escort you people off the property. If you refuse to go, you leave me no choice but to place you under arrest."

Nicky's lips parted as she sucked in air. Joe could almost hear the sizzle as her fuse ignited. Her big brown eyes shot sparks at him. Then, *boom*, she whipped around and took two long strides, which put her right in his face.

"That's it," she said, her eyes blazing. "I've had it with all the aggravation. *You* I don't need. Take a hike."

Joe blinked as he absorbed the full impact of her ire, but stood his ground. As Vince had reminded him, he was Chief of Police. Vince, as mayor, was his boss. If Vince wanted these people gone, then it was up to him to make them disappear. All things considered, though, it had been more fun being an innocent bystander.

"Ms. Sullivan . . ." he began. Too late. She'd already turned her back to him and was marching back toward the door.

So much for reason. He sighed inwardly.

"You in there." He raised his voice, talking over her to the cameraman, whom he could see just inside the house. "Shut off those cameras. We're closing you down."

She whirled and came back, heels clicking furiously. "I don't *think* so."

He crossed his arms over his chest, and looked her over. "You're backing me into a corner here."

"Is that so?"

"Do you *want* to get arrested?"

Her lips thinned. Her face tightened. Her eyes blazed. They were practically shooting out fire now, like twin flamethrowers. *Yikes,* she was mad.

Holding that scorching gaze, Joe practically felt the hairs on the back of his neck stand up.

"Listen up, you," she said. "We're on TV, live, in about ninety seconds. Anybody who interferes with this broadcast, from this moment onwards"— her glance slid toward Vince, who, with Dave, was standing just behind him, then snapped back to skewer Joe like meat on a shish kebab—"will be looking at a lawsuit. A huge one, I promise. Do you understand me?"

"One minute," the voice called warningly from inside the house.

"Okay," she called back. Her eyes narrowed, then glittered. She was in Joe's face again, glaring up at him, radiating menace despite the fact that the top of her head reached approximately to his mouth and he outweighed her by, he guessed, at least seventy pounds. "You hear that, Barney Fife? We're on the air in one minute. That means you've got a choice. You can go ahead and arrest me on live TV with millions of people watching, or you can *back off.*"

She jabbed a slender forefinger toward his nose for emphasis. It stopped about six inches short of its goal and stayed there like a pale arrow frozen in the air.

After this, Joe reflected as his gaze lifted from that well-manicured finger to her eyes, he was going to have to lose the shirt. She was making the Mayberry connection, too.

"Nicky, we need you in position *now.*" The black-haired woman gestured frantically from the doorway.

"Coming," Nicky answered, glancing around. Then she refocused on him.

"Your call," she said through her teeth. Her fists were clenched. Her eyes dared him. This, Joe decided dispassionately, was a woman on the edge. All it would take was one tiny little push to shove her over.

And he wasn't about to be the one doing the pushing—not without a much better reason than he'd been given so far. Not with a live TV audience getting ready to tune in at any second. No way. No how.

She must have read the answer in his eyes. With a final warning look at him, which she then widened to include Vince and Dave, she turned on her heel and hurried toward the door.

"You gonna let her buffalo you like that?" Vince demanded under his breath. "Quit pussyfooting around. Arrest her ass."

"Ten, nine, eight . . ." The countdown, in a woman's voice, was coming from somewhere behind the cameraman.

"Vince, we don't want to do this. Trust me," Joe said, grabbing Vince by the arm when the mayor, with a fulminating look that made clear his opinion of his police chief's lack of resolve, started to go after her himself. "Not on live TV."

". . . four, three, two, one . . ."

Vince hesitated. "Goddamn it," he said bitterly.

"This is *Twenty-four Hours Investigates*," Nicky said into the camera, and Joe realized that she was on the air. Her body language had changed completely in the last few seconds; she now looked comfortable, relaxed almost, and even managed to produce a smile for the audience at home. "Thank you for joining us for this special *live* broadcast. I'm Nicole Sullivan . . ."

4

"THERE IS NOTHING IN the hall . . . nothing in the living room . . . nothing in the dining room," Leonora intoned.

As Nicky had anticipated, once the camera was focused on her, Leonora had turned into the consummate professional. She was no newcomer to TV, after all, and she'd been a practicing professional psychic since the age of sixteen. Only someone as intimately acquainted with her as, say, her younger daughter, would have caught the nervous flicker in her eyes, the tension in her jaw, the jerkiness of her gestures. For whatever reason—psychic's block or something else—Leonora was not *on* tonight. But she was trying, gamely walking through the house with increasingly rapid footsteps that Nicky knew signified her impatience with the lack of paranormal activity to pick up. The camera panned the magnetometer—standard ghost-hunting equipment that measured the magnetic field generally associated with the presence of spirits—that had been set up in each room: nothing. The temperature sensors likewise revealed a steady 72 degrees: no cold spots to be found. Since the house had no air-conditioning, they couldn't even hope for a temperature drop due to a helpfully positioned vent, Nicky reflected gloomily. They were going au naturel, whether they liked it or not.

The plan was for Leonora to walk through the house, room by room, encountering and interacting with whatever ghosts were present, while the cameras rolled. So far, the plan had yielded approximately twenty-two minutes of the opposite of must-see TV: just nothing, nothing, nothing. And more nothing.

Call it Al Capone's Vault Part II: the ghostless séance.

And Nicky's worst nightmare.

"This is the library," Nicky said quietly into the camera as her mother glided toward the small room next to the dining room. Despite the tall light set up in one corner specially for this broadcast, it was gloomy as all get out with its empty, dark shelving and shuttered windows. Dust lay over everything, and a cobweb adorned one corner of the coffered ceiling. Like the rest of the house, it smelled faintly musty, as if it had been shut off from light and air for a long time. If she'd been a ghost, Nicky thought, *she* would have wanted to hang out here.

Like the camera, her eyes followed as Leonora moved around the room, touching the fireplace mantel, a windowsill, the paneled wall itself. Behind her, out of range of the camera, Nicky was conscious of Karen and the rest of the crew watching with bated breath. If, through sheer willpower, they could have conjured a ghost out of thin air, it would have been materializing before them at that very moment. But they were as helpless to change what was happening—or, rather, what was not happening—as she was.

"Nothing. I'm getting nothing in this room," Leonora said at last, her voice tight. Her eyes met Nicky's for a long moment. Nicky knew that look. If the program bombed as badly as it seemed like it was going to, the bigwigs at the network weren't the only ones who would be howling for her head: Her mother would be, too.

In the end, when the show was over and the backlash hit, this whole unbelievable debacle was going to turn out to be all her fault, Nicky realized bitterly. Why, *why*, hadn't she seen this coming?

Because she'd been too eager to make tonight's program happen, and the reason she'd been too eager was because she had known they were looking at her: CBS. They were searching for a new co-host for *Live in the Morning*, the long-running chatfest that most of America consumed along with their morning coffee. Quite apart from the fact that *Twenty-four Hours Investigates* was in crisis mode, *Live in the Morning* was a gig that every female television personality in the country would sell her laser-whitened teeth for. At their request, she'd sent in her audition tape, which had made enough of an impression that she'd been flown to New York for an interview. Things had gone well.

But she hadn't been offered the job. They were keeping her in mind, they said, but they were continuing to look.

A friend in a position to know had told her that they liked her but had reservations: As a foil to Troy Hayden, the handsome, buttoned-down male host, they had envisioned a perky little suntanned blonde, not a tall, milky-skinned, sometimes too-composed redhead; the bulk of her reporting had been for news-oriented shows, from Channel 32 in Charleston where she'd gotten her start to *Twenty-four Hours Investigates* for A&E; and she had no experience with live TV.

Well, thanks to her own machinations, now she did. And it looked as though it was going to bite her in the butt.

After this, not only was she not going to get the job, she probably wasn't going to be working for *Twenty-four Hours Investigates*, either. If she didn't get fired, it would be because they would have no reason to fire her: The news magazine would be cancelled. She would go down in the annals of broadcast history as the reporter who killed the program.

If CBS ever talked about her again at all, it would be because she was to *Twenty-four Hours Investigates* what the iceberg was to the *Titanic*.

"Leonora James—who, as most of you know, also happens to be my mother—has an amazing record as a psychic medium. On her late, much-lamented-by-fans show *The Great Beyond*, she was able to put hundreds of families in touch with their deceased loved ones. She has talked to Marilyn Monroe, to Elvis, to John Ritter . . ."

With the camera now zooming in on Nicky, Leonora felt free to give her daughter a baleful look, which Nicky, still talking, did her best to ignore. Then, head high, posture regal, purple caftan swirling, Leonora glided past Nicky and back out into the hall while the camera, once again focused on her, rolled silently behind.

". . . investigated literally hundreds of hauntings," Nicky continued. "Including Ford's Theater in Washington, D.C., where the ghost of Abraham Lincoln's assassin, John Wilkes Booth, is said to still walk the boards. . . ."

In a group just inside the front door, clustered well out of camera range, Nicky caught a glimpse of the onlookers craning their necks to follow the (non) action: several members of the technical support crew; a miniskirted woman she thought was with the local weekly newspaper; the scowling, bulldog-like mayor; and the mayor's puglike pal, a short, chunky, balding guy she took for a cop. Barney Fife, tall, dark, and brooding, was standing at the rear, arms crossed over his chest, shoulders propped against the wall. He was watching her with a sardonic twist to his mouth: She hadn't made a friend there. He was probably planning to pounce on her once the broadcast ended and haul her off to jail—which, at the moment, was the least of her worries, she decided as her gaze scanned the group. Their expressions ranged from worried to bored to skeptical. Unfortunately, there was not one enthralled face in the lot.

The flushing sound she heard in her mind was her career going down the toilet.

She had always felt uncomfortable in this house, Nicky reflected dismally as she trailed Leonora through the hall, doing her best not to trip over the myriad cables that snaked across the floor, courtesy of the *Twenty-four Hours Investigates* crew. As a young girl, she had been inside it on several occasions when her parents had socialized with the people who had owned it way before the Schultzes. At the time, she'd thought her discomfort had been due to the inferiority she had felt as a scrawny, freckle-faced nonentity who was simply awkward at the parties that were Livvy and Leonora's lifeblood. Now she wondered if it had something to do with the house itself. There was still a vibe—a dissonance—in the atmosphere that made her skin feel almost clammy.

Or maybe it was because the crime hit too close to home. She hadn't known any of the victims or their families—Leonora had remarried, and they'd moved away to Atlanta years before the Schultzes had come to live in the Old Taylor Place. But since Tara Mitchell and the other girls had been around Livvy's age and the island was the place that Nicky and Livvy and their mother had always thought of as home, the crime had been a major topic of conversation within their family when it had happened. Though the details had faded over the years, the crime had resonated with Nicky, and it had remained part of her internal landscape ever since. When *Twenty-four Hours Investigates* had been looking for a blockbuster crime to feature, it had popped back into the forefront of her mind.

And the rest, as they said, was history.

So here she was, taking charge of her life, going after what she wanted, making a grab for the brass ring—and the sad fact was that she was falling flat on her face. She knew, from the expression on Karen's face, from the sidelong glances being exchanged among the crew, from her own experience with what went on behind the scenes, that the feedback they were getting from the control-room producers, who were in Chicago watching right along with the audience at home, wasn't good.

"Nothing's happening!" they were probably screaming into Karen's earpiece at this very moment. "Do something! Fix it! We need *action*!"

The thought made Nicky's stomach knot.

One ghost. Please, God, just send us one ghost. Casper, where are you when you're needed?

Nicky had never known her mother to fail to find a ghost when she went looking for one. Usually, ghosts practically pushed one another aside in their eagerness to come through for her. But not tonight. *Oh, God, not tonight.* Wasn't that the way life worked, that the one time Leonora's link to the Other

Side went on the blink would be on live TV, with her daughter's professional life on the line?

"Leonora is now entering the kitchen," Nicky said to the folks at home, just loudly enough so that the microphone would pick it up. She hoped it didn't also pick up the despair that she was starting to feel. They were looking for ghosts in the *kitchen?* That was, in a word, pathetic. She had never in her wildest imaginings expected to get this far; she'd been sure that way before now they would have encountered enough otherworldly presences to fill up the hour, and more. Lucky thing she'd had the whole house prepped, just in case Leonora's sometimes-unpredictable wanderings brought them this way.

Leonora walked across the kitchen, her flat, gold slippers making shuffling sounds on the tile floor. It felt cooler in here, Nicky realized as she stepped into the room in her mother's wake, probably because it was mostly white: white floor, white cabinets and appliances, long expanses of smooth, white counters. The only thing that wasn't completely white was the wallpaper in the breakfast nook. It featured a tangled green vine covered with huge red cabbage roses that for some reason looked to Nicky at first glance like splashes of blood.

She shivered, realized what she was doing, and glanced hopefully at the temperature sensor. It showed an unpromising 72 degrees.

Damn.

Leonora was almost to the back door when she stopped and clasped her hands in front of her waist. For a moment—one of the longest moments in Nicky's life—Leonora stood perfectly still, an arrested expression on her face.

Nicky held her breath.

"I am getting a great sense of unease," Leonora said at last. "Fear . . . pain . . . something terrible happened in this room."

Leonora went silent, staring unseeingly in front of her.

Cue the ghosts. Please.

"The emotions are still here," Leonora said, her eyes glassy as they fixed on a point directly in front of her. "Surprise . . . disbelief . . . *terror.* Absolute terror. Waves of terror, swirling up all around me. Someone was afraid for their life."

Leonora shook her head slightly, as if to clear it. Then she moved. The camera followed her on soundless wheels as she walked seemingly at random around the kitchen. It was a large room, about fourteen by twenty-five feet, rectangular, with an island in the center and the octagon-shaped breakfast nook angling off it. Another set of the French doors that were a feature of the house opened onto a patio at the far end, opposite the swinging door through which they had entered. Once jaunty white curtains, now faintly yellowed with time, still hung from the windows, blocking out the night; Nicky wondered, fleetingly, if they were holdovers from the Schultzes' time.

Were they, like the house itself, silent witnesses to the tragedy that occurred here?

Okay, so she was a veteran of encounters of the paranormal kind. The thought still gave Nicky the creeps.

"Someone . . . someone else was here, too. Hiding," Leonora said, her voice echoing hollowly off the walls as she walked toward the French doors. Her caftan swished around her legs as she moved. Her slippers whispered over the floor. Other than that, the room was absolutely silent, as everyone, including Nicky, focused on Leonora. Staying just enough behind her to be out of the shot, Marisa followed with the machine on which Leonora always recorded her sessions so that anything she said could later be checked and, hopefully, verified. Not that she didn't trust other people's recordings, as she had explained to Nicky countless times, but editing happened. She wanted her own, independent record of events.

"I can feel that person waiting. Feel the heart pounding—fast, *thump-thump, thump-thump* . . ." Leonora pressed a hand to her heart, tapping out the rhythm with her fingers. "The person is nervous, excited almost, breathing hard. Listening."

One look at her mother's rapt face told Nicky that Leonora had found her groove at last. She let out a silent breath of relief.

"Who's hiding?" Nicky asked softly. "Is it a man or a woman?"

Leonora hesitated. Then she shook her head.

"I can't tell," she murmured in a distracted tone. "I can't see. What I'm getting is what I *feel*."

Nicky nodded her understanding. Leonora closed her eyes. The lights threw Leonora's shadow against the wall and blanched her pale complexion until it appeared almost corpse-like. Had it not been for her flaming hair and vivid makeup, she would have looked like a ghost herself. The deep purple of her caftan and the glinting gold of her jewelry added additional touches of the exotic to what Nicky knew from experience would be an arresting TV image.

On TV, as in life, Leonora James was nothing if not compelling.

"Happy, lighthearted—the emotions of the one entering the room are buoyant. Then . . . fear." Leonora's eyes popped open. "Just overwhelming shock and fear."

Frowning slightly, Leonora started walking, stopped in front of a wall of cabinets, and pulled one door open. It was about six feet tall, narrow, no shelves—a broom closet, Nicky guessed.

"Here," Leonora said. Her voice was softer, almost sounding as if it was coming from far away. "The person was in here. Hiding. Waiting. I'm getting waves of anger. Hatred. This person came to do harm. The feeling I'm getting is of evil . . . *evil* . . ."

Leonora glanced over her shoulder, then turned away from the broom closet, leaving the door standing open. She took one hesitant step toward the center of the kitchen, then another, and a third.

"So afraid . . . so afraid . . ." Leonora murmured mournfully, clasping her hands together in front of her waist again and staring into space. She took another faltering step forward. "The emotions are so strong, I—" Stopping, she sucked in her breath sharply. "It was here—a girl, I think . . . she was surprised . . . she turned around and saw someone . . . a man, I'm getting that it was a dark-haired man . . . jumping toward her and she screamed and then . . . the knife went in . . . oh, oh—" Leonora clutched her arm just below her shoulder. "Somebody help me! He's killing me! No . . . no . . ."

Those last horrified cries, uttered in a voice totally unlike her own, stopped abruptly. Leonora's eyes closed. Her chin dropped to her chest. A long shudder racked her body from head to toe. Watching, Nicky felt a prickle run down her own spine. No matter how many times she had witnessed her mother at work, it still occasionally had the power to make her blood run cold. Like now, when she knew her mother was reaching into the past, reliving the horror of that long-ago night as if it were happening to her at that very moment. She only hoped the TV audience was having the same visceral reaction that she was.

"Tara. That's the name I'm getting: Tara." Leonora looked up suddenly, blinking. Her lips parted, and she drew in a long breath. "Tara was first attacked in the kitchen. Someone hiding in that cabinet jumped out at her. She fought, and was stabbed . . ." Leonora squatted, her purple gown scrunching up around her knees, to touch the floor near her feet. The tile was white, pristine. Watching, Nicky could almost feel the hard, cold smoothness of it beneath her own fingers. "There was a puddle of blood here, right here. She bled and bled—so much blood. I can feel it . . . it's warm, sticky . . ."

Leonora's voice started to go soft and distant again, and Nicky knew she was once again being drawn into the past.

"Can you talk to Tara? Can she tell you who attacked her?" Nicky prompted softly. This was good. Vintage Leonora James at last. The eyes of the audience at home should be glued to their screens.

"No." Leonora rose, glancing around the room with the slightly bewildered air of one who had just become aware of her surroundings. "Tara's not here. No one's here. We need to go upstairs."

Nicky heard the slightest of whirring sounds and glanced around. The camera was being pulled back out of the way fast, and repositioned so as not to impede Leonora while at the same time capturing everything she did. The cameraman was Gordon Davies. He was around forty, short and thick-bodied, with strong, coarse features and thick, dark hair that he wore in a ponytail at his nape. They'd been working together since August, and Nicky considered him a friend as well as the ultimate professional. His expression was intent, absorbed. It was clear that he was focused, not just on his job but on Leonora herself and the story she was telling. Beyond him, crowding around the open doorway, a strange group of observers had gathered. Nicky glimpsed Livvy, Uncle Ham, and Uncle John; the Schultzes, who'd asked permission to be present; Mario, Tina, and Cassandra, the hair and makeup crew; Karen—even the mayor, pug-dog cop, and Barney Fife were watching. Every single one now looked engrossed to their back teeth.

Yes. Even as she gestured at them to get out of the way, Nicky mentally gave a pumped-fist salute. Al Capone's vault was empty no longer. Welcome to Ghosts-R-Us.

Appearing oblivious to her surroundings—which was a good thing, as the impromptu audience fell back in front of her with the approximate grace of a herd of cows on ice—Leonora turned and walked out of the kitchen, heading for the beautiful curving staircase at the end of the wide entry hall. She was moving swiftly, purposefully, paying no attention whatsoever to the entourage now following on her heels. Knowing her mother, Nicky doubted that Leonora was even aware that they were there.

"We're heading for the second floor," Nicky said quietly to the TV audience as she trailed Leonora up the stairs. When Leonora was in the zone, long stretches of silence broken by rapid verbal bursts of information were the norm. And as silence was anathema to gripping TV, it was up to Nicky to fill in the gaps, which was tricky but doable, as long as she kept her eyes on the ball—or, in this case, her mother. "The house has three stories in all, with the family living areas downstairs, the family sleeping quarters on the second floor, and what were once servants' rooms on the top floor."

Another camera in the second-floor hall rolled into view as Bob Gaines, the second cameraman on the shoot, got into position. He was in his mid-thirties, average height and build, with close-cropped brown hair and an open, friendly face that matched his personality. Nicky waited for the light on his camera to come on to indicate that the filming was now over to him. There it was: He was zooming in for a close-up just as Leonora reached the top of the stairs.

Nicky continued, "Leonora is now in the upstairs hallway. There are five bedrooms and two bathrooms on this level. Leonora is walking toward the front of the house. If you remember from our exterior shots, the front of the house overlooks a lawn that pictures show was abloom with colorful dog-woods and crepe myrtle and oleanders at the time of the crime. At the bottom of the yard is a private street, and just on the other side of that is Salt Marsh Creek. By day, the creek is busy, providing local boaters with a channel to the Atlantic Ocean. By night, its waters are dark and mysterious, teeming with wildlife. . . ." Nicky paused and took a breath as she reached the top of the stairs. The camera panned to capture its surroundings. Like the downstairs hall, this was a once-grand space that had been allowed to deteriorate through neglect. The ivory damask wallpaper was peeling away from the wall in spots, and there were several stains on the ceiling that spoke of possible leaks in the roof.

"Leonora's at the end of the hall now." Having followed her mother, Nicky was almost at the end of the hall, too. "On her left is the master bedroom, which at that time would have been shared by Andrea and Mike Schultz, Lauren's parents. To her right is what would have been Lauren's bedroom. If you remember from our earlier broadcast, Elizabeth and Susan Cook talked about the ghostly encounters they experienced in this room. . . . Clearly, Leonora is being drawn to it. She is entering Lauren's bedroom now."

Nicky stopped talking as she followed Leonora—and Marisa and the camera—inside. It was a corner room—large, as bedrooms went—with three large casement windows, two overlooking the front of the house and the other overlooking the side yard. The floor was uncarpeted hardwood, and a paneled closet door bisected one wall. Other than the windows, there were no distinguishing features. The walls were painted pale lavender, the trim white. Floor-length white sheers hung at the windows. Their hems flut-tered slightly.

Fluttered? The windows were closed. There shouldn't have been any moving air in the room at all. But, Nicky realized, she was definitely feeling a draft around her feet. A *cold* draft.

A hopeful glance at the sensor confirmed it: the temperature, a constant 72 degrees in every other room they'd visited in the house, was 68 degrees.

As Nicky pointed out this hopeful sign in a quiet voice to the audience at home, Leonora stopped in the center of the room and closed her eyes.

"There was a bed—here, against this wall." Leonora's eyes opened. She moved forward, waving a hand to indicate the outside wall. "Between the windows. It's a double bed, with a pink-striped bedspread that reaches to the floor. There's a chair in the corner—an armchair, pink floral upholstery, with a"—she hesitated for a moment—"a stuffed dog on it. The dog is long and white—a dachshund—with writing on it: signatures. Lots of signatures, in ink. Of course, it's an autograph hound. There's a dresser over there." She turned to point at the wall beside the closet. "It's white, kind of . . . kind of French provincial. Two lamps, white bases, pink shades with fringe, on either end. There's a mirror over the dresser. An oval mirror with a gold frame."

Stopping, she took a deep, slow breath. "There's someone in the room. A girl, I think. I can . . . I'm getting just a glimpse of her reflection in the mirror."

Leonora turned around swiftly, as though to catch sight of someone standing behind her.

"Is anyone here?" Leonora called softly. Nicky knew she wasn't talking to any living person. "Tara! Tara, are you there?"

Silence.

"Lauren? Becky?" Leonora's voice dropped into the husky, rasping timbre that told Nicky that she was once again in a dimension of her own. She was frowning, concentrating, as she called out to the spirit world.

"Yes, I can see you," Leonora said, sounding as if she was talking to someone only a few feet away. Her voice sharpened. "Who are you?"

She was looking at a point near where she had said the bed had once been located.

Nicky found herself looking there, too, although so far as she could tell, there was nothing but empty room to see. But . . . the draft moving around her ankles had turned icy.

A quick glance at the temperature told her that it had fallen to 65 degrees. And the magnetometer was showing unmistakable signs of activity as well. Soundlessly—she didn't want to disturb her mother when she was obviously on a roll—she indicated to the cameraman that he should pan to the sensors. The camera's digital clock indicated that they were running out of time: only six minutes left. The way her night was going, the three dead girls would materialize right in front of them—exactly thirty seconds after they were off the air.

Ah, well. There was no speeding this up, no regulating it. As Uncle John had pointed out to the mayor, Leonora, once set in motion, was like a runaway train. Nicky was on board now, which meant that all she could do was hang on for the ride and try to shape the experience so that it was as exciting for the viewers as possible.

"You don't like us being here?" Leonora's voice was barely audible now. "I understand. We're trying to help you. Can you tell me your name?" Leonora frowned, then glanced at Nicky. "Tara. It's Tara. She says she's looking for the other girls—Lauren and Becky. Are they here in the house with you?"

That last question was clearly addressed to the unseen Tara. Leonora nodded, as if she was listening to someone's reply.

Watching, Nicky discovered that she was holding her breath. She had witnessed her mother's interactions with the spirit world for so many years that they had long since ceased to be anything out of the ordinary. Leonora talked to the dead as regularly as some mothers baked brownies. But tonight, something, some combination of the echoing emptiness of the room and her mother's deepening voice and the knowledge of the atrocity that had been committed in this house, gave her the willies.

Thank God. It had to be good TV if her mother was succeeding in unnerving *her.*

"You can't find them? You think they might be in the kitchen?" Leonora paused, seeming to listen intently. "Yes, I know it's Lauren's birthday . . . you think they're having birthday cake without you?" Leonora frowned, then shook her head. "Tara, wait. Don't go. Please, we want to talk to you. The other girls aren't in the kitchen now, Tara, they're . . ."

Leonora's voice trailed off. She turned, as if watching someone go out of the room. Standing between her mother and the door, Nicky felt a rush of icy air go past her face. Her eyes widening, she took a reflexive step back. Her hand flew to her cheek.

Spooky.

Her skin felt normal—warm, dry.

Her heart, on the other hand, was suddenly racing.

"She's gone," Leonora said, sounding disappointed as she turned to look at Nicky. "Tara. She was here and now she's gone. I think . . . I think what's happening here is that she's reenacting the events that occurred before she was attacked in the kitchen. I think on that night, she got separated from the other two girls, for whatever reason, then came up to this bedroom— Lauren's bedroom—looking for them. When they weren't here, she went down to the kitchen and . . ."

She never finished speaking. Instead, the air was split by a woman's blood-curdling scream.

5

TWO MORE SCREAMS followed in quick, terrifying procession, jagged twin shards of sound that sliced through the floorboards to hang in the air like an icy mist. The dreadful, haunting shrieks were faintly muted, as if they came from a little—but just a little—distance. They were unmistakably human, unmistakably female, juiced with the gut-wrenching terror of an animal unexpectedly falling victim to a predator. As caught by surprise as everyone else, Nicky sucked in her breath as goose bumps raced over her skin. Automatically, she looked down, because down was the general direction from which the sounds seemed to have sprung. Time seemed to stand still as the last shivering notes slowly faded away.

"What the hell?" Bob the cameraman muttered.

Nicky glanced at him in surprise. It was a measure of how unnerving the cries had been that he had forgotten himself enough to speak at all. Usually, he and Gordon were about as loquacious as their cameras. In fact, so much were they appendages of their equipment that everyone, herself included, tended to forget that they were there. But now he was staring down, just as she had been seconds before, his job momentarily forgotten.

Nicky caught a quick glimpse of herself reflected in his lens as the camera, temporarily without a guiding hand, lurched drunkenly. Her eyes were wide with surprise. Her mouth hung open.

"Unprofessional" didn't do her demeanor justice. She looked shaken up, shocked. To make matters worse, she wasn't talking. In fact, no one was talking. No one was filming. No one was doing anything. Everybody, followers hanging just outside the door included, was just standing there looking as if they'd been poleaxed. In the meantime, *Twenty-four Hours Investigates* was transmitting that bane of live TV: *dead air*.

The horror of that, Nicky found, was as instantly restorative as a faceful of cold water. Whoever—whatever—had screamed, it was up to her to put the best possible spin on it for the audience watching at home, and worry about the details later. Hissing to get Bob's attention—realizing his lapse, he looked as appalled as Nicky felt as he quickly grabbed and refocused his camera—she spoke in hushed, confidential tones to the audience at home.

"There you have it, people. You heard those screams right along with us. I have no idea who screamed, or why, but, given everything we've learned here tonight, everything we've experienced together, I'm willing to make a guess. I think what we just heard—those dreadful, soul-shattering screams— are the same screams that Elizabeth and Susan Cook reported hearing one terrifying night as they huddled together in this bedroom, the same screams that others have heard on dark nights when they ventured too near this house. I think they are the screams of a terrified girl being slashed to death in the living room directly below us. I think they are Tara Mitchell's screams. . . ."

Sixty-eight seconds left. That left her with a little more time to fill than she would have liked, Nicky calculated even as she spoke, but not enough so that it would be obvious that she was trying to stretch her sign-off to fill it. After those screams, anything else would be an anticlimax. They were the perfect endnote to a program that had, in the teeth of her earlier fears, finally turned out to be, if not everything she'd been hoping for, close enough. And if she did say so herself, it was definitely damned good TV.

Nicky turned to her mother. Leonora was standing perfectly still, hands clasped, lowered lids veiling her eyes, lips compressed. Since glancing down as they all had in automatic response to the screams, she didn't appear to have moved so much as a muscle. Leonora was undoubtedly still a little shaken, Nicky realized, just as she was herself. Whatever their origin—and now that the last chilling echo had died away and her brain was once again able to function properly, Nicky suspected that she might not want to inquire too closely into exactly where they'd come from—the screams had been as terrifying as they had been unexpected. Nevertheless, the oldest rule in the entertainment business still applied: The show must go on.

"Leonora, thank you for being our guide tonight as we crossed the threshold between life and death. You've taken us with you on a journey that few have made. It was fascinating. Enlightening. Chilling. I'm sure everyone watching with us at home was as absolutely blown away by the experience as I was."

When Nicky had started talking, Leonora had looked up. Her expression had been cloudy, vague, her eyes unfocused. Nicky had gotten the definite impression that her mother was still off in ghostland somewhere. Now, though, as Nicky wrapped up, Leonora's eyes sharpened, narrowed, and locked on her daughter.

Nicky knew that look, and felt her stomach tighten in response. Leonora was not pleased. It didn't require genius to deduce that Leonora suspected, just as Nicky was beginning to, that the screams weren't necessarily supernatural in origin. They had been so loud, so shattering, so *human*. So eerily appropriate. And the timing—the timing couldn't have been better. Nicky couldn't be sure, of course, but she suspected that astral beings had little interest in TV ratings, and thus couldn't be expected to scream precisely on cue. Had someone—God forbid it was one of her crew—decided to give the program the finale it deserved? It was possible, she had to admit. Nicky only hoped that, discombobulated as her mother generally was after an encounter with the spirit world, she would remember that they were on live TV and behave accordingly.

She wasn't prepared to count on it, however.

"One more time, thank you, Leonora James," Nicky said quickly, taking her mother's hand in both of hers. It was flaccid, icy. Leonora's eyes, on the other hand, were anything but icy: They were beginning to burn.

No doubt about it: Her mother was in a snit.

"I'm glad I was able to help," Leonora replied, her tone slightly stiff. Then her fist clenched in Nicky's hands, and she pulled her hand away.

Uh-oh.

Still smiling, Nicky walked away from her mother, signaling for Bob to keep the camera on her. Whatever was riling Leonora—and Nicky was pretty sure she knew what it was—the time to find out about it was in exactly twenty-seven seconds—in other words, *after* they were off the air.

"As always, we go the extra mile to try to solve cases that have left other investigators baffled. We'll take the information provided by Leonora tonight and see if it opens up any new leads, and we'll keep you updated on our progress on subsequent shows. For now, I'm Nicole Sullivan. Thank you from all of us here for joining us tonight on this special live edition of *Twenty-four Hours Investigates*."

A beat passed, during which Nicky determinedly smiled into the camera, and then the red light that warned them they were on the air blinked off. Bob pulled out his earpiece and grinned at her. The monitor showed the credits rolling. A quick glance at the sensors told Nicky that the readings were back to normal: Any and all ghosts had apparently vacated the premises. There was a smattering of applause from the onlookers crowding the door, and she glanced toward them with a smile that froze on her face as her gaze encountered her mother's.

An explosion was clearly imminent. Thank God they were off the air.

"Nicky. That was awesome," someone called. Nicky thought the voice might have been Mario's. He had been looking on from the hallway and was probably now one of the group streaming into the room, but she was too busy bracing herself for what she knew was coming to definitively identify the speaker or do more than acknowledge the compliment with a wave.

Leonora's eyes blazed into hers. Her lips parted. . . .

"I have to tell you, everything you said tonight was exactly on target." Andrea Schultz saved her. Nicky had been so focused on her mother that she hadn't even noticed that people were forming a knot around them. Slender in jeans and an embroidered vest over a pale green T-shirt, Mrs. Schultz looked far older than her fifty-five years. Her face was pale, and her eyes were bright with unshed tears. She took Leonora's hand and clung to it. "Lauren's room—the way it was—you described it perfectly. How did you *know?* And the blood in the kitchen. There *was* blood on the floor, just where you said."

Leonora refocused on Mrs. Schultz. Faced with someone who had suffered a loss, someone who was turning to her for help, she was always *on*, always compassionate. As angry as Nicky could tell she was, this was no exception.

"I'm sorry for your pain." Leonora gripped Mrs. Schultz's hand. "I wish I could do more to help you."

"Just . . . tell me one thing." Mike Schultz, looking slightly out of place in a navy business suit, white dress shirt, and striped tie, stood behind his wife. Based on her previous dealings with the couple, Nicky would have described him as stolid: the rock supporting his wife through her grief. But his shoulders were slumped now, and his face seemed to have crumpled during the course of the broadcast. Where before he had appeared comfortably middle-aged, he now looked impossibly old. "Where is my daughter? You seemed to see Tara—what about Lauren? Where is *Lauren?*"

The pain in his voice was palpable. Nicky felt her throat constrict in the face of such obvious grief. That was the thing about the line of work she was in: It was easy—too easy sometimes—to forget that real people and real heartbreak lay behind these shows.

Leonora shook her head. "I can't tell you that. I'm sorry. It wasn't shown to me."

"Oh, God . . ." His face turned red and tears formed in his eyes. He abruptly turned away, covering his face with his hands.

"Excuse us. Mike . . . ." His wife went to him, sliding an arm around his waist and murmuring something to him. Together, they moved toward the door.

Marisa, who'd been hovering around the edges of the room, had joined them in time to hear that last exchange.

"Should I . . . ?" she asked Leonora quietly.

Leonora nodded, and Marisa hurried after the grieving couple. From long experience with her mother's work, Nicky knew that Marisa would offer to set up an appointment for a private reading, free of charge, at some future date. Presumably, when she was no longer "blocked."

"That was *great*," Tina breathed, unclipping the microphone from Nicky's lapel. Nicky got the feeling that she would have been jumping up and down in her platform shoes if the soles hadn't been too heavy to allow it. "Your mom *rules*." She let Nicky go and turned enthusiastically to Leonora. "You are the absolute *bomb*," she told Leonora as she removed her microphone. "Do you think you could do a séance for me sometime? My grandmother died last year and . . ."

Tina was part of Nicky's usual team, too, and ordinarily, Nicky loved the tiny blonde to death: Her bubbly enthusiasm could be counted on to inject a note of cheer into any shoot, no matter how nerve-racking the conditions. One glance at her mother's face, however, confirmed her gut instinct: For Leonora, now was definitely not the moment.

"Maybe next time we're in town," Nicky intervened hastily before her mother could answer, and took Leonora's arm. Her mother didn't actually pull away, but the resistance—to her daughter's touch, not to leaving—was there. At least her mother's annoyance served a purpose: It kept Nicky from dwelling on her uncomfortable conviction that in that icy brush of air across her face, she'd just had her own up-close-and-personal encounter with the resident ghost. "We need to get packed up and out of here pronto, before Barney Fife and company"—she nodded toward the two cops, who were cautiously entering the bedroom at that moment—"really do arrest us."

"Can they do that?" Tina spotted the newcomers and frowned.

Already tugging her mother toward the door, Nicky shrugged. "I don't know about you, but I'd just as soon not find out."

The room's lighting suddenly went from blazing bright to normal overhead fixture bright, and the temperature dropped at least a couple degrees. Nicky blinked and glanced around automatically, but realized even as she did it that the reason had nothing to do with the paranormal: The plug had just been pulled on the TV lights. The gang was already bustling about, doing their jobs. She knew from experience that they'd have the whole house restored to pre-broadcast conditions in less than half an hour.

"Nice show," a man commented dryly, and Nicky looked up to find Barney Fife in her path. He was good-looking enough to be described as hunky, she discovered now that she got her first real look at him in decent lighting: wavy black hair, bronzed, chiseled features, a broad-shouldered, lean-hipped body that was all muscles and sex appeal. In fact, all the usual clichés applied, and her female radar gave its standard hot-guy-in-the-building heads up, but the dorky shirt coupled with the expression on his face helped her keep things in perspective. This was a small-town cop with a bad attitude. In fact, if she'd had to describe him now, she would have said tall, dark, and *nasty*. There was a glint in his eyes and a twist to his mouth that told her that he believed in what he'd just seen and heard about as much as he believed in Santa Claus. "It sure sent chills down *my* spine."

"Thanks." It required considerable effort, but she took the high road and ignored the not-so-subtle sarcasm. *Screw you* was what she felt like saying, but at the moment, she had bigger problems than an ignorant cop. Problems such as her mother, whom she steered carefully around him. She could feel Leonora's arm stiffening beneath her fingers. If she looked—which she didn't dare do—she knew she'd see her mother swelling up like a puffer fish.

If he'd asked, she would have warned him that Leonora was not in the mood to suffer fools gladly—fools being him.

Barney Fife turned to follow them with his gaze as they passed him. "You're not planning on filming any more shows around here, are you? Because if you are, next time I'd check into getting that permit we were talking about."

"We're flying out tomorrow, so you can quit worrying." Nicky resisted the urge to tell him to go stuff himself in favor of getting her mother out of the room before she could explode. She pulled Leonora into the hall and practically pushed her toward the stairs.

"What was *that?*" Leonora hissed a moment later, and Nicky knew she wasn't talking about the insufferable cop. To give her mother credit, at least she'd waited until they were on the stairs and—relatively—alone. Nicky's hand tightened on the smooth oak banister. A glance told her that twin spots of hectic color burned in Leonora's cheeks; her jaw was tight; her eyes flashed. Leonora stopped halfway down the staircase—she was one step ahead—to glare up at Nicky. "How dare you put those screams in there? Didn't we already have this conversation once tonight? You of all people know I *do not fake it.*"

Fortunately, having sensed the way the wind was blowing, Nicky had already had time to think this one through. There was only one possible answer that wouldn't result in Leonora blowing sky-high.

"What makes you think they were faked?" Nicky hissed back, nudging her mother with her knee to get her going again. Below them, a small crowd was clustering around the foot of the stairs watching them descend. All eyes—of course—were on Leonora. Nicky was careful to keep a smile on her face and her voice down. "As far as I know, nobody put those screams in there. *We* didn't fake them."

Becoming aware of her audience, Leonora smiled, too, and resumed descending with regal grace. But that didn't mean that things were all better. Nicky could practically hear the snap, crackle, and pop of her mother's fuse burning toward detonation.

"Bullshit," Leonora said out of the side of her mouth.

"Truth," Nicky shot back, just as discreetly.

A smattering of applause distracted them both. A glance down confirmed it: The group waiting for them was applauding. For one of the few times in her life, Nicky was actually glad to see her mother's public. The good news was that it shut her up and got her the rest of the way down the stairs.

"Ms. James, I have to tell you, I am the *biggest* fan." The mini-skirted woman stepped forward as Nicky and her mother reached the first-floor hall. "I'm Marsha Browning with the *Coastal Observer*. We cover all the local news for Pawleys Island, Litchfield, and Murrels Inlet. That was just remarkable. Could I possibly get an interview?"

"I'd be honored." Every inch the gracious diva now, Leonora smiled and shook hands.

"You'll need to call her assistant and set up an appointment for another time. I'll get you the number." Nicky ran interference with the ease of long practice. As her mother accepted congratulations all around, Nicky was relieved to see Livvy, flanked by Uncle Ham and Uncle John, who were each holding one of her arms, slowly approaching. Livvy's face was pale and puffy, and she was moving as though each step was an effort, but at least she was no longer red-eyed and weepy.

Nicky's gaze locked with her sister's. A moment of wordless communication passed between them. During the course of their growing-up years, they'd been the opposite of close, as popular boy-magnet Olivia had queened it over gawky wallflower Nicky. Even as adults, though the three years that separated them seemed to shrink with each passing birthday, they weren't exactly friends. The fact was, they had very little in common except genes. Livvy had married right out of college, married Ben Hollis of the Charleston Hollises, which in this part of the country was akin to marrying a god, and had spent the last ten years living in Charleston sixty miles from where they'd grown up, queening it over local society just like she had once queened it over Nicky, being the perfect wife as her husband had risen in the family business, volunteering, lunching, doing things that were inexplicable to Nicky, such as serving as president of the Junior League. Nicky, on the other hand, hadn't been able to shake the dust from this little corner of the South off her feet fast enough. Since college, she'd been doing her best to carve out a career in television, moving frequently, as she'd gotten jobs in bigger TV markets in bigger cities until she'd wound up in Chicago last August on *Twenty-Four Hours Investigates*. It was her big break, she'd thought at the time, but as the show had failed to take off, she finally was forced to amend that thought. She and Livvy saw each other maybe twice a year, and the rest of the time communicated basically through their mother. But sometimes, particularly when their larger-than-life mother was concerned, they found themselves in accord and able to work together, especially when something was to their mutual benefit.

Like now. Livvy wanted to go home; Nicky wanted to get their mother out of her hair. Their needs dovetailed perfectly.

Raising her voice slightly, Nicky called to her sister over the heads of the assembled company, "Oh, Liv, don't you feel well?"

Everyone turned to look at Livvy, something which Nicky knew her sister, in her present condition, would not appreciate. But to Livvy's everlasting credit, she kept her game face on.

"I have a headache," Livvy said in the pathetic little-girl voice that never failed to get their mother's instant attention—and never failed to set Nicky's teeth on edge. Now, though, as Leonora looked past her public to frown at her older daughter in concern, Nicky blessed Livvy's acting ability. "I need to go home. *Now*."

"You should go with her, Mama," Nicky said in her mother's ear. She herself couldn't leave yet—there were lots of things that had to be finished up before she could call it a night—but getting her mother out of the way before Leonora could blow a gasket was absolutely Job One. "She needs you."

"Yes. Yes, I will." Without the turbulence of an upcoming TV appearance to distract her, Leonora was once again ready to concentrate on her elder daughter's well-being. With a gracious smile and a few more handshakes all around, she moved toward Livvy.

"Take my car," Nicky called after her. Without the bright light that was Leonora to hold them, the little knot of her admirers started to flutter away in various directions. "The keys are in it. There are some things I need to do here, so I'll just catch a ride with somebody."

Uncle John acknowledged that with a wave. Nicky watched with relief as the four of them headed in a tight little cluster toward the door. Then

Leonora looked back over her shoulder. Her eyes were once again baleful as they met Nicky's.

"Nicole," she said. *"Find out."*

Nicky sighed. She should have known that she wasn't going to get off quite that easily.

"I will," she promised, knowing that her mother meant find out where the screams had come from.

"And then you come straight home and tell me."

"I will," Nicky said again, although her voice was a little fainter. So much for the peaceful solitude of her hotel room in Charleston, she thought, wistfully picturing the airport Holiday Inn accommodation with its two queen-sized beds and a TV. Oh, well, she had never really expected to use it anyway. She'd last seen her mother and sister during a whirlwind Christmas visit, and she'd known even when she'd checked in that the chances that she would actually sleep there were slim. Her mother would never forgive her if Nicky came home and stayed in a hotel. One night of family-centered chaos wouldn't kill her.

On the other hand, if it turned out that the screams had been faked and somebody on the TV crew was responsible, Leonora might.

As if she could read Nicky's mind—well, she probably could—Leonora gave her a final sharp look before Livvy and the uncles managed to take her with them out the door.

"Looks like we get to keep our jobs one more day," Gordon said cheerfully from behind her. Nicky turned around to see that he was winding up cable. A big orange coil of it was looped over his arm, and he was adding more to it by the second as he moved through the downstairs, taking it up from the floor. "I've been hearing good things."

"Yeah?" That was good news.

"That was one hell of an ending."

"Yeah." If this time she sounded slightly dispirited, it was because she was. She lowered her voice. No point in letting anybody who wasn't on the payroll know that there was some question about the authenticity of their blockbuster finale. "Those screams—you were down here. You didn't happen to see anybody screaming, did you?"

Gordon shook his head. Then, pausing in the doorway between the hall and the dining room, he frowned at her. "It was some kind of ghost or something, wasn't it?"

Nicky wrinkled her nose. "I don't know. I'd like to think so. They just sounded so . . . real."

"All I know is, I was right here in the hall, and I didn't see anybody screaming. I sure heard 'em, though. Made me jump, I don't mind telling you."

Nicky made a wry face. "That good, huh?"

"Hey, last time I jumped like that was when my ex-wife walked in while I was scoping out the babysitter."

Nicky laughed. Gordon grinned and resumed his task. Feeling a little better, Nicky headed for the kitchen, where, she presumed from the sounds that were emanating from it, she would find the rest of the crew. Maybe the screams had been legitimate. After all, she'd certainly thought they were at the time. It could be just that after her negative experience with her own TV show, Leonora was paranoid. And Leonora hadn't been totally herself tonight. Maybe she was enough off her game not to recognize a ghostly shriek when she scared one up.

A group was coming down the stairs as Nicky went by: Tina, Marisa, the Schultzes, Barney Fife, and his sidekick. Nicky grimaced inwardly at the sight of those last two, and picked up the pace in a bid to avoid any further encounters of the unpleasant kind.

The show was over. Time to get out of Dodge while the getting was good.

When Nicky entered the kitchen, Cassandra and Mario were packing up their supplies and guzzling their favorite cranberry Snapple, while Bob was setting a partially dismantled camera down on the counter near the sink. They suspended their conversation to greet her with high fives, low fives, and a variety of other variations of "Great show!"

"Okay, I've got a question for you guys," Nicky said when the accolades had died down. She was leaning back against the center island, trying not to remember that her mother had said that fifteen years ago, there had been a puddle of blood about six inches from her right foot. *Tara Mitchell had been stabbed in this room.* . . . Nicky gave an inner shiver, found her gaze resting on the vivid scarlet roses that adorned the wallpaper, and tried her best to dismiss all thoughts of violence and gore from her mind. After all, the murders and the subsequent reports of ghostly sightings were the sole reason they were in the house to begin with. It was ridiculous, at this late date, to let the whole haunted-house thing start to freak her out. "Did somebody on our team get a little creative and fake those screams?"

A beat passed. Three pairs of eyes looked at her, clearly surprised.

"No way," Bob said, his hand suspended over the lens cap he'd been tightening. "That wasn't in the script. Anyway, here on location, we don't have the technical capability to digitally come up with anything like that."

"I'm not talking high-tech." Nicky folded her arms over her chest and gave him a level look. "I'm talking somebody screaming."

Bob frowned. "Not that I know of."

Nicky looked at Cassandra. She shook her head, her chocolate-brown eyes wide and innocent. "Girl, believe me, if I could scream like that, I'd be looking for a career in slasher movies," she said, and took a swig from her Snapple. "Those were some eerie-ass screams."

"*I* thought it was a ghost for sure." Mario snapped a makeup case closed. "Gave me the—what do you call them?—Williams, let me tell you."

He shivered theatrically.

"Willies," Cassandra corrected.

"You mean it *wasn't* some kind of paranormal thing?" Bob asked, his frown deepening. Like Nicky, the bulk of his experience was with hard news, and the idea that something on their program was less than authentic, once digested, wouldn't sit well with him, she knew.

"I don't *know* that it wasn't," Nicky said cautiously. "I'm just trying to make sure. Isn't there some saying, like, *trust but verify?*"

"I never heard of that." Mario, who, as a fairly recent immigrant from Guatemala, was constantly trying to perfect his English, looked interested. "Is that on one of your coins?"

"No," Cassandra said. "It's, like, a famous quotation or something."

"Ah." Mario nodded. His expression made it clear that he was storing up the expression for later reuse.

She'd known this group long enough and well enough to tell when they were lying, Nicky decided, looking from one to the other. They weren't.

"Where's Karen?" Nicky asked, as the next likely possibility occurred to her.

"She got a call on her cell phone and took it outside," Gordon said. Pulling a camera dolly behind him, he'd entered the kitchen just in time to hear her question and jerked a thumb toward the French doors. "From the way she acted, it was important. I kinda got the impression that she was talking to His Highness the Head Honcho."

His Highness the Head Honcho was Sid Levin, *Twenty-four Hours Investigates*'s executive producer.

"Oh, yeah?" Nicky knew she sounded apprehensive, but she couldn't help it. Her job—her *career*—rose and fell on Sid Levin. "What did he say?"

Gordon shrugged. "Don't know. You'll have to ask Karen."

"I will." Nicky headed toward the patio. Her exit was hastened by the fact that Barney Fife and his little cop buddy entered the kitchen just as she reached the French doors.

"You guys need any help closing up shop?" he asked.

With one hand on the door latch, Nicky glanced over her shoulder to find his eyes on her. Gordon said something to him by way of a reply, but Nicky missed hearing it as she pulled the door open and stepped outside. She'd had enough stress and worry for one day, she thought as she closed the door behind her. She felt emotionally and physically drained, tired to her toes, used up, worn-out, empty. Dealing with the pain-in-the-patootie local fuzz was more than she could face at the moment.

Let somebody else do it for a change.

She stopped just outside the door as darkness and the sweet night air enfolded her. For an instant, she simply stood there on the small stone patio with her eyes closed, savoring the heady aroma of flowers and sweetgrass and the sea, the faint taste of salt on her tongue, the gentle wafting breeze. It was warm, even warmer than it had been in the house, but the breeze kept it from being hot. On this part of the island, the gurgle of the ocean was muted, distant: a backdrop for the calling of the night birds that nested in Salt Marsh Creek. Their fluting cries, along with the whirring of the insects and the rustle of the leaves high up in the trees, made an eerily beautiful chorus that was as much a part of her as her bones.

The night music of Pawleys Island. In all the years she'd been away, she'd never, ever forgotten what it sounded like.

Tonight, it called to her, made her think of ghosts—not the ghosts that might or might not be hanging around the Old Taylor Place, or the ghosts that popular tradition said had long walked the island, but her own ghosts: the ghosts of her past.

She had to hold them at bay only a little while longer, she reminded herself, even as, unwanted and unsolicited, they began to unspool themselves from the deepest recesses of her mind. *Her father . . . the boat . . . torrents of cold, dark water . . .*

No. She refused to remember. By this time tomorrow night, she would be safely back in her apartment in Chicago.

Mission accomplished.

It was a good feeling, and as she savored it, Nicky felt some of the tension that had built up in her neck and shoulders begin to ease. As impossible as it had earlier seemed, they'd done it: put on at least twenty minutes (and never mind that it was an hour-long show) of must-see *live* TV.

Pay attention, CBS.

With that thought, Nicky opened her eyes and looked around for Karen.

There she was. Nicky spotted her almost at once. The moon was brighter now, a pale white disk that gave off just enough light so that Nicky could see Karen's slender shape walking slowly down the inky black asphalt path that was the driveway. It was too dark for her to be able to make out any details, but from the way Karen was moving, Nicky guessed that she was still talking on the phone: Her pace was slow, and there was a certain aimlessness to it that made her appear to be walking more for the sake of being in motion than with any destination in mind. Certainly, she did not seem to be heading anywhere purposefully, such as toward her car, which, like the others, was parked out of sight around the bend in the driveway.

After I ask her about the screams, I need to tell her she's giving me a ride, Nicky reminded herself, and crossed the patio to head down the driveway after Karen.

She felt herself growing tense all over again at the thought of what she might be getting ready to hear.

Please, let the news from Chicago be good.

Once she was away from the warm, yellow rectangles of light that spilled from the house's windows, the driveway became unexpectedly dark. First, the solid bulk of the garage to her right, and then the trio of magnificent live oaks that stood sentinel beside it, blocked out the moon. The night sounds were louder now, as if being away from the house somehow amplified them. The breeze seemed to have picked up, so suddenly Nicky was almost chilly, despite her suit jacket. She could see Karen's shadowy figure in front of her, moving into the bend of the driveway now, and she almost called to her to wait. Then she remembered that Karen was on the phone, probably on a business-related call, possibly even talking to the Head Honcho himself, and refrained. How unprofessional would she sound if the phone picked up her voice in the background, yelling at Karen to stop?

Nicky stepped up the pace, determined to silently catch her. A smile tugged at the corners of her mouth as she imagined how pleased the home office must be with how the program had turned out. Karen was probably listening to somebody—or maybe several different people—extol its praises. She could probably expect a congratulatory call herself, just as soon as she retrieved her phone from her purse and turned it back on again.

There was no—okay, almost no—possibility that the news could be bad.

As she hurried after Karen, Nicky made up her mind about something: Even if the screams turned out to be anything other than paranormal in origin, *she* wouldn't be telling—not her mother, not the rest of the crew, not anybody. When and if she discovered the culprit—if there even *was* a culprit—she was going to impress upon them the wrongness of what they had done, and then swear them to eternal secrecy. That way, her mother's integrity would be preserved, her wrath would be averted, and Nicky herself would not have to make any uncomfortable and possibly career-damaging admissions to anybody.

The show was over: Let it rest in peace. It would be best for all concerned if it was allowed to go down in the annals of television history exactly as it had been experienced by the viewers: with the origin of those chilling final screams forever a mystery.

Nicky had almost reached the bend in the driveway when she realized that she couldn't see Karen anymore. She frowned and slowed her steps, peering intently ahead. A number of tall pines with shaggy branches that reached clear to the ground clustered together to her left a few paces ahead, just as the driveway made its swooping turn to slope down toward the street. One of the gnarled and bearded live oaks on the other side seemed to reach out toward the pines, its branches arching above the pavement some twenty feet overhead. The shadow that the trees cast was so dark that it seemed to swallow up everything, even the faint gleam of the asphalt itself.

Even Karen.

No, wait, there she was—a stray moonbeam glinted off something metallic deep in the shadow of the trees that could only be Karen's cell phone. Karen was closer now—surprisingly close. She must have stopped to finish her conversation, and Nicky had been so deep in thought that she hadn't noticed that she was rapidly catching up.

Relieved, Nicky hurried toward her. Darkness dropped over her like a blanket as she stepped into the shadow of the trees, and it suddenly became almost impossible to see anything at all. She realized that there was a reason for the thick gloom—the swaying canopy overhead completely blocked out the night sky—but that didn't stop the prickle that ran over her skin as a breeze that was several degrees cooler than the night swirled around her, caressing her face, lifting the hair from the back of her neck.

Taking a deep breath, she inhaled the scent of pine, faint but unmistakable. The sounds of birds and insects and rustling leaves that she'd been so attuned to were muted now; so still was it there beneath the trees that she could hear the faint click of her own high heels on the pavement—the increasingly hesitant click as her pace slowed . . .

Karen had to be right in front of her. Why couldn't she hear her talking?

To hell with it.

"Karen?" she called. Her heart was pounding, she realized with some surprise, and her breathing came fast and shallow. For what reason? She didn't know. But . . . "Karen?"

No answer.

From somewhere in the distance, somewhere out there in the general direction of the marsh, rose the faint, lonely howl of a dog.

Nicky stopped dead as the hair stood up on the back of her neck.

"Karen?" she tried one more time, but even to her own ears her voice sounded weak. Her pulse raced; her skin prickled. The dip in the temperature sent a chill racing over her from her scalp to the soles of her feet. She could see nothing of her colleague now, not even the glint of Karen's phone. The night sounds had mutated into a curious roaring that filled her ears. Darkness was all around her, darkness that now felt alive and threatening, darkness that suddenly seemed to be peopled with terrible things that meant her harm. She had the sudden overwhelming sense that someone—some*thing*—was watching from the shadows. . . .

An icy gust of air brushed her cheek. The sensation was almost identical to the one she had experienced in Lauren's room. It felt, she thought as her heart clutched, like the touch of cold, dead fingers.

For the space of a heartbeat, Nicky couldn't move as her breathing suspended and the bottom dropped out of her stomach. Then she turned and ran.

And not a moment too soon. Even as she fled, stumbling a little as her high heels slipped on the pavement, there was a sound, a rush of movement, an unmistakable sense of a *presence* hurtling along behind her. Someone—some*thing*—was chasing her, she realized to her horror. She could hear running footsteps, breathing, a kind of rustle as if two layers of cloth were rubbing together rapidly. Daring a glance over her shoulder, dreading what she might see but compelled to look, she saw nothing: It was too dark. But every instinct she possessed shrieked that she was in mortal danger.

It was closing fast.

Her heart thudded in her ears. Her knees went weak. Her lungs cried out for air, but she was so terrified that she couldn't fill them, couldn't breathe. Just ahead, beyond the shadow of the trees, she could see that the world was silvered with moonlight, that it was alive and warm and promising safety. But she was trapped in darkness—cold, stygian darkness that seemed to wrap itself around her and claim her, turning her feet to lead and making her feel as though she were running through the deep black water that was the stuff of her worst nightmares, as though she were moving in slow motion, as though she was caught up in one of those hideous dreams in which there was no escaping the monster in never-ending pursuit. . . .

A scream, sharp as a knife and quivering with fear, split the night.

Then something slammed hard into the back of Nicky's knees, and she fell.

6

IT SEEMED TO NICKY that she had been suspended in space for an incredibly long time, although in reality it could not have been more than a split second. The world seemed to slow down around her. Her senses seemed to heighten. The scent of pine needles, faint before, was suddenly as strong as if a bottle of Pine-Sol had been opened directly under her nose. The sounds of the night seemed to intensify, as if the birds and insects and wind had chosen that precise moment to reach their crescendo. The intense blackness of the pavement seemed to rush up at her, yet her eyes were so keen that even through the darkness they could discern each tiny, individual jet crystal in the macadam. She was aware of the blood racing through her veins, of the dryness of her throat and mouth, of the thudding of her heart.

Most of all, she had this overwhelming sense of danger, of evil, of a terrifying dark *presence*. . . .

Her knees crashed painfully into the driveway. Her palms skidded over the rough asphalt. She screamed, a pitiful, choked sound, as something huge and heavy came down on top of her, flattening her, driving the air from her lungs and cutting off her scream almost before it left her throat.

She'd been caught, brought down, she realized to her horror. Unbelievably, against all the rules of nightmares, the phantom monster had succeeded in claiming its prey.

I'm going to die, she thought with a flash of icy clarity. Then her forehead smacked the pavement hard, and her world went black.

SMOKING HAD MANY DISADVANTAGES, Joe reflected as he stepped out onto the patio to light up. It was expensive; it was politically incorrect; it was bad for his health. But it was also, as he had found on many previous occasions, useful. Now it provided him with an excuse to follow Nicky Sullivan outside.

The look she had shot him over her shoulder just before she'd left the kitchen had been an unmistakable mixture of dislike and contempt. He wasn't used to having women look at him like that; he was a lot more accustomed to "come hither" than "get lost." But, as he had just discovered, "get lost" definitely had its charms. It had, in fact, brought him out onto the patio on this dark and breezy night to further his acquaintance with her.

But she wasn't there.

Which was probably just as well, he reflected as he walked to the edge of the patio and took a deep, revivifying drag on his Marlboro Light. Beautiful redheads who hated him might be a whole new category of female, but exploring it further was almost certainly a bad idea.

Number one, he hadn't had a woman—not so much as a kiss, a date, even a conversation with one that wasn't either casual or business-related—since his life got nuked, so starting small, say, with a woman who actually seemed to like him and was going to be around for a while, seemed a reasonable thing to do. Women were undoubtedly a lot like bicycles: Once you learned how to ride, you never really forgot. But all his experience of women had been before, when he'd been a cocky, badass babe-magnet who'd perfected "love 'em and leave 'em" until his particular version of it had approached the level of art. Now it was after, and he was broken: fragile and tentative and unsure of the world and his place in it in a way he had never been before.

He'd experienced his share of extreme emotion, and it had left him with a distaste for it. Finding out that he had a heart after all had taught him something else, too: that hearts, even hardened stainless-steel ones like his used to be, could be broken.

All he'd wanted since he had started to heal was to keep himself in the calm and steady place that he'd finally managed to achieve. He'd had his fill—and more than his fill—of turbulence, of heat, of danger. If, as someone had accused him long ago, he once had been an excitement junkie, he was over it.

Which brought him to point number two: Nicky Sullivan had piqued his interest more strongly than any woman had since he'd woken up to discover to his dismay that his life had an after. She was a redhead, which in his estimation was always a plus. Add to that the fact that she had a killer bod and a beautiful face, and that put her squarely on his A-list. Then she'd glared at him; she'd yelled at him; she'd stood nose to nose with him and called his bluff.

And won.

The show she'd been so determined to get on the air was a joke: He'd watched with interest as the supposedly great psychic Leonora James had walked through the house, claiming there were no ghosts present, while Brian, who Joe knew for a fact was certifiably dead, paced along beside her; then, later, she'd *pretended* to see a ghost in the bedroom while Brian had practically done the frug in front of her to get her to notice him. Okay, it was possible that Brian hadn't really been there at all; maybe he didn't exist anymore outside of Joe's head. And, okay, probably most television of that sort was a joke. He could live with that. But the kicker was that even after that joke of a show was over, Nicky, who had just finished assisting in the perpetration of a fraud that undoubtedly had an audience of millions, had continued to regard *him* with disdain.

In short, he thought wryly as he took another drag on his cigarette, she was his kind of woman: a challenge. A gorgeous, sexy, redheaded challenge.

Which was downright scary when he thought about it, as he now had a few minutes of leisure time to do. Because that was the kind of woman he would have been attracted to before—the kind that had no place in his life now.

When he got around to looking again—and if he was that attracted to Nicky Sullivan, it was probably time to start checking out the local chicks—what he wanted was the girl next door; Mom and Pop and apple pie; sweet, wholesome, uncomplicated.

He'd experienced enough emotional highs and lows to last him forever. All he wanted from here on out was a calm and peaceful life.

That being the case, he was going to finish his cigarette and go back inside. Just because Nicky Sullivan was a challenge didn't mean he had to take it up.

Never trouble trouble till trouble troubles you, as his foster mom had been fond of saying. Words to live by.

Taking a final drag on his cigarette, Joe dropped the butt, crushing it under his heel. He glanced up, noted the heavy cover of charcoal-gray clouds that was rolling in from the sea to systematically blot out the few stars that still twinkled in the midnight-blue sky, and guessed there would be rain before morning. Then he bent to pick up his discarded butt.

That's when he heard it: a high-pitched squeal, almost instantly cut off. Something about it made him straighten, the butt forgotten, and frown into the night. He waited, listened, strained his eyes trying to see something past the light spilling from the windows. Nothing. Silence. Black-velvet darkness.

The cry had probably come from an animal that had fallen prey to some nocturnal hunter. What else could it have been?

FOR SOME UNKNOWABLE expanse of time, Nicky drifted in and out of consciousness, not quite sure of what had happened or where she was or anything except that she hurt. Pain brought her slowly back to awareness. Her head throbbed; her hands and knees stung; she ached all over, she realized, and then realized, too, finally, that if she was in pain, she had to be alive.

Alive: It was as she remembered how unlikely and wonderful that was that she opened her eyes.

At first, all she saw was darkness. Her vision was blurry, and she blinked, trying to clear it, trying to focus. It didn't help. The darkness swirled around her; a stabbing pain shot through her head. She felt dizzy, nauseated. Closing her eyes again, she lay perfectly still to try to get it under control. There was a roaring in her ears that rendered her effectively deaf: She could hear nothing beyond it. Breathing deeply, trying to get her bearings, she inhaled the scent of damp earth, and pine, and—something else. Something that she couldn't quite define, although she knew she had smelled it before. Something earthy and pungent that her subconscious mind recognized even if her conscious mind did not.

It was something vaguely recognizable yet alien and frightening enough that just breathing it in sent a prickle of unease rippling over her skin.

She was afraid, Nicky realized, and that knowledge scared her even more. *Afraid of what?*

As soon as the question popped into her mind, memory returned in a tidal wave of horror. She'd been chased, caught, brought down.

By what? By whom? The jumbled image her subconscious came up with was of something leaping at her from behind. A man? She wasn't sure, but she thought so. She hadn't been able to see a thing, but all her senses other than sight told her that it had been human.

Where is he? Is he close by? Is he watching me at this very moment, waiting for me to wake up?

Nicky's eyes popped open. At the thought, panic gripped her even as she warned herself not to move. Her heart began to thud. Her pulse slid into overdrive. Her muscles tensed as every nerve ending she possessed prepared for instant flight.

Wait.

She took a slow, careful, soundless breath. *If* he was nearby, *if* he was watching, she did not want to give away the fact that she was awake. Before she did anything, even so much as lift her head, even so much as try to move her arms or her legs, she needed to know where she was, where he was, and if she was injured or hampered in some way that might prevent her from getting to safety.

The darkness no longer swirled around her, but it was still there, still impenetrable. Her right hand was splayed out flat not far from her face—she could feel her own breath feathering across her knuckles—but it was so dark that she couldn't see it. Her other hand was trapped beneath her body. It tingled slightly, as if it had gone to sleep. She didn't dare move to try to ease it out from beneath her. The good news was, she didn't seem to be bound in any way. The bad news was, she ached all over.

She was lying on her stomach on an uneven surface. Some kind of hard ridge ran beneath her hipbones, and a small, sharp object jabbed into her left shoulder. Her head was turned to one side, and what lay beneath her cheek and outflung right hand felt cool, faintly damp, and a little prickly.

Pine needles?

Her fingers pressed down experimentally, testing what was beneath them: pine needles. Their scent was suddenly acute.

Her memory returned in its entirety, and with it came a realization: She was in all probability outside the Old Taylor Place, lying under the low-hanging branches of the cluster of pines at the curve of the driveway.

But she had fallen on the pavement. How had she gotten under the trees?

She'd been out cold. She hadn't crawled to where she was lying. Someone had to have dragged or carried her there.

He had to have dragged or carried her there.

Is he still here?

The thought made her blood run cold.

Any second now, he might do whatever he means to do to me. Rape me . . . kill me . . .

She was breathing too fast, she realized. If he heard it, would he guess that she was aware? Without moving, unable to see in the dead darkness beneath the pines, Nicky tried to slow her breathing down to the steady, untroubled pattern of unconsciousness, tried to focus her senses, tried to listen for something that would tell her if he was near, tried to *feel* another presence. It was hard when her head was throbbing, when her blood was pounding in her ears, when her heart was racing so that the frenzied beat of her own pulse was all that she could hear, but she tried—and she got the hideous sense that *she was not alone.*

If she screamed, someone in the house might very well hear. If she screamed and he was close, he would be on top of her before the sound escaped her throat.

She wasn't even sure she *could* scream. Her throat was so dry. Her mouth was dry, too.

What if she tried to scream, but the only sound that came out was a strangled croak?

Forget screaming. Her best bet, her only bet, was to run for it, to gather up every bit of strength she could possibly muster and catapult herself out from under the trees, then race like a greyhound toward the house.

But could she even run?

Her ears were ringing. Her head pounded. When she tried to focus her eyes, she got nauseated. Her legs, her hands, her whole body felt achy and bruised. She was hurt, though how badly she couldn't be sure. Too badly to run for it?

The alternative was to lie where she was and simply wait. But for what? Nicky was as sure as she had ever been that she didn't want to find out.

Then she made a terrible discovery: Over the din in her ears, over the racing of her pulse, over the panicked thud of her heart, she was almost sure *she could hear someone else breathing.*

He was there. He was close. She could feel him. On her right, down near her hipbone. He seemed to be sitting, or crouching, although she couldn't be sure because she couldn't see him.

But she could hear him breathing.

And she could hear something else, too—a strange sawing sound that made no sense. She couldn't imagine what it was, but it was weird enough and spooky enough to make the hairs stand up on the back of her neck.

Oh, God, oh, God . . .

She heard the rustle of branches, felt something nudge her hip. The breathing—harsh, uneven breathing—came closer. He was turning toward her.

He was crouched beside her now, leaning over her. . . .

Terror washed over her like an icy wave. Her heart gave a great leap, then seemed to lodge in her throat. Her stomach knotted.

Don't move.

"Nicky," he muttered, and touched her hair, stroking it.

A scream exploded into her throat, where it remained trapped and silent. Her skin crawled. Her head spun. Her pulse surged until it was as loud as thunder in her ears. She felt like she might be going to pass out. . . .

If she did, she would be helpless.

Something warm and wet seeped beneath her right hand. A liquid with some body to it, sticky like paint, with a faint but distinctive smell. It oozed beneath her fingers, pooled beneath her palm, crept toward her body.

The surprise of it froze her for an instant. Then, in a compulsive movement that she could no more have stopped than she could have stopped her heart from beating, her hand jerked, recoiling from the warm wet pool.

And brushed something.

Another hand lying, palm upturned, on the ground just inches away. Warm but motionless, unresponsive . . .

"You're awake, aren't you?" he asked, his voice a low, guttural rasp.

Oh, God, no. Help me. . . .

Twin beams of light speared out of the darkness, raking through the branches, throwing his shadow, hunched and black, against the trunk of the tree, illuminating the unmoving hand and the body to which it belonged in a freeze-frame of horror that could have lasted only a scant fraction of a second. But it was long enough for the image to stamp itself indelibly in Nicky's brain.

The body was Karen's. Her face was turned away, but her shiny, black hair was unmistakable. She lay on her back not two feet away in a dark-red pool of blood that rolled outward in a flood tide over the brown bed of pine needles. Nicky saw Karen's slim, pale hand lying limply in the crimson lake, and realized in that instant that the liquid that had puddled beneath her own hand had been Karen's blood, that the smell she had become aware of immediately on regaining consciousness had been the meat-locker aroma of blood, that Karen was in all probability dead, murdered, and that she was going to be murdered, too, probably in the next few seconds, right here under the pines beside Karen.

The sheer horror of it galvanized her. The shriek that tore out of her throat would have done Jamie Lee Curtis proud. With her heart pounding so hard she feared it might explode, and fueled by a huge surge of adrenaline, she reared up on her poor bruised knees and shoved him with every bit of strength she possessed, catching him off guard, thrusting him away hard enough so that he gave a surprised grunt and fell back, toppling over on his butt, she thought from the sound of it, although she didn't wait around to make sure. In almost the same instant, she launched herself forward like a missile, scrambling on all fours through the maze of entwined branches, scuttling like a terrified crab toward the dim silver moonlight that shimmered just beyond the trees, toward the car that was purring its way up the drive, its headlights having slashed through the pines and moved on.

"Bitch."

Lunging after her, he grabbed at her, caught her jacket, but, infused with a strength born of terror, she hit and kicked and fought and somehow managed to win free. Then, in a last desperate lunge, she leaped out through the branches, throwing herself toward the edge of the driveway, which was no more than six feet away. Something slammed hard into her side just above her hipbone as she dove out of the tree, but she made it anyway. Screaming like a banshee, she hit the ground hard, rolled, and came to rest on the asphalt right in the dazzling brightness of the headlight beams.

Brakes screeched. Tires squealed. The car slewed sideways as it tried to stop. . . .

JOE HAD JUST STARTED walking down the driveway when the scream ripped through the night. It was loud as a siren, unmistakably female, and so full of terror that it froze him in his tracks and made his heart skip a beat. He'd almost gone back inside, having done a pretty thorough job of convincing himself that his best course of action was to get things wrapped up here as fast as possible and then head on home to bed where temptation would be safely out of reach, but he hadn't been able to get that aborted little squeal out of his mind.

It was almost certainly an animal. But Nicky had gone out into the dark, and unless she had walked around to the front—quite a trek in her three-inch heels, given that the ground was uneven and the grass high—she was still outside. The one thing he knew for sure was that she hadn't gone back inside the house via the back door, because if she had, he would have seen her. Of course, it was very possible that she'd walked to where the cars were parked, hopped in hers, and taken off.

It was also possible that she'd fallen or . . .

He didn't have a clue what the *or* could be. But with that choked-off little squeal in mind, and just in case, he'd decided to take a quick stroll down the driveway.

He'd only gone about four yards when he saw headlights cutting through the darkness toward him. The car wasn't in sight yet, but the headlights were coming on steadily, illuminating the big pines at the curve of the driveway and turning them into giant black silhouettes of Christmas trees. On the other side of the pavement, the live oaks looked like huge, twisted hands. Someone was driving up from the street, possibly Nicky herself. He could just hear the soft whine of the engine over the muted murmurings of the night.

He stopped, watched the car coming, and figured that if there was anything to see on the driveway, the driver of the car would see it. No need to trek down to the street at all. He listened to the faint *swoosh* of tires on the pavement and breathed in the warm, briny air and thought about what to have for dinner.

The roast chicken at Dave's place was probably out. Given that it was past ten-thirty now and any place with food worth eating on the island was closed, that meant his choices were pretty much limited to what he could cook himself or . . .

The scream came out of nowhere, ripping through the darkness, stopping his thought process in its tracks.

Joe was already racing down the driveway when more gut-wrenching screams and the squeal of brakes split the air. By the time he reached the scene seconds later, the night had already descended into chaos. The car had stopped so fast that it was slanted across the driveway. Its headlights lit up the night. He could smell exhaust and burnt rubber from the tires. His gaze followed the path of the lights, and he saw that someone lay on the smooth, black asphalt in front of the car. A woman, curled on her side, her body slender and clad in black, her legs pale and bent at the knee, her long hair gleaming a rich, deep red in the twin beams of white light: Nicky.

"Shit," he said, moving fast. He crouched beside her. She gasped out something that he didn't understand, and tried to roll onto her hands and knees, tried to get up. Her glorious hair spilled over her face, hiding it from him. She was breathing hard, obviously in distress, and her shoes were gone. The silky material of her suit was covered with dirt and some kind of debris, like grass or pine needles or something. There seemed to be smears of something, mud or blood—God, he hoped it was the former—on her hands and legs.

"Stay still," he ordered, and caught her by the upper arms, easing her back down onto the pavement. His hands slid over her, quickly checking for injuries. He could feel her body—slender, shapely, warm—shuddering beneath his palms. There was a rip in her jacket just above her right hipbone. He investigated further. The cloth around it was wet and tacky: blood. *Shit.* "You just got hit by a car."

"No . . ." Nicky's head slewed round, and her hair fell back from her face. She tried to get up, but he once again caught her arms and this time didn't let go, holding her down on the pavement as she strained to be free. She was on her back now, looking up at him, wild-eyed, shaking her head violently. "Karen . . ."

"She jumped right out in front of me," a woman cried. Obviously the driver, she'd left the car door standing wide as she ran around to the accident scene. The quick *slap-slap* of her feet hitting the pavement was surprisingly jarring. "Is that *Nicky?* Oh my God, did I hit her? Is she dead?"

"Not dead," Joe said, sparing the woman—it was the tiny, blonde makeup artist—only the briefest of glances.

"*Karen.*" Nicky's hands, cold and slender but surprisingly strong, grabbed at his, closed around his wrists, held them tightly. Her expression was desperate, frantic. "She's hurt! You've got to help her!"

"What?" He didn't understand.

"He's got her," she cried, struggling to sit up again. Her eyes were wide and glassy with shock or fright, or some combination of the two. Her mouth shook. The words tumbled over each other, spilling out so fast that they were almost incoherent. Her hands had his wrists in a death grip now. He could feel them trembling.

"It's all right," he said, thinking to calm her. "Everything's all right."

"*She's under the trees. There's a man . . .*"

"Just stay still, okay?" He kept his voice gentle, sort of half-listening to what she was saying as he did his best to keep her in place without exacerbating any injuries that she might have sustained. That he was able to control her with relative ease said a lot about her physical state, he thought. She was obviously weakened, and he feared she might be going into shock.

"He's under there, too—he attacked me. . . ." She was still babbling, but the expression on her face as she pointed toward the pines said more than a thousand words could have. She looked absolutely terrified. Then her eyes locked with his and her expression grew fierce. "Are you *listening?* The car barely touched me. There's a man under the trees—he's got Karen. . . ."

Joe looked around at the trees with a frown.

"Karen?" the makeup artist repeated blankly, her expression doubtful as she, too, glanced at the pines. She was crouched down beside him now, her pixie face a study in concern as she touched a bruise or a smudge or something on Nicky's cheek.

"She's under there—*hurry, she's bleeding.*" The note of hysteria in Nicky's voice told its own tale. Her legs were moving restlessly, and she was trying to get up again, shoving at his hands and pushing up off the pavement with a pathetic lack of strength.

"Whoa, there." He tightened his grip on her. Her shoulders were narrow, her bones delicate; her arms felt surprisingly fragile beneath his hands. "You don't want to be moving just yet."

We need an ambulance here, he thought, and he started to reach for his cell phone, which was in the front pocket of his jeans.

"He'll get *away*—" Taking advantage of his movement, she tried to twist free. He forgot the cell phone for the moment in favor of keeping her still. With both his hands on her again, she seemed to realize it wasn't happening and gave up. Defeated, she lay there on the pavement, breathing hard, her eyes dark with agitation as she looked up at him, her face white as paper, her hair a bright burst of color against the black asphalt.

"Karen's under the trees?" The makeup artist's voice betrayed stark skepticism, but Joe was suddenly starting to understand and believe.

Unless Nicky was hallucinating, which was always possible if the car had knocked her to the pavement and she'd taken a hard blow to the head, something bad was hidden under the dusty skirts of the pines.

"Stay with her," he said abruptly to the makeup artist, and stood up.

"Do you have a gun?" The question was sharp, and there was a hysterical edge to Nicky's voice. Without his restraining hands on her, she finally managed to struggle into a semi-sitting position. Her legs curled beside her, and she leaned on one elbow. Her hand was pressed to the spot above her hip where he'd detected the oozing blood. Her eyes stayed glued to the pines. "I think . . . I think he has a knife."

"Yeah."

Hell, he *always* had his gun. It was a SIG Sauer, smooth and black and shiny, lightweight and small enough to be tucked away in a pocket or the small of his back—or in the ankle holster he was wearing tonight to keep it well out of the way of Amy's kiddies. He'd had it a long time, so long that by now it was almost as much a part of him as one of his hands. During his previous life, it had saved his ass more than once. It wasn't his department-issued weapon. That one was tucked away in the glove compartment of the squad car out in front of the house. That one was a Glock, relatively big and clumsy, and he didn't much like it. The SIG was his own. Even on this tiny bit of paradise, where nothing—before tonight—ever seemed to happen, he kept it with him. It was habit. Like the cigarettes. Two things he couldn't—wouldn't—give up.

He stepped away into the dark and started to hike up the leg of his jeans to free his SIG—just in case.

"Tina, hurry. We need to lock ourselves in the car," he heard Nicky say urgently. Glancing over his shoulder, he saw that the makeup artist had hold of one of Nicky's arms and was trying to help her get to her feet. Given that Tina, big shoes, long blond hair, and all, was about the size of a mosquito and Nicky, while reed-slim, was about five-seven or so, they were struggling. Despite her panicked efforts, Nicky couldn't seem to get her legs beneath her.

Until the extent of her injuries was determined, letting Nicky move was probably a mistake. On the other hand, if there was a hurt woman under the trees, finding her and helping her was urgent. And if some kind of creep was indeed lurking beneath the pines, getting the women out of harm's way before checking things out was obviously the prudent thing to do. It was always possible that the guy might manage to sneak around his flank, or, God forbid, take him out. Then the women would be at his mercy.

Joe left the SIG in its holster, retraced his steps, and scooped Nicky off the pavement in a single economical movement.

"What—?" She clutched at his shoulders in surprise, her eyes wide as she looked at him.

"Just a precaution," he said as he lugged her around toward the passenger-side door. As he had expected, she didn't weigh all that much, certainly not more than a hundred twenty pounds or so. Her hair smelled faintly of some floral shampoo, and her body felt firm and supple in his arms. This close, he could see that there was a huge knot on her forehead just above her left eye. Whatever had hit her, she had been dealt quite a blow.

"You've got to help *Karen*." She sounded on the verge of losing it. Her nails dug into his shoulders. Even through his shirt, he could feel the sharp crescents pressing into his skin. He had a brief flash of insanity in which he imagined those manicured nails sinking into the muscles of his bare back, and he gritted his teeth at the effort it took to dismiss it.

You need a woman, Franconi, he told himself grimly as he bundled Nicky into the passenger seat.

"Get in the car," he said to Tina, who had been bobbing along at his elbow, watching him and Nicky, wide-eyed, as if not quite sure whether or not he meant Nicky harm. At his words, Tina appeared to realize that he was on their side. At any rate, she nodded, ran around to the driver's side, and got in.

"Lock the doors and drive on up to the house," he said to Tina, who was now behind the wheel. He was leaning into the car, speaking across Nicky, who was looking up at him with eyes as big and round as Frisbees. "When you get there, start blowing the horn until somebody comes out. If nobody comes out, or if you don't like the look of whoever it is who does come out, just sit tight until I get up there. Understand?"

Tina's eyes were now as wide as Nicky's, and she looked just about as scared. She nodded.

"Go," he said.

His eyes met Nicky's for the briefest of instants—her pupils were huge and made her eyes look shiny black—and then he shut the door and stepped back, listening for the click of the locks. He heard it, and then the car—it was a Dodge Neon, he saw—was on its way up the driveway.

Now for the SIG.

With the familiar weight of the weapon in his hand, he felt ready to take on all comers, but Nicky's obvious terror stayed with him and made him cautious. Moving toward the pines, he reached the outermost tips of the shaggy branches and paused, his senses shifting to high alert. The scent of pine wafted around him, borne on the breeze. He heard the usual night sounds but nothing else, nothing out of the ordinary. Without the headlights for illumination, it was dark as pitch: He couldn't see a thing. He didn't have a flashlight on him, not a real one, but, he remembered with satisfaction, he did have one of those tiny penlight key rings. Under the circumstances, it would have to do. Fishing his keys from his pocket, Joe grabbed the thing, squeezed it, and eyed the narrow beam of white light that shot out with satisfaction. It wasn't much, but it should be enough for what he had in mind.

He looked at the trees again.

"Police," he barked in his best cop's voice. "Come out with your hands where I can see them."

Right. Like he really expected that to work. Only in the movies did bad guys come out with their hands up. In real life, at least, in his real life, they either started shooting or ran like hell.

Still, he waited. The breeze stirred the branches, and the slight rustling sound of it was the only reply. Joe waited a moment longer, then sighed. Of course. Nothing was ever that easy.

Gun in one hand, penlight in the other, he started shining the light through the branches, peering in at the rough, gray trunks, the branches like dark, extended arms, the carpet of fallen golden-brown needles.

Beneath the third tree, he struck gold: Just within the outer edge of the branches, the tiny beam illuminated a trickle of viscous red liquid rolling slowly along a downward slope that ended at the driveway.

Not good.

His heart started pumping faster; his stomach tightened; his jaw clenched. Using the light, Joe followed the ominous trail upward until he found himself looking at a lily-white hand lying lifelessly in a pool of dark-red blood.

7

NICKY WAS IN SHOCK. She knew it, could tell from the way everyone else in the kitchen seemed to be far away, even though her mother and Uncle John were sitting right there at the table with her, and Livvy was at the refrigerator, and Uncle Ham was at the stove, frying up bacon and eggs, and Harry, having ventured into the center of the action just moments before to fetch himself a beer, was directly in her line of sight as, bottle in hand, he hot-footed it back into the relative peace and quiet of the den. It was just after two a.m. Monday morning, the start of a whole new week. She was scheduled to be on a plane to Chicago at ten-fifteen, and back in her office by three.

Karen was dead.

"Drink your hot chocolate," Uncle John said, sounding as if he were at the other end of a long tunnel rather than directly across the table from her. The steady *fwump-fwump* of the ceiling fan echoed the pounding in her head. Funny, nothing really hurt: not the long but shallow knife wound just above her hipbone, not her bruised thigh that had endured a close encounter with Tina's car, not her poor thumped head, not her scraped-up hands and knees. Maybe shock had something to do with that, too. "You need the sugar."

Nicky nodded and looked at the cup, which was sitting on the table di-rectly in front of her. The hot chocolate was thick and milky brown with a little puff of steam rising from it. Uncle Ham, who was arguably the best cook in the world, had garnished it with a dollop of whipped cream and some chocolate chips. Ordinarily, Nicky loved Uncle Ham's hot chocolate. Right now, she thought she might throw up if she drank it. Drinking was easier than arguing, however, so she picked up the cup and took a tiny sip.

It tasted chalky in her mouth. Her stomach knotted with revulsion, and she quickly set the cup down again, to find Uncle John watching her with concern.

"I can't believe I didn't see it. My own daughter," Leonora said in an aggrieved tone, as she had at least a dozen times since she and the rest of the family had met Nicky at the island clinic, where Dave the deputy had driven her directly from the Old Taylor Place. At the clinic, the knife wound had been identified as what it was, cleaned, and bandaged; she'd been diagnosed with a mild concussion, for which she'd been told to rest; and a sedative, which she hadn't yet taken, had been given to her to help her sleep. She'd still been on the examination table when the call had come in confirming what she'd known intuitively all along: Karen was dead. That was when she'd gone numb, she remembered. After that, nothing had seemed quite real.

An hour later, she'd been released to her family. In the approximately forty-five minutes since they had arrived home, she'd showered—carefully, so as not to get her bandage wet—and tried not to think about the fact that at first the water running off her body and swirling away down the drain had been brown with blood, some her own, some undoubtedly Karen's. After noticing that, she had gotten out of the shower much more quickly than she had originally meant to, toweled off, dried her hair, and dressed in a pair of silky pink nylon pajamas and, because she was freezing, a thick pink terry-cloth robe and a pair of white ankle socks. All the clothes belonged to Livvy, because the clothes Nicky'd been wearing when she was attacked had been taken for evidence, and her suitcase, along with practically everything else she had brought with her from Chicago, was still in the trunk of her rental car. The car was parked by the garage—she'd noticed it when they had arrived home from the clinic—but by the time she'd thought about her things and remembered that they were in the trunk, she was naked and wet. It had been easier après shower to simply wrap herself in a towel and scamper into Livvy's room and help herself to her sister's clothes. Livvy hadn't objected: Her only reaction upon seeing Nicky padding into the kitchen in her clothes had been a slight narrowing of her eyes. To her surprise, Nicky had found wearing her big sister's clothes oddly comforting, almost like going back in time to their teenage years, when if she'd really wanted to get back at Livvy for something, all she'd had to do was "borrow" some of her cherished clothes. As if some rule of ancient karmic payback was in effect, though, now

Livvy's things were miles too big, to say nothing of being Pepto-Bismol pink, which was definitely *not* Nicky's color. Fortunately, the pajama pants came equipped with a drawstring waist, which she had cinched tightly, and the color was the least of her worries at the moment.

Her hand had lain in a puddle of Karen's blood.

Nicky shivered, and of its own volition, the hand in question curled into a fist in her lap.

"Drink up," Uncle John urged her again. "You're cold."

"You never *can* see anything to do with family," Livvy reminded Leonora impatiently while Nicky took another tiny sip of hot chocolate. "We could all be dying and you wouldn't know it. You didn't even know that Ben was screwing his head off with his secretary. Face it: You're just not that psychic when it comes to us."

"Olivia Jane." Leonora stiffened in her chair to fix Livvy with an affronted gaze. "That's not true."

"Is too," Livvy said, unrepentant.

"You forget I saw Harry all covered with blood, and Charlie sitting on a beach when he should have been in New York, and poor, dear Neil—well, you know how I saw your father."

"They're not blood kin, Mama. You can see them a little, but you can't see blood kin. Not at all. It's the truth, and you know it."

"Even if your mother *had* seen what was happening with your husband, what good would it have done?" Uncle Ham intervened over his shoulder as he expertly cracked eggs into a skillet. They slid into the hot grease with a loud sizzle. The bacon, done now, lay draining on paper towels by the stove. The homey scent of breakfast filled the kitchen. It made Nicky's stomach churn.

"I could have caught the bastard in the act." Livvy closed the refrigerator door with more force than the action called for and shuffled toward the table. Like the rest of the family, she'd been getting ready for bed when the call to meet Nicky at the clinic had come in. She was fully dressed in the same clothes she'd been wearing earlier, only now her T-shirt was on inside-out and she had backless pink slippers—clearly the companions to the robe Nicky was wearing—on her feet.

"I'm sorry I didn't see either one of you in trouble." Leonora's chin quivered. "I keep telling you, I'm *blocked.*"

"You're getting better: You saw something tonight." Uncle John's tone was comforting.

"It was an imprint—a loop." Leonora shook her head. "Sometimes terrible events leave their imprints on their surroundings. That's obviously what happened in this case and thank goodness I was able to pick up on it, because otherwise, I was getting *nothing.* I wasn't communicating with Tara's spirit in the usual way at all. And Dorothy still didn't come through."

There was a forlorn note to her voice as she said that last.

"Here, you might want to put this on your forehead. You look like you're growing a horn." Livvy dropped something—a bag of frozen peas, Nicky realized after blinking at it confusedly for an instant—on the table in front of her.

"Oh. Thanks."

The bump on her forehead *was* big, having grown to about the size of a golf ball. That being the case, the peas were probably a good idea. She picked up the bag and applied it to the bump. In the meantime, Livvy walked around the table and lowered herself, grimacing, into her seat. The oak ladderback chair was old, having been around since they were kids, and it creaked warningly as she settled into it. All eyes immediately shot to Livvy, who fortunately seemed to be too preoccupied to notice either the protesting chair or the apprehensive looks on the faces of her family. Another attack of the "I'm too fat to live" blues was probably more than any of them could take, Nicky thought. Certainly, it was more than *she* could take at the moment.

"If I'd caught him in the act, I would have left him flat. Instead, he waited until I was pregnant, and then the bastard left *me.*" Livvy dug savagely into the banana pudding she'd extracted from the refrigerator. "Until then, I was Little Miss Clueless."

"The eggs are ready," Uncle Ham announced from the stove. "Who wants breakfast?"

"I do," Livvy said, while Uncle John stood up to help Uncle Ham carry the plates to the table.

"Livvy, you've done nothing but eat for the past two months. You're going to make yourself sick." Leonora looked meaningfully at the pudding that Livvy was scarfing down.

"I'm going to make myself *fat,* you mean, don't you? Well, too late, Mama. I *am* fat. And you know what? It doesn't matter. I worked like a dog for years to keep my figure, and he left me anyway, and now I'm pregnant and big as a moose and *I don't care.*" Livvy shoveled a defiant spoonful of pudding into her mouth, then reached for one of the plates that Uncle John had just brought to the table. "Bring on the bacon."

"You'll be sorry later on," Leonora warned.

Livvy fixed her big blue eyes on their mother, opened her mouth wide, and shoved in an entire piece of bacon.

"Olivia." Leonora's tone made it a reproof.

"Leave her alone, she's eating for two," Uncle John said, sitting down.

Uncle Ham, after bellowing at Harry to come and get it, took his place at the table, too.

"Not two. Two hundred. Pounds, that is," Livvy said. "I only have ten more to go. Want to bet I make it?"

She took a ferocious bite of egg on toast.

Unreal, Nicky thought. Here her family was, having a perfectly normal—for them—conversation when she had been attacked and Karen had been brutally murdered just a few hours earlier. For her, the remembered horror seemed to hang in the air like an icy cloud, and yet—the world just kept on keeping on.

"Eat," Uncle John said, and tapped his fork against the edge of Nicky's plate for emphasis. Automatically, she glanced down at the glistening fried egg on toast, at the two strips of crisp bacon, at the twisted orange slice he'd used for garnish. Perfection on a plate. She should have been hungry; she'd had nothing to eat since . . . breakfast? She and the rest of the team had made do with airplane food on the flight from Chicago. Karen had sat across the aisle from her, picking gingerly at an omelette. They'd meant to grab lunch when they landed, but as it turned out, they hadn't had time. That tasteless airplane omelette had been Karen's last meal. . . .

Nicky's stomach turned inside out. Suddenly the hot, greasy smell of the food was more than she could bear.

Before she could do more than glance up from her plate, a brisk knock cut through the desultory talk that was still going on around her.

All conversation ceased as everyone in the room looked toward the sound. It came from the back door, which stood open so that the cool night breeze could blow in.

"Something smells good," a male voice Nicky didn't recognize said through the screen. Since it was bright in the kitchen and dark on the other side of the door, it was impossible to see who was there. "Mind if we come in?"

"That depends on who you are." Leonora slewed around to look at the door while Uncle John got up to unlatch it. "And what you want."

"It's Dave O'Neil, Miz Stuyvescent," Dave said in the drawling accent typical of area natives as he stepped into the kitchen.

It was, Nicky saw, Deputy Dave—and right behind him came his boss, the nasty cop. But he'd come to her aid back there on the driveway, so thinking of him as the nasty cop was probably something she might want to reconsider. "Barney Fife" was probably out now, too.

"I don't think I had a chance to introduce myself earlier," the no-longer-quite-so-nasty cop said, glancing around the kitchen. As she'd noticed when she had first heard him speak, he clearly wasn't from around there. *Yankee* was the word that popped into her mind upon hearing him now, which showed her just how far back into her deep Southern childhood she had temporarily regressed. "Joe Franconi, Chief of Police."

He was clearly taking everything in, and for a moment, Nicky imagined the scene from his perspective: the homely smell of breakfast still lingering in the air, the uneven thumping of the paddle fan overhead, the outdated avocado-and-gold kitchen with its dark cabinets and harsh lighting, countertops cluttered with eggshells and paper towels and the various implements Uncle Ham had used to cook with, the ancient black iron skillet that was one of Uncle Ham's prized possessions still smoking slightly on the only modern appliance in the room, the six-burner, stainless-steel, professional-quality gas stove. In the center of the room, directly beneath the lazily rotating fan, the table stood, crowded with plates of bacon and eggs and hot-chocolate mugs and Livvy's nearly empty pudding bowl. Around the table sat Leonora, who, having rid herself of the overdone makeup and purple caftan sometime before arriving at the clinic, was dressed in a very ordinary-looking blue-flowered shirt and matching slacks, her only makeup a barely-there trace of deep red lipstick, with a pair of the oversized tortoise-shell-framed glasses she wore when she took her contacts out slipping down her nose; Livvy, with most of her two-toned hair having now escaped from its wispy little knot to straggle toward her shoulders, her top on wrong side out, her face almost as pink as her top, her mouth crammed full of bacon, which she continued to defiantly chew; Uncle Ham, in a turquoise Hornets T-shirt and loose plaid flannel pants, a strand of his thinning red hair hanging limply across his forehead, his face flushed and sweaty from working over the stove; and Nicky herself, dressed in Livvy's way-too-bright pink pajamas and robe, her undoubtedly pale and shiny face scrubbed clean of makeup, her still slightly damp hair pulled back and secured in a ponytail at the nape of her neck . . .

With a white plastic bag of frozen peas pressed to her forehead.

Realizing that, Nicky hastily lowered the peas, only to discover that the police chief's eyes were on her. His mouth quirked slightly as his gaze touched on the plastic bag. Then his eyes slid back up to her forehead, and suddenly there was no trace of amusement at all on his face.

"John Nash." Uncle John, looking as natty as he always did in the same black T-shirt and khaki slacks he'd been wearing earlier, introduced himself, distracting the police chief's attention from the knot on Nicky's head. As they shook hands, Uncle John nodded toward Uncle Ham and continued the introductions. "Hamilton James"—with a slightly sour expression on his face, Uncle Ham stood up, shook hands, and immediately sat back down again—"Leonora James Stuyvescent"—Leonora nodded regally—"Olivia Hollis"—Livvy swallowed and waggled her fingers by way of a greeting—"and I know you've met Nicky."

"Yeah." His eyes met hers again. As before, his expression was impossible to read. He had the kind of lean, hard-featured face that the harsh lighting sharpened and filled with shadows. It also picked up on lines around his eyes and mouth which she hadn't noticed previously. The whites of his eyes were bloodshot, and his mouth was grim. He'd changed his dorky uniform shirt for a ratty black Chicago Bulls T-shirt that looked nearly as old as he was. It struck her as an odd thing to have done, given that he'd almost certainly been conducting some kind of investigation into what had happened, until it occurred to her that maybe he'd gotten blood on his uniform shirt.

Her blood . . . or Karen's blood.

Suddenly, Nicky felt light-headed.

"Y'all know me," Dave the Deputy said comfortably, which was true; he'd been a resident of the island for so many years that even Nicky, whose visits as an adult had been sporadic at best, could vaguely remember seeing him around. He wandered over to the table as he spoke and stood eyeing the food while Nicky, gripping her chair seat on the off chance that she might slide right off it if she didn't, took a couple of discreet breaths as she fought to recover her equilibrium. "We're real sorry to bother you at this time of night, folks, but . . ."

"So where's the . . . oh," Harry interrupted. Having finally managed to tear himself away from whatever program he was watching in the den, Harry paused in the doorway as he realized that there were strangers in the kitchen. His thick hair looked parchment-white under the fluorescent light, which also seemed to leach some of the golf-course tan from his face and made the lines running across his forehead and down his cheeks look deeper than they actually were. Dressed in rumpled khakis and a short-sleeved blue dress shirt, he had smallish blue eyes, a large, triangular nose, thin lips, and a square chin. About six feet tall and in reasonable shape, he was an attractive man for his age.

No surprise there: All Leonora's husbands had been attractive. Physical beauty was important to her, and she wouldn't have settled for anything less.

"Harry Stuyvescent," Uncle John introduced him. "Leonora's husband. Harry, this is Joe Franconi. You know, he took over Barry Mead's job."

"I guess that would make you our new Chief of Police then." Harry moved on into the kitchen and they shook hands. "Welcome to the island, Mr. Franconi. You've been on the job since—what? Christmas?"

"January. And call me Joe."

His glance included everyone in the room in the invitation.

"Terrible business tonight." Harry shook his head as he headed for the table. "Unbelievable thing to have happen."

"That poor girl," Leonora chimed in with feeling. "And to think it could have been my darling Nicky. . . ." She broke off, pressing her lips together, her gaze shooting to the bump on Nicky's head. *Her darling Nicky* was keenly aware of the injury now. It was throbbing and swelling and felt as though it had grown to about the size of a tennis ball since she'd last checked it. Livvy was right, she decided, as all eyes in the room suddenly seemed glued to her forehead. She *felt* as if she were growing a horn.

She had to resist the urge to clap the bag of peas over it again just to hide it from view.

"So, what's going on?" Harry sat down at the table where his plate of bacon and eggs was waiting at his usual place, and directed his question up at Joe. "You got any idea who the sick bastard is who would do something like that?"

"Not yet," Joe said.

"Harry!" Leonora frowned at her spouse. "Would you please watch your language at the table?"

That was rich, Nicky thought, coming from somebody who, when the occasion warranted, could and did swear like a sailor. Of course, there was a Yankee stranger in the room, and her mother was a great one for keeping up appearances.

"Oh. Right. Sorry, dear." Harry, looking suitably abashed, subsided and turned his attention to his plate. In the six years he'd been married to her mother—Nicky never could manage to think of him as her stepfather; she simply didn't know him well enough—he'd clearly learned that the best way to deal with Leonora was simply to not resist her. She was a force of nature, not to be denied—at least not without a fight.

Nicky didn't think any of them were up to any more fights tonight. At least, she knew *she* wasn't. She was bone-tired, nauseated, physically and mentally hurting—and afraid to allow herself to acknowledge any of it. If she did, she would have to face the hideous truth of what had happened.

Karen had been butchered.

She shuddered inwardly as her mind immediately shied away from the thought.

"Can we offer you two some breakfast?" Uncle John asked, having moved back to stand behind his chair. "You don't know it yet, Joe, but Ham's the best cook in these parts, and he always makes plenty."

Indeed, Nicky noticed as she determinedly focused on the here and now again, there were three untouched helpings of egg on toast on a plate in the center of the table, and another plate—only about a third full now, since Livvy had been helping herself—of bacon. In case, as Uncle Ham would have said, anybody should want seconds. Or thirds.

"Appreciate the offer," Joe said, eyeing the food with what looked to Nicky like considerable regret. "But I actually came by to talk to Ms. Sullivan, if she feels up to it."

Nicky's stomach sank. *No, Ms. Sullivan doesn't feel up to it. Definitely not.*

"Now?" Uncle Ham's brows snapped together. Could he read her reaction in her face? "It's nearly two-thirty in the morning, and she's been through a lot."

"I know." Joe looked at Nicky. "I understand from some of the people you work with that you're planning to fly out later today. Otherwise, I'd just ask you to stop by the office tomorrow and give us a statement."

"*Are* you leaving today? I would have thought—after what happened . . ." Leonora's voice trailed off and her brows slowly met over the bridge of her nose as her gaze touched Nicky's. "Maybe you *should* go."

Because she might be in danger. Her mother's expression as much as her words crystallized the fear that Nicky had until that moment refused to face.

She had nearly been killed along with Karen tonight. If things had happened just a little bit differently, she would be dead right now.

And the killer was still out there.

Wild horses couldn't keep her off that plane.

"Now is fine," Nicky said, pushing her chair back and standing up. Her scraped and bruised knees ached, the cut in her side reminded her of its existence with a sharp twinge, and her head swam unexpectedly. Tottering a little, she caught hold of the back of the chair for support, then gritted her teeth and fought to pull herself together. Talking to the police was unavoidable, and if she meant to be on that plane at ten-thirty A.M., then now was the moment to do it. From her own work as a reporter, she knew that as the person who had found the body—*Oh, God, "the body" would be Karen*—any evidence she could give would be of vital importance to the investigation. And beyond that, she had been attacked, too, presumably by the same man, presumably for the same purpose.

Could she identify the killer?

Her skin turned to gooseflesh at the thought.

"Is there someplace we can talk in private?" Joe asked, and the confused images that had begun to swirl through her mind receded.

"Use the den," Leonora suggested, peering at him over the top of her glasses.

Fighting not to shiver, Nicky glanced at Harry—the den was his secondary place of refuge after the garage—and he nodded.

"Game's over," he said. "Feel free."

"This way." Taking a deep breath, Nicky squared her shoulders, let go of the chair, and started to lead the way out of the kitchen. Joe followed. Out of the corner of her eye, she watched him pause to look back at the group around the table.

"Dave will be taking statements from the rest of you while we're here, if you don't mind. Your whereabouts during the last fifteen minutes or so that the show was being broadcast, anything unusual you might remember, things like that."

There was a murmur in response, but Nicky was too far away to hear what was said. Anyway, she didn't care. Walking was much harder than she remembered it being, and just putting one foot in front of the other without collapsing required all her concentration.

By the time she reached the den, Nicky was freezing. It was a small room, paneled in rare longleaf pine, with an elaborately carved fireplace built into one wall and a single tall window that looked out into the side yard in the middle of another. A pair of shabby leather armchairs flanked the fireplace; a tapestry-covered couch had been placed opposite them. The faint smell of wood smoke from decades of fires hung in the air. Harry was a Civil War buff, and paintings of the Blue and Gray engaged in various epic battles adorned the walls. The drapes—once-grand gold damask panels that were now so old that they were almost see-through in places—were closed. The only light, a faint bluish glow, came from the small jabbering TV in the entertainment center that took up nearly the entire wall beside the door. Unable to bear its too-cheerful noise, Nicky switched the TV off as soon as she entered, then found the sudden near darkness unexpectedly unnerving.

Get a grip, she told herself, and walked steadily across the shadow-filled room to the lamp on Harry's big desk, which was positioned in front of the window about as far away from the door as it was possible to get. Turning on the lamp, relieved at the soft yellow glow that banished the shadows, she didn't realize that she had been holding her breath until it escaped in a soft *whoosh*.

Then she sank down in one of the armchairs by the fireplace, wincing a little as the tape that held the bandage in place tugged at her skin, and pulled Livvy's too-pink robe closer around her throat.

She was so cold. Cold as death . . .

"Do you mind?" Joe asked. He'd closed the door while she was turning on the lamp, and he was now standing beside Harry's desk. Nicky frowned a little in incomprehension, then saw that he had something in his hand, which she discovered on closer inspection was a small portable tape recorder. Clearly, he was asking if she minded if he taped their conversation, and her permission, just as clearly, was something that he took for granted, because he turned on the machine even before she nodded.

He identified himself, identified her, and gave the time, place, and date.

"So, how are you feeling?" That was his first question. He was leaning back against Harry's desk now, his arms crossed over his chest. Besides the ancient T-shirt, he was wearing sneakers and worn jeans that hugged his lean hips and long, muscular legs.

It occurred to her that he looked sexy as hell standing there like that. It also occurred to her that he looked pretty unprofessional for a police chief.

In which capacity he would undoubtedly be heading the investigation into Karen's murder. She pursed her lips.

"Fine," she lied, electing to concentrate on the subject at hand, then added, "considering," because of course it was obvious that she wasn't *fine*. Then she ended up changing the subject by asking him about something that had been bugging her since she'd heard him say it in the kitchen: "Why ask my family their whereabouts during the last fifteen minutes of the show? What happened to Karen—it happened after we were off the air."

"What makes you think that?"

"Why . . . I followed her down the driveway, and I didn't go outside until the broadcast was over. Probably at least *ten minutes* after the broadcast was over."

"You followed her down the driveway." He was watching her closely, his brows drawn together above the faintest of frowns.

"Yes."

"All right. Before you followed her down the driveway, when was the last time you saw her?"

Nicky thought. "In the hall, right before I followed my mother upstairs. We were on the air. Karen"—she swallowed as the memory came back to her—"was in the downstairs hall, and I walked past her."

"And this would be about what time, do you think?"

"Probably about fifteen minutes before we finished. If you look at the tape of the show, the time should be easy to fix. My mother would have been going up the stairs to the second floor."

"I'll keep that in mind." His tone was noncommittal. "What was Karen doing? Who was she with?"

Nicky tried to remember. "She was watching my mother, like everybody else. And . . . smiling, because things were finally going well. Actually, she gave me a thumbs-up." The memory hurt. "She was with . . . oh, gosh, I don't know. I think . . . Cassandra? And maybe Mario. There was a group standing together near the bottom of the stairs, but I wasn't really paying attention."

He nodded as if to say he understood.

"So when I saw you in the kitchen after you were off the air, you hadn't seen Karen since right before you'd gone upstairs about fifteen minutes before the end of the broadcast?"

"That's right."

"Why did you go outside?"

Nicky frowned. She had to think a minute. Then she remembered: She'd been looking for Karen, and *he* had entered the kitchen, and she hadn't wanted to deal with him—two very good reasons, only one of which she meant to tell him.

"Gordon said Karen had gotten a phone call, and that he thought it was Sid—somebody important—about the show, and I wanted to know if it was, and what he said. Also, I wanted to tell her that she was giving me a ride home in her car."

"Gordon?"

"Gordon Davies, one of our cameramen."

He nodded. "Okay. So you went outside. Then what?"

"I stood on the patio for a few seconds." Nicky felt herself starting to tense up. She didn't want to remember this—but for Karen's sake, and her own, she had to. "Then I saw Karen walking down the driveway. And I followed her."

"Did you call out to her or anything?"

Nicky shook her head. She was so cold now, it was all she could do not to shiver openly.

"No?" he prompted.

"No," she said, realizing that he wanted her to respond out loud for the benefit of the tape recorder. "I thought she was probably talking on the phone. I didn't want to interrupt."

"What makes you think she was on the phone? Could you hear her talking?"

Nicky thought. A flash of memory crystallized in her mind's eye: Karen ahead of her in the dark, moving down toward the shadow of the pines . . .

Clenching her teeth, she did her best to remain objective.

"No," she said. "I couldn't hear her. Not ever. Even when I was close enough, when we were both . . . under the trees. I remember thinking I should have been able to hear her."

"So you never heard her. Let me ask you something: Did you ever actually see her? Well enough to positively identify her, that is?"

"What?" Nicky blinked at him. "I told you: I followed her down the driveway."

"Are you sure?" He was watching her intently. "That it was her, I mean."

Nicky stared at him. The possibility that whoever she had followed down the driveway might not have been Karen had never occurred to her until now. Her brows knit. What had she actually seen?

"I think it was," she said at last. "I saw *some*one walking away from me down the driveway, moving kind of aimlessly, like you do sometimes when you're talking on the phone, and it looked like Karen to me. I'm almost positive that it was a woman. Slim, with kind of a swaying walk. But no, now that you mention it, I didn't actually see enough of her to be absolutely positive it was Karen. It was too dark."

"So the person you saw could have been anybody."

"Well—" Nicky frowned. "I guess. Are you saying that you think it *wasn't* Karen?"

He shook his head. "I don't know. I'm just trying to get things right here. If it was Karen, then she had to have been killed after you saw her, and that makes the time frame kind of tight. If it wasn't Karen, then the possibilities open up some."

"Who else could it have been?"

"At this point, I don't have any idea." He hesitated. "Let me ask you something: How well did you know Karen?"

"We were colleagues. Friends, but work friends, if you know what I mean. Outside the job, I didn't ever see her. We all—the crew I have here with me—started working together in August, when *Twenty-four Hours Investigates* was being put together. I didn't know her before that."

"So you wouldn't know if there was someone in her personal life who might want to do her harm?"

"No, probably not. But I never heard of anything like that."

"Okay." He paused for a moment, glancing over at the tape recorder as if to make sure it was still working. Then his gaze switched back to Nicky. "I realize that this might be tough for you, but . . . I want you to take me down that driveway with you. Tell me everything that happened."

Nicky simply looked at him for a moment without saying anything. Then, when she tried to speak, her lips parted but her throat wouldn't work.

"Take your time." His eyes flicked over her face. He was still frowning slightly, but it was impossible to tell what he was thinking. "You walked out the back door onto the patio and saw someone you thought was Karen. Then what?"

"I started walking down the driveway toward her, sort of following her, not wanting to call to her until she got off the phone." Her voice had come back, she was relieved to discover, but she was suddenly so cold that she had to tuck her hands into the sleeves of her robe while her toes curled up in their fuzzy socks. "The big pine trees there at the turn of the driveway, they cast this enormous dark shadow over the pavement, and when I stepped into it, everything seemed to . . . *stop*. It was just unbelievably dark, so I couldn't really see anything, and for some reason, I couldn't hear anything, either, not the birds or the insects or anything that I'd been hearing before. It was kind of like I'd fallen down a hole, a black hole, and then I realized that I couldn't hear Karen."

The memory came back in a rush, and for a moment, Nicky was back under that pine tree, alone in the silent dark. "She was right in front of me, I thought, and I should have been able to hear her. But I couldn't. Then . . . I don't know why, exactly, but I got scared and turned and ran." She took a deep breath, remembering. Her heart began pumping faster, and goose bumps slid to prickling life over her skin. "Someone jumped me from behind. A man, I'm almost sure. I didn't see him, but . . . anyway, I think it was a man. Then I must have hit my head on the pavement and blacked out, because the next thing I remember is waking up under that tree."

Remembering, she started to feel dizzy and closed her eyes. Reconstructing what had happened next as a continuous sequence was impossible, she discovered, when she tried. It was too terrifying, too painful. Instead, snippets of memory swirled into her consciousness like quick snapshots of horror.

"Go on." His voice was deep and low, steadying, a verbal lifeline anchoring her to the here and now, and she latched onto it thankfully. She could feel his eyes on her, feel the weight of his gaze, hear his occasional encouragement when she paused or her voice broke, but she kept her eyes steadfastly closed. In halting phrases broken up by pauses in which fragments of scenes so graphic that they took her breath away flashed on the screen of her mind, she told him everything she could remember.

When she finished at last, he said nothing. For a moment, she didn't move but simply sat there with her head resting back against the smooth leather upholstery while she breathed carefully in and out and fought to drag her mind back to the present. Then, as the terrible images finally began to recede, she opened her eyes to discover that he was crouched in front of her, his brows drawn together and his mouth grim as he looked at her.

His hands were big, long-fingered, and tan, with smooth, well-kept nails. They were warm, and strong, with faint calluses on the palms. She knew this because she was holding on to them tightly, though she had no memory of reaching out to him or having him reach out to her. He was close enough so that she could see the exact pattern the fatigue lines made around his eyes, and each individual whisker in the stubble that darkened his cheeks and chin. The width of his shoulders blocked her view of much of the room, and his shadow fell across her like a blanket. That he was able to get that close without her even having been aware that he had moved, to say nothing of the fact that she hadn't even known that she was clutching his hands, said volumes about just how deeply into the recesses of her mind she had plunged, she realized. She realized too that she was huddled against one wing of the chair now, with her legs drawn up beside her, having made herself into almost as small a package as physically possible. Her skin felt cold and clammy, and she was shivering so hard that her teeth began to chatter.

"Hey." Joe said it very gently as their eyes met. His were a warm, golden hazel, flecked with green, dark now with concern for her. "You okay?"

8

No. That was the short, brutal truth, but Nicky didn't say it. Instead, she clenched her teeth to stop them from chattering and swallowed hard, fighting to regain her composure. But the horror, once summoned, was hard to shake.

She nodded.

"Sure?"

Still too upset to speak, she nodded again and concentrated on steadying her breathing and letting the hideous images go. She felt so cold that the sensation was like a physical ache; the only warm spot on her entire body was where her hands touched Joe's.

"I'm sorry I had to put you through that," he said after a moment. The nasty cop was being kind now, and she appreciated the change, but it didn't really help. What she needed was strength, and for that she had to dig deep inside herself. It required a physical effort, but she finally managed to stop shivering and relax her jaw. Then she took a deep breath and drew the remnants of her composure around herself like a tattered garment.

And she let go of his hands. He didn't seem to notice as she folded her arms across her chest instead.

"The thing is . . . he knew my name. He said 'Nicky' and t-touched my hair." Her voice sounded hoarse, croaky, not like her voice at all.

"You're on TV. Lots of people know your name."

There was that, of course. The thought didn't exactly make her feel any better.

"Did you recognize the voice?" He didn't sound particularly hopeful.

She shook her head. Just remembering that whispered "Nicky" made her skin crawl.

"Can you . . . tell me something?" she asked after a moment. "How exactly did Karen die?"

He regarded her steadily. He was still crouched in front of her, so close that she thought she could feel a little of the welcome warmth of his body heat radiating toward her. His hands now rested lightly on the arms of her chair, so that he was in effect closing her in. Under the circumstances, his position was comforting rather than claustrophobia-inducing.

"The autopsy hasn't been performed yet, but from what we could see, she suffered multiple stab wounds."

Nicky nodded. She had guessed it, of course, but having it confirmed made her feel sick all over again.

"The sound I heard—the sawing sound I told you about," she managed after a couple slow breaths. "Do you have any idea what that was?"

For the space of a heartbeat, he simply looked at her without replying. She got the impression that he was debating whether or not to answer.

"Please," she said. "I need to know."

He made a face. "I can't say for sure, of course, but . . . it looked like he cut off some of her hair. There was just a little bit of stubble left around her face. At a guess, I'd say that the sound of him hacking her hair off with his knife was what you heard."

"Oh, God." At the picture this conjured up, Nicky felt herself going all light-headed again. The thought of it was too awful . . . and then she remembered the killer touching her hair. She started to shake. The room seemed to tilt. Everything started slowly revolving around her. She closed her eyes in self-defense. Her head suddenly felt impossibly heavy, as if she had a boulder attached to the top of her neck, and she let it drop sideways to rest against the wing of the chair.

"You've been through hell tonight, haven't you?" He sounded as if he was kicking himself for answering her question. He touched her cheek, his warm fingers sliding over the cool smooth surface of her skin, and she realized that he was brushing stray strands of her hair back from her face. "But it's over, and you're safe now. Take a few deep breaths and . . ."

The realization that suddenly burst in her mind like an explosion of fireworks had to be shared that instant. She opened her eyes. He was leaning in toward her, closer now.

Their gazes met, and his hand, which had been tucking her hair behind her ear, dropped away.

"It's just like what happened to Tara Mitchell," she gasped, appalled.

"Yeah," he said, easing back on his heels so that he was no longer so close. "I know."

"He's back." Her throat seemed to have constricted. She could hardly force the words out. "It's the same guy. Oh my God."

He stood up then, tucked his hands in the front pockets of his jeans, and looked down at her almost meditatively.

"Is it?"

"It has to be, don't you see?" Her tone was urgent. She shifted positions so that she was sitting upright, her feet on the floor, leaning forward a little as she pointed out the obvious to him. "It's the same house, the same M.O., the same everything."

"Looks like it."

"What do you mean, 'looks like it?' It *is*. The program—maybe he saw the promos or something. Maybe he was out there in the dark the whole time, watching through the windows, waiting for his chance—" Nicky broke off with a shudder.

"That's certainly one possible explanation."

Nicky looked up at him with a frown. He was tall, so it was a long way up. If she'd been feeling stronger, she would have gotten to her feet just to lessen the height differential. There was something in his voice. . . .

"What other explanation could there be?"

He shrugged.

"A copycat? Is that what you're thinking?"

"Could be." A beat passed. "I understand from talking to some of your crew that your program is on the verge of being cancelled."

"Maybe." She hated to admit it aloud, even under such dire circumstances. "So what does—?" All of a sudden she saw where he was going with that. Her eyes widened. "You're not suggesting—you don't think—*nobody* would kill Karen and attack me just to jack up the *ratings.*"

He shrugged again. "Probably not. It's just something to look into." He turned and moved back to the desk. After a glance at the tape recorder— Nicky presumed to make sure that it was still functioning—he perched on a corner of the desk, one leg swinging, and looked at her again. "Let me ask you a question: The screams at the end of the program—I'm assuming they were computer-generated, or something like that?"

Nicky frowned. She was still trying to get her mind around the idea that he could even for a moment consider that someone connected with *Twenty-four Hours Investigates* might have done it, much less for a rise of a couple points in the Nielsens.

"No." Okay, time to be scrupulously honest here. "At least, not as far as I know."

"But they were scripted, right? A planned part of the program?"

"No."

Their gazes met.

"You're saying the screams were not scripted?"

"That's right."

"Oh, come on." The skepticism in his voice was unmistakable. "You can tell me, you know. I'm a cop, and I've got no interest in the hows and whys of how TV shows are put together. Any information you give me won't go any further than this room, I promise. But I need to know the truth for the sake of the investigation, so I'm going to ask you one more time: Were those screams part of the act?"

"Act?" As the implications of the word slowly but inexorably penetrated, Nicky stiffened. She could feel her strength returning, could feel the blood flowing through her veins again, could feel her skin warming. She wouldn't have suspected it, but annoyance, she was discovering, was positively therapeutic.

"You know, your mother's shtick."

"My mother," Nicky said with more than a hint of bite, "does not have any *shtick*."

He looked impatient. "Whatever you want to call it then. The question I'm asking you is this: What was the source of those screams?"

"Did you ever think it might be . . . a ghost?" Nicky wasn't convinced of it herself, but he was so obviously incredulous that she couldn't resist.

"No," he said. "I never did."

"Maybe you should open your mind a little and consider it, then."

He crossed his arms over his chest. There was a wry twist to his mouth now. "Hey, I'm a cop. If my choice here is to believe that those screams came from a ghost or from some other source, I'm going to have to go with the other source every time."

"That's your prerogative." Nicky smiled. It wasn't a particularly nice smile. A great deal of her life had been spent listening to people snicker when they found out who her mother was and what she did. She no longer had much patience for it. "All I can tell you is, the screams weren't scripted. I have no more idea where they came from than you do. Tara Mitchell's ghost is the best I can do."

"Right."

The nasty-cop sneer was back, and Nicky found herself disliking him all over again.

"Is there anything else?" she asked, gathering herself together in preparation for standing up and ending the encounter. "Because I'm really very tired."

It was the truth. Her head throbbed, her body ached, and her poor sore heart was in even worse shape than all the rest. And she was so exhausted that she felt practically boneless. All she wanted to do now was crawl into bed and try to sleep until it was time to get up and go to the airport. The question was, though, what would she see when she closed her eyes? The thought made Nicky shiver inwardly. Then she remembered the sleeping tablets that the doctor had given her. With any luck, they would totally zonk her out. The idea of being mindless, oblivious, unconscious of everything that had happened for a few hours was suddenly enormously appealing.

"Just one more thing," he said.

She looked a question at him.

"Did you get any phone calls after the program ended? On your cell phone, I mean?"

Nicky frowned. "I don't know. My phone's in my purse. I turned it off and put it there before we went on the air, and I haven't looked at it since."

"Would you mind checking it now?"

"All right." Nicky stood up and took a step, then caught at the curved wing of the chair as her head swam unexpectedly. Rising fast was clearly not going to be on the program for a while.

He came off the desk as she faltered, then stood irresolute in front of it, his gaze sliding over her. "You've had a rough night, remember? You might want to sit back down."

"My purse is in the kitchen." In the midst of the bedlam that had descended on the Old Taylor Place after Karen's body had been found, someone had nevertheless managed to locate Nicky's purse and bundle it, with her all-important insurance card, off to the clinic with her, and it was now hanging from the coat rack by the kitchen door.

"I'll get it. Just tell me where."

She told him.

"Sit down," he said, making it sound like an order, then clicked off the tape recorder and left the room.

Instead of sitting, which, given the way she felt, was undoubtedly what she *should* do, she took a few deep breaths and waited for her head to clear. When it did, she let go of the chair and walked the few paces to the desk, where she was staring down at the small silver tape recorder on the desktop when he came back with her purse.

"I thought I told you to sit back down." He handed over her purse, which was a big, black leather tote, a designer knockoff that was a whole heck of a lot less expensive than it looked, crammed with the minutiae of her life.

As her hand closed around the smooth leather straps, she met his gaze.

"Do people always do what you say?" she asked in a pseudo-interested tone.

"Usually." His eyes crinkled slightly at the corners, as if he was fighting a smile. "If they're smart."

Touché, she thought as her knees gave a warning quiver, and she put her purse down on the desk without replying. Leaning a hip against the heavy piece of furniture for unobtrusive support and digging a hand into the side pocket, she found her phone and held it up for him to see. He was standing maybe three feet away, watching her, his expression unreadable.

His gaze flicked to the phone. "Mind checking your call record?"

"Why?" Even as she asked the question, Nicky flipped open the phone and pressed a button: There were four missed calls. She glanced up at him. "Who do you think might have called me?"

"We found Karen's cell phone in some bushes across the street from the Old Taylor Place. The last incoming call, at least the last one she answered and that we can use to verify that she was still alive, was from Sid Levin, who I understand is some big wheel with your show's production company, at nine fifty-two P.M." He paused. "The last outgoing call on it was to you."

"Oh." The information was like a knife to her heart. Nicky remembered Karen calling to warn her that the local fuzz was trying to shut down the broadcast. The conversation seemed like it had taken place a lifetime ago. "But that was earlier. Before we went on the . . ."

Her voice trailed off as she studied her call record. The missed calls—one of which was from Sid Levin's private number, she felt a brief flicker of excitement to see—had all been logged after the broadcast ended. Karen's number was listed last.

"Karen called me at ten forty-seven P.M.," Nicky said slowly, staring at the data on the glowing screen. The truth hit her like a fist to the stomach: By 10:47 P.M., Karen had been dead. Nicky would have been in Dave the Deputy's car on her way to the clinic.

Her breathing suspended. She looked up to meet Joe's eyes. She didn't have to point out that Karen had been dead by the time the call had been placed. It was clear, from his expression, that he knew.

"Hang on a minute."

He took a step forward and reached around her to turn on the tape recorder.

"Miss Sullivan confirms that her cell phone received a call from Miss

Wise's cell phone at ten forty-seven P.M. Miss Sullivan's phone was, at that time, turned off." He looked at her. He was so close that she could have reached out and touched him if she chose, and his body now seemed to radiate tension. She was reminded, suddenly, that he was a cop. "Do you have any messages?"

Nicky nodded. She'd just discovered that she was unable to speak.

"Miss Sullivan indicated that she has messages," he said for the benefit of the tape recorder. Then, to her, "Mind playing them?"

Nicky shook her head, remembered the tape recorder, and managed a husky "No."

Then she pressed the *replay messages* button.

The first message was from Livvy. "Nick, I just remembered: We're out of ice cream. Would you mind stopping by Baskin-Robbins and picking up a quart of Rocky Road on your way home? Thanks."

The second was from Sarah Greenberg, *Twenty-four Hours Investigates*'s overworked supervising producer. "Wow! Home run! You did it! We're already starting to get floods of calls and e-mails. From what we can tell so far, viewers loved it! Tell your mom thanks from all of us here. Talk to you later."

The third was from—*Be still my heart*—Sid Levin. "An impressive piece of work, Ms. Sullivan. When you get in tomorrow, stop by my office. Maybe you can do something more along that line for us."

The warm little thrill with which she heard that last message was immediately vanquished as the next message came up. It was from Karen. Her name and number blinked on the screen. Nicky held her breath as she waited.

She had known, of course, that it couldn't possibly be Karen's voice, and it wasn't. The deep tones belonged to a man.

All he said was, "Are you superstitious?"

But just hearing that hoarse, raspy whisper again was enough to make Nicky go light-headed. She knew immediately who it was: Karen's killer, the man who had attacked Nicky herself, the evil presence under the pines. Her knees gave out, and she would have fallen if Joe hadn't caught her. He grabbed her elbows, said "Hey" in a surprised tone, then took one look at her face and pulled her into his arms.

If she hadn't had the solid wall of his body to collapse against, she would have crumpled to the floor at his feet. Her muscles seemed to have turned to Jell-O. Her legs threatened to fold beneath her. The room whirled. For a moment, all she could do was close her eyes, hang on to the only available solid support, and breathe.

"It's okay." His voice was low and faintly husky in her ear, and his arms were warm and strong around her. "Just stay put a minute."

"It's him," she managed finally. Her head was turned to the side so that her cheek rested against the sturdy width of his shoulder. For all his leanness, he was much bigger than she was, wider, taller, taut with muscle. She could feel the warmth of his body heat, smell the faint aroma of—*What was it? Cigarettes?*—hear the steady whisper of his breathing. He felt hard and strong and unmistakably masculine against her, and as her mind began to function again, it occurred to her that she was clinging to him like icing to a cake.

She opened her eyes to discover that they were just inches from the strong, brown column of his throat. His jaw and chin were dark with stubble and stubbornly male. As she looked at him, he slanted a glance down at her, and their eyes met.

"I figured." He inhaled, more deeply than before, and she felt the rise of his chest against her breasts. They were pressing warmly into the wide, firm contours of his pectorals. In fact, she was practically lying against him, her fingers curled into the front of his T-shirt, and if it hadn't been for the thickness of Livvy's industrial-strength robe, she would have been able to feel every inch of him. And vice versa. "You any closer to recognizing the voice?"

Oh, God. She didn't want to think about that voice.

"No." Instead, she pulled herself together, released his T-shirt, and, with her hands flat against his chest, pushed out of his arms. He let her go without resistance. His hands lingered on her arms only long enough to make sure that she could stand without collapsing. Then they dropped to his sides, her hands dropped to her sides, and for a slightly awkward moment, they simply stood there, looking at each other.

"Thanks for keeping me from hitting the floor," she finally said.

"Anytime." He folded his arms over his chest.

"It was just the shock."

"I understand." The merest suggestion of a smile touched one corner of his mouth. "Just for the record, next time I tell you to sit down, you might want to think about doing it."

Nicky's eyes widened as she realized that he was teasing her. Before she could reply, her mother appeared in the doorway.

"Joe, there's some reporter here asking for you."

IN THE END, Joe didn't get to sleep at all that night. By the time he finished with Nicky and her family, then returned to the Old Taylor Place to supervise his willing but inexperienced-in-homicide-investigations police force in the painstaking gathering of evidence, oversaw the loading of the victim's body into the county coroner's van, dealt with the rain he had foreseen by jury-rigging tarpaulins over the crime scene, then made sure said crime scene was taped off and a guard was posted to await the coming of daylight—when he hoped additional evidence that might have eluded them in the darkness and still managed to survive the downpour would be discovered—it was well past dawn.

He was still hoping to recover the murder weapon, but so far it wasn't looking good.

"You wanna stop by IHOP?" Dave asked hopefully as they drove away from the scene at last. They were basically facing Hobson's choice, because it was the only eating establishment in the area open at such an ungodly hour.

Joe was so tired that his head ached and his eyes felt grainy, but, he realized as he thought about it and remembered his and Dave's missed dinner, he was hungry, too. That was one of the things he liked best about the South: They went in for breakfast in a big way. In Jersey, if he'd had breakfast at all, it had been coffee and a cigarette grabbed on the fly, but here it was a meal big enough to sustain a man for the rest of the day.

"Sure."

The sun was rising over the ocean now, and that was a truly beautiful sight. What made it even better was that it was there to be savored every single day, no matter how dark and disturbing the night before had been. When he had first arrived on the island, Joe had been unable to sleep for more than a few hours at a time. In consequence, he had spent many a dawn nursing a cup of coffee on the small deck behind his house, letting the glorious pinks and purples and oranges that heralded the coming of a new day do what they could to soothe his troubled soul. Now, as he drove over the narrow stretch of highway that connected the island to the mainland, he glanced automatically at the heavens. The Technicolor pinwheels swirling across the deep lavender sky spread their mirror image across the midnight blue of the slice of ocean he could see off to both sides and the black waters of the creek beneath the causeway. The creek was up, as it rose some ten feet or so every night when the tide came in, and the surface of it was dotted with a flock of Canada geese that were late flying north for the summer. Gulls and herons and egrets wheeled among the gray stretches of cloud left over from the previous night's downpour, then swooped down low under the bridge, fishing for their breakfast in the relative stillness of the creek. As he had slowly and painfully learned to do over the last few months, Joe took what comfort he could in the sheer splendor of the newborn morning, then spared a brief thought for the irony of it all. That a world of such immense physical beauty could harbor the kind of evil it did was one of the great mysteries of the universe. Sometime, when enough years had passed so that he had attained some perspective, he was going to try to fathom the whys and wherefores of it all.

But not now, he told himself as he pulled into the IHOP parking lot. Now he was going to lock the horrors of the night away in that special place in his mind that he had learned to reserve for such things, and concentrate on doing the job he was being paid to do.

"Think we're going to be able to solve this?" Dave asked uneasily after they had placed their orders. They were seated in a booth in front of the window, nursing steaming cups of coffee. Joe was looking out through the glass, watching an eighteen-wheeler maneuver carefully into a parking place. The pavement was still wet from the earlier rain; oil mixed with the puddles to form shimmering rainbows on the macadam. There were four other patrons in the restaurant, all men, all, from the look of them, either truckers or fishermen. At just after six A.M. on a Monday morning in May, half a dozen customers was probably about as good as it got for this particular IHOP. Pawleys Island, like the entire oceanside area of the Strand in which it was located, wouldn't start to get really busy until the tourists started pouring in by the carload right around the first of June.

After the May sweeps were over. Joe had been about as vaguely familiar as the average TV viewer with the concept that in certain designated months, television stations rolled out their best programming in hopes of attracting a large number of viewers, which would then enable them to hike the rates that they charged advertisers. But he had heard—with great interest—about the May sweeps again last night when he had talked to the *Twenty-four Hours Investigates* people at the crime scene before heading over to interview Nicky at her mother's house. From what he'd understood from his discussion with them, TV people lived and died (maybe literally in this case?) by the ratings that their programs generated during the sweeps. As a motive for murder, juicing TV ratings wasn't the best one he'd ever heard, but then again, it wasn't the worst, either.

"We're going to do our best," Joe said, turning over various possibilities in his mind. The truck's lights went off, and the driver emerged, tromping through rainbows as he headed toward the entrance. Dave made a sound that was sort of like an under-the-breath snort, and Joe pulled his gaze away from the view outside the window to look at him. His second-in-command was pale and tired-looking, with bags under his eyes and smudges and smears of Joe-didn't-want-to-think-about-what on his once-white shirt.

"To tell you the truth, I've never been involved in a murder investigation before. I don't think any of the guys have." Dave said it low-voiced, as if he were imparting a slightly shameful secret.

"I'm aware." It wasn't exactly Joe's area of expertise, either, although early in his career, he'd spent six months on the homicide squad before moving on to vice. On the other hand, vice encompassed a lot of territory. He'd seen his share—more than his share—of killings, and had gotten involved in their investigations as necessary. He knew the basics, the rudimentary procedures to be followed, and he had a veteran cop's keen nose for things that didn't smell quite right. Since the island had had only one confirmed murder—Tara Mitchell's—in the last several decades, experience in conducting homicide investigations had not been a very high priority when the town council had hired its new police chief.

They might very well be rethinking that about now. As the saying went, though, hindsight was always twenty-twenty.

"Have you—?" Dave began, only to be interrupted as the waitress arrived with their meals, slapping plates of bacon and eggs and toast—Joe's—and pancakes and sausage and biscuits with a little bowl of white gravy—Dave's—down on the table in front of them. Joe was secretly glad for the interruption. The question he assumed Dave had been in the process of asking him—something along the lines of "Have you ever conducted a homicide investigation?"—was better off being left unanswered if possible, Joe judged. He was still the outsider, the new guy in town, the stranger in a place where most people had known each other all their lives. The job was his to do, and it would be easier all around if he had the confidence of his department—to say nothing of the community—while he did it.

"Can I get you boys anything else?" the waitress asked. She was an older woman, late fifties maybe, a little on the stocky side, with short, dark-brown hair and tired eyes. Her uniform was limp and tired-looking, too, as if it had been washed way too many times.

"No, ma'am," Dave said, already tucking into his food with relish.

Joe shook his head and picked up his fork, digging into his eggs. The smell of breakfast made him think of the kitchen at Twybee Cottage, and for a moment, the image of Nicky Sullivan appeared in his mind's eye. In a few hours, she'd be on her way to the airport, and that, all things considered, was probably a good thing. With her gone back to where she'd come from, he wouldn't have to deal with the strong attraction she engendered in him; and, more important, unless the perp was a jet-setter, it would keep her safely out of harm's way while he tried to figure out who had killed her friend and attacked her.

The driver of the eighteen-wheeler walked past and slid into a nearby booth just then, and the waitress moved away to offer him coffee.

"So what do we do now?" Dave asked after a few minutes, during which he'd managed to make most of the food on his plate disappear.

His Number Two was looking at him with utter confidence, and Joe tried not to grimace. *Better get used to it*, he told himself. He was now the quarterback, as it were; it was his team, and the plays were his to call. Wishing that, at a minimum, he was hitting on all cylinders mentally was an exercise in futility.

Taking a swallow of the truly awful coffee gave him a moment to think.

"Go over the crime scene with a fine-tooth comb to make sure we didn't miss anything." He was ticking off the necessary steps to be taken in his mind as he spoke. "Go over the evidence we've already collected, and send off anything that needs to go to the FBI crime lab. Verify witness statements." Dave was looking eager but slightly bewildered, so Joe clarified. "Make sure everybody was where they said they were last night. If we find inconsistencies, we'll know where to start looking for our perp."

"More coffee?"

The waitress was back. Joe shook his head—the stuff was bitter as gall—and Dave declined, too. Joe was just about to ask for the check when the waitress frowned at him.

"Say, aren't you that new police chief from over at the island?" Eyes brightening, she was openly looking him over now.

"Yeah," Joe replied, cherishing a faint hope that she might offer him a freebie meal. His salary wasn't all that big, and in his view, every dollar he didn't have to spend today was one more that he had to spend tomorrow.

"Honey, you're on TV," she told him. He must have looked surprised, because she stepped back and pointed to a small television set mounted on the wall behind the counter. He hadn't noticed it before, probably because the volume was turned down so low that he couldn't hear it even now, when he was looking right at it. But he didn't have any trouble seeing it, and what he saw appalled him.

There he was, standing in the dark driveway of the Old Taylor Place, talking to Vince while, behind him, Karen Wise's sheet-wrapped body was being loaded into an ambulance that waited on the driveway, its orange lights flashing. Her body hadn't been taken away from the crime scene until nearly one-thirty A.M., so he knew approximately what time the piece had been filmed. The pine trees to his left and the big house behind him told him that the camera crew had been located down near the street. There had been a lot of chaos at the time, a lot of comings and goings. He hadn't even been aware that a local news crew was on the premises.

But there, in front of him, was the unmistakable evidence that indeed it had been.

"Hey, we made the morning news," Dave said with evident pleasure. Joe didn't even bother telling him that making the news was not necessarily a good thing, especially under the circumstances. Instead, he stood up and headed for the counter. He was vaguely aware of Dave and the waitress following.

"Mind turning that up?" he asked the fat guy behind the counter. The guy wiped his hands on the apron he was wearing and complied.

All of a sudden, the pretty blonde who'd been moving her lips soundlessly on the screen was given a voice.

". . . ghost story come to life," she said. "In an eerie coincidence, a member of the *Twenty-four Hours Investigates* team down here in Pawleys Island to take a psychic look into the fifteen-year-old murder of a local teenager and the related disappearance of two of the girl's friends was herself murdered last night. The butchered body of Karen Marie Wise was found minutes after the conclusion of a broadcast involving a séance that purported to make contact with the spirit of previous murder victim Tara Mitchell. What makes this tragedy so bone-chilling is that the murder of Ms. Wise appears to be nearly identical to the long-unsolved murder of Ms. Mitchell, which begs the question: What's going on here? We'll be talking to the local police later today in an effort to get the answer for our viewers. In the meantime . . ."

"Crap," Dave said in an appalled tone as it seemed to finally occur to him that their untested, untried, inexperienced-in-anything-much-besides-DUI-and-disorderly-conduct-arrests police force was now smack-dab on the hot seat.

Joe would have expressed his dismay a little more strongly. He'd already been braced to see the story written up in all the local morning papers; the reporter who had appeared at the door of Twybee Cottage last night had been from the Savannah *Morning News.* Good news might travel fast, but bad news traveled faster.

"So we got ourselves a woman-killer around here now?" the fat guy asked, looking at Joe and shaking his head. "A hell of a thing for business."

The dull ache that the bad coffee had almost gotten rid of was back, pounding behind Joe's temples.

"Frank, you watch my tables for a minute," the waitress said. "I gotta go call Pammy—that's my daughter"—that was an aside to Joe—"and tell her to be sure and lock her doors. Her idiot of a husband always leaves them unlocked when he heads off to work." She started for the back, then paused to lay a hand on Joe's arm. "Honey, you catch him quick now, you hear?"

"I hear," Joe said, hoping he sounded less sour than he felt. Then, with Dave on his heels, he slapped some money down on the counter and beat a hasty retreat, thinking, *So much for a peaceful life.*

9

THE NEXT FEW DAYS were some of the most difficult of Nicky's life. She flew back to Chicago on Monday. On Tuesday, she went in to work, where the atmosphere was a weird dichotomy of the somber—because of Karen's death—and the jubilant—because of the buzz the show had generated. On Wednesday, she flew to Kansas City, which was Karen's hometown. On Thursday morning, she, along with a whole contingent from *Twenty-four Hours Investigates*, attended Karen's funeral. By Thursday night, she was alone again, back in her apartment in Chicago.

There, at ten minutes before eleven, exhausted and wrung out with emotion, she was wearing a pair of ratty old sweatpants, a baggy T-shirt, and thick, gray sweatsocks—her favorite sleeping gear—with her hair twisted into a haphazard knot on the top of her head and her face shiny with the intensive-moisturizing pack that she sometimes used to fight the skin-damaging effects of too much air travel. She was sitting cross-legged in the middle of her queen-sized bed with her laptop balanced on her knees, checking what was almost a week's worth of e-mail.

With every light in the place blazing. Since Sunday night, she hadn't been able to stand being alone in the dark. When she wasn't getting creeped out about a monster who wanted to kill her lurking in the shadows, she was hearing the whispers of a chorus of faceless ghosts.

She was safe in her apartment, she knew. The door was double-locked and chained, the security system was on, and the house of horrors, as she had come to think of it, was roughly a thousand miles away.

None of it could touch her here. And even her memories could be held at bay—as long as she kept the lights on.

She had received hundreds of e-mails, most of them from fans of *Twenty-four Hours Investigates* who had gotten her e-mail address from the show's website. Nicky scrolled down through them with one eye on the screen and one eye on the TV, on which one of the many incarnations of *Fear Factor* was playing. She wasn't really paying attention to it; she didn't even particularly like the show. She just had the TV on because, for one of the few times in her life, she needed its noise, along with the illusion it provided that she wasn't alone.

Her apartment was a cozy—okay, make that tiny—one bedroom on the twelfth floor of a way-too-expensive high-rise that *almost* had a view of Lake Michigan. Sometimes on a clear day, if she rode up to the exercise club on the top floor and used a little imagination, she thought she could see the flinty blue waters of the lake. Other times, she wasn't so sure. At any rate, she'd sublet the place, furnished, for the allowed minimum of one year, because TV was an iffy business and by the time August rolled around again, she might well be out of a job, or working on a TV show that was based somewhere other than Chicago.

At any rate, the apartment had all the essentials: a comfortable bed in a bland, white-walled bedroom that was just about big enough to hold it; a white-tiled bathroom; a galley-sized kitchen; and a white-carpeted, white-walled, white-draped combination living-dining area sized so that parties of maybe a dozen or less could crowd into it if they stood really, really close together. Not that she ever had parties. Unless she was attending a work-related function—and she went to a fair number of those—she was strictly a late-to-bed, early-to-rise working girl.

For the first time, Nicky wondered if maybe she was missing something. In Chicago, she had neighbors with whom she exchanged good mornings or good evenings, depending on the time of day when they ran into each other in the halls or elevators, and the occasional piece of misdirected mail; work friends; dozens of acquaintances; and a couple guys she'd gone out with once or twice before deciding that the relationships weren't going anywhere and were, in fact, more trouble than they were worth. She had lots of friends scattered about the country from other places she had lived, other places she had worked; a fair number of ex-boyfriends, some of whom she actually still spoke to; and more family than any one human being could reasonably be expected to cope with for any extended period of time.

That was her life. That was how she liked it. Neat, uncomplicated, focused on work and getting ahead. Money put away for a rainy day. A substantial enough income—at least as long as *Twenty-four Hours Investigates* stayed on the air—so that she could actually live on it and have money left over.

In other words, it was the exact opposite of the chaos in which she had grown up. Her father had died when she was seven years old. From that time on, the household had been as volatile as Leonora herself. "The gift," as they all called Leonora's psychic ability, was a capricious master. It tended to manifest itself without warning, and when she felt it speaking to her, Leonora was liable to forget mundane things, like daughters who needed to be picked up from school or dinner cooking on the stove. Strangers were constantly coming to the house for readings, or, nearly as often, Leonora was being called away to assist with this or that investigation. As young girls, Nicky and Livvy had never known, from one day to the next, if they were going to be spending the night at home with their mother or at Marisa's house across the island, or at Uncle Ham's in Charleston. Boyfriends and husbands had moved in and out of Leonora's life on what was practically a revolving-door basis; Nicky and Livvy had learned not to get too attached to them, because one morning the girls would wake up and the latest man in their mother's life would be gone.

Money had been a constant problem as well. The other thing that no one seemed to quite get about being a psychic was that it didn't come with a regular paycheck. Sometimes, as when Leonora had her TV show, money had been plentiful. Other times, it had been a struggle just to keep the utilities on. If it hadn't been for Twybee Cottage, which Leonora and Ham had inherited from their parents and which, through all the turbulent years, had served as Leonora's base, many times they might not even have had a home. Leonora had never been less than a loving mother, and Nicky was devoted to her. But wherever Leonora was, turbulence reigned, and Nicky had discovered years ago that turbulence was just not her thing.

So she'd done her best to construct her life so that it held as little turbulence as possible, occasional visits to her mother notwithstanding.

Before tonight, she'd never felt even the tiniest bit lonely.

But now, sitting on the bed in her clean, neat, orderly apartment with only her computer and the TV for company, suddenly she did. She didn't know what it was, exactly. Maybe Karen's untimely death and the knowledge that except for the vagaries of fate, her own life could have ended then, too, had suddenly made her conscious of how short life really was. Maybe what she was feeling were the reverberations of that night's fear, lingering like a bad aftertaste once the danger was over. Maybe she had just been exposed to one too many ghosts. But for whatever reason, she was feeling uncharacteristically on edge.

It would have been nice to have somebody to talk to, she reflected— somebody to discuss the e-mails with, for example, or to share the shock and fear and grief of the last week, or even just to keep her company.

Somebody special.

What she was missing, she concluded as she thought about it, was some kind of significant other in her life. A steady boyfriend. A live-in lover. A *man*.

She imagined someone tall, lean, and muscular, black-haired, totally hot . . .

Joe Franconi.

She made the ID in an instant. Then, annoyed at herself, she banished the image from her mind.

Maybe, she thought wryly as she focused on the e-mails with renewed determination, she should get a cat.

". . . *love* the show," gushed the e-mail she was reading.

Smiling a little, Nicky scrolled down to the next.

". . . think Leonora James is *amazing*. Where can I get in touch with her?"

That one she would forward to her mother—or, rather, to Marisa, as Leonora didn't do e-mail.

". . . do more shows like that? Paranormal stuff is so *in*."

Glad you think so, Nicky thought, and clicked on the next message.

> *Never forget the rule of three*
> *Three times will death come to thee*
> *Three who were connected in daily life*
> *Will walk close together into death's dark night.*

Nicky blinked and read the e-mail again. Slowly.

No salutation, no signature, nothing except the rhyme itself.

Then she looked at the sender's name.

Lazarus508.

And felt her heart start to pound.

Lazarus—the dead man reborn. And 508 could only stand for May eighth—the day Karen had been murdered.

She realized it with a thrill of horror: The message almost certainly had been sent by the killer.

THE ONLY TIME when sleep steadfastly eluded him was when he desperately needed it. There was irony in there somewhere, Joe knew, but he was too damn tired to care. This was Thursday—a glance at the digital clock glowing from the cable box atop his TV, and he amended that to Friday, because it was now forty-three minutes past twelve—and since Sunday night, he had been working practically around the clock. Everybody was on his ass, from Vince growling at him to solve the case yesterday to little old ladies corralling him in the street to ask things like, "Do you think I should get a dog?" to reporters of various stripes and persuasions, who seemed to have seized Karen Wise's murder with all its sensational aspects as an antidote to what must obviously be a slow news week. Tonight, he'd said to hell with it shortly after eleven, and had come home to fix himself canned chili and hot dogs, grab a shower, and roll into bed.

Fifteen minutes ago, fed up with lying there in the dark, counting possible killers instead of sheep, he'd rolled right back out again. Now he was sprawled on his couch, channel-surfing, hoping to clear his mind enough so that sleep would come.

The Tonight Show . . . *Letterman* . . . a *Seinfeld* rerun . . . CNN (hell, no, the current state of the world was *not* conducive to sleep) . . . Comedy Central . . .

His cell phone rang. As it was in the pocket of his pants and his pants were draped across the chair in his bedroom, the sound he heard was more like a muffled bleating. He got up, hotfooted it in bare feet and boxers across the living room's hardwood floor to the larger of the house's two bedrooms, stubbed his toe on the jamb, and limped, cursing, to the far corner of the dark bedroom where his ancient Barcalounger reigned supreme. Grabbing his pants, he fished out the insistent phone and snapped it open.

"Joe Franconi," he growled into it, pissed about his toe and his inability to fall asleep and the generally sucky turn his life had taken lately, and not caring if he sounded like it.

"Um, hi." The woman on the other end of the phone sounded slightly hesitant. "Did I wake you up? I'm sorry."

"I was awake." He was sitting in the Barcalounger now, his ankle resting on his knee as he massaged his sore toe. The only light in the whole house was the faint blue glow of the TV in the living room, and the corner where he sat was dark as a cave. The tiny air-conditioning unit that he had personally bought and installed in the bedroom window—why no one on Pawleys Island seemed to have heard of central air was a continuing mystery to him—rattled nearby. "What can I do for you?"

"This is Nicky Sullivan."

Nicky Sullivan. He'd been doing his best *not* to think about her since he'd left her mother's house early Monday morning.

"Hey," he said.

"I know you're working on Karen's murder, and I thought I ought to let you know that I just found a weird e-mail."

He tried not to picture her—red hair, satiny skin, slim, supple body—and failed miserably. It was the middle of the night—she'd be dressed for bed. An instant image of her in a slinky black nightie with her hair hanging all smooth and shining to her shoulders and her full, red lips pouting at him popped into his head. It took the self-discipline of a Jedi master to banish it. Recalling that the only time he'd actually *seen* her ready for bed, she'd been wearing a pony-tail and a granny robe in antacid pink should have helped. It didn't.

The sad part was, she'd looked sexy, even in that.

"Oh, yeah?" he said.

"Yeah. Do you want me to read it to you?"

"Sure." And never mind that the husky cadence of her voice made him think of about a hundred and one other uses for her lushly beautiful mouth.

" 'Never forget the rule of three/Three times will death come to thee/Three who were connected in daily life/Will walk close together into death's dark night.' "

Joe straightened in the chair. His foot hit the floor. He'd been casting about for some way to get his mind out of the gutter, and she'd just supplied it.

"You want to read that to me one more time?"

Nicky complied. Joe could feel the way-too-familiar tingle of adrenaline start to burn through his veins. Excitement had always been his drug of choice. Once he'd lived for it, for the thrill of the chase, the danger of discovery, the rush of knowing that death lay right around the next wrong turn.

All that was behind him now, but there was nothing he could do to stop his body's long-conditioned response.

"The sender was Lazarus508," she continued when he apparently didn't respond fast enough to suit her. "You know, Lazarus, like from the Bible? He was dead, and came back to life. And 508—May eighth? The day Karen was killed."

"Yeah," he said. "I get it. Did you send a reply?"

"N-no."

"Good. Don't. Don't do anything with it until I've had time to think about it a little. Save it, but leave it alone. Where are you?"

"In my apartment. In Chicago." She sounded slightly impatient. "Does it matter?"

"It might." Joe's head rested back against the cool slick Naugahyde, and his gaze slid to the window. The mini-blinds were closed, but through the slats, he could see slivers of starry sky. "If that was sent by the guy who did this, and from the sound of it, it may very well have been, you realize that this would be the second time he's contacted you directly?"

A beat passed.

"So what does that mean?" Her voice held a sliver of uncertainty now.

"Nothing good," Joe said grimly. "I'm glad you're in Chicago. How'd he get your e-mail address?"

"I don't know. From the show's website, I guess."

"Your physical address wouldn't be on there, would it?"

"Of course not."

"Good. You just now got the e-mail?"

"I just now found it. It was sent on Monday, at three-seventeen A.M. I haven't checked my e-mail since—"she hesitated briefly—"Sunday."

"Monday at three-seventeen A.M.," Joe mused. "That's only a few hours after the murder. You were still on Pawleys Island at the time it was sent, right?"

"Yes."

"And we had your cell phone." He'd confiscated her phone, with its original message, as evidence, just as he had the clothes she'd been wearing at the time of the attack. She hadn't objected. He'd gotten the impression that she would rather have carried a snake around in her purse than keep that phone with her after she'd heard the message that the perp had left for her on it, and the clothes had been torn and bloody, unusable. "So e-mail was probably the easiest way for him to get in touch with you at that particular time."

"I guess."

"The question is, who knew we had your phone?"

There was a pause.

"I don't know. Lots of people. My family, probably most of the staff on the show, whoever knew in the police department—it wasn't a secret."

"No." In retrospect, it probably would have been better to have made it one. Too late.

"You have a new phone now, right?" With a new number, while they monitored the old one in case the perp should call her again. So far, no luck.

"Yes."

"Nothing?" Obviously, she would have told him if there had been, but . . .

"No."

Joe was silent as he turned various possibilities over in his mind.

"You understood what the message was saying, right?" she said after a moment. He could hear the anxiety in her voice. "He's planning to kill three people who are connected, and the murders will happen close together. It's like before—Tara Mitchell and her friends."

"I understood that." His response was faintly dry.

"He's already murdered Karen. So that means . . ." Her voice trailed off.

"One down, two to go," Joe finished for her.

"Yes," she said. He could hear her breathing. "I think . . . I think I was meant to be the second victim."

"Looks that way."

"Is that why he's contacting me?" The words came out in a rush. "Do you think those messages mean he's going to come after *me* again?"

That was a hard one to answer. She sounded scared. His natural protective instincts—and he was surprised to discover that he still had any—made him want to assure her that she was home free, out of the woods, safe. Unfortunately, honesty wouldn't let him. "Three who were connected in daily life" implied that the other two victims would know the first. "Close together"—hell, what did that mean? As a time frame, it was vague. But Nicky had been attacked within minutes of the first killing. . . . By accident, because she had stumbled across the crime scene at just the wrong moment, or by design? There was no way to be sure. But one thing he was sure of: If the message was legitimate—and that was a big *if*—Nicky had reason to be concerned. On the other hand, since she was safely out of the way, there was no reason to confirm what she already knew and in the process possibly scare her senseless.

"Maybe," he said. "I'm not an expert on nutcase killers."

There was the briefest of pauses.

"Great," she said.

Something about her tone made him smile.

"From everything I've been able to learn, though, these kinds of perps tend to operate within a comfort zone. They choose victims within at the most a few hours' drive from their home. If we assume that this is the same guy who killed those three girls fifteen years ago—and that's assuming a lot at this point—then I feel pretty safe in saying that he's from the local area. In other words, I don't think you have to worry about him showing up in Chicago anytime soon."

"Unless you're wrong."

There was that tone again. It wasn't quite sarcasm, but it was close.

"I gotta admit, that's always a possibility." He couldn't help it. He was smiling again. "Are you alone?"

"Yes."

"Then I suggest you keep your doors locked."

"Oh, thanks. I wouldn't have thought of that one."

He laughed out loud. "I really do think you're safe. Chicago's a long way away, and as far as I've ever heard, jet-setting serial killers are pretty rare."

A beat passed.

"So you think this is a serial killer?"

"At this point, it's kind of looking that way."

"So why is he contacting *me*?" The undertone of fear was back in her voice, and it effectively banished his smile.

Again, he wanted to reassure her. Again, he couldn't.

"I don't know. Some of these guys like to brag. Maybe that's what he's doing. Maybe he chose you because of the TV thing: You know, he's seen you on TV and he feels a connection. Or maybe he feels a connection to you because he targeted you and you got away."

As he spoke, Joe caught a glimpse of movement out of the corner of his eye, and automatically glanced toward the opposite side of the bedroom. A shadow, slightly denser than the rest, seemed to take on a vaguely human form as it slid through the bedroom doorway before vanishing into the living room. Joe grimaced, then deliberately looked up at the ceiling just so he wasn't watching shadows anymore. Ignoring things he didn't want to see was getting to be an art with him.

"Or maybe he thinks I can identify him."

"There's that."

She made an impatient sound. "Do you have any idea *at all* about who might be doing this?"

"Statistically, serial killers are overwhelmingly white males in their thirties and forties. Other than that, the field is wide open."

"What are you doing, reading up on it?" She sounded vaguely scandalized.

"Google's a wonderful thing."

"You're *Googling* serial killers?" Okay, there was no vague about it now. She was definitely scandalized.

"It's a place to start."

"You're joking—aren't you?" There was the tiniest note of uncertainty in the last two words that told him that she was not entirely sure. Since he *wasn't* joking, at least not entirely, he chose to leave the matter ambiguous.

"Maybe. Think you could send me a copy of that e-mail?"

"Yes." She sounded relieved, as if she'd taken his *maybe* as reassurance. "What's your e-mail address?"

Joe told her. Then, because he got the sense that she was getting ready to end the conversation and he wanted, however stupidly, to keep her talking just a little bit longer, he asked, "How's the head?"

"Better. I've got a black eye."

"I'm not surprised." Picturing it, he frowned. "What about the knife wound?"

"It's healing. It itches, though."

"That's a good sign."

"So I've been told."

"You back at work yet?"

"Yes."

There didn't seem to be a lot more to say. And he wasn't doing himself any favors by trying to prolong the conversation. She might be what the before part of him wanted, but she wasn't what the after part knew he needed. Anyway, she was in Chicago, and he was stuck down here in paradise.

End of story.

"Well, I'll be watching for you on TV."

"Thanks."

Just when the pause stretched out to the point when Joe knew it was time to say good-bye and hang up, she spoke again.

"Really, how's the investigation going?"

Really, he'd told her the truth the first time. "Okay."

"Has the FBI gotten involved? Or anybody like that?"

The saying about *hope springs eternal* popped into his mind. Thanks to shows like *Law and Order* and *CSI*, everybody always thought that once a major crime, such as a murder, was committed, armies of specially trained investigators swarmed the case like ants at a picnic. *Wrong*.

"Murders generally fall under the jurisdiction of the local police force. That would be me and my guys. The FBI's involved only as far as we've sent some evidence off to their crime lab."

"What kind of evidence?"

"We found a couple of hairs on the victim that weren't hers. There was some stuff under her fingernails. I'm hoping it's human tissue—that she clawed him—so that we can get some DNA, but it might just be dirt. Footprints, things like that."

"*Were* there footprints?"

Joe grimaced. Actually, by the time they'd gotten to the point of trying to preserve evidence, there'd been *dozens* of damned footprints. In the rush to get cops and paramedics and ambulance workers on the scene, to say nothing of the continually growing number of onlookers who had converged on the spot as soon as word had started spreading about what was going on, everybody and their mother seemed to have trampled that particular patch of earth. But there had been one footprint partly under the pines—and from the looks of it, he would have guessed that it had been made by a man's tennis shoe or walking shoe. The others he'd had photographed; that one had been photographed and had a plaster cast made of it. The plaster cast had been sent off to the FBI crime lab along with everything else.

"A few."

"Can you tell"—there was a catch in her voice—"was she sexually assaulted?"

"No." The autopsy findings had been very clear about that.

"Neither had Tara Mitchell."

"I'm aware." Joe had, in fact, already spent hours going over that autopsy report and comparing it to Karen Wise's. There were a number of similarities—multiple stab wounds, shorn hair, the general location of the crime—but also some dissimilarities. For example, Tara Mitchell's face had been practically destroyed. Karen Wise's face hadn't been touched—but then, in the case of Karen Wise, the killer had been interrupted. Maybe he just hadn't gotten around to the facial-mutilation part yet.

"Did you ever find out who screamed?" she asked. "During the broadcast, I mean?"

Joe couldn't keep the mock surprise out of his voice. "Don't tell me you don't think it was a ghost?"

"That's just it," Nicky said, refusing to rise to his bait and sounding unhappy. "I don't know. I've been thinking about it a lot over the last few days. You don't think it could have been Karen?"

He had been wondering that himself, almost from the moment he had realized he had a dead woman lying under the Old Taylor Place's pines. From what he'd been able to determine so far, the timeline made it possible. As far as anyone was admitting, Karen had last been seen in a good light with a positive identification in the kitchen, just before she had headed out the back door to take a call on her cell phone. That had been some six and a half minutes before the screams had ripped through the night. The call, which had come from Sid Levin, who confirmed that Karen had been alive and well at the end of their conversation, had ended in a normal fashion approximately one minute and fifty-eight seconds before the screams. He'd checked the timing against tapes of the TV show; again, nothing to rule Karen out as the screamer. He'd even conducted a few impromptu tests of his own—having Dave stand in various places in the yard and shriek at the top of his lungs while he listened and recorded the sounds from different locations in the house—but none of the screams he'd been able to capture had matched the ones that had provided such a shattering finale to *Twenty-four Hours Investi-*

gates. But then, of course, he had to take into consideration the fact that Dave wasn't a woman shrieking in mortal fear for her life, either.

"I don't know," he said. "So far that's kind of up in the air. You'd tell me if those screams were part of the show and you knew it, right?"

He heard her draw in a breath.

There was no mistaking the bristle in her tone. "I've already told you—"

"I know, I know," Joe interrupted before she could finish. "I just had to ask again, that's all. Because I'm really not coming up with a source for those screams."

"So maybe you should look harder." Bristle had turned to bite.

"I mean to," he said amiably.

A beat passed.

"My mother is a genuine psychic medium, you know." Nicky still sounded a little hot under the collar. "She truly is able to tap into energies and emotions that the rest of us can't."

"You're saying she can talk to the dead." If he sounded skeptical, it was an accident. The tone he was going for was strictly neutral.

"Yes."

"Then would you do me a favor?"

"What's that?"

"Would you have her get in touch with Karen Wise and ask her who killed her? It would sure save me a lot of time and effort here."

This time, the ensuing pause practically crackled with ill feeling.

"You're not funny," Nicky said, sounding as though she was talking through her teeth.

Joe couldn't help it. He grinned. Maybe not, but at least he was succeeding at amusing himself. The truth was, he was getting more enjoyment out of this phone call than he had out of anything in days.

"Sorry."

"I'm hanging up now."

He was surprised at how much he didn't want her to. "Don't forget to send me a copy of that e-mail."

"I'll do it right now. Good-bye."

"Nicky—"

"Hmm?"

"If your mother *should* get a message from the Great Beyond, you'll let me know, right?"

An indrawn breath, followed by a sharp click, was his answer.

She'd hung up on him. Joe was still grinning as he followed suit.

In his before days, he wouldn't have been able to resist putting some moves on her. But now it was after—and fortunately for his good intentions, she was in Chicago, and therefore out of reach.

Joe tried to tell himself that that was a good thing as he padded back through the living room to the kitchen, where his computer was set up on the part of the kitchen table that he didn't use for eating. Moonlight filtered in through the uncurtained glass top half of the back door, making the scratched metal countertops and scarred oak cabinets look almost presentable. The appliances were white and cheap, the floor was linoleum in a speckled gray faux-stone pattern, and the rectangular dark pine table with four matching chairs that took pride of place in the center of the room was a ninety-nine-dollar special from Wal-Mart.

Like the rest of the house, which was one of the small, single-level dwellings located in the interior of the island, the kitchen looked better with the lights off. Not that that was the reason he didn't bother turning them on. It was simply that he could see well enough to move about without them—and turning on the lights no longer served any purpose for him other than that.

Turning them on did not, for example, make the things that went bump in the night go away.

Not for him. Not anymore.

Ignoring the shape-shifting shadows lurking in the corners had gotten relatively easy, Joe reflected as he sat down at the table, lit a cigarette, turned on his computer, and checked his latest messages. Ignoring Brian—

"Whoever this dude is, he's one bad poet," Brian observed right on cue from behind him, apparently reading Nicky's e-mail, too.

—was harder. The guy popped up without rhyme or reason, with unnerving unpredictability, looking and sounding as real as he ever had when he was alive. When Joe had finally, hesitantly, told the doctors at the hospital where he was being treated about seeing Brian, they'd hemmed and hawed and adjusted and readjusted his medication to control his "hallucinations," and finally referred him to a damned psychiatrist. At the time, Joe had been so bothered by the sudden appearances and disappearances of his new best buddy that he'd actually gone along with that and unburdened himself to the sympathetically nodding shrink. But when he'd seen where that was heading—they were writing him off as a nutjob, saying that he was suffering from post-traumatic stress disorder and should be relegated to desk work or retired from the force altogether—he'd seen the handwriting on the wall.

If he ever wanted to get back to living a normal life, to say nothing of being a cop, he was going to have to suck it up and learn to live with his life as it was after, Brian and the shadows and all.

With that in mind, he told the shrink, and the doctors, and everyone else he'd been stupid enough to mention the matter to, that Brian and the shadows were gone, that he didn't see them anymore.

The shrink had been pleased, chalking it up to the success of his therapy. The doctors had been pleased, assuring him that no more Brian meant that he was getting well. The department had been pleased, because before he'd been a hell of a cop and even now, even in the after, he still had a lot of good friends in the brotherhood who were looking out for him.

Which was how he had gotten offered this sinecure position on this sleepy little island. When the situation had been made clear to him, when he realized he couldn't go back to his old job, the powers-that-be had gone into networking mode and come up with this. He had, in effect, been retired at age thirty-six.

Not that he had protested. Instead, at the time, being shuffled off to paradise had suited him just fine. The slow pace, the undemanding job, the sun, the sea, the beach, the bikini-clad babes at the beach—hell, what was not to like? Ninety-nine percent of the guys he'd hung with back in Jersey would have killed for a gig like this. Every time he talked with one of them, which was less and less often these days, they told him so.

But the truth was, he was starting to get bored.

Printing out a copy of the e-mail that Nicky had sent him—without so much as a "hi" or a "nice talking to you" of her own added on, which he interpreted to mean that she was definitely ticked off—Joe reluctantly faced facts: Paradise was in the eye of the beholder.

Brian—ghost or hallucination or whatever the hell else he was—notwithstanding, he was clearly recovering. First Nicky, then the murder, had proven that all the usual juices were starting to flow again. He'd gotten a taste of the intensity that had once been as much a part of his life as the air he breathed, and he rediscovered what he'd actually known all along: He craved it.

"Hang on a minute, I was looking for something," Brian said as Joe started the process of turning off the computer. The protest—which might or might not have been in his head, but sure as hell sounded as though it had been uttered right next to his ear—made Joe realize that the computer had been scrolling crazily back through his e-mails, even as the newest one, the one from Nicky, was printing out.

Joe gritted his teeth and punched the final button that made the screen go dark. If he hadn't seen Brian dead himself, he thought savagely, he would have had real trouble believing that the guy wasn't actually standing right there in the kitchen with him, being the same damned nuisance he had been in life.

But he *had* seen Brian dead, which meant that Brian couldn't be there in the kitchen. That being the case, Joe ignored whatever *was* there in favor of standing up and collecting his printout.

He would put it in the file that he'd carried home from the office with him, and then he was going to go back to . . .

There was someone in his backyard.

10

J OE'S HEAD WHIPPED AROUND as he caught just a glimpse of movement, a flash of moonlight on metal, like a watch or something, through the ratty mini-blinds that covered the glass-set-into-a-wooden-frame back door. It wasn't much, but it was enough to send another revivifying jolt of adrenaline through his nervous system. Stubbing out his cigarette, he moved as silently as a cat to the door to look out.

Careful to stay out of sight, he scanned his moonlit backyard, which was about as big as a postage stamp. There was a fence around it, a would-be privacy fence of rickety upright wood pickets that might actually have provided some privacy if about half the pickets hadn't been broken or missing— something he'd been meaning to fix ever since he'd moved into the rental property five months before. As it was, three other households—the two on either side of him and the one directly behind him—had at least a partial view of his little patch of earth whenever they were out in their yards. The deck, which was a long, narrow, low-to-the-ground oasis of treated wood planks, took up about a fifth of the available space. Beyond the deck, short tough beach grass, green as a dollar bill when seen in the daylight, fought with a profusion of taller weeds and the remains of the previous owner's perennial garden for supremacy. A six-foot-tall stand of sunflowers grew wild against the north side of the fence, and a trio of thick old blackberry bushes, their dusty boughs heavy with leaves and thorns but devoid of berries, huddled together in one corner. A black gum with a gnarled trunk and low, spreading branches grew just beyond the deck on the south side of the yard. Its thick foliage partially obscured Joe's view.

But there was no doubt about it: There was someone in his backyard. He—Joe was willing to bet dollars to doughnuts it was a man—was over by the blackberry bushes now, bending low, clearly up to no good. The darkness kept Joe from seeing more of him than his crouched shape outlined against the broken pickets. He spared a thought for his Chief, which rested on the small table beside his bed, and his department-issued weapon, which was at that moment tucked away in the glove compartment of his cruiser. But fetching even the Chief would take precious seconds, by which time the intruder might well have gone.

That being the case, Joe opened the back door, stuck his head out, and yelled, "Hey, you! Freeze!" into the dark and hoped to hell whoever it was wasn't armed.

The intruder jumped at least three feet in the air and gasped out, "Crap!" as he whirled around to face the door.

Even before Joe heard that "crap," he knew who it was.

"Jesus Christ, Dave, what the hell are you doing prowling around in my backyard in the middle of the night?" he demanded with disgust as his Number Two started walking toward him. "You're lucky I didn't shoot you."

"I would've called, but I didn't want to wake you up." Dave sounded sheepish. Joe's eyes narrowed as he observed that something was trotting along beside Dave, something a little less than knee-high and about a yard long and round as a barrel. "I guess you were already awake, though, huh?"

"Looks like it," Joe said grimly, eyeing Dave's companion. "What's up?"

"Well, see, it's, um, Amy." Dave stepped up onto the deck, and his barrel-shaped friend came right along with him. The do-it-yourself deck creaked under their combined weight. "There was an, um, accident, and she's madder than a wet hen. She said I had to choose between her and Cleo. So I brought Cleo over here to stay for a day or two, just until Amy cools down. I knew you wouldn't mind."

"Like hell." Cleo was Cleopatra, Dave's beloved potbellied pig. *That* was what was trotting along beside him, and *that* was not spending a day or two in Joe's backyard. Paradise he could deal with if he had to. Paradise with a pig in it he could not.

"Joe, *please*. Amy said that if I come back with Cleo, then she's throwing *me* out."

Joe stared at his Assistant Chief. Dave's eyes were wide and pleading. His round face was as innocent-looking as a little kid's. He was dressed in what looked like cotton pajamas, some dark color, complete with button-up shirt, with his work shoes on his feet.

The guy was so clueless that you had to feel for him.

"Get in here." Joe stepped back so Dave could enter, then glared down at the pig, which was kind of a grayish-black with floppy ears and a squiggly tail. He blocked it with his legs when it gave every indication that it intended to trot inside the house at its master's heels. It looked up at him then, with little black eyes that he was ready to swear gleamed with intelligence.

"Not you," he said to it, and shut the door in the animal's face.

"Hang tight," he said to Dave as he flipped on the light. The sudden brightness made Dave blink, and did the small kitchen no favors. "I'll be right back."

Joe headed for the bedroom to throw on some clothes, glad to realize as he did so that Brian seemed to have vanished. That was the thing about his experience with the undead: There seemed to be no rhyme or reason to it. Brian and the shadows just popped up at random. If he'd been the kind of guy who lost his cool easily, the whole thing would have been damned unsettling.

The worst part was that there didn't seem to be a whole hell of a lot he could do to make it go away. Basically, the only thing left that he hadn't tried was an exorcism.

"Want a beer?" Dave asked morosely as Joe, now clad in jeans and a T-shirt, rejoined him in the kitchen. Dave was sitting at the clear end of the table, nursing a bottle of Bud Light. And yes, he was wearing pajamas, a matching set of pants and top: smooth, navy cotton piped in white with big white buttons up the front. Joe hadn't even realized they made those anymore. "There's plenty in the fridge."

"Yeah." And never mind that he was being offered his own beer out of his own refrigerator. Joe helped himself.

"Love sucks, don't it?" Dave took a swallow of beer.

Watching Dave swig beer was sort of like watching Mister Rogers do it, Joe discovered, but his Number Two looked so thoroughly miserable that Joe felt sorry for him anyway.

"So, you want to tell me about it?" Beer in hand, Joe leaned back against the counter and settled in to listen. The role of father confessor was not one he wanted to assume, but Dave was so far out of his depth with Amy that it was like watching a minnow swimming around all unknowing in a tank with a shark. Having already over the course of the past few weeks had his nerves stretched to the limit as he waited for the inevitable moment when the poor guy was devoured, Joe discovered that he couldn't just watch and wait anymore.

"Amy says Cleo attacked her."

Go pig! was what Joe almost said, but he managed to swallow it in time. Instead, he went with a neutral "Oh, yeah?"

Dave nodded, swilling his beer and looking despondent. "Amy had to work late tonight, see, and when she got home, she came in through the back door so she wouldn't wake anybody up. Cleo was sleeping in the kitchen, and she must have thought Amy was a burglar or something, because Amy says she went after her."

Since Amy's "late nights at work" had been arousing Joe's suspicions for some time, Joe's sympathies remained firmly with the pig.

"Oh, yeah?" he said again for want of something better.

Dave took another swallow of beer. "I was sound asleep, and then I heard Amy screaming and cussing a blue streak and Cleo squealing and all this commotion like you wouldn't believe. So I jumped up out of bed and ran into the kitchen, and there was Amy, standing up in the middle of the table hollering her head off, and Cleo up on her back legs with her front hooves on the table trying to get at her."

Dave shook his head, remembering. Joe couldn't help it: At the picture this conjured up, he had to smile.

"Go ahead and laugh if you want to. I don't blame you." Dave didn't miss the smile. It was a measure of his distress that he managed only a half-hearted grimace in return. "It was a sight, let me tell you. So then the kids come running in screaming, and Amy is screaming, and I'm yelling, and it all must have scared the daylights out of poor Cleo, because she hopped right up on the table with Amy."

By this time, Joe's smile had turned into a full-fledged grin.

"Amy must have loved that," he said as Dave paused to take a fortifying sip.

"Oh, yeah." Dave rolled his eyes. "So she shrieked like somebody was killing her and jumped off the table. Then, wouldn't you know, as soon as she hit the floor, her feet slipped out from under her and she sat on her butt and cracked her elbow on a chair. That's when she said Cleo had to go. I thought after I got Cleo outside and her and the kids calmed down that she'd kind of get over it, but she didn't. She said either Cleo was leaving or she was."

Joe barely managed to contain his amusement. "That's cold."

"Yeah." Dave made a face, took another swallow of beer, and burst out, "I don't blame Amy for being mad, I really don't. But Cleo didn't just attack her. She's not that kind of pig. And anyway, she wouldn't have been sleeping in the kitchen if Amy's brats—uh, kids—hadn't broken the gate off its hinges by swinging on it. You know she always stays in the backyard." He looked at Joe appealingly. "I was going to fix that gate first thing in the morning, too. But then this happens."

Joe shook his head. "Ain't that always the way?"

Dave narrowed his eyes at him. "It might be funny to you, but it isn't to *me*. Now Amy says that either Cleo goes or she does. So what am I supposed to do?"

A beat passed in which Joe took a reflective chug from his beer.

"How long you been living with Cleo?" he asked.

"About eight years."

"How long you been living with Amy?"

"About a month."

"There you go, then."

Dave stared at him. "You saying I ought to get rid of *Amy?*"

Joe shrugged. "Unless you want to get rid of Cleo."

"I can't do that." Dave looked hunted. "Amy'll get over it. She just needs a little time. If you'll just let Cleo stay here for a day or two . . ."

"No," Joe said. Until he'd moved south, the only contact he'd ever had with any sort of pork had been in the supermarket, all wrapped up in neat packages and ready to eat, and that was the way he liked it. "No way. Sorry, but I don't do pigs."

"What's to do?" Dave argued. "She just stays in your backyard. I'll come over and feed her and clean up after her and everything. You won't even know she's here."

"No," Joe said. "She's not staying."

"If I take her back home with me, Amy says she'll throw me out."

"It's your damned house."

"I know, but I can't say that to Amy. She'll hit the roof."

Joe looked at Dave for a moment in silence.

"Dave, buddy, did it ever occur to you that maybe you and Amy aren't exactly a match made in heaven?"

"What do you mean?"

Clueless wasn't the word.

"Well, she's . . ." Joe floundered, looking for a tactful way to put what he had to say. The whole Big Brother thing was not his style. He wasn't good at it. He didn't want to be good at it.

"Hot?" Dave supplied.

Definitely not the description he'd been looking for. *Mattress-tested* was more on the order of what he'd had in mind, but he didn't think that would be particularly sensitive.

"Experienced" was what he settled on. "More experienced than you."

Dave made a face. "Like, who isn't?" Joe's expression must have changed, because Dave added in a rueful tone, "In case it's escaped your notice, there aren't exactly dozens of hot women hanging around my house, wanting to take me home to meet Mama. I'm lucky Amy's willing to take a chance on me."

She's the lucky one, and you can bet your ass she knows it was what Joe wanted to say, but no sooner had the words formed in his brain than they stuck in his throat. Getting into a conversation like that was way more male bonding than he wanted to do here.

"So, will you keep Cleo for a day or two?" Dave asked hopefully, having apparently read something in Joe's face that he interpreted as a softening of Joe's already firmly stated position.

"No," Joe said. "Get somebody else."

"There isn't anybody else. Who? Most of the guys I know have a wife, kids, a dog, a *family*. Families don't mesh with pigs."

"I don't mesh with pigs."

"Joe, come on. You're the only single guy I know with a fenced backyard. Anyway, you owe me, remember?"

"I *owe* you?"

"Remember down at Linney's Bar when those two girls were drunk and throwing up in the parking lot and *somebody* had to drive them home in his patrol car? I did it, and you said, 'I owe you one.' Remember that?"

"It was a friggin' figure of speech, and you know it."

"Just for tonight." Dave's voice, his eyes, his whole demeanor was pleading. "Just so I can go home. Tomorrow I'll find someplace else, I swear."

"Oh, for God's sake . . . all right, for tonight. Tonight *only.*"

"Thanks, man." Dave jumped up from the table and rushed him. For an alarmed moment Joe thought he was going to be the recipient of a big ole Southern bear hug, so—since his position smack against the counter ruled out retreating as an option—he stuck out his hand. Dave grabbed it and wrung it vigorously. "I appreciate this. Anytime you need a favor, all you gotta do is holler, and you got it. I'll just go out and make sure she's comfortable now, and then I'll get out of your hair." He frowned as though remembering something. "By the way, weren't you going to turn in early? I kinda hoped—thought—you wouldn't even know Cleo was here until in the morning."

"Yeah," Joe said dryly. "Something came up. I'll tell you all about it in the morning."

"Sure, okay." Dave was already headed for the back door, clearly eager to be on his way home now that his problem had been solved—or had been turned into *Joe's* problem.

"Wait a minute," Joe said as Dave opened the door. "What do I do if the pig gets hungry or something?"

"Oh, you don't have to worry. I already put her food dispenser and water dispenser in your yard. Like I said, when I got the idea of bringing her over here, I thought you were going to be asleep. I was going to leave you a note."

"That would have been something nice to wake up to."

But Dave was already out the door and missed the sarcasm.

A glance at the clock in the microwave told Joe that it was one-thirty-eight A.M.

So much for getting to bed early.

He wasn't tired now. Or, rather, he was too tired, wound, his mind racing a mile a minute just like it had been almost continually since it had occurred to him that the murder of Karen Wise was his problem to solve. Method plus opportunity plus motive equals a viable suspect, but the problem was that nobody'd been able to find the weapon, too damned many people had the opportunity—so far, the pool included practically everyone on the island except the few people in and around the Old Taylor Place at the time whose alibis he'd (tentatively) been able to verify—and the motive could have been anything. Or nothing at all. A psycho on the loose was the scariest possibility, but it wasn't the only one.

The sick bastard—if it was Karen Wise's killer who was doing it, which at this point was nothing more than an assumption, and one thing he had learned over the years was that assumptions could be dangerous, because they sometimes blinded you to the truth—was sending messages to Nicky. That added a new twist, and a new kind of pressure, to the investigation. He was pretty sure that she was safe in Chicago, but . . .

But the message seemed to promise two more killings. *Close together.* Whatever the hell that meant, it could not be good. With a renewed sense of urgency, Joe picked up the file, extracted the printed-out e-mail, frowned down at it, and discovered that he couldn't read it: The words were blurring on the page.

For a moment, he almost panicked. Then he realized that his eyes were probably just too tired to focus properly, and the panic subsided.

But the dull throbbing behind his temples didn't. *Face it,* he told himself. After five nights of practically no sleep at all, he needed a minimum number of hours of sleep tonight to continue to function at anything near optimal capacity. If he didn't sleep, he was worthless to the case.

He hated to do it. It felt like backsliding, like a failure. But otherwise . . .

Padding barefoot toward the bathroom, he let the thought trail off.

The bathroom was small, basic, and ugly. Everything from the tiled walls to the toilet, sink, and bathtub was puke-green. As a nice contrast, the floor was a mosaic of tiny gray, white, and pink tiles, and the little bit of wallpaper that covered the untiled portion of the wall around the medicine cabinet was a pink-and-green floral. Instead of a shower curtain, the tub was enclosed with frosted-glass sliding doors with big plastic daisies stuck to them.

Some long-ago resident had clearly been more concerned with safety than aesthetics.

But ugly or not, the bathroom was his and it worked, and in the end, that was all that mattered. Pulling open the medicine cabinet, he picked up the bottle of prescription sleeping pills that the hospital had sent him home with.

That had been more than eighteen months ago now, and the bottle was still almost full.

The first couple weeks at home, when sleep had been absolutely impossible, he'd taken them dutifully, night after night. He'd told himself that he needed sleep, that sleep would help his body heal, help him recover faster. But the real reason he'd taken the damned things was that he had craved oblivion, craved falling into a dark hole for a few hours every night, when he knew nothing and remembered nothing and regretted nothing.

As soon as he had realized that, he'd quit with the pills. What had happened had happened. The only thing he could do was face the truth of that, and learn to deal with it.

But now he needed sleep, and he knew himself well enough to know that the kind of sleep that came in those little yellow pills was the only kind he was going to get tonight.

So enough with the soul-searching, he told himself, and he popped a pill and washed it down with a swallow of water from the sink without further ado. Then he walked through the house, turning off the lights and TV and checking the doors, shucked his clothes, and fell into bed and lay there on his back with his eyes open and his hands folded behind his head, staring up at the ceiling so that he wouldn't have to see anything else as he waited for the pill to work.

NICKY ARRIVED in her office on the third floor of the Santee Productions building promptly at eight A.M. the next morning, and breathed in the familiar scent of stale air and coffee with resignation. The term "office" was really a misnomer; "cubicle" described her workspace better. It was beige with charcoal carpet, maybe six feet by eight feet, with a continuous desk surface built into three walls, and a shelf running around the same three walls about four feet above the desk. The desk, the surface of which was beige laminate, was home to an assortment of work-related objects including a computer, scanner, and printer, two telephones, an overflowing in basket, and an assortment of neatly stacked files. The latest ratings chart had been pushpinned onto the bulletin board on the wall beside her computer, with *Twenty-four Hours Investigates*'s position circled in red. The shelf, also beige laminate, was crowded with videotapes and a row of small TV sets in case she wanted to watch several channels at once, as she sometimes did in the case of, say, breaking news. The fourth wall, the one with the door, was also the only one with a window. It was a very nice window, quite large, complete with short beige-and-charcoal-striped curtains and a pull-down shade. Its only drawback was that it didn't face the outdoors. Instead, it provided her with an excellent view of the corridor that separated her office from the offices just like it across the hall.

The ones with real windows.

Around Santee Productions, which was the company that owned and produced *Twenty-four Hours Investigates* and many other made-for-TV programs, office space was allocated by virtue of an individual's status within the company. Nicky had realized early on that her cubicle said it all. The *Twenty-four Hours Investigates* gang had been given the interior rectangle of offices on the third floor. This was a clear indication that they, and their program, were very small, unimportant cogs in a very large, very results-oriented organization. A closer glance at the chart confirmed that *Twenty-four Hours Investigates* was number 78 in the latest ratings. Not good, but better than the 89 it had been the previous week. It had fallen from number 42 in the fall, when the network had opted to keep it around because (a) it was relatively cheap to produce, and (b) they didn't have anything better to replace it with.

But unless something turned around fast, her chances of ever getting an office with a real window didn't look good.

Fortunately for her morale, she wasn't in her office all that much. She was just as likely to be out somewhere working a story, or in a meeting, or downstairs on the set, which was a good thing. It kept her from getting claustrophobic and depressed.

CBS, take me away.

"Morning, Nicky. You doing okay?" The speaker was Carl Glover. She didn't even have to look around to be sure: She would recognize that deep, velvety voice anywhere. As one of the two other on-air reporters for *Twenty-four Hours Investigates*—the third was Heather Hanley—Carl was both coworker and rival.

Nicky dropped her purse into the drawer in which she kept it, then turned to smile at Carl. A shade under six feet tall and about her own age, he was leaning a broad shoulder against her doorjamb, looking gorgeous, as always, in a navy pin-striped suit that had probably cost the earth, white shirt, and pale blue silk tie, his dark blond hair brushed until it gleamed and worn long enough so that it flipped up at the ends, his baby-blue eyes—they almost exactly matched his tie, which had been chosen, no doubt, to bring out their color—sliding over her.

Lasciviously. He barely bothered to try to hide the lecherous gleam in them.

"Sure," she said, although it wasn't entirely true. But despite his calendar-boy looks, Carl was a snake—no, a shark—and to show him any weakness at all was to invite getting eaten. "How about you?"

"Oh, *I'm* fantastic." He smiled at her. "But you look like hell. Maybe you should think about taking a few days off. To recover, you know."

Okay, Nicky told herself as she fixed him with a cold stare, she probably did look like hell. A dying yellow-and-purple bruise formed a semicircle around her left eye, and various other scratches and contusions were hidden beneath her well-tailored black pantsuit. Getting to sleep the night before had proved almost impossible, which probably meant that she had visible bags under her eyes and lines of fatigue around her mouth. But concern for her well-being was not his motive. This was a cutthroat business, and Carl was a player. Did the insufferable egotist really think she didn't know the score? If she took a few days off, that would mean more stories and more airtime for him, to say nothing of Heather. Of course, it was always possible that if Nicky took his advice and stayed home, he would push Heather under a car.

"Don't you have some place you need to be?" she asked.

"Actually, I do." His smile widened as he straightened and saluted her. "I have an eight-fifteen appointment with Sid. See you later."

He turned and disappeared down the hall. It was all Nicky could do not to glare at the empty doorway in his wake. Dropping that disturbing pebble into the previously smooth pool of her morning had been the reason for Carl's visit, Nicky realized. *Sid* could only be Sid Levin, and telling her that he had an appointment with him was akin to announcing an appointment with God. Nicky narrowed her eyes. Carl never did anything without a purpose, and therefore, his needling of her had a point. The question was, what?

It took her a minute, but she finally realized that frowning into thin air wasn't going to help her figure it out. If it concerned her, the point would be revealed in its own good time.

Doing her best to dismiss Carl from her mind, Nicky tried to throw herself into her routine and almost immediately ran into another problem. Usually when she got in to work, she dropped off her stuff in her office and made a beeline for coffee before coming back to start her day by checking her messages. But today was different. Today, she wasn't going to be able to do that. To get to the coffeemaker, which was in a small break room at the south end of the hall that also housed vending machines and assorted goodies, it would be necessary for her to walk past Karen's cubicle.

She wasn't up for it. Not yet. The sheer shock of Karen's death was beginning to wear off, but the pain and sense of unreality remained strong. Last Friday morning when she had passed Karen's office on her way to get coffee, Karen had come out and gone with her. They had talked about the upcoming trip to Pawleys Island. Karen had been excited about it. . . .

Nicky closed her eyes and willed the memory away. The impulse to just turn around and walk off the floor and out of the building was suddenly all but overwhelming. She had sick days, personal days, and vacation days that she could use to stay home and, in Carl's words, recover. But with Carl and Heather and the realities of television and sweeps month in mind, she rejected that option almost at once. She was at work and staying at work and, since that was the case, the only thing to do was get busy. Reliving the nightmare over and over again in her mind was useless. It had happened, and there was no undoing it.

As callous as she felt even thinking it, the cold, hard reality was that life— and *Twenty-four Hours Investigates*—went on.

As if to prove it, the third floor was its usual Friday-morning hive of activity. People walked down the hall chatting and calling to each other as they passed open doors. Phones rang. TVs droned. One of the overhead lights buzzed a little behind its metal grate, as if the tube was about to burn out. Her computer hummed as she turned it on. She almost hated to check her messages—the one from Lazarus508 was seared into her brain—but e-mail was vital in her line of work, and she couldn't avoid it.

The little thrill of fear that slid down her spine as she opened her mailbox was unnecessary, as it turned out. A quick scan of her new messages revealed nothing alarming. Unless, of course, she considered an e-mail from jfran conipawleysisland.gov scary.

"Thanks, and good-night to you, too," it read. He'd signed it, "Joe."

Nicky was reading it again, her back to the door, when someone walked into her office.

"Nicky. I wasn't sure you'd be in. Nobody would have blamed you if you'd wanted to stay home today, you know."

So engrossed was she that the interruption was startling. She almost jumped, but managed to catch herself in time. Feeling ridiculously self-conscious about the message she was reading, which suddenly felt way too personal in nature, Nicky clicked it away before turning to smile at Sarah Greenberg. *Twenty-four Hours Investigates*'s supervising producer was a no-nonsense type in her early fifties, about five-five, with short, dark brown hair and hazel eyes. As a behind-the-camera type, she had allowed herself to age naturally, which meant that her face had all the usual wrinkles and her waist and hips bore some extra poundage. Today, she wore black pants with a pale blue sweater set and sensible, low-heeled shoes.

"I'm fine," Nicky said. It was beginning to feel like her mantra. If she said it often enough, it might even start to feel true.

"I'm glad to hear it." Sarah's tone was brisk. "Sunday's special got the highest ratings we've had all spring, by the way, so congratulations again. And your mother was wonderful. We might want to do something else with her down the road."

"Thanks. I'll tell her."

"Well, no point in beating around the bush. The reason I'm here is to pass on a message: Sid wants to see you in his office as soon as you can get up there."

"He does?" Nicky would have been excited, anticipating praise for Sunday's special if nothing else, if she hadn't known that Carl was also meeting with Sid just then. And there was something about Sarah's choice of words and tone. . . .

Nicky frowned at her. "So what's up?"

Sarah shook her head. "You'll have to talk to Sid."

Horror pierced Nicky's soul as a hideous possibility occurred to her. "Oh my God, we haven't been cancelled already, have we?"

A smile touched Sarah's mouth. "It's not as bad as that, but I'm not telling you anything else. Go on, go up and talk to Sid."

There was no moving Sarah when she looked like that, and, anyway, begging was unprofessional. But something was clearly awry. Turning all possibilities over in her mind as she rode the elevator to the top floor, Nicky was still drawing a blank by the time she arrived in the reception area of Sid's penthouse office.

Whatever was coming her way—my God, was she going to be fired?—she was going to face it with her head up, her shoulders back, and her stomach in a knot.

"You can go in now," the receptionist said after phoning Nicky's name through to her boss.

Nicky thanked her, did a quick check of her appearance in the brass-framed mirror behind the desk—no hair straggling from her smooth updo; makeup in place; slim black pantsuit meeting the triple test of being unobtrusive, flattering, and businesslike—then, taking a deep breath, she walked past the receptionist, opened the door, and strode into Sid's lair.

If office space was allocated according to an individual's status within the company, Sid was clearly master of this particular universe. His office was huge, with three walls of floor-to-ceiling windows that looked out over the tall skyscrapers and narrow, canyon-like streets of the city. Outside, the sky was gray and overcast, and light rain blew against the building, pattering against the glass. Inside, the incandescent lighting was warm and welcoming. Plush cream carpeting stretched beneath an elegantly upholstered seating arrangement that consisted of two full-sized charcoal-gray couches and four pale gray chairs around a bathtub-sized glass-and-brass coffee table, then led on to a pair of navy leather wingback chairs that she could see only the backs of because they faced, as a kind of grand finale, Sid's desk. It was the size of a pool table, a solid block of gleaming, dark wood that was probably ruinously expensive, and was punctuated by the presence, behind it, of the great man himself.

"Nicky, good to see you," Sid said heartily, getting to his feet and coming around the desk to shake hands with her, his square, heavy-featured face breaking into a smile. His accent was Upper Midwest urban, and he looked as though the closest to the Mason-Dixon Line he'd ever ventured was Chicago's South Side. Nicky knew from the office grapevine that he was fifty-four, twice married, and the father of five children ranging from adult to kindergarten age. About five-eleven, average weight, a little stoop-shouldered, and a little flabby around the middle, he had black hair with liberal flecks of gray in it and mild gray eyes behind steel-rimmed glasses. His brows were his most arresting feature—thick, black brows as furry as caterpillars that almost met above his nose. For the rest of it, he had jowls, a receding hairline, and a rumpled gray suit, and was pasty-skinned from too much time spent indoors. In other words, he was your basic average-looking office schmo.

Only he wasn't.

Around Santee Productions, he was king. In the *Twenty-four Hours Investigates* credits, he was listed as Executive Producer. He was also listed as Executive Producer on eleven other shows that Santee Productions owned. That meant that he had the power to hire and fire pretty much everybody in the building. He could axe programs; he could axe personalities. He could also, if he took a personal interest in somebody, ignite a rocket booster under their career. Nicky had met him exactly four times: her first day on the job, when he had personally welcomed her to the team; at the office Christmas party; at Karen's funeral; and now.

As she and Sid shook hands, Carl rose from one of the wingback chairs. He was smiling at her, which, in Nicky's experience of him, had never yet meant anything good. She acknowledged him with a curt nod. His smile broadened.

"So, what's this about?" Her question, which was addressed to Sid, was perhaps a little more abrupt in tone than it would have been if Carl hadn't been standing there, looking at her like the cat who was getting ready to swallow the canary.

"Sit down, sit down." Sid waved her toward a chair as he walked back around his desk to take a seat himself. Though she would have preferred to remain standing, Nicky sat in the nearer of the two wingback chairs, perching almost on its edge, while Carl sank back down comfortably into its twin.

Never let them see you sweat.

With that oldie-but-goodie in mind, Nicky took a discreet but deep and calming breath—the place even *smelled* expensive, she noticed as she inhaled—and deliberately relaxed back into her chair, too, letting her hands rest on the chair's smooth arms as she crossed her legs.

Carl wasn't going to beat *her* in the body-language department. She could project cool confidence, too.

"So." Sid clasped his hands in front of him on his desktop and leaned forward as he looked at Nicky. "First, I want to tell you again how pleased we are with your special. It was excellent work, just excellent, and it's performed really well for us in the ratings."

"Thank you." As hard as she tried to look relaxed, she wasn't. She was, instead, waiting for the other shoe to drop. It was all she could do not to dig her nails into the leather and swing her high-heeled foot.

"Sad as it is to say, there's also been a lot of interest in Miss Wise's murder," Sid continued. "The AP picked up on some local reporter's coverage and sent it out over the wire, so that the story wound up in dozens of newspapers across the country. The murder got featured on *Entertainment Tonight* and several other entertainment/newsmagazine-type shows, one or two of which we don't even own." He grinned briefly, and Nicky, realizing that this was his idea of a joke, managed a weak smile, too. "It's all over the Internet. The whole tie-in with the earlier murder and disappearances of those teenage girls, the ghost thing with the séance and the psychic—that was your mother, wasn't it? She's a real spark plug—the fact that our reporter—you—was also attacked and lived to tell the tale . . . this is a good story. This has legs. This we can build on. Our viewers want to know more."

He paused, looking at Nicky as if he expected some sort of reply.

I'm sure Karen would be glad to know that she basically took one for the team was the thought that popped into Nicky's head, but she had a feeling that it might be a less-than-politic remark. Sid seemed to feel no shame, or even remorse, about considering Karen's murder sort of like found treasure as far as the ratings were concerned.

"It was a horrible crime" was the best Nicky could come up with. She hoped it was supportive enough.

Sid nodded as if she'd said something wise. "It was indeed. And don't think for a moment that we're not going to do our best to make sure that Miss Wise—and you—get the justice you both deserve. Given the realities of small-town police departments, though, this crime is very likely to remain unsolved—unless we stay on top of it. Put some pressure on them. Keep their feet to the fire, as it were. What I want to do is have *Twenty-four Hours Investigates* follow the ongoing investigation into Miss Wise's death. I want a reporter down there on the scene full-time, working right along with the police department, letting our viewers inside the case. We'll do a fifteen-minute segment on the next two shows, promote the hell out of them, do some spots on our other shows—you know, tie-ins, cross-promotion, that kind of thing—then do a wrap-up—probably a full hour special like the one you just did—in which we solve the crime. Last week of sweeps. We'll promote the *hell* out of that. There's no telling what kind of numbers we'll get."

Just thinking about it made his cheeks flush and his eyes gleam. If ever a man could be said to gloat, Sid was gloating then.

Nicky wasn't. The purpose of her summons to Mount Olympus was becoming all too horribly clear. Sid wanted her to go back to Pawleys Island, back to where Karen had died and where she had nearly been killed, deliberately putting herself in harm's way, raking up the dreadful memories, exposing her raw and at the moment painfully gun-shy psyche to the terror that waited for her there.

To juice the ratings.

"I'm not sure three weeks is going to be enough time to actually identify the murderer," Nicky pointed out in as neutral a tone as she could muster. She could feel her palms growing damp, feel her insides start to twist and tighten.

She couldn't go back. Not now. Maybe not ever. Just considering the possibility made her woozy.

Sid waved a dismissive hand. "As long as we give 'em something—a theory, a profile, maybe even another psychic session with your mother . . . now there's an idea; that'd be great—we're covered. At the end of the day, the point isn't what we give 'em. The point is to get them to tune in."

I can't do it.

The words popped into her head out of nowhere. Nicky swallowed them before they could be said, but they scrolled through her mind in bright neon letters nonetheless.

Lazarus508 would be there on the island waiting. She felt it, *knew it.* . . .

Gritting her teeth, she tried to fight back the threatening tide of panic.

"You're looking kind of pale, Nicky. Are you all right?" Carl asked.

Her gaze slid sideways to him. He was leaning toward her, looking oh-so-solicitous. Anybody who didn't know him—like, say, Sid—might actually think he was concerned about her well-being.

But she knew him.

"Which brings me to the other thing I wanted to say to you," Sid continued smoothly, his eyes, like Carl's, on her face.

Nicky tried to keep her face unreadable. Day in and day out, for the entire eight years that she'd been in television, she had been working with predators. The entire industry was rife with them. They were everywhere, waiting like jackals to pounce on those who became weak and vulnerable.

There was no way she was going to let herself even seem to falter in her present company.

"What's that?" she asked.

"The idea for the special, the whole séance angle, it was all yours, and I want you to know that I won't forget your good work on it. But given what you've already been through with this, we sure as God can't ask you to do more. That being the case, I'm giving this assignment to Carl."

11

"**W**_HAT?_" Nicky shot up out of her chair. "No! You can't do that!"

"I had an idea you might be upset," Sid began, but Nicky interrupted, planting both hands flat on his desk and leaning toward him.

"Upset? I'm not upset. I'm damned _mad_," she roared, and had the momentary satisfaction of seeing Sid's eyes widen as he rocked back in his chair to, it seemed, put as much space between them as possible. "That's _my_ story!"

"It's just . . . it would be much _safer_ for a man," Sid said, blinking at her, seemingly taken aback by the vehemence of her response. "And . . . and Carl's had more experience with crime reporting. . . ."

Nicky's head snapped around so that Carl was in her sights. He was looking at her, his expression faintly alarmed. Or, at least, she would have thought it was faintly alarmed if she hadn't seen the glint of satisfaction lurking in his eyes.

That glint gave her pause. Carl had known about this. Carl had probably lobbied hard for this. Carl had, in fact, played Sid like a fish. He was being vintage Carl: underhanded, backstabbing, and _smart_.

Okay, maybe blowing up at the Head Honcho wasn't the best way to handle the situation, especially when she was fighting for her professional future here. Carl, the snake, would ride the wave of interest in Karen's death as far as it would take him. As far as Nicky was concerned, the general idea of exploiting that horrible tragedy for ratings was all but unthinkable. It was sordid. It was repugnant. For her, the prospect of returning to Pawleys Island to investigate the murder was terrifying. It would be psychologically traumatic. It would probably be physically dangerous. In theory, she wanted nothing whatsoever to do with it.

But if she didn't do it, Carl was going to.

Reining in her temper with an effort, Nicky swung her gaze back around to Sid.

"I grew up on Pawleys Island," she said in an even tone. "I know the layout and history of the Old Taylor Place—the house we did the show in, where Karen and those three girls were murdered—because I was there as a guest as a child. I know just about everybody on the island, certainly all the old-timers. My mother—the psychic you want to get to do another séance on the wrap-up show—owns a house there. In addition, she is *my mother*." She resisted the urge to glance at Carl again. "You tell me how Carl can compete with that."

"Miss Wise was murdered, and you were attacked," Sid said, sounding unhappy. "We just can't take a chance on sending you back down there."

"The killer might try to take you out again," Carl added. He was leaning forward in his chair now, his hands gripping the ends of the arms, his gaze intense as he transferred his attention to Sid. "Not only am I the more experienced reporter, but I won't have that problem. No serial killer who's interested in chicks is going to mess with me."

"I have access. You don't," Nicky shot back, straightening to glare at Carl. "You'll find you have a hard time getting the locals to open up to you. You don't know who anybody is, or where anything is. And if you think *my mother* is going to do a séance for you, you're wrong." Her gaze switched back to Sid. "She won't do it. Trust me."

"There are lots of psychics out there," Carl growled. "Psychics are a dime a dozen. As for *access*, all it takes is a good reporter, which you would know if you were one."

"Oh, yeah?" Nicky planted her fists on her hips and smiled at him. It wasn't a nice smile. "I already have a source in the police department and inside information that you'll never get. Inside information that *no one* has but me."

"She's lying," Carl said to Sid.

"He wishes," Nicky said to Sid.

Sid held up a stubby-fingered hand, looking from one of them to the other with a frown.

"You've done a good job on this for us," Sid said to Nicky. "I have absolutely no problem with anything you've done on camera the whole time you've been working for *Twenty-four Hours Investigates*, and the special was fantastic. Taking you off the story is not a punishment of any sort. I want you to understand that. We just want to keep you safe while providing our viewers with the best information we can."

Carl looked smug. Nicky, who interpreted this speech to mean that she was about to be told that the story was now irrevocably Carl's, felt desperate.

"He's been contacting me," she said. "The killer."

A beat passed while both Sid and Carl stared at her.

"What?" Sid said finally.

Nicky nodded. "First he called me. Then he sent me an e-mail."

"You're lying," Carl said.

Nicky shook her head.

"Now that's a story," Sid said. "What did he say?"

Nicky smiled.

"I'll talk about it on the air—*if* the story is mine. If not, I'm afraid I can only talk about it to the police. Carl can try to develop a source in the police department who'll tell him all about it, of course, but . . ." Her voice trailed off, and she shrugged. "These things take time. And you said three weeks?"

"That's blackmail," Carl burst out angrily. To Sid, he added, "You aren't going to let her get away with that, are you?"

Sid looked reflective for a moment.

"If she doesn't want to tell us something, I don't see how we can make her," Sid said in a reasonable tone. "And she's right about the local access. And the psychic being her mother. And the time frame. And if she's in contact with the killer . . . admit it, Carl, you can't compete with that. And if *she's* not concerned about her safety . . ." His voice trailed off as he shrugged. He looked at Nicky, snapped his fingers, and pointed a stubby forefinger at her. "Okay, Nicky, the story's yours. Go get it."

HAVING A PIG WATCH HIM while he ate his breakfast was the antithesis of a digestion aid, Joe reflected as he sat at his kitchen table, downing a plate of bacon and eggs while the possible kin of half his meal stared at him through the glass window in his back door. The damned thing must have been able to see through the mini-blinds—hell, he could see through the mini-blinds, so there was no reason it shouldn't be able to. Its round, black snout was pressed to the glass, and its beady little black eyes were staring right at him. The really weird thing was that it hadn't appeared in the window until the bacon had started sizzling and splattering in the skillet. Then he had gotten the prickle-between-the-shoulderblades feeling that meant he was being watched and whipped around, the fork with which he had turned the meat still in his hand. There the damned pig had been, looking at him almost as though it knew what he was cooking.

By now Joe was almost willing to swear that its expression was accusing.

"Get lost, pig," Joe said to it, as he had at least half a dozen times in varying forms in the last five minutes. The pig didn't budge. It either couldn't hear, didn't understand, or was plotting its next move.

Joe felt like an idiot for talking to it. To compensate, he ostentatiously picked up a crispy brown slice of bacon and opened his mouth.

The pig grunted. He could hear it through the door.

He eyed the pig. He eyed the bacon.

The pig grunted again.

"*Goddammit,*" he said bitterly, and put the bacon down.

The pig stayed put. He could feel its eyes on him as he pushed his still half-full plate away and, taking a sip of coffee and lighting a cigarette instead, returned his attention to the file that was spread out on the table. The e-mail that Nicky had sent him was on top.

He'd already read it so many times that he could recite the lines from memory.

The question was, what the hell, if anything, did they actually mean?

It was eight-forty-seven A.M., he'd gotten more than six hours of sleep, and he should have been wide awake, clearheaded, and filled with fresh enthusiasm for the job he had in front of him. Instead, he felt about as fresh as last week's garbage. His mouth was as dry as if it had been stuffed full of cotton, his eyes burned, and he had a killer headache, which half a breakfast, two cigarettes, and his coffee so far hadn't touched.

The damned e-mail tortured him with its possibilities. He turned them over in his mind, trying out various interpretations without being convinced by any of them, and finally ended up sitting with his head in his hands, staring at the pig in frustration.

Outside, the sun was shining. The sky was a beautiful baby blue dotted with fluffy, white clouds that looked like sleeping lambs. Beyond the less-than-lovely visage of the pig, he could see that the stage was set for one more glorious day in paradise. The purply foliage of the black gum fluttered like blackbirds' wings, ruffled by what he knew from experience would be the warm, salt-tinged breeze that regularly blew in from the ocean in the mornings and evenings. The golden-yellow sunflowers had already shaken off the morning dew and were turning their dinner-plate-sized faces toward the sun. The gulls would be calling, the tide would be going out, and fishing boats and small yachts would be making their way down Salt Marsh Creek toward the ocean. The clam-diggers and early-morning joggers would be coming in from the beach, while the day-trippers and sun baskers would be heading out for a day in the sun.

Inside, the kitchen looked like crap, smelled like coffee and cigarette smoke and grease, and felt airless. Joe probably looked like crap, smelled like coffee and cigarette smoke and grease, and felt airless, too. In the jacket and tie that Vince insisted he wear since the two of them were scheduled to talk to the local media at nine-thirty, he was already too hot. The cooling effects of the bedroom air conditioner didn't do a thing for the kitchen, which was at the other end of the house, and the kitchen's windowless state precluded installing a second air conditioner in there.

Ordinarily, he opened the back door while he cooked to air the place out.

Ordinarily, there was not a pig with its snout pressed to his door.

A loud banging on his front door—the bell had been broken when he had moved in, and he hadn't yet gotten around to fixing it—distracted him, and he got up to answer it. It was Dave, as expected, and about time, too.

Joe opened the door.

"You got that in-depth background stuff back on the TV people yet?" was how he greeted Dave. In Joe's experience, investigation was best done in concentric circles. Start with the people nearest the victim, physically and emotionally. Nicky had discovered the body. Other TV people who worked with the victim had been present at the time of the crime as well. As far as he'd been able to determine, the members of that small group were the only ones on the scene who had known Karen Wise before she had come to Pawleys Island. Ergo, they were the place to start digging.

"Some. Employment records are still coming in."

Joe led the way back into the kitchen. "I want to see the files this afternoon, whether they're complete or not."

"You got it."

They reached the kitchen, and Joe rounded the table. As he did so, he glanced up and found two beady, black eyes watching him through the door.

"You're taking the damned pig, right?"

"We-ell . . ." Dave drew the word out.

In the act of reaching toward the e-mail so he could show it to his Number Two, Joe froze. He turned his head and fixed Dave with hard eyes.

"What do you mean, 'well'? There is no 'well.' "

"I'm taking her, I'm taking her," Dave said hastily.

"Good."

As Joe turned back to the table, Dave walked past him, making disgusting kissy noises at the pig, which, Joe saw at a glance, was practically dancing with excitement at seeing him.

For the first time ever, Joe found himself in agreement with Amy about something.

"We got a new development in the case," Joe began, turning back to the e-mail. "Last night . . ."

The pig began to scratch frantically at the glass with a hoof. Joe broke off, frowning at it.

"You finished with that?" Dave asked, nodding at Joe's unfinished plate of bacon and eggs.

"Yeah," Joe said.

"Do you mind?" Without waiting for Joe's reply, he picked up the plate, walked to the door, opened it, and, with the pig nudging his trouser leg with its snout and wagging its wormy little tail like an ecstatic dog, dumped the contents on the deck.

Joe watched, dumbfounded, as the pig lowered its snout to the food and started gobbling it up, bacon and all.

"She loves breakfast," Dave said by way of an explanation, and came back into the kitchen.

Cannibal, Joe said silently to the pig just before Dave shut the door on it.

"So, what were you saying?" Dave carried the plate to the sink, turned on the water, and started rinsing it.

Recalled to himself, Joe returned his attention to the matter at hand. "Nicky Sullivan called me last night. She got an e-mail she thought I ought to see." He tapped the e-mail. "This is it right here."

"Oh, yeah?" Dave opened the dishwasher, stuck the plate in, closed it again, then came toward the table, drying his hands on a paper towel. He took the e-mail from Joe, scanned it, and whistled.

"Sounds like our guy."

"Does, doesn't it?"

Dave frowned at him. "You don't think so? Seems to me like that handle is pretty convincing. Lazarus is the guy in the Bible who died and was brought back to life. And 508—that's the date the Wise girl was killed, you know."

"Yeah, I know." Joe's voice was dry. "The thing is, at the time this e-mail was sent, just about everybody else on the island knew that Karen Wise had been murdered on May eighth, too. To say nothing of the people at the TV station where the girl worked. And her family. And God knows who else."

A beat passed.

"I didn't think about that." Dave sounded slightly chagrined. "So, you think somebody else maybe sent it?"

"Somebody else *could* have. I don't know that they did. I'm just saying that it doesn't necessarily have to have been sent by the perp."

"Good point."

"We got anybody on the force that maybe has some computer expertise? What we want to do now is trace this back to its source, if we can."

"I don't know." Dave looked doubtful. "Not me, for sure. And not Bill Milton; he can't even send an e-mail. And not Jeff Roe, or George Locke, or Andy Cohen, or——"

"I get the picture," Joe said, interrupting. What he didn't need was a recitation of all the people on the force who *couldn't* do it. "Don't feel bad; I can't do it, either. I already tried all I know how to do, which is basically contact the service provider. It was forwarded through one of those free Hotmail accounts, but that's all they could tell me. They're trying to trace it back, but it's not looking good."

"Did she send a reply?"

Joe shook his head.

"How about if we get her to, then? Maybe he'll write back to her, and we can use it to trap him somehow." Dave sounded eager.

Joe kept his opinion on the possibilities of that succeeding to himself. Anyway, even if it worked, it involved widening Nicky's exposure to the possible perp, which he was loath to do. "I tried sending a reply myself. What I got, basically, was something like 'e-mail address not found on server.' "

"Crap," Dave said.

"Yeah." Joe reached for the e-mail. "I know it goes without saying, but keep the fact that Nicky got this to yourself. If it gets out all over the place, she'll probably start getting copycat e-mails by the dozens. If the perp writes to her again, we might miss his message in the avalanche. In fact, pass the word around the department: Nobody tells anybody anything concerning this investigation without running it by me first."

"I know better than to talk about an ongoing investigation." Dave sounded injured. "We all do."

"Just making sure." Joe gave him an apologetic grimace, and glanced up at the clock over the refrigerator. "I gotta be at the mayor's office at nine-thirty. What I want you to do is start checking out that list we had put together of known violent offenders in the area. The key question is, where were they Sunday night? Also, we need to know about anyone just released from prison, or out of the military, or back from anywhere that might have kept them out of circulation in this area for a number of years."

"Got it."

"We probably also need to start pulling in files on any murders involving women and knives in the last fifteen years within, say, a two-hundred-mile radius."

Dave groaned. "You realize that we're sixty miles from Charleston, right? And then there's Columbia and the whole Myrtle Beach–Grand Strand area and—"

He broke off, waving his hands to indicate the magnitude of the search.

"I know," Joe said. "But if we're dealing with a serial killer, something related should turn up. They don't kill and just stop for fifteen years, then start up again. Unless he's been out of circulation for some reason."

"Yeah." Dave made a face. "Well, I'll get on it."

He turned and started walking out of the kitchen, obviously heading toward the front door.

"Whoa, there." Joe saw where he was going and straightened away from the file he was putting back together. Dave turned to look at him, his face suspiciously innocent. "Aren't you forgetting something?"

"Oh, yeah." Dave snapped his fingers like he just then remembered. "Cleo." He started walking back toward Joe. "Well, I'll just take her home, then."

"Good idea." Joe's voice was dry.

Dave had a hand on the back doorknob when he looked back. "Unless she could just stay one more night?"

"No," Joe said. "N-O. I mean it."

Dave sighed. "Okay."

Then he went out the back door.

Joe waited until he saw Dave leading the pig—it had a harness-type collar and leash just like a dog—out through the gate before he left the house. It was a little after nine as he walked across his lawn toward the curb, where his cruiser was parked. Sure enough, there was a nice tropical-scented breeze, enough to make the temperature, which was probably in the mid-seventies, feel five degrees cooler. The sunshine was blinding, reflecting off the worn, gray asphalt and the sidewalks and the cars parked along the street. A couple of women were out walking their dogs, and one old guy was cutting his grass with a push mower that had a roar like a chainsaw—the yards in this part of the island were way too small for anything as fancy as a riding lawnmower—but other than that, the neighborhood was quiet. On this block of small, neat, well-kept homes—his, he noticed with a sweeping glance up and down the street, was the only one that obviously needed its grass to be cut—adults worked and kids went to school. There were few residents around during the day.

One of the women waved—plump, middle-aged, a bubble-haired blonde in tight black capris; who the hell *was* she?—and he, having had five months of conditioning in the ways of the South, waved back. Then the other woman waved, and the old guy, and he waved back to them, too, then opened the door to his cruiser and got in and shut the door again with a feeling of relief.

Like everything else here in paradise, the waving-to-the-neighbors thing was different from what he was used to.

Where he'd lived before, in Trenton, he'd never even so much as grunted at his neighbors. If he had started waving at them, they would have thought he was a nut and stayed the hell away from him. His neighborhood had been a little run-down, but he'd had a decent enough apartment. Gunshots could frequently be heard in the middle of the night, pigeons had roosted in the eaves of his building and pooped on his windowsills, and trash was nearly as ubiquitous in the streets as kudzu was in any untended open spot here, but, hey, he had damned sure had air-conditioning.

The mob, the druggies and the dealers who sold to them, the hos and pimps, the petty thieves and thugs—they'd all been part of the landscape of his life. He'd dealt with them on an as-needed basis, and the rest of the time he'd alternately ignored or arrested them, depending on the circumstances.

He'd never thought he'd actually miss them.

But he did.

The almost perpetual sunshine, the slow pace, the laid-back, whacked-out locals, such as Nicky's supposedly psychic mom and his pig-owning, lovesick assistant chief, were as foreign to his experience as penguins to a Texan. This wasn't his town, and these weren't his people. He didn't have an instinct for how the place worked, which meant that he was operating at a disadvantage before he even got started.

If he'd been back in Jersey and this murder had happened on his watch, he would have known where to start. He would have leaned on the neighborhood homies until somebody gave some information up, and then he would have had an idea about where to begin looking for the perp. That was the thing about crime: It never happened in a vacuum. Criminals didn't just spring up out of the ether. They were people, with jobs and families and neighbors just like everybody else. Same thing with victims.

In other words, somebody always knew something. The key was finding who and what.

He'd already talked by telephone to Karen Wise's parents, her two brothers, her friends, and her coworkers. None of them professed to have a clue as to any reason why anyone might want to kill her. She'd been only twenty-two years old, in her first job, with a boyfriend who had an airtight alibi in Chicago at the time of the crime.

At this point, it wasn't looking as though the crime was personal.

On the other hand, a whole slew of factors, from the similarity of Karen Wise's murder to the earlier murder of Tara Mitchell (and keeping in mind here that no one knew the actual fate of the other two teenagers), to the site of the killing, to the tie-in of the television show, pointed to a link between the slayings.

Which led to another question: If the murders were related, were they dealing with the same perp, or a copycat?

And if this was the same perp, where the hell had he been for fifteen years?

At this point, with the coroner's report on Karen Wise still unavailable for comparison with the autopsy findings on Tara Mitchell, and any possible DNA or forensic evidence still being processed by the respective labs to which it had been sent, all Joe could do was speculate.

But he did have at least one semisolid lead: Nicky's e-mail, which, if legit, promised two more killings. Two more "close together" killings. Two more close together killings that it was his job to prevent.

The first order of business for the day was to find out where that damned e-mail had originated.

Joe started the engine, cranked the air-conditioning, and pulled away from the curb. As he drove down the street, he started punching numbers into his cell phone.

He might not personally have the expertise to trace the e-mail back to its source, and his department might be equally lacking in technical know-how, but fortunately, he knew someone who could get the job done.

He'd been away for a while, but they wouldn't have forgotten. It was time to start calling in some chips.

THE OLD SAW about being careful what you wished for kept running through Nicky's mind as she nosed her rented silver Maxima over the South Causeway Bridge to Pawleys Island. It was Saturday, about six-thirty P.M. After leaving Sid's office, she'd spent the remainder of the day Friday filming her segment of Sunday's show—all except for the lead-in, which would be done on-site at the Old Taylor Place in just a few minutes—making travel arrangements, and packing. Today had been spent in transit, first flying from Chicago to Atlanta, then taking another, smaller plane from Atlanta to Charleston, and finally driving from Charleston to Pawleys Island. She was tired, hungry, crabby, and increasingly scared to death.

She'd wanted to come back here. She'd fought to come back here.

And now here she was.

Right within Lazarus508's orbit.

It was possibly not the smartest thing she'd ever done.

But she couldn't have *not* done this story. It was hers, dammit—not Carl's or anyone else's. *Hers.*

If it killed her. Which she hoped—no, prayed—it wouldn't do.

But the thought of what might be waiting for her here made her pulse accelerate until she could hear the too-rapid beat of it drumming in her ears.

It was only for three weeks, she reminded herself, and she was going to take every precaution to make sure that she didn't die, such as taking care that she was never alone, and staying nights with her family at Twybee Cottage, where the usual state of constant chaos and influx of visitors should be enough to keep her safe. For a tantalizing moment or two, as she'd been going over the travel arrangements, she'd considered staying in the Best Western on Highway 17 with Gordon, who was traveling with her as her cameraman and was at that moment driving the red minivan behind her, as they were going to take advantage of the remaining light to film the "live on tape" opening bit for Sunday night's show before staggering off to their respective lodgings to recuperate from the rigors of a day spent traveling. But as appealing as the prospect of peace and privacy was, Nicky had decided to forget the hotel almost as soon as she'd thought about it. She knew herself well enough to know that she'd never be able to sleep for constantly picturing Lazarus508 creeping into her room in the middle of the night. The rest of the team, shaken by Karen's murder, had been given the choice about whether to return to the island or not, and Nicky wouldn't have blamed them if they'd chosen to stay away. But every single one of them had agreed to come when they were needed, which was for the hour-long finale in three weeks' time. For the shorter preceding segments, Nicky would do her own hair and makeup. She'd done it lots of times before. But she'd be glad to have Tina and Cassandra and Mario, and Bob the cameraman, too, with her and Gordon nevertheless. She liked them, they were a good crew, and at this point, she felt as though there was definitely safety in numbers.

There had been no more e-mails, no more phone calls, no more communication of any kind from Lazarus508. But she couldn't escape the feeling that he and she were somehow connected now. Every time she closed her eyes, it was almost as if she could *feel* him. And when she slept—which she did very badly—he stalked her dreams.

If it hadn't been daylight still, she would have been nervous as hell about the spot they were getting ready to shoot. She would be standing in front of the Old Taylor Place, pointing out the spot beneath the pines where Karen had died, and she had almost died, for the folks at home.

Just thinking about it made Nicky's stomach knot and her throat go dry.

So she deliberately put it out of her mind and concentrated, instead, on her driving.

The sun was getting ready to sink beneath the horizon, but it wasn't gone yet. Since she was heading due east now, it hung low in the sky behind her, a bright yellow ball that radiated light and heat and limned the shaggy treetops ahead of her in neon orange. As she neared the center of the causeway, she could look to either side and see the Atlantic and the rush of frothy surf where it merged into the calmer, darker waters of Salt Marsh Creek. At this hour, the tide would be starting to come in, she knew. As it rose, the creek beneath the causeway was busy with cabin cruisers and houseboats and Jet Skis returning to their docks. The sky was just beginning to darken from the afternoon's halcyon blue to indigo. Soon it would deepen to purple, and then, when the sun finally disappeared altogether, to midnight blue.

It would be night once more.

It was the nights that scared her. The killer was a creature of the night.

But he didn't know that she was back, Nicky reminded herself as her heartbeat started to quicken at the terrifying images that conjured up. There was no way he could know she was back.

But as soon as Sunday's program aired, he would.

At the thought, Nicky's hands tightened on the steering wheel.

Maybe she should think about buying some pepper spray.

Maybe she should think about buying a gun.

Picturing herself packing heat, Nicky made a wry face. She'd never fired a gun in her life. Her best bet was to stick to pepper spray or some similar nonlethal weapon, and to being very, very cautious.

There was quite a bit of traffic on the causeway, most of it going the other way. Locals from off-island frequently spent Saturday afternoons at the beach and then returned to their homes on the mainland as the sun sank. Except for a few slightly seedy bars and the restaurants and lounges in the hotels, there wasn't a lot of nightlife, which Uncle Ham, with his proposed restaurant-cum-nightclub, hoped to change.

Which had prompted her mother to call her about a TV gig, which had prompted Nicky to remember the Tara Mitchell murder, which had prompted her proposal at the staff meeting, which had led to last Sunday's special and Karen's murder.

Was life a series of terrible coincidences or what?

Her cell phone rang. Though she knew them well, the melodious tones were unexpected and made her jump. Fumbling for the phone, which was in the pocket of her elegant knit jacket because she now felt safer with her phone on her person rather than in her purse, she glanced nervously at the incoming number as she kept one eye on the road.

Her mother.

Considering other even more dire possibilities, her reaction to that was *Thank God.*

"Where are you?" Leonora wanted to know when Nicky answered.

"Just coming across the causeway. I'm going to stop by the Old Taylor Place to do a quick shot, and then I'll be home."

"Did you bring it?"

It being the spare blazer Karen had kept at work. Inexpensive black polyester, it had been overlooked in the hall closet when her things were being packed up after her death to be sent to her parents. Nicky had remembered it only this morning, when she had called her mother to tell her that she would be coming home and Leonora had expressed a need to have something personal of Karen's to use as a possible aid to making contact with her. Although Leonora usually had no need for such conduits, the gravity of the situation made her willing to try anything at this point, including what she considered "primitive" methods, such as holding a possession of the deceased's in her hands in an effort to pick up vibes from it.

"Yes," Nicky said. "It's a blazer. Do you think it'll work?"

"It's worth a try." Nicky could almost see her mother's shrug.

"Yeah." Neither one of them was exactly exuding confidence.

"Nicky." Leonora sounded worried. "I have a bad feeling about this. I wish you'd go back to Chicago."

"Mama, we talked about this."

"I know, but I've had a splitting headache all day. Practically a migraine, and you know I never get migraines. And I have this *feeling.* Like there's a dark cloud hanging over me. Like something bad is getting ready to happen."

Coming from Leonora James, this was not a pronouncement to be taken lightly. Nicky felt a prickling rush of goose bumps over her skin.

"Did you see something?"

"That's just it. I can't see anything. Anything at all. I've tried and tried and *tried.* Nothing is coming through—except this *feeling.* And that's one thing that makes me worry so much. I've never, ever in my life been blocked like this. There's something wrong, and I don't know what it is, but you know how hard it is for me to see anything that has to do with family. What if it means that something's going to happen to *you*?"

Okay, Nicky's heart was knocking against her ribs now. Her one hand on the steering wheel—the other was gripping her phone—had tightened until she was practically white-knuckling it. If she wasn't careful, what was going to happen to her was that she was going to crash through the guardrail and plunge into the deep, dark waters of the creek thirty feet below from sheer bad driving.

"You're scaring me, you know," Nicky said.

"Well, then, that makes us even, because you're scaring *me.*"

Nicky hadn't told Leonora about the e-mail yet, knowing that it would only make her worry. When she did—and she had to soon, because it was part of the segment that was going to be broadcast on Sunday's program—Leonora would go into orbit.

"I promise I'm going to be really careful." Nicky tried for a soothing tone.

A beat passed.

"You're going to give me a nervous breakdown, you know, you and your sister," Leonora burst out. "You with your job where you go around chasing after murderers all day long, and her with her obsession with that piece of shit Ben Hollis. You know where *she* is right now? Out somewhere spying on him and that tramp he's taken up with. Oh, she told me she's going shopping, but I know her. I know what she's up to."

As far as Nicky was concerned, it was almost a relief to focus on Livvy for a moment instead of indulging in an all-new bout of worry regarding herself.

"When I get home I'll talk to her, okay?"

"Always provided you live long enough," Leonora said bitterly, and disconnected.

Nicky slipped the phone back into her pocket and then turned off the air-conditioning. Her mother's *feeling* had left her chilled to the bone.

For a long, hard moment, she thought about taking her mother's advice and just making a U-turn at the end of the causeway and heading back to the airport.

Then she remembered Carl. And Sid. And CBS.

And Karen. If Nicky hadn't suggested doing a show on the Mitchell murder, the *Twenty-four Hours Investigates* team wouldn't have come to Pawleys Island in the first place, and Karen would be alive right now. That was the cold, hard truth that she'd been trying not to face for most of the past week.

But she *had* suggested it.

And now she owed Karen, too.

She was going to be really, really careful. But she was going to stay and see this investigation through.

For Tara and her friends. For Karen. And for herself.

Then Nicky had no more time to ponder, because she was over the causeway and at the intersection where she needed to turn left, and when she did, the Old Taylor Place came into view.

12

―

"AS YOU CAN SEE behind me, the yard is still cordoned off with yellow crime-scene tape," Nicky said into the camera that Gordon had focused on her. Since the entire property was, as she had just noted for the audience at home, indeed still roped off with the plastic tape that warned away the curious, strung between green metal stakes that had been driven into the ground, she'd been able to get no closer to her goal than the street in front of the house, which, if truth be told, suited her just fine. In front of her, a wall of tall marsh grasses and a dense tangle of dogwoods and birches and crepe myrtle and spirea separated her from the steep bank that led down to the rising waters of Salt Marsh Creek. Behind her, queening it on its slight rise, the Old Taylor Place caught the last golden rays of the sun. It was the very picture of faded grandeur with its peeling white paint and boxy double porches and old-fashioned gingerbread trim. With the sky behind it the deepest of indigos now, and the live oaks with their silver beards of Spanish moss looming tall in the background, and the lengthening shadows of approaching twilight creeping across the overgrown yard, it looked like the quintessential haunted house.

Which, as far as Nicky was concerned, was just what it was.

It was *not* exactly where she wanted to be, especially since it would be dark in an hour and the idea of being at the Old Taylor Place after dark scared the pants off her. But she had to admit that having the scary haunted house where the crimes had taken place in the background made for damned good TV.

Anyway, five minutes and she and Gordon were *gone*.

"There, beneath the stand of Norfolk Island pines at the curve of the driveway . . ."

She couldn't see through the camera lens, of course, but because they had discussed the spot in advance, she knew that Gordon would be taking a long view of the driveway leading up to the curve and then closing in on the pines themselves for a close-up of the lower branches. As for herself, Nicky couldn't bear to look, lest she be overwhelmed by terrifying memories. Fortunately, she didn't need to. All she had to do was keep her eyes on the camera, ignore the pounding of her heart and the nervous churning of her stomach, and get the job done.

". . . is where Karen was brutally stabbed to death, and I was also attacked. Tonight, we'll walk you through the crime, second by terrifying second. We'll give you the *real* inside view, in a way no program or reporter has ever been able to do before, of a murder as we investigate the horrific slaying of our dear friend and colleague Karen Wise. Using what I know from my own experience as the intended second victim that night, we will reconstruct the crime for you and reveal secrets known only to those involved in the investigation. And we'll take you inside the Pawleys Island Police Department, too, as they search desperately for who they believe at this point may also be the killer of three teenage girls fifteen years ago. Stay with us, and right after this break, you'll hear how I got this"—knowing that the camera was focused on her again, Nicky touched the bruising around her eye—"and *this* at the hands of the man we're calling the Lazarus Killer."

Much against her instincts, which tended toward the frugal, Nicky had traveled in one of her best on-camera outfits, an expensive St. John pantsuit, in anticipation of just this moment. To begin with, the silky knit was thin enough to be cool, and it never wrinkled, which made the garments ideal for a long day of travel, which was to be followed immediately by some on-camera work. In addition, the pull-on construction of the pants made doing what she needed to do for this shot easy. With the air of a magician pulling a rabbit out of a hat, she pushed her single-button black jacket back behind her hipbone, pulled her white shell up a few inches, and shoved down the waistband of her black pants. Approximately six inches of creamy hipbone was exposed, along with the red-edged, scabbed-over slash where the killer's knife had sliced through her flesh.

Just looking at it made Nicky's chest tighten. But like it or not, her own wounds were part of the story, and she wouldn't be doing her job if she left them out.

Besides, she reminded herself, *the shock factor was key.* The whole point was to grab the audience's attention, whether it made her feel queasy or not.

She gave Gordon a couple seconds to get a tight shot of her hip before he refocused on her face again, and then she pulled her clothes back together and concluded with, "I'm Nicole Sullivan. Stay with me as *Twenty-four Hours Investigates* launches our own investigation into this horrifying crime."

Gordon pushed a button and looked up from the camera. "That was great."

Nicky summoned a smile for him. "Thanks."

Gordon had been a trouper to come with her, and the last thing she wanted to do was have her lousy mood rub off on him. The thing was, she didn't feel particularly good about what they were doing. The little spurt of satisfaction that usually came when she had just wrapped a spot that she knew was a ratings-grabber was missing, although she was well aware that she'd never been involved with a bigger ratings-grabber in her life. But as far as this story was concerned, the thrill was definitely gone, probably because the subject matter now hit too close to home. And then, *she'd* never been part of one of her own stories before, and there was that whole exploitation-of-Karen's-death thing. To say nothing of the fact that basically every time anything moved within the range of her peripheral vision, she felt like jumping out of her skin. For the first time ever, being back on the island just felt wrong. The familiar warm, perfumed breeze seemed tainted now with a musky, half-rotted undernote from the marsh, the distant murmur of the ocean sounded more like a warning growl, and the bright crayon colors in which nearly everything on the island was rendered seemed inappropriately garish, like someone wearing red at a funeral.

The sense of homecoming that she always experienced upon returning to the island was gone, too.

It had been replaced by a gnawing apprehension that ratcheted up to an icy sinking sensation that she recognized as dread, as she squared her shoulders and turned around for a final, almost defiant look at the house.

She would get past the feeling, she told herself sternly. She had to.

Because, like it or not, the Old Taylor Place, like the island itself, was part of the fabric of her life. Her earliest memories were of this island. They had been happy here once, she and Livvy and their parents. Every picture she had of her father had been taken on or around this island. When she remembered him, the island was there, too, its warmth and scent and exotic colors inextricably entwined with each precious moment that her mind could dredge up.

She would not permit a crime, no matter how hideous and violent, to spoil those memories for her, to spoil this island for her.

The Old Taylor Place was just a house, after all, just a slightly run-down relic that had suffered the misfortune of being the site that an evil man had chosen for his crimes. The house itself was blameless. Nicky looked it over, absorbing such *un*-scary details as the untidy masses of overgrown pink-and-white oleanders crowding against the lower porch and the eight identical casement windows on each floor, and the slightly sagging black shingle . . .

As Nicky's eyes touched on the roof, it hit her that something was off-kilter. In her quick scan of the house, she'd seen something that had registered with her eyes before it could be processed by her mind. As her mind finally caught up, her breathing suspended. Her eyes widened, her gaze dropped, and she looked disbelievingly at the second-floor window.

The corner one, Tara Mitchell's bedroom window.

A girl was standing at that window, looking out.

Even though Nicky's view was from the street, with the outside light now uncertain as the sky continued to darken, she could see the girl quite clearly. The golden-blond shade of the hair that flowed over the girl's shoulders almost to her waist, the pale oval of her face, featureless at such a distance, the slim curves of her body dressed in what looked like a cream T-shirt and jeans—Tara Mitchell.

Nicky's mind reeled. Her heart gave an uncontrollable leap. The world seemed to stop spinning on its axis as she stared upward—and then Tara Mitchell turned her head and looked back as though she had felt Nicky's gaze.

Then she vanished.

Just like that. *Poof.* One minute she was there, the next she was not.

For a split second, Nicky stayed frozen, her eyes glued to the window, her mouth agape. There was nothing to be seen there now but dark, unfathomable panes of glass, glistening black and empty like the eyes of a fly.

"*Gordon.* Gordon, did you see?" Released from the spell at last, Nicky fell back a couple paces on legs that felt about as solid as rubber bands, practically babbling as she looked around for the cameraman. "Oh, God, tell me you had the camera running."

"What? What are you talking about?" Gordon looked at her, clearly confused. As she had interrupted him in the process of tucking the camera back in its bag, it seemed pretty obvious that the camera had not been recording during the crucial seconds, which meant that there was no chance that he had gotten Tara Mitchell on film, even accidentally. But had he seen?

"I just saw Tara Mitchell in that bedroom window." Nicky pointed. Even she could see that there was no one there now. Like all the other windows, it was at that moment reflecting the last orange burst of the sinking sun—no more, no less. "I mean, a girl. A girl with long, blond hair. Damn it, I'm *sure* it was Tara Mitchell."

Gordon looked where Nicky pointed, then glanced back at her. Even in her agitated state, she had no trouble deciphering his doubtful expression.

"You saw something in the window?" he asked. "Besides a reflection, I mean?"

"Yes. Yes. *Come on.*"

Consumed with getting what she'd seen on record, Nicky charged toward the house. The yellow crime-scene tape didn't even slow her down. A nimble hop, and she was over. A glance told her that Gordon was right behind.

"Set up right here." Nicky stopped about three-quarters of the way up the weed-infested lawn, where she judged that Gordon would have the best view of the window in question. "I'm going to describe what I saw, and then I want you to focus in tight on that window. Then pan the house. Who knows, we might even get lucky and catch her on film this time."

Gordon was already getting out his camera. "If we get a ghost on film, I'm retiring. I'd be able to put all three of my kids through college with the money I could make off of it."

"BEST THING WOULD BE if this was some kind of boyfriend-girlfriend thing," Vince said. He was walking Joe down the steps of a relatively modern three-story brick office building where the town council had just concluded an emergency meeting. Part of the commercial corridor across the causeway from the touristy part of the island, it was on the other side of Highway 17 from a strip mall featuring various outlet stores, doctor's and dentist's offices, and a pizza parlor. In front of the pizza parlor there were perhaps half a dozen parked cars. The rest of the parking lot was deserted. This time of year, things were slow. In a couple weeks, when the high season got under way, the shops would be busy until eleven.

Provided that the talk of a serial killer on the loose didn't scare the tourists away.

"That would be best," Joe agreed. They were just leaving a meeting in which Joe had updated the town elders on the progress of the investigation. As, so far, there hadn't been a whole hell of a lot of progress, it hadn't been an entirely happy meeting. The councilmen, all businesspeople, wanted the murder to just go away. Barring that, they wanted it solved yesterday.

"So?" Vince said.

Joe paused on the bottom step to look back at Vince, who was a step behind. It was twilight now, and the breeze blowing in from the ocean was picking up. Joe's tie—he was wearing a navy sport coat, gray slacks, a white shirt, and a red tie—and the tails of his jacket flapped in the wind. "Boyfriend's got a rock-solid alibi."

"Shit." Vince stuck his hands in the pockets of his khaki slacks and rocked back on his heels. He, too, was wearing a coat and tie, forest green and striped, respectively. Since reporters had started popping up on them without warning, they were all dressing better, Joe reflected. Talk about silver linings. "You sure?"

"Yeah."

"Maybe some guy she hooked up with who wasn't her boyfriend, then. In a bar or something. You know, one of those *Looking for Mr. Goodbar* things. Only not an island bar."

"You're fishing, Vince."

"Damn it, Joe—"

Joe's cell phone rang, interrupting. Not that Joe was sorry. Vince, the councilmen, practically every business owner he came in contact with, his neighbors—everybody on the island, it seemed—had their own theory about the murder, which they weren't at all shy about sharing, and everybody wanted it solved. Not that anybody particularly gave a shit about a poor innocent girl viciously murdered in the springtime of her life. The consensus was that the thing had to be solved so the rest of the island could get on with their lives and the tourist season could happen unimpeded.

"Hang on a minute," Joe said to Vince, holding up a silencing hand. Then, into his phone, "Joe Franconi."

Joe listened, grinned, said, "I'll be right there," and disconnected.

"Gotta go," he said to Vince.

Vince frowned. "You got to understand, Joe. There's a lot at stake here. This thing is a monkey on our backs. We got to get it off. Whatever it takes."

"I understand." Joe started moving toward his cruiser, which was parked just a few yards away. He understood, all right. Vince and the rest of them wanted a perp ASAP. The right perp would be ideal. But ultimately, any halfway-plausible perp would do.

Just as long as the vacationing public could be reassured that the island was safe.

NICKY WAS SITTING, not very happily, beside Gordon in the back of a patrol car parked at the bottom of the Old Taylor Place's front yard when she saw, through the rearview mirror, a pair of headlights coming toward them. It was a measure of just how dark it had become that the approaching car had its headlights on, she realized. A quick glance around confirmed it—the light was almost gone. The purple shadows that had enveloped them what seemed like scant minutes ago were deepening to charcoal gray now, and beyond the tangle of undergrowth, the surface of the creek glinted a smooth, shiny black. Looking at it, Nicky shivered.

She was trapped out in front of a haunted house where she had just, personally, for the first time ever, seen a ghost, and where just about a week ago she had almost been killed and her friend had been viciously murdered, in the damned dark, with rising black water nearby.

As far as she was concerned, scary didn't get much more unnerving than that.

Even as she had the thought, from somewhere in the distance, the sound so faint that she could barely hear it over the nearer sounds of the night beyond the car and the people shifting, breathing, and exchanging desultory comments inside, a dog started to howl. Nicky listened to the mournful crescendo with widening eyes and a thudding heart as the memory hit her like a sledgehammer: A dog had been howling on the night Karen had died, too.

Okay, she'd been wrong. Scary had just gotten cranked up to a whole new level.

"Um," she began, meaning to do her best to alert the two dunderheaded cops in the front seat to the howling dog. But the thought of trying to explain the significance to two men who had looked at her like she was a raving lunatic when she'd told them she'd seen a ghost in an effort to explain why she and Gordon had crossed the crime-scene tape was daunting, to say the least.

"Here he comes," the cop in the driver's seat said before Nicky could get out more than that one indeterminate syllable. She didn't know him or his partner, which made trying to explain why she took ghosts way more seriously than they seemed to more difficult than it might otherwise have been. Under the circumstances, she decided to let the whole dog thing go in favor of trying to guess who *he* was. She knew who she was hoping for, anyway, although she probably shouldn't have been hoping for any such thing.

The driver had called somebody on his cell phone after locking Nicky and Gordon in the car. As the conversation had taken place outside the car, and she and Gordon had been inside it, she hadn't been able to overhear what was said. But that it concerned them was pretty obvious by the way the driver had kept looking in at them as he talked. Nicky had thought at the time that he was reporting the situation to somebody, and logic had dictated that the person he was reporting to was probably the Chief of Police. But it could have been his shift supervisor, too, or even his wife, whom maybe he'd called to ask what he should bring home for dinner.

"'Bout time," his partner grumbled, and Nicky definitely agreed with that. At this point, the tension in the car was so thick, you could have ladled it into soup bowls. Nicky—with only an occasional assist from Gordon, who at times during their little walk on the wrong side of the law had seemed to be almost on the side of the cops—had argued, cajoled, and done her best to explain as they were marched down the yard and herded into the patrol car, finally falling silent only when the cops had threatened them both with handcuffs and arrest if she didn't shut up—and Gordon had elbowed her hard in the ribs. Since then, she'd sat in stony silence, waiting for . . . she didn't know what.

The same thing the cops were waiting for, apparently, because after the driver had finished his call, both cops had slid into the cruiser, and there they'd all sat.

Nicky had a feeling that this oncoming car—which she now saw was, as she had suspected, another police car—was what they were waiting for. As the vehicle they were in was facing away from the arriving car, she had to slew around in the seat to watch as the newcomer pulled to a stop behind them. A masculine figure got out and slammed the door. Nicky took one look and felt her pulse quicken—in a good way, this time.

It was too dark now to see his face—the back windows of the cruiser were tinted, which didn't help—but there was just no mistaking that tall, lean form.

The first cop rolled down his window. Nicky heard the muted crunch of footsteps on gravel, saw a shape walk past her window, then found herself staring through the metal grille that separated the backseat from the front seat at Joe, as he leaned down to look in the driver's-side window.

"I don't believe it," Joe said as their eyes met. It was almost full night now, and his face was in shadow, so she couldn't really read his expression, but she could see the dark glint of his eyes. "What the hell are you doing here?"

Nicky was surprised by how very glad she was to see him—even under the circumstances.

"My job," she said, sticking out her chin.

"Is that so." His gaze moved from her to Gordon, who waved and said a wry "Hi there," then back to the cops in the front seat.

"They were trespassing," the driver said, and jerked a thumb toward the Old Taylor Place. "Up there."

Nicky leaned forward so that her nose was just inches from the grille and spoke to Joe through it. "Could you please tell them we're harmless and that they can let us go now?"

He flicked her a glance. "Depends." To the driver, he said, "So, is trespassing all you've got?"

"That, and crossing police lines. When we got here, they were up there on the porch, taking pictures through the windows."

Joe glanced back at Nicky.

"We were trying to catch something on film," Nicky said.

"A ghost," the driver said, his tone carefully neutral.

Joe glanced at her again. "Oh, yeah?"

There it was: skepticism in spades. She was getting fed up to the back teeth with it.

Nicky narrowed her eyes at him. "Yeah. I saw a ghost. You got a problem with that?"

"Nicky thought she saw a figure that looked like Tara Mitchell in the upstairs bedroom window when we were filming from the street earlier. We were trying to get it on camera," Gordon intervened hastily. As he'd already told Nicky, he knew how these small-town Southern lockups went: Go to jail on the weekend, and you'd be there until some good ole boy judge got into the courthouse on Monday. And he did *not* want to spend the next two nights in jail. Neither, if she had any sense, did she. "Would've been a money shot if we could've gotten it."

"But you didn't." Joe's tone made it a statement rather than a question.

The one cop whose face she could see smirked. Nicky bristled.

"I know what I saw," she said. "Could we please go now?"

"You got any problem with letting them off with a warning?" Joe asked. The other cops shook their heads. Joe looked back at Nicky. "Next time you see crime-scene tape, don't cross it," he said, and straightened away from the window. A moment later, he opened the back door.

Nicky slid out, followed by Gordon a few seconds later. Joe shut the door.

"Good job, guys," Joe said to his subordinates. "Wait for backup, and when it gets here, you two go in and check out the house."

"Sure." The driver grinned at Joe and lowered his voice. "I got a question for you, though: If we find a ghost, should we arrest it?"

Nicky heard and stiffened. Gordon shook his head at her warningly.

"Call me." Joe's voice was dry.

"Will do."

"Thanks for getting us out of that," Gordon said, hefting his camera bag over his shoulder as he started walking toward his and Nicky's vehicles. Nicky contented herself with shooting Joe a dirty look as she, too, started walking, heading toward her Maxima, which was some thirty feet away. Gordon's van was about ten feet beyond that. Joe was wearing a jacket and tie, she noted, and looking handsome enough to *almost* make up for his rotten personality. Now that it was dark, though, she was more interested in getting away from the scary haunted house with the howling dog—which, incidentally was no longer howling—than she was in quarreling with Joe, or in drooling over him.

"Not a problem." Joe fell into step beside her. Gordon was a couple paces ahead. "So you want to tell me why you're not holed up all safe and sound in your apartment in Chicago?"

"I told you: I have a job to do. And just so you know, I saw what I think was Tara Mitchell's ghost looking out of her bedroom window. And I heard a dog howling."

"A dog howling?" Joe sounded faintly bemused.

"I heard a dog howling Sunday night. Right before I was attacked. And just a little while ago, I heard one again."

"And that's supposed to mean?"

She could feel him looking at her, but she refused to look back, marching along with her eyes straight ahead. The musky scent of the marsh grew stronger as she reached her car. It was full dark now, and a bass choir of bullfrogs was just getting keyed up somewhere near the water. Cicadas and katydids and crickets whirred, and mosquitos buzzed, one or two around her head. She waved at them absentmindedly, barely noticing. Bloodthirsty insects were the least of her worries at the moment.

"How do *I* know? I'm just telling you," she snapped, curling her fingers around her car door handle. She jerked the door open, then paused—okay, she wasn't stupid—to make a quick survey of the interior before sliding inside.

"You heading for the airport?" Joe asked, stopping beside the car to look down at her.

"Nope." She shut the door and hit the lock button. As the sharp click sounded, she felt marginally safer.

Gordon was outside her door now, too. He had paused to say something to Joe. Lips tightening, keys already in her hand, Nicky rolled down her window.

"I'll call you in the morning and we'll set up a schedule for the day, okay?" she said to Gordon, the words brusque because she was in a hurry to leave. Besides being aggravated at Joe—and the other cops and Gordon and, basically, most of the rest of the world—for being such a doubter, she wanted to get out of there. Now that it was dark, the place was creeping her out to the point where she had cold chills running up and down her spine every time she glanced around.

"Yeah, okay," Gordon said, and started walking again.

"So, where are you headed?" Joe asked her. "Somewhere far away, I hope."

"Home. Twybee Cottage." She started rolling up her window.

"I'll follow you," Joe said. It wasn't a question. It was, instead, more of a grim statement, with the unspoken corollary *to make sure you get there alive.*

Nicky's finger paused on the button. The window stopped moving. Their eyes met through the gathering gloom.

She wanted to say "There's no need." Pride dictated that she say "I'll be fine." But nerves won out. *Face facts,* she told herself glumly: She was now officially afraid of the dark. She wasn't going to feel safe until her fanny was parked inside her big, noisy, chaotic house right in the middle of her big, noisy, chaotic family. Having a cop follow her until she got there would make her feel a whole lot better, especially since the cop in question was Joe.

She might not especially like him right now, but she trusted him.

"Thanks," she said. He nodded.

A few minutes later, the minivan with Gordon driving went past. Nicky pulled behind him, and Joe pulled behind her.

They lost Gordon with a honk and a wave at the first intersection, when he went west toward the South Causeway and she turned east toward the heart of the island. But Joe stayed behind her all the way to Twybee Cottage. She knew, because she snuck occasional glances in her rearview mirror just to make sure.

Nicky hated to admit it even to herself, but she was really, truly glad he was there. Still, she couldn't help it: She felt as jumpy as a grasshopper in a field full of lawnmowers as she drove through the dark, past fields crowded with tall grass and scrub pine and palmettos, past oncoming cars that were no more than a brief flash of headlights before they were gone, and finally past the big, old houses that lined Atlantic Avenue, only some of which were starting to glimmer with a few dim interior lights.

Coming back to the island was much worse than she'd thought it was going to be, she was discovering. *Everything* was starting to creep her out.

Nicky snorted. Was there any wonder? Within the last two hours or so since she'd arrived on the island, she had seen Tara Mitchell's ghost and heard something that sounded like the Hound of the Baskervilles howl. And she could almost *feel* the presence of evil.

Good God, she thought, appalled, as the words took on shape and substance in her mind—she was starting to sound like her mother.

That notion was so mind-boggling that she barely noticed that the Maxima was crunching up the pea-gravel driveway to Twybee Cottage until she swung around the garage and into the parking area and her headlights caught her mother, clad in loose black slacks and a short-sleeved floral blouse, upswept red hair gleaming brightly as the beams caught it, and her sister, wearing tight pink cropped pants and a pink-and-white gingham tent with her blond hair swinging loose around her face, leaning together into the open driver's-side door of a big black Mercedes-Benz sedan that was parked alongside Livvy's silver Jaguar. Since they both seemed to be looking at something in the Mercedes's front seat, all she saw of them at first was their backsides. But as the headlights hit them, their heads came out of the Mercedes faster than corks out of a champagne bottle. Almost in perfect unison, they swung around to face the oncoming car, looking like deer caught in the headlights, their eyes and mouths identically big and round as sand dollars.

Nicky frowned. Sliding the transmission into park and killing the engine and lights, she got out. She'd seen her mother and sister in all their moods, and this one she recognized easily: extreme guilt.

"So, what's up?" she called. The front end of the Maxima was between her and them as she walked toward them, which meant that she could see them only from about the hipbones up.

"Oh, Nicky, thank God it's you." Leonora sagged against the open car door behind her.

"You scared the *daylights* out of us," Livvy added, throwing her sister a disgusted look before turning and thrusting her head back inside the car.

"Look what they've got me doing. Just look at this." The tone was one of bitter complaint. The voice was Uncle John's, and it came from somewhere on high. Glancing up, Nicky's mouth dropped open. Framed by the glossy green leaves of the big magnolia by the porch, he was a good twenty feet off the ground, inching his way out along one of the arm-thick branches, one hand clamped around the smaller branch over his head, the other grasping a silver-bladed hacksaw that gleamed faintly in the yellow porch light. A metal ladder leaned against the trunk of the tree, mute evidence of his method of ascension.

"It'll be a miracle if I don't break my neck," he added.

"Here's the ice." Uncle Ham banged out through the screen door, then checked on the porch for an instant as he first saw the Maxima, and then Nicky. "Nicky! Sweetie! Welcome home!"

"It's not my fault." Livvy said. She no longer had her head inside the Mercedes, and was instead leaning against the closed back door, one hand pressed to her swollen belly. Only Leonora's backside now protruded from the car. Livvy looked appealingly at Nicky. "He called me *Shamu*."

Uh-oh. Did somebody have a death wish, or what?

Uncle Ham was moving again, running down the back steps, bulbous white dishcloth presumably filled with ice clutched in one hand. Uncle John was moving, too, creeping farther out along the branch and asking plaintively if they thought that was far enough. Leonora had withdrawn from the Mercedes again and was shaking her head at Livvy, whose lower lip quivered ominously.

Nicky registered these things only peripherally because, as she rounded the hood of her car and got a full view of her mother and sister and the driver's side of the Mercedes, her attention was instantly riveted by something else. A man's feet in medium-sized black dress shoes were planted side by side in the pea gravel. His legs, in pin-striped black dress pants, rose from the feet to bend at the knee and then, at about mid-thigh height, disappeared inside the car. The interior light was on, and there was no mistaking what she saw, but still Nicky stared for a few seconds, dumbfounded. Then it hit her that there was indeed a man lying motionless on his back across the Mercedes's front seats. It also hit her that she knew that car: She'd last seen it at Christmas, when her sister and her sister's husband had arrived in it.

The supine man could only be her soon-to-be-ex-brother-in-law. And he had called Livvy Shamu.

"Ohmigod." Nicky clapped a hand over her mouth as she hurried forward to survey the damage. It was Ben, all right. With her mother and Livvy blocking access to the car door, she couldn't see much, but she got a glimpse of a (now pale as white bread) strong-featured male profile and meticulously groomed dark blond hair. His eyes were closed. His mouth was slack. His body was limp. Her horrified gaze encountered her sister's. Her hand dropped away from her mouth. "Liv, what did you do?"

"Coldcocked him with a candlestick," Uncle Ham said, not without a certain amount of satisfaction as he pushed past Nicky to hand the makeshift ice bag to Leonora. "I always knew she had the James temper in there somewhere."

"I didn't mean to really hurt him," Livvy said in a small voice. "It's just— I was upset. I was at our house, getting some of my things, and he came home and said I couldn't take anything and then I went ahead and jumped in my car—it was pretty full by then—and took off, and he followed me all the way home. And then he started yelling about how *immature* I am and how Alison"—Alison being, as they all knew, the homewrecking bimbo—"is what he needs, and then he called me *Sh-Shamu.*"

Listening to Livvy's voice quaver, Nicky would have given her brother-in-law a sharp kick in the kneecap if he'd been aware enough to feel it.

"And then she beaned him. We were having supper, and we all saw it through the window," Uncle Ham said with relish.

"I was carrying Grandma's candlesticks in from the car," Livvy said to Nicky. "You know the ones."

Nicky did indeed. A pair of pre–Civil War sterling-silver candelabra, they had held pride of place with a matching epergne on Livvy's dining-room table since she'd married. They were about two and a half feet tall, and had to weigh at least fifteen pounds each.

Nicky stared at her sister, then looked at the motionless legs.

"Is he—?" "Dead," was what Nicky was going to say, but the sound of tires crunching up the driveway coupled with the sweep of headlights across the parking area made her jump and whirl around to face them. Everybody in the group—with the exception of Ben, of course, who was incapacitated, and Uncle John, who was up in the tree—followed suit with a collective indrawing of breath.

"It's Joe," Nicky said, having just then remembered that he was behind her. "Joe Franconi. He followed me home."

"The police chief?" Leonora pressed a hand to her bosom.

"Look out below!" A magnolia branch as long as Nicky's leg crashed down right in front of the open Mercedes door, making them all jump again.

"We're going to tell Ben that a branch broke off the magnolia and hit him in the head. I don't think he saw the candlestick coming," Uncle Ham told Nicky hurriedly. "If he ever wakes up, that is." Then, glancing skyward, he hissed, "Dammit, John, be quiet up there. Can't you see what just pulled up the driveway?"

"Oh, shit."

The cruiser had them all pinned in its lights now as it pulled up beside Nicky's Maxima and stopped. She could only imagine the tableau they must present, with her, Livvy, Leonora, and Ham frozen in place beside the Mercedes and, in her case at least, staring bug-eyed in the newcomer's direction. Guilt had to be written all over all of them. And that was before Joe got around to spotting Uncle John in the tree—or Ben's legs sticking out of the car door, for that matter.

"I won't have to go to jail, will I?" Livvy sounded petrified. "He called me Shamu."

It occurred to Nicky then that what Livvy had done could probably be considered assault, the Shamu comment notwithstanding—unless, of course, Ben was dead.

"Hush," Leonora hissed at her older daughter. "You're not going to jail." Then, giving Nicky a little push in the center of her back as the cruiser's headlights went out and its door opened, she added under her breath, "Get rid of him. *Now.*"

Okay. Nicky started to move as her mind went into semi-hysterical overdrive. *Once more into the breach . . .*

"Evening, folks." Joe was out of the car now, slamming the door behind him as he walked toward them. His tall form was in deep shadow. Nicky realized with a thrill of horror that *they* were in the light.

"Hi, Joe," her family chorused. A lightning glance over her shoulder told Nicky that they were all clustered in front of the telltale legs now, forming what amounted to a human wall that unfortunately failed to hide Ben's feet. Uncle Ham smiled; Leonora smiled. And Livvy—white as flour, round as the Great Pumpkin, eyes as big as Toll House cookies, and grinning like she had rigor mortis—Livvy leaned against Leonora's shoulder and gave a little three-fingered wave.

Nicky couldn't see Uncle John in the tree. Hopefully, Joe couldn't see him, either.

But those of her relatives that she could see looked about as relaxed and natural as *American Gothic*.

Horribly conscious that as soon as Joe rounded the hood of his car he would be able to see Ben's feet, Nicky moved faster.

"Everybody okay?" Joe asked. He was close enough now that Nicky could see that he was frowning a little. Presumably something about her relatives' posture was starting to pique his interest.

"Just fine."

"Sure thing."

"Absolutely."

The responses came in an almost simultaneous chorus—and sounded false as hell to Nicky.

Joe had almost reached the edge of his front bumper.

She rounded the hood of his car and stopped dead in his path, successfully blocking his forward progress.

Yes.

He looked down at her, and his expression changed. His eyes took on a dangerous glint, and his lips compressed. He looked, in fact, like a man in a snit. With her.

Well, good. Come to think of it, she was in a snit with him, too, and, moreover, she was going to beat him to the punch.

"We need to talk." She glared up at him with all the ferocity she could muster.

"You're damned right we do." He kept his voice down, so that his response went no farther than her ears.

"Great." Then, having just had another one of her patented eureka moments, she added, "In private."

"Honey, you read my mind."

She was ticked off at him, scared of ghosts and killers, and worried that her temporarily psychotic sister might be headed for either the loony bin or the pokey, whichever got to her first, but still, something about him calling her "honey" in that sexy Yankee voice of his sent a little thrill curling through her stomach—or somewhere thereabouts.

"We're going for a walk on the beach," she called over her shoulder without looking around. Then, with her mother's falsely cheery "Y'all have fun" echoing in her ears, she caught Joe's hand and dragged him away from the scene of the crime, toward the front of the house and the rickety wooden walkway that led over the dunes and down to the beach.

13

BEING DRAGGED OFF into the dark by a gorgeous, sexy woman he was developing a considerable jones for wasn't the worst thing to ever happen to him, Joe reflected as Nicky towed him along like a dog owner with a recalcitrant mutt, but under the circumstances, it was damned suspicious.

"So, what was going on back there?" he asked as they left the shelter of the house behind and started down the rickety wooden walkway that connected Twybee Cottage to the beach. A considerable number of the old houses that fronted the ocean had private boardwalks rising over the constantly shifting dunes and tall drifts of sea oats that separated the houses from the beach, making access to the ocean easier. Like the houses, most were in the "arrogantly shabby" mode of the island, and some were wobblier than others. This particular one was pretty wobbly, creaking underfoot, its supports as cockeyed and insubstantial-looking as a smashed spider's legs.

"Nothing out of the ordinary," she said, then she seemed to realize that she was literally pulling him along, and she slowed down and dropped his hand.

Joe was surprised at how keenly he felt the loss of those warm, silky-skinned fingers.

"Just a typical Friday night at home, *hmm?*"

Her mouth twisted a bit as she glanced up at him. "For my family? Oh, yeah."

For a moment, the issue hung in the balance. Then, because her voice carried the ring of truth, and because he'd much rather be heading down toward the ocean with her than be back there sorting out her family anyway, he let the matter go.

"I don't quite get the setup," he said, feeling some of the tension start to leave his shoulders and neck as the night enveloped them like a whisper-soft blanket. For one of the few times in the past week, he was enjoying something. And what he was enjoying was, quite simply, her company. "Do they all live there together?"

Nicky made a face. "Not usually. But we're having sort of a . . . family crisis, and everybody's kind of circling the wagons right now."

They were walking side by side now, and he was loath to ruin the companionable mood so soon by launching into the argument that he knew he was going to have to have with her. Besides, he was curious. "What kind of crisis?"

"You mean you haven't heard? I thought everybody on the island knew."

He shrugged. "I'm a newcomer. I'm out of the loop."

"Yes, you would be. Well . . ." Her voice trailed off as they reached the peak of the walkway, and the sea, dark and wild in the light of the rising moon, came into view. The tide was coming in, and waves thundered toward shore like rows of galloping black horses with tossing white manes. The roar was hypnotic. The wind—it was too strong to be called a breeze—hit Joe in the face. It smelled and tasted briny, like oysters. It caught his tie and sent it flapping off to the side.

Nicky's glorious hair blew all over the place, whipping around her face, getting in her mouth, and she paused to deal with it. Joe watched with some pleasure as she pulled a strand away from her lips, then caught the top section of it up and held it back with one hand. Etched by pale moonlight, her profile was as fine and delicate as a cameo's, except no cameo he had ever seen in his life had possessed such long lashes—or such full, seductive lips.

Watching them part, he felt his body tighten and wrenched his eyes away.

"Livvy—my sister—is getting a divorce."

It took him a second to get his mind back in gear again so that he was actually able to make sense of her words.

"And she's pregnant," she continued, "and her husband's being a real prick, and she's having a really hard time dealing with everything. So she moved back in with my mother and Harry. Harry's pretty much horrified by the whole situation, and does his best to stay out of the way, but Uncle Ham and Uncle John have been really supportive. They actually live in Savannah, but they've been spending a lot of time at Twybee Cottage lately to help with Livvy—and because Uncle Ham's going to be opening a restaurant here. He owns Hamilton House in Savannah, you know."

There was an unmistakable touch of pride in her voice as she said that last sentence.

"I heard." Hamilton House was one of the best-known restaurants in the region, as Joe had learned while having everyone who'd been present at the Old Taylor Place on the night of Karen Wise's murder checked out. Hamilton James had been described to him variously as a highly respected businessman, a temperamental artiste of the kitchen, and a Southern aristocrat to his fingertips. His partner in life, John, was also his partner in the restaurant business, as well as being his accountant and, by all accounts, a much less combustible type.

"Plus, my mother's having a small crisis of her own, because she thinks she's suffering from psychic's block, as she calls it. She hasn't been able to get through to the Other Side properly for a while now, and it's making her slightly nuts."

Joe thought about that for a second.

"So if the psychic hotline's down, as it were, how was she able to talk to Tara Mitchell's ghost on your TV show the other night?" He did his best to keep the whole "got ya" vibe out of his voice.

Apparently, he didn't entirely succeed, because she gave him a sharp look.

"You know what? Since I'm not psychic myself, I don't understand precisely how it works all the time, either. But if my mother said she saw Tara Mitchell, she saw Tara Mitchell. My mother is many things, but she is *not* a liar."

Combustibility must run in the James family genes, Joe thought, with a wry glance down at his now-bristling companion. Wasn't there some saying about fiery hair equaling a fiery heart (which, for his money, wasn't necessarily a bad thing)?

The thing about playing with fire, though, was that it was way too easy to end up getting burned. . . .

Which, he reminded himself firmly, was why he was opting not to play.

"Hold on. You're putting words in my mouth here. I never said she was. I only asked the same question any other reasonable human being would."

That earned him another sharp look.

"Just because *you* don't believe in ghosts doesn't mean they don't exist, you know."

Joe thought of Brian, who was, fortunately, nowhere in evidence at the moment. "Believing in ghosts is a pretty big stretch for a guy like me. What can I say? I need proof."

They reached the end of the boardwalk then, and the white beach stretched before them like a pale highway. The moon hung just above the horizon, big and round as a hubcap and the color of milk in an inky sky. Its reflection shimmered on top of the waves like the squiggle of icing on a snack cake. A sprinkling of stars peeped through a layer of shredded gray clouds.

"Careful." Joe paused to let Nicky proceed down the steps. She hesitated at the top, one hand on the rail, the other still holding back her hair as she glanced cautiously up and down the beach. It wasn't quite empty. He could see, in the distance, outlined by moonlight, a couple walking shoulder to shoulder, and a woman jogging while her dog—something big, a Lab, maybe—raced in and out of the surf.

But it was deserted enough so that for all intents and purposes, they were now totally alone.

That was not necessarily a thought he needed to be having, Joe told himself. The problem was, though, he *was* having it, having thoughts about making some moves, about doing something concrete about this attraction he felt for her, which wasn't doing a thing but getting hotter and more difficult to resist with every moment that he spent in her company. He wanted her: There was the truth of it. And the thing was, going after what he wanted seemed to be hardwired into his nature.

Sleeping with her would do nothing but complicate his life, which was way too complicated already.

There were lots of women—lots of nice, pretty, local women—who'd given him every indication that they would be willing to share his bed anytime he felt the urge. Taking one of them up on it would be a whole hell of a lot easier. It would be the smart, safe, get-your-life-back-on-its-new-peaceful-track choice.

He had some control: The excitement junkie in him didn't have to win out.

Then Nicky glanced around at him, and just looking at her blew him away. Her eyes were wide and dark, her skin luminous in the moonlight. The wind was plastering the black sweatery thing she was wearing against her body so that he could see her every exquisite line and curve. In general, he liked his women to be shaped like women, he reminded himself in a desperate bid to keep from being totally bedazzled: big boobs, nice round ass. And she was definitely lacking in that department. Instead, she was almost impossibly slender. Her breasts were small and firm and high, probably no more than a B-cup, certainly real. Her waist was slim, her hips almost boyish. And her legs seemed to go on forever in the clingy black pants.

Looking at her, he was reminded of Spencer Tracy's line about Katharine Hepburn: something to the effect of "There's not a lot of meat on her, but what there is is choice."

And sexy. Sexy as hell.

"You've got your gun, right?" she asked then, and with that, the whole warm-and-fuzzy ambience that had been building up between them went straight to hell.

His brows twitched together as he met her gaze. The fear-fueled anger that had almost been overshadowed by the unexpected rush of wanting her came back in spades. Okay, the sweet little getting-to-know-you interlude was now officially over. Time to get her the hell out of Pawleys Island—and, if he had any sense at all, his life.

FOR A MOMENT, Joe didn't say a word. He just stood there against the backdrop of night sky and waving sea oats and the peaked roof of Twybee Cottage and frowned at her. Then, still wordless, he pulled open the left side of his jacket and let her see his shoulder holster, stark against his white shirt. She could just make out the dull black gleam of a businesslike pistol peeking out of it. The sight was reassuring.

"Feel better?" he asked. His tone had a snarky quality to it that told her he was once again in a snit. Apparently, he hadn't liked her asking about his gun.

Luckily, his mood swings weren't her problem.

Nicky nodded tranquilly and, since she really had no choice, considering the drama that was no doubt still playing out back at the house, turned and went down the steps to the beach. The wind was much less intense once she was no longer ten feet above the earth, and she was able to let go of her hair by the time her feet touched the sand. She tucked it behind her ears, which was enough to keep it out of her face. Joe followed her down, joining her as, from habit, she started walking toward the little cluster of hotels and bars and souvenir shops that anchored the north end of the island. For as long as she could remember, there had been commercial development of one kind or another on that site; as little girls, she and Livvy had often walked down there to play games in the long-since-vanished arcade, or to get ice cream at the also long-since-vanished sandwich shop. The distant glow from the lights of the establishments there now made a small oasis of brightness in the dark.

"You know that coming back here was stupid, obviously, or you wouldn't have asked me if I had a gun," Joe said.

She'd been right. He was in a snit.

"Probably."

The thing was, *she* no longer felt like quarreling. She was tired, still a little shaken from her first bona fide ghost-sighting, worried about her sister, worried about her job, and worried about dying—probably not exactly in that order. Plus, he was the first man in a while who had the ability to make her heart go pitter-pat, even while he was scowling at her. That, she decided, was something worth exploring. How long had it been since she'd had any kind of romance in her life? The short answer was, way too long.

"*Probably?* You think it's *probably* stupid to put yourself within reach of a vicious killer who's already tried to murder you once and seems to have you parked right at the top of his buddy list? What does it take to make stupid a certainty for you? Imminent death?"

Of course, sarcasm wasn't her favorite male trait. It wasn't even in her top ten.

"Look, it's really none of your business, is it?"

"The hell it isn't. I'm the Chief of Police, remember? It's my job to keep people from getting murdered around here. Even criminally stupid ones. That being the case, I'm going to ask you very nicely to do us both a favor and go back to Chicago."

He said it as though he actually expected her to do it just because he was telling her to. Oh, wait, he probably did.

"No."

That shut him up for a moment. She could feel him fuming, see him scowling at her from the corner of her eye, but she didn't meet his gaze. Instead, she looked past him and out to sea. She could see, just faintly, the boxy, black outline of a trawler against the horizon and, farther away, the twinkly lights of what was either a large private yacht or a small cruise ship. They were walking close to the ocean's edge, just beyond the place where the tide ebbed and flowed. She watched the frothing water curl and retreat, curl and retreat, just inches from his black-shod feet. The sand where they were walking was wet with spray and nearly as firm as asphalt. The breeze had died down to a whisper now, and stars were popping out all over the sky. Nicky had known the island in all its moods in every season, and May was one of her favorite months. Bright, hot days; warm, soft nights; and few tourists. Around here, it didn't get much better than that.

Except for the fact that a killer was on the loose, of course.

"You can't *want* to be here," he said, clearly trying hard to sound reasonable. "You were smart enough and scared enough to call me when you got that e-mail—and smart enough and scared enough to practically collapse when you heard the message he left on your cell phone. Why would you even think about coming back here until he's caught?"

Nicky didn't like being reminded how scared she had been—and still was. "You're wasting your breath." Her tone was short. "I'm not leaving. You can't talk me into it, and you can't make me, so why don't we find something else to talk about?"

A beat passed in which he said nothing. The bald truth was, if she didn't want to leave the island, there was nothing he could do about it. And they both knew it.

"Damit, Nicky . . ."

She could hear the frustration in his voice, but that wasn't what got to her. It was, she realized, the first time he had called her by name. The sound of that sexy Yankee voice of his saying "Nicky" made her go all soft and buttery inside. It also prompted her to at least try to make him understand her position.

"My producer was going to send someone else, all right? Another reporter to cover this story instead of me. But I talked him out of it because it's *my* story. Yes, okay, I admit it: I'm a little bit afraid. And no, I'm not giving it up. It's important to me."

"I don't have enough manpower to assign somebody to watch over you twenty-four-seven, you know." He still sounded testy.

"I'm not asking you to."

"Oh, so I'm just supposed to go on about my business while you cross your fingers and hope you won't be attacked again?"

"I'm planning to be careful."

He snorted. "Yeah, right. You've been on the island for—what? Maybe two, two and a half hours? And you've already been almost arrested for trespassing at the Old Taylor Place, which, under the circumstances, is the very last place you should have been. And right now you're walking on the beach at night with an armed man you don't know from Adam. How do you know *I'm* not the killer?"

"You're a cop."

"So? Believe me, that doesn't mean a thing."

"You ran down the driveway to rescue me while the killer was still under the trees. You couldn't possibly have done it," she pointed out triumphantly.

He paused. "Okay, I give you that. Say we stipulate that you're safe with me. That just leaves you about another five hundred men on the island to worry about. To say nothing of the tens of thousands of men *off* the island. In Murrels Inlet, say, or Litchfield, or even Savannah."

She slanted a look up at him. Despite the darkness, she could see that his jaw was tight and his eyes were intense. It was clear that he was truly worried about her safety, and that made her already-soft-and-buttery insides practically melt. They were walking so close together that their arms brushed. She could see the hard line of his mouth, the stubby silhouette of his lashes, the worried vee of his brows.

Her heart beat just a little faster as she again tried to explain.

"See, the thing is, in TV you're either hot or you're not. Lately I've been kind of on the *not* side. And I'm twenty-nine years old."

"Well, hello there, Grandma."

There he went with the sarcasm thing again. But he was smiling a little, and an answering smile quivered around the corners of her mouth.

"Believe me, that's old for TV. If I don't make it big soon, I won't make it. If *Twenty-four Hours Investigates* is cancelled, my next gig probably won't be as good. But if it does well, if *I* do well, I may have a shot at the cohost's seat on *Live in the Morning.*"

Clearly, he wasn't a TV person; he looked singularly unimpressed. "None of that is worth dying for."

"But, see, I'm not planning on dying."

"Nobody ever is."

There was something in his voice—a faint bitterness, maybe—that made her cast a quick, questioning look up at him. Their eyes met, and he grimaced.

"Which brings me back to my original point: You need to leave the area until this guy is caught."

"Which brings me back to my original answer: No."

He studied her. "Are you always this stubborn, or am I just getting lucky here?"

"Is that one of those trick questions, like 'When did you stop beating your wife?' "

He laughed. "I take that as an 'always.' "

"Feel free to take it any way you like."

They had almost reached the yellow pool of light cast by the cluster of commercial buildings by this time. More people were on the beach now, most, from the look of them, early vacationers. An elderly man sat in a plastic beach chair drawn to the very edge of the surf. A couple in going-out-to-dinner clothes strolled across the circle of light and then moved on into the dark, clearly intent on taking their own private walk along the beach.

"You ever been here?" Joe gave a jerk of his head toward the buildings. Nicky identified with a glance one of the hammock shops for which the island was famous, a jewelry store, a dive shop, and a bakery—all of which formed part of the island's premier tourist trap. It was anchored by what the glowing neon sign on one wall proclaimed was the Seaside Resort and Spa. This, Nicky knew, was the island's newest hotel complex, built on the site of a former hotel that had been torn down to make way for it. The trio of four-story white stucco buildings had red tile roofs, Spanish arches, and dozens of wrought-iron balconies. A profusion of palmettos and yuccas and hibiscus and bright blue phlox crowded around the walkways and the patios and the swimming pool, making the area an enticing oasis of color against the sugar-white sand.

All the better to take your money with, my dear. . . .

Nicky shook her head. "My sister and I used to walk up here for ice cream when we were little girls, but there was nothing like this here then."

"Want to try it?"

She frowned at him. "What?"

"For dinner," he said. "I haven't eaten. Have you?"

"No."

"So, you want to have dinner with me?"

"Well . . ." Rather to her surprise, Nicky realized that the short answer was *yes*. She looked down at herself. Her clothes were fine—thank goodness for fabrics that didn't wrinkle!—but there was sand on her low-heeled, boxy-toed, airport-friendly shoes, and probably, though she couldn't be sure, on the hem of her pants. From the way her lips felt, she doubted that she had any lipstick left, and her hair was a windblown, tangled mess.

"You look beautiful," he said, clearly having correctly interpreted her hesitation.

Their eyes met. At what she saw in his, her heart started beating just a little bit faster. They were dark and hot, and made her think of sex. And thinking of sex—with him—made her breathless.

She could if she wanted to. . . .

"Thank you," she said, trying to sound more composed than she suddenly felt. "I'd love to have dinner with you."

He grinned at her, a slow and charming grin that went a long way toward dazzling her. She smiled back. Then they walked through the circle of light into the hotel.

While Joe went to see about getting a table, Nicky made a quick stop in the gift shop, where she bought a few necessities with the twenty-dollar bill that she always kept tucked in her pocket for emergencies. Armed with those, she adjourned to the ladies' room and made some badly needed repairs to her appearance. Feeling better with her hair restored to at least a semblance of its former style and her nose powdered and lipgloss in place, she headed for the dining room. It was lovely, small and intimate, with marble floors, smoked mirrors covering the walls, and candles flickering in the center of each table. Potted palm trees placed strategically about the room gave each table the illusion of privacy. The hostess was a girl—well, a woman now—who had gone to elementary school with Livvy. She greeted Nicky with delight, assured her that she watched

Twenty-four Hours Investigates every week and couldn't wait for the upcoming episode, then dropped her voice to commiserate with her over the awful thing that had happened (meaning Karen's death), all as she showed Nicky to the small table in the corner where Joe was waiting. He stood up as she approached, and Nicky was impressed all over again by how handsome he looked in a coat and tie. Then he pulled her chair out for her. She had always been a sucker for a guy with good manners, Nicky reflected wryly as she sat, and a gorgeous guy with good manners was simply piling it on. The hostess was clearly impressed as well: As Joe returned to his seat, she gave him the kind of once-over that told Nicky that (a) she thought he was hot, and (b) the news of their "date" would be all over the island by this time tomorrow. Then she sent Nicky a wicked, congratulatory grin before leaving them to the waitress's tender care.

"I hope you don't mind being gossiped about," Nicky said when the waitress, having finished taking their order, had left, too.

Joe shrugged. "I guess that's what I get for having dinner with a woman who's famous."

Nicky made a face. "I'm not really very famous, believe me. In Chicago, I can go to the mall, to the movies, out to eat, anywhere, and people hardly ever recognize me. It's just here, because of the whole hometown-girl-makes-good thing. Anyway, I think you're the one she's primarily going to be talking about. As in, 'You know who I saw Chief Franconi having dinner with last night?' "

"That's the thing about the South." Joe's mouth quirked into a faint smile. "Everybody butts into everybody else's business."

"Hey," Nicky said. "At least people talk to each other."

Joe grinned. "You say that like it's a good thing."

Nicky's cell phone rang just then. Grimacing apologetically, she pulled it out of her pocket, glanced at the number, and sighed.

"Sorry," she said. "It's my mother. If I don't answer, she'll go insane with worry."

"Smart woman," Joe said dryly.

Nicky narrowed her eyes at him as she said "Hello" into the phone.

"You've been gone forever. Where are you?" Leonora asked.

"We're having dinner. At the new hotel down the beach."

"You're having dinner?" Leonora sounded taken aback. "With Joe Franconi? As in a *date?*"

"Yes," Nicky said, smiling at the waitress as she arrived with their drinks and salads, set them down on the table, and left again. Fortunately, only two other tables were occupied, both at some distance from theirs, so as long as she kept her voice down, she didn't have to worry about bothering the other diners.

"Oh, my. Well, that's fine, I guess. I mean, he seems nice enough, and he's certainly good-looking, but . . ." Leonora's voice trailed off. Then, belatedly, she asked, "Is he right there with you? Can he hear me?"

"Can you hear her?" Nicky asked Joe.

"Don't ask him that," her mother hissed, while Joe, smiling, shook his head.

"No," Nicky said into the phone. "At least, he says not. Did you want something in particular?"

"I just called to tell you Ben's gone. You can come home anytime." There was the briefest of pauses. "What time are you coming home?"

"I have no idea."

"Oh." Leonora absorbed that. A touch of anxiety crept into her voice. "He's not married or anything, is he? I mean, we don't know anything about him, except he's from up north somewhere. He could be—"

Nicky interrupted ruthlessly. Joe was eating his salad, his expression totally innocent as their eyes met. *Too* innocent? She suddenly wasn't sure he'd been telling the truth about not being able to hear. Anyway . . .

"Everything's fine, Mother. Don't worry. I have to go, my salad's here. Bye."

She disconnected, tucked the phone back into her pocket, took a bite of her salad, and reflected.

Okay. Sometimes—just sometimes—Mother had the right idea.

"So-o," she said on a drawn-out note as her eyes met his across the table, "are you married?"

His lips twitched. "She told you to ask me that, didn't she? The answer is no, I'm not."

Considering the direction her thoughts had been taking, that was a relief.

"Ever been?"

"No."

"Engaged? Steady girlfriend?" she asked with a lift of her brows, and took another bite of salad. The lettuce was iceberg, the dressing a light vinaigrette, probably from a bottle. Decent, but nothing special, was her verdict. Certainly nothing to distract her from the conversation—or the company.

He grinned. "No. And no."

"Good," she said.

At the implication implicit in that, his eyes darkened—and heated. She caught her breath. . . .

Before either of them could say anything more, the waitress arrived with their meals. She chatted to them both comfortably as she served the food, and the moment passed. In the low country, seafood, as the menu had stated, was king. That being the case, Nicky had ordered grilled shrimp and grits, Joe soft-shell crab. Joe dug into his hungrily, like a man who'd been catching meals on the fly for some time, and Nicky followed suit, although with considerably less enthusiasm. Like the salad, the food was good, but not, Nicky was pleased to discover, great. When it opened, which probably wouldn't be until the season was well under way at the rate things were going, Uncle Ham's restaurant would blow this one away.

"So, have you gotten any hot leads since we talked Thursday night?" Nicky asked as she delicately dissected a shrimp.

Joe looked up from his crab. His eyes slid over her face. "You trying to pump me for information?"

Nicky grinned. "Maybe."

"Maybe nothing. You are. You can forget it, too. I've got nothing to say about an ongoing investigation."

"Too late. You already told me stuff. When I called you."

"It was the middle of the night. You caught me by surprise." Without warning, his brows met over his nose and his jaw hardened. Clearly, he'd recollected his grievance with her.

Uh-oh, Nicky thought. She was already starting to recognize that look.

"Whoever this guy we're dealing with is, he's a very bad guy. I want you off the island. For your own safety. I'm begging here. Please."

Nicky sighed and put down her fork. "We've already had this conversation."

"Yeah, well, we're going to keep on having it, believe me."

"Joe . . ." His eyes darkened and flickered, and she realized that it was the first time she had called him by name. It was clear from his expression that he registered it, too.

"Nicky," he said, his tone gently mocking hers. Their eyes locked. A strange new intimacy seemed to shimmer in the air between them, as if they'd taken a step through a door that led to—what? A relationship?

Nicky's heart beat faster at the thought.

"I told you. . . ." she said.

"Yeah, you told me." His voice was dry. "Basically, what you're saying is that your career is more important than your life, right?"

Nicky narrowed her eyes at him. "There you go again with another one of those 'heads I win, tales you lose' things."

For a moment, they all but glared at each other. Then, almost reluctantly, he laughed.

"All right," he said. "So tell me about *Live in the Morning*. That's the one with Troy Hayden and Angie somebody, right? If you get it, you gonna be moving to New York?"

"Yes. *If* I get it. That's a very big if."

"And why is that?"

She was surprised, a little touched, and more than a little charmed that he remembered so clearly what she'd said earlier. Very few people knew that she was interested in the job, even fewer knew that she had auditioned, and what she had said to him about it had been only a passing remark. Getting ahead in TV-land was a game best played close to the vest, she had learned, and telling people she worked with that she was being considered for the *Live in the Morning* spot would only result in (a) them questioning her commitment to her present job, and (b) her stock going down if the job wasn't offered to her, which, realistically, it probably wasn't going to be. But Joe wasn't in TV, and that was why she had felt safe in mentioning it in the first place. Now he watched her with smiling dark eyes as she talked, and asked all the right questions, so she ended up telling him all about it. By the time she finished, their plates had been cleared, the check had been presented and taken care of, and they were lingering over coffee.

"You ready?" he asked. "I can't smoke in here, and I need a cigarette."

She nodded, pushed her chair back, and stood up. "You shouldn't smoke."

"I know." He followed her from the dining room. "It's one of my bad habits."

"You say that like you have a lot of them."

"I have a fair number."

They were out in the open-air courtyard now. He paused to light a cigarette, and she watched with some disapproval as he cupped a hand around the flame of his lighter to shield it from the wind, then took a drag deep enough to make the tip of the lit cigarette glow red. Then he dropped the lighter back into his pocket along with the pack of cigarettes, and they started walking along the path between the pool and the hot tub, heading for the beach. His hand curved around her elbow, as casual and possessive as if it belonged there. She was very aware of it, even though, cool to the end, she pretended not to have even noticed. It was after ten now, she guessed, and beyond the reach of the tiki torches that lit the courtyard, the night was as soft and dense as black velvet. There were two couples in the hot tub, and a lone swimmer carved out laps in the pool. The smell of smoke was in the air, from Joe's cigarette and the torches. The sound of the sea made gentle background music for the laughter and splashing of the tourists.

"I've been wondering," she said, because her tension level was climbing as they reached the beach and headed toward the edge of the circle of light, and she felt a sudden nervous need to break the silence that had fallen between them, "how you ended up as the island's police chief. It just doesn't seem like the kind of job you'd like."

His hand tightened on her elbow.

"What's not to like? The sun, the beach, babes in bikinis everywhere you look—this place is practically paradise."

They were crossing the line now, stepping from warm yellow light into cool darkness, and Nicky felt an anticipatory shiver race down her spine. It took a second for her eyes to adjust, but when they did, she saw that the old man in the chair was gone, as were the children who had played in the surf earlier. If there were other people strolling along the sand—and there had to be, it was that kind of night—she didn't see them. All she saw was that the moon was high in the sky and the beach was washed in otherworldly light, and the white-capped waves rolled toward shore in an endless, hypnotic rhythm that was as old as time.

"Still . . ." she murmured.

He stopped walking, tossed his cigarette away, and pulled her around to face him.

"I've been wondering something, too."

His eyes gleamed at her through the darkness. The top of her head barely reached his chin. They were now standing so close together that she had to tilt her head back to see his face. With the moonlight glinting off his black hair and silvering his hard, high cheekbones and the strong lines of his nose and jaw, he looked so handsome that he stole her breath.

"What?"

He held both her elbows lightly now, and her hands rested on his upper arms. His jacket was some kind of lightweight summer material, not linen but something smooth and cool, probably a synthetic. Through it she could feel the well-developed firmness of his biceps. Her heart started to beat just a little bit faster.

"What you meant back there when you said 'good.' "

"Good?" She looked down. Distracted as she was by her own shivery reaction to those admittedly impressive muscles, she didn't follow at first.

"I said I'd never been married, that I wasn't engaged and I didn't have a steady girlfriend, and you said 'good.' "

"Oh," Nicky said, remembering now. "Well, I probably said 'good' because that meant there was a job vacancy."

"Oh, yeah?" He smiled, a little, and she suddenly found her eyes fixed on his long, mobile mouth. Electricity seemed to sizzle in the air between them. Heat curled somewhere deep inside her body. Her heart began to thud in her chest.

"Yeah," she said, looking up to meet his gaze. Then, because the suspense was killing her and she'd never been very good at just passively waiting for anything anyway, she went up on her toes and kissed him.

14

HIS LIPS WERE WARM and firm, and tasted faintly of cigarettes. He stood perfectly still for a moment, just letting her kiss him. Nicky would have thought that maybe she was striking out if it hadn't been for the gradual tightening of his hands on her elbows. They were looking at each other from beneath lowered lids, watching each other's eyes while her lips plied his, and even when he started to respond, the kisses stayed hot and soft and only faintly demanding. Her body did a slow burn. Her nipples tightened. An insistent, throbbing excitement sprang to life deep inside her. As they kissed, the feeling just kept spiraling tighter and tighter until her toes were curling in her shoes. Dizzy with the heat that they were generating, she leaned into him, kissed him harder. The sudden fierce flare in his eyes was all the warning she got before soft and gentle was suddenly abandoned as he took control of the kiss, pulling her close against him with his hands now hard on her elbows, slanting his lips over hers and sliding his tongue deep into her mouth. Her head spun. Her heart slammed against her rib cage. Her eyes closed. She kissed him back while her body went haywire with excitement, and he let go of her elbows and slid his arms around her and took her mouth with a hungry carnality that practically dissolved her bones.

Oh, God. She'd forgotten what it felt like to be kissed like this.

Her arms slid up over his shoulders to wrap around his neck. She pressed close, flattening herself against him, and kissed him as if she'd die if she didn't. Sex had never been high on her list of priorities, but suddenly it was, suddenly it was all she could think about, suddenly her body was in the grip of a hot, sweet fire that made her absolutely mindless—or, rather, absolutely single-minded.

She wanted him.

"Nicky." He lifted his head, trailing his mouth across her cheek until it came to rest, hot and damp and unbelievably erotic, in the soft, sensitive hollow below her ear.

"Joe," she breathed. Her fingers stroked the warm skin at his nape, slid into the cool, thick hair that curled there, as his mouth crawled down her throat to press a hot, steamy necklace of kisses around the base of her neck. The breeze caught her hair, blew it in front of her eyes. She tucked it back behind her ears to get it out of the way, then slid her hands sensuously over the solid expanse of his shoulders. Her breasts snuggled into the firm wall of his chest. There was a protrusion—hard, unnatural—his gun. As she identified it, her body quaked all over. It was a personal first: She was wanting to get naked and horizontal with a man who carried a gun. A cop. *Joe.* At the thought, her head spun and her knees turned to Jell-O. If he hadn't been holding her up, chances were good that she would have gone down.

"That thing won't go off, will it?" she managed.

"What thing?" His head lifted, and he looked down at her. His eyes were dark, restless, gleaming. She could see the wanting there, feel the tension in his arms, his body.

"Your gun."

Their mouths were just inches apart. His big body was curved protectively around her, and she could feel the heat of him seeping through the layers of their clothes. His arms were hard bands holding her against him; his hands felt large and strong as they splayed out across her back.

Behind his head, the night sky was aglitter with stars.

"Oh. No. The safety's on." His voice was thick and low. The warmth of his breath feathered her cheek.

"That's good," she said.

"*Mmm.*" His eyes moved over her face. "Just for the record, you have the sexiest mouth I've ever seen."

She started to smile at him but got no further than a slight upturn at the corners of her lips before he was kissing her again, so expertly and thoroughly that she quivered with pleasure. She kissed him back shamelessly, on fire for him and not caring if he knew it, wanting him to know it. Her hips rocked into his. Her thighs pressed against his thighs. She could feel how turned on he was, feel the hot, urgent bulge beneath his zipper, and she pressed closer yet, moving sensuously against him.

"God, I want you." His voice was a rough whisper. Nicky opened her eyes to discover that he was looking down at her. His face was hard, his eyes dark and hot. He almost looked like a stranger—a tough, aggressive stranger—and it struck Nicky then that she really knew very little about him, and maybe she should be careful and . . .

His hand found its way between them, unbuttoning the single button that secured her flimsy jacket with practiced ease, then sliding over her breast. Nicky felt the jolt of it clear down to her toes. Her body tightened instantly. Arching her back, she kissed him feverishly and pressed closer into that caressing hand. His thumb found her nipple. Even through the thin layers of her shell and bra, she could feel the heat of it brushing back and forth over the sensitive nub. She quaked, she quivered, she melted, she burned.

The one cohesive thought that managed to form in her passion-stupefied brain was, *The man knows his way around women.*

He tugged her shell out of the waistband of her pants. His hand slipped beneath it. She felt the hard heat of that hand sliding up the cool skin covering her rib cage and moaned into his mouth.

In answer, he pulled her closer yet, and his thigh pushed between her legs. *Wait. Hang on. Get a grip. Slow down.*

Even while that niggly little voice in her mind tried to tell her that this was a mistake, that she was going way too fast, that if she didn't call a halt soon, this was going to turn into one of those you're-going-to-hate-yourself-in-the-morning kind of situations, she ignored it in favor of abandoning herself to sensation. It had been so long since she'd felt anything like this. Had she *ever* felt anything like this? She tried to remember. . . .

Then her instant mental replay of past boyfriends crashed and burned as her thrice-damned phone began to ring.

The sound came out of nowhere, shocking her with its incongruity. It took her passion-fogged brain a moment to figure out what it was. Then she realized, and stiffened.

He lifted his mouth from hers, met her gaze with eyes that were narrow and gleaming with desire.

"Let it ring," he said.

She wanted to. Oh, she wanted to. But as much as she would have liked to ignore the strident summons, she couldn't. It was her mother, she knew it was her mother, and the idea that it was her mother was like having a bucket of cold water dumped on her head. It was stupid, it was maddening, it was probably childish as all get out, but there it was: She couldn't fool around with a man knowing that her mother was at the other end of her phone.

"I can't."

By the time she started wriggling to get free, it was on its fourth peal.

His eyes blazed, his jaw clenched, his body went taut and still—but he let her go.

"Sorry," she said distractedly as a glance at the caller's number confirmed her suspicion. Joe's fists were on his hips, he was breathing hard enough so that she could hear it, and he was looking tall and dark and dangerous in the moonlight. She discovered that she especially liked the dangerous part.

I'm going to kill you, Mother.

She sent the thought winging its way toward Twybee Cottage, and tried not to sound as ticked off as she felt as she answered the damned phone.

"Are you on your way home yet?" Leonora demanded.

"Yes, I am, Mother." Okay, she probably sounded just a little annoyed. Anyway, Joe, who was now about three feet away, lighting a cigarette, smiled a little as he listened.

"Did I interrupt something?" Her mother wanted to know. Clearly the edge in Nicky's voice had told her more than her daughter would have voluntarily imparted.

"Not at all."

"Oh," Leonora said. "Well, you're an adult, but I would have thought you might want to wait just a little bit longer. . . . But that's your decision to make, of course."

"I'm hanging up now."

"Wait. The reason I called is Marisa's here at the house. She brought the tape from Sunday night. There are voices on it. Tara and Lauren and Becky, I'm almost sure. You can hear them whispering things like 'He's here' in the background. They mean the man who murdered them, of course, and I thought Joe ought to come and have a listen."

Nicky glanced at Joe. He was watching her, the smile gone now, his expression impossible to read as he puffed away at his cigarette. At the thought of conveying this news to him, Nicky's stomach tightened.

And not in a good way.

It was hard to discuss ghosts in a reasonable manner with a man who patently didn't believe in them.

Her mother was still talking. "I *knew* they were there that night. I just couldn't see them. All I could do was pick up Tara's imprint. Nicky, what on earth am I going to do if I don't get over this?"

"You'll get over it," Nicky said, added a quick "We're on our way," and then disconnected.

"I think that took 'saved by the bell' to a whole new level," Joe said as she dropped the phone back into her pocket. His tone was light; his eyes were anything but. They still gleamed hotly at her in the moonlight. He had, she saw, finished his cigarette. At least, it was nowhere in evidence.

"Joe," she said, and stopped. Her legs were rubbery, she still felt flushed and way too warm, her breasts tingled, and there was an ache deep inside her that had not yet had the decency to even begin to subside.

"Yeah." He moved toward her then and picked up her hand and carried it to his mouth. While she watched, faintly mesmerized, he pressed his lips to her palm. The heat of them made her fingers curl so that her fingertips just brushed his cheek. His skin was hot, and the faint stubble there was prickly to the touch. The tiny contact sent heat shooting through her body. Her heart started beating faster again. The steady blaze in his eyes told her that he, too, was still feeling the glow.

"So-o," he said, drawing the word out, "how do you feel about sex on the beach?"

Okay, knock off some points in the romantic department.

Nicky narrowed her eyes at him. "You're taking a lot for granted, aren't you?"

To her surprise, he lowered her hand and grinned a little at her.

"That's what I thought. In that case, maybe you better tell me what your mother wanted."

Nicky sighed. The night was bright with stars, waves were crashing toward the shore, and the beach was bathed in moonlight. He was looking like the embodiment of every erotic fantasy that she had ever had, she was feeling sexy as hell, and the thought of simply taking up where they had left off was extremely appealing.

On the other hand, it was a *public* beach—with sand, which, if she followed through on her imaginings, was probably going to end up in some very uncomfortable places. And, besides, she really didn't know him all that well.

Wrong time, wrong place. Maybe not the wrong man, but jumping in the sack on a first date was never a good idea. She could almost hear her mother saying it: *Be careful, or he'll think you're easy.*

She practically ground her teeth. Being back on the island was causing her to regress. It had been years since she'd heard her mother's voice in her head like that.

Forget sex on the beach. For her, it was clearly destined to forever remain just a drink.

"Marisa—my mother's assistant—made an audio recording of the program Sunday night," Nicky said, knowing as she did so that she was probably doing the verbal equivalent of shooting the remainder of the evening in the foot. "There are voices on it. They say 'He's back' a couple of times, and my mother says that by 'he' they mean the man who murdered Tara Mitchell.

And the other girls, too. Which means that their killer is probably Karen's killer, because whoever he is was at the Old Taylor Place Sunday night." From the corner of her eye, she saw a couple—elderly, from the shape of them—silhouetted by moonlight as they walked toward the hotel. They were still a little distance away, down near the edge of the surf. But if she could see them, they almost certainly could see her and Joe. It was a good thing she had decided against sex on the beach.

Joe frowned. "Wait a minute. Whoa. Back up. *Whose* voices are on the tape?"

Nicky sighed again. "Tara and Lauren and Becky's."

A beat passed.

"*Ghost* voices?" There was so much incredulity in his tone that Nicky stiffened and glared at him.

"Yep."

Pulling her hand from his, she turned and started marching away down the beach, toward home, passing the elderly couple on the way. *Chalk the last little interlude up to the triumph of sexual chemistry over innate incompatibility,* she thought angrily. *Okay, make that* sizzling *sexual chemistry.*

Not that it made any difference.

"Wait. Hold on. Okay." Joe caught up with her. A sideways glance told her that he was smiling. Her visceral reaction was, *not* a good idea. "Let me get this straight: Your mother's assistant has ghost voices on tape."

"Are you *laughing?*" She shot him an outraged glance.

The smile vanished. His face was immediately as solemn as a judge's.

"No, I am not laughing. See me not laughing?" He pointed at his own face. Nicky caught the teasing gesture from the corner of her eye.

"It's good you're not laughing," she said in a dangerous tone. "Because if you were, I might just have to deck you."

At that he did laugh, unmistakably, and she made a furious sound under her breath and stalked on.

"I was joking, all right? Don't tell me you're one of those girls—women, whatever—who can't take a joke? Damn it, Nicky, quit walking away from me. You have to admit that ghost voices on a tape sounds pretty far-fetched."

"Go screw yourself," she said pleasantly. A playful little wave shot spray at her as if in reprimand, and she dashed the droplets from her face with an impatient hand, even as she kept on trucking—and at a pretty brisk pace, too.

"Nicky. Honey." He caught up with her again. He was looking at her; she was looking straight ahead—though she was monitoring his expressions out of the corner of her eye. Lucky for the length of his life span, he looked—sort of—contrite. "If you say there are ghost voices on tape, then I am absolutely willing to believe there are ghost voices on tape." There was the briefest of pauses. One corner of his mouth quirked up. "What, you can hear them but not see them?"

For a man who was not laughing, there was a hell of a lot of amusement in the question.

"Sometimes," Nicky said, shooting him a killer glance.

"I've got to admit, that's a new one on me."

"But then, you don't know much, do you?"

"So ghosts aren't my area of expertise. Sue me." He grinned at her. "Are we quarreling again?"

"Yeah, I think we might be."

He was keeping pace with her without any visible effort at all, despite the fact that she was now striding along like a power-walker on a mission, which was annoying. There were two other couples in view now, youthful silhouettes splashing through the surf in a close, laughing quartet as they headed in the direction of the hotel, and Nicky skirted closer to the undulating rows of sea oats that lined the dunes in an effort to stay well out of their way. She had always loved walking along the beach at night. Despite everything, it was still a joy to feel the ocean spray on her face again, to taste the salt in the air, to watch the waves surge toward shore. Without Joe's solid presence, she would have been afraid tonight, she knew—certainly too afraid to venture out onto the beach. Generally speaking, though, she couldn't ask for a more reassuring bodyguard than a cop with a gun. Specifically speaking, Joe with a gun was even better. The fact that he was tall and dark and handsome was not the point. The fact that with him beside her, she felt safe was. Even if, at the moment, she kind of wanted to throttle him.

"And by the way," she added, "while we're quarreling, did I mention that I'm getting plenty tired of the way you practically roll your eyes anytime anybody says anything to you about ghosts or spirits or psychic phenomena?"

"I do not roll my eyes."

"You do. Practically. Anyway, you know what I mean."

"You mean I exhibit healthy skepticism when somebody tells me they've seen a ghost?"

"Not somebody." Nicky narrowed her eyes at him. "See, that's the thing. We're talking about my mother here. And me. Take, for instance, earlier. When I told you I saw Tara Mitchell in her bedroom window, you quite clearly didn't believe me. What, do you think I made it up?"

"No." He shook his head. "I do not think you made it up. But . . ."

"But what?" Her tone dared him.

He grimaced. "Okay, you want the truth? I think it's possible—mind you, I'm only saying 'possible'—you were mistaken. I mean, how likely is it that dead people are just hanging around out there in the atmosphere somewhere, popping up to show themselves to the living whenever they feel like it?"

"I don't think that's *quite* how it works."

"So how *does* it work?" He sounded genuinely curious. "Explain it to me. Let's say, for the sake of argument, that there are such things as ghosts. Why would only certain people be able to see them, for instance? You'd think they'd want everybody to know they were there."

"All I can tell you is that some people are more sensitive to psychic phenomena than others."

"What about the people who *aren't* sensitive to psychic phenomena? What does it mean if they see a ghost? Like that kid on your TV show, for example, who was cutting grass at the Old Taylor Place and supposedly saw Tara Mitchell. I talked to him the other day. He *seemed* pretty normal."

"He *is* normal," Nicky said, exasperated. "Normal people see ghosts all the time. It could be an accident, a onetime thing, sort of a disturbance in the atmosphere, so to speak. Or it could be the ghost is trying to give that person a message. See, the thing is, a lot of times ghosts—and, just for your information, 'spirits' is the term my mother would use—don't know they're dead, especially if they passed suddenly, like in an accident—or, like Tara Mitchell, in a murder. Other times, they have unfinished business."

"Such as?"

Nicky glared at him. "How do I know? It could be anything."

"So, exactly how sure are you that you saw Tara Mitchell's ghost in that window?"

"Sure," Nicky said.

"No possibility of mistake?"

"There's always the possibility of mistake," Nicky conceded reluctantly. "But I don't think I'm mistaken. I think she was there, and I think it's a bad omen." *Like I think the howling dog is a bad omen,* she almost added, but she didn't want to muddy the issue. As far as ghosts and Joe were concerned, the best policy was clearly KISS: Keep it simple, stupid.

"You don't think you just could have . . . imagined it? Especially considering the fact that your mother is always going around seeing ghosts everywhere, you might be more susceptible than most to things like that."

The look she threw him sizzled.

"Before today, I have never in my life seen a ghost, or imagined I saw a ghost, and the reason my mother sees ghosts is because she's a *psychic medium*," Nicky said with bite. "If you would take the trouble to check her out, you'll find that police departments all over the country call her all the time for her input on cases. She's amazingly accurate. She finds people who are lost. She picks up on clues that help solve crimes. She saves lives. And yes, she *does* see ghosts. If you're a psychic medium—and sometimes even if you're not—it happens."

"Actually, I did check your mother out." Joe's tone was mild. "I have to say, she seems to have a pretty impressive track record. Of course, she has some misses, too."

"Nobody's right one hundred percent of the— *You checked my mother out?*"

"Crime investigation 101: I had everybody who was at the Old Taylor Place the night of the murder checked out. You included."

Nicky drew in a breath. "*Did* you? And what did you find out about me?"

He grinned tantalizingly. "Besides the fact that you're beautiful, and an amazing kisser, and—?"

"Yeah, besides that." Her voice was tart.

"Well, let's see. Your father died when you were seven. You lived here on the island until your mother remarried when you were ten, and then you moved with your family to Atlanta. Your mother divorced that husband when you were sixteen. You were kind of a wallflower in high school, but you graduated with honors, attended Emory University, where you majored in broadcast journalism, got your first job in television in Savannah. You've been working your way up the TV food chain ever since. Oh, and your mother married for the third time somewhere in there. Your personal life hasn't been all that spectacular, although you've had some boyfriends. The last was a lawyer named Greg Johnson. You broke up with him right before you moved to Chicago last August. Since then, you've—"

"Stop." They had reached Twybee Cottage's boardwalk by that time, and instead of starting up the steps, Nicky turned to face him, stopping him with an up-flung hand just inches from his chest. The dunes rose in undulating waves at her back, and she could hear the sea oats rustling in the wind behind her. The bottom step brushed the back of her calf through the thin knit of her pants, and her other hand rested on the smooth, gray plank of the handrail. Joe blocked a lot of her view, but on either side of him, she could see the blue-tinged beach and the ebony gleam of the sea.

"I don't think I like the idea of this. I can't *believe* you checked me out."

His eyes slid over her face. He took a step forward so that her up-flung hand rested against his chest. Beneath the smooth cotton of his shirt, she could feel firm muscles and heat. The part of her mind that had trouble focusing in situations like this segued to the whole sex-on-the-beach question again. But nothing had changed—except that she was mad at him now. *Definitely not a plus in the sex column,* she thought, and clenched her hand into a fist and let it drop to her side.

The gesture, and the hesitation that preceded it, wasn't lost on him. A faint smile curved his mouth. "Honey, that's what us cops do. Especially when we're investigating a murder."

Okay, so she liked the way he said "honey." And the way he smiled. And . . . never mind. Nicky gritted her teeth as she did a quick mental review of their previous conversations. Come to think of it, he had really asked her for very little personal information—because he basically already knew everything there was to know about her.

"Okay," she said, glaring up at him, firmly in no-sex mode now. "So you know all about me. In that case, I think it's only fair that I know something about you."

"I have no problem with that." He stuck his hands in his pockets and rocked back on his heels. "Anyway, you already know the important stuff. I'm a cop. I'm not married. I think you're cute."

She narrowed her eyes at him. He smiled.

"How old are you?" she asked.

"Thirty-six."

"Where are you from?"

"Jersey. Trenton."

"How long have you been a cop?"

"Twelve years." There was something in his face that told her she was amusing him. That did not make her feel any friendlier toward him. Quite the opposite, in fact. "You know, it would be easier if I just sent you my résumé."

She ignored that. "Parents?"

He sighed. "Deceased."

"Siblings?"

"Deceased, too. Think you could save the rest of your twenty questions for another time? Shouldn't we be heading on in and listening to your mother's assistant's tape about now?"

She ignored that, too. "All your family is dead?"

"That's right." There was a sudden underlying hardness in his voice that told her she'd hit on something that he didn't want to talk about—which, as any reporter worth his or her salt knew, was the place to start digging.

"So you're—" she began, only to be interrupted by the ringing of her phone.

"I told you we should be heading on up to your house," Joe said in a smug tone as Nicky, frowning, fished her phone out of her pocket again.

"Mother . . ." she said into it impatiently.

"Nicky."

The husky whisper shocked her into silence. Everything seemed to be whirling away: the sights and sounds of the night, the feel of the wooden step against the back of her leg, even Joe's solid, reassuring presence in front of her. It was as if she was alone suddenly in a huge, dark void. Terror, cold and immobilizing as death, shot through her veins.

"Nicky." This time the voice was Joe's. She scarcely heard it, scarcely registered his sharp tone or suddenly intent gaze or the fact that he was reaching for her. The world was spinning away fast, and as it receded, all she was conscious of was the voice that had haunted her nightmares since she had first heard it under the pines the previous Sunday.

"Having fun on the beach?" it asked.

The words seemed to vibrate, echoing through her head as though she was hearing them across a vast distance. Even as Joe caught her by the upper arms, she dropped the phone and sat down hard on the bottom step of the boardwalk.

NOT EVEN THE distorting effect of moonlight could hide the fact that she had gone utterly white. She said "Mother" in an impatient tone into the phone, and then her eyes widened, her lips parted, and her phone fell from fingers that seemed to have gone suddenly nerveless. Joe grabbed her by the arms as she was going down, but she didn't faint as he had feared. Instead, her legs folded beneath her as though her knees had suddenly given out, and she sat abruptly on the bottom step. Then she bent almost double as her head dropped forward to rest on her knees.

"Nicky, what?" Alarmed, he crouched in front of her, sliding a hand over the silky disorder of her hair to push it out of the way so that he could see her face. Her eyes were closed, but they opened as he touched her, and he breathed a little easier. Even as he ascertained that she was breathing, that she was conscious, that she didn't seem to have sustained an injury, he knew that something was still horribly wrong. He just didn't know what.

"It was him," she said, her voice so soft and shaky that he could barely understand her over the murmur of the waves and wind. "Oh, Joe, it was him."

It was impossible to mistake who she meant. "Him" could only be the sick bastard who had called her before. The killer. Joe's eyes cut to the phone, now resting on the sand near her feet. His pulse shot into overdrive as he scooped it up.

"Hello?" he said sharply into it. Nothing. A void. If somebody was there—and he didn't think anyone *was* there any longer—he stayed silent. "Hello? Who is this?"

"It was him," Nicky said again, sounding as if she was speaking from somewhere far away. "He said . . . he said . . ."

She broke off with a shudder.

"What did he say, honey?" His voice was gentle as he brushed the hair back from her face again, this time tucking it behind her ear in hopes that it would stay put. His fingers slid down to the pulse below her ear. It was beating way too fast, like the wings of a trapped and terrified bird. Her skin, which only a little while ago had been warm and vibrant to his touch, was now cool and pale as milk. Gasping breaths shook her slender form. Then her head lifted suddenly, and she looked quickly, fearfully, all around.

"What?" he asked urgently.

"He's watching." Her voice was a terrified thread of sound. The gleam of her eyes was feral as the moonlight struck them.

Joe had to work to keep his voice even. "Is that what he said?"

She looked at him. Her pupils had dilated to the point where her eyes seemed almost black. "He said . . . he said . . ."

Even as Joe listened, he pressed the button to check her phone's call log. The screen glowed in the dark as a number came up. . . .

" 'Having fun on the beach?' " she blurted out in a shaking voice.

"Shit," Joe said, looking at the number. Then, to Nicky, in a different, gentler tone, "It's all right. Everything's all right."

"Joe—"

"I'm right here. You know I'll keep you safe." He was looking around warily. What he saw was a whole lot of dark, shadowy nothing—and also a whole lot of dark, shadowy places where someone could be hiding.

Just about the only way the caller could know that Nicky was on the beach was if he had seen her there, which meant that at some point during the evening—possibly even right now—he had to have been close by.

When Joe remembered the steamy little interlude that had just concluded between him and Nicky, his blood ran cold. An entire division of men could have snuck up on him during that, and he wouldn't have noticed, or cared, until it was too late.

The last time he'd been that careless, a whole bunch of people he cared about had wound up dead.

It wasn't going to happen again.

The phone number, and what it might signify, was going to have to wait. His first priority was to make sure Nicky was somewhere secure. Dropping her phone into his jacket pocket, he drew his Glock. Her eyes touched on the weapon and widened. She audibly sucked in air.

"Just a precaution," he said. "Come on, we need to get you off the beach."

He could carry her if he had to, but that would be tricky if he wanted to be able to react at an instant's notice. Hoping that she was not too shaken to walk, he slid a hand around her upper arm.

"Can you stand up?"

"Yes," she said.

Taking her at her word, he rose, pulling her up with him. To his relief, she seemed steady enough on her feet now, able to climb the stairs and, a moment later, hurry down the boardwalk at his urging. The echo of their footsteps joined with the steady drone of the waves and wind to, he feared, block out just about any other sound short of a scream that might be out there. The rolling dunes beneath them were probably eight feet tall in places, and the sea oats grew in among them in thick, dark clumps that swayed and rustled continuously. Anything—anyone—could be hidden among them. That being the case, he stayed close behind her, protecting her to the best of his ability, scanning their surroundings for something, a telltale gleam, a movement, anything that might betray the presence of a watcher.

Nothing. He saw nothing. The guy wasn't a sniper, he reminded himself. A shot coming out of nowhere wasn't his style. He liked butchering his victims. And terrifying them.

Still, by the time they reached the house, Joe felt as though he'd aged ten years.

The large bay windows at the front of Twybee Cottage were only dimly illuminated, as if the light inside the house emanated from somewhere besides the rooms fronting the beach. Nicky headed around the side of the house, back the way they had come, and Joe followed her lead. They emerged in the parking area, which was full of cars but empty of people. Joe spotted another police cruiser behind his, frowned, then realized that he and Nicky were now caught in the yellow glow of the porch light and were clearly visible to anyone who might be watching.

Vulnerable.

"Inside." He hurried her along with a hand in the small of her back as her steps slowed and she glanced around at him.

"How did he get my new phone number?" she asked over her shoulder.

It was an intelligent question, and one he had no answer for at the moment, although it was certainly an angle he meant to explore as soon as he could. He had confiscated her phone on Sunday night. She had gotten a new phone, complete with a new number, presumably either Monday or Tuesday. This was Saturday. Somehow, the perp had learned her new number in that length of time. The question was, who would have access to that information?

"No idea. But we're going to find out."

He was practically pushing her toward the steps as he spoke. Gravel crunching underfoot sounded hideously loud to his suddenly hypersensitive ears. The keening of the tree frogs and whirring of the crickets and cicadas and mosquitoes and other assorted insects in the vicinity bombarded his eardrums. A heavy perfume with notes of crepe myrtle and magnolia and the sea assaulted his nose. The taste of salt was sharp on his tongue. He saw everything—the cars, the garage, the house, the hedge and overhanging trees, and the shifting shadows beyond—with a kind of clarity that had been beyond him just moments before.

He knew what had happened. The adrenaline had kicked in.

For the first time in a long time, he felt like himself again.

"Joe—"

"Tell me inside."

He stayed right behind her as they went up the stairs, knowing that a sniper shot was unlikely but unable to totally discount the possibility, and meaning to provide her with what cover he could. The glimpses he'd gotten of her face told him that she had her color back now and no longer looked like death on the hoof. In fact, she seemed to be more or less fully functional again, which was a good thing, because as soon as he made sure she was safe, he was going to have to leave her.

"There you are at last," Leonora said in a tone of mild reproach as Nicky, with Joe right behind her, pushed through the unlatched screen door into the brightly lit kitchen. The paddle fan was rocking unevenly overhead, the scent of coffee and something chocolate hung in the air, and a tangle of voices and laughter broke off abruptly as all eyes focused on the newcomers. Leonora was seated at the kitchen table along with what Joe was starting to think of as the usual suspects, plus a couple. Even as the gang greeted the new arrivals and everyone started talking practically in unison, he broke the group down into its component parts: Nicky's mother, uncles, and sister; another woman—ah, yes, he remembered her now—Leonora's friend and assistant, Marisa; and Dave. What his Number Two was doing in Nicky's mother's kitchen he couldn't at the moment begin to fathom, but he had no doubt that he would shortly find out.

A tape recorder rested in the middle of the table. Joe's gaze touched on it and moved on: Ghost voices were going to have to wait. Instead, his eyes fastened on Dave, who was standing not far from the door.

Joe jerked his head at him in what he hoped was a subtle *come here*.

"Uh, we got a call about a possible assault on the premises," Dave explained in an undertone as he sidled close. The babble from the rest of the group was so loud that he could have shouted and they probably wouldn't have paid any attention, but Dave clearly considered the information he was imparting sensitive enough to warrant a whisper. "Livvy's husband claims—"

"I don't care." Joe cut him off ruthlessly. "Come with me. We got a problem."

As Dave's eyes widened, Joe looked at Nicky, who had sunk into a chair at the table and was now the center of the group's fascinated attention. He had no doubt at all that she was regaling them with an account of the fright she had just experienced.

So much for keeping certain details secret to the investigation.

"Nicky," he said, sharp enough to cut through the chatter, and she broke off what she was saying to look up at him with raised brows. "I have to go. Stay in the house. Don't go outside. Understand?"

She frowned, then nodded.

"And for God's sake, somebody come lock the door. And keep it locked."

What kind of damned clueless community routinely leaves their doors unlocked anyway? Joe thought savagely, then answered himself: *Oh yeah, paradise again.*

John pushed back from the table, clearly intending to do as Joe had requested and lock the door. Joe registered this and headed out, fishing Nicky's phone from his pocket as he went. He was outside, and the heavy wooden door was being closed and locked behind him as he checked Nicky's phone log again.

"The perp called her," he said over his shoulder to Dave, who had followed him out the door as he strode along the porch. Joe was dialing out on his own phone even as he spoke. "He knew she was on the beach."

Joe was already halfway down the steps when the dispatch operator answered. His gut tightening, he gave her the name and address from which the call Nicky had received on the beach had originated.

"Get somebody over there *stat*," he said.

"Yes, sir," the operator answered.

Despite the cooling effects of the brisk ocean breeze, he was starting to sweat as he ran for his car. And the reason was that he remembered much too vividly the only other phone call Nicky had received from this guy.

It had originated from the phone belonging to his victim.

15

THE HOUSE WAS a small stucco-and-frame bungalow much like the one Joe lived in, but instead of being blue like his, it was painted a cheerful lemon yellow, and it was shaded by a leafy pawpaw tree and located on a quiet side street full of houses just like it except for the color. The only difference was the pair of black-and-whites parked in the driveway.

The blue flash of their stroboscopic lights lit up the night.

Too late, too late, too late. The refrain beat through Joe's head in time with his quickened heartbeat as he pulled in behind the cruisers, parked, and got out. Neighbors were already starting to emerge from the surrounding houses, some standing on their stoops, peering at the action, others venturing toward it. Joe ignored them as he loped toward the front door, where, he saw at a glance, a third of his force was milling around, waiting for him. From the corner of his eye, he saw Dave's cruiser pull to a stop on the curb in front of the house. He heard the door slam as Dave got out, and then he, too, was hurrying across the yard.

"She's not answering," George Locke greeted Joe. Locke, Andy Cohen, Randy Brown, and Bill Milton were clustered on the stoop, looking tense. Locke, Cohen, and Brown were middle-aged white guys. Milton was a middle-aged black guy. They'd all been on the force for years. It was the kind of job where you took it, you got comfortable, and you stayed until retirement, unless something happened to screw you up. Shoplifting, simple assault, public intoxication, DUI, domestics, the occasional bust for possession: That's what they were accustomed to.

Homicide wasn't supposed to be part of the program. They weren't trained for homicide. They weren't prepared for homicide. But all of a sudden, homicide seemed to be the name of the game.

"It's locked," Cohen added. "So's the back door. I tried it, too."

The house was dark, not a light on anywhere inside. It was always possible that the owner wasn't home, but . . .

There was a car in the driveway.

That, coupled with the call to Nicky, was good enough for Joe.

"Break it down," he ordered.

"Wait, wait, don't do that, I have a key." The speaker was a seventyish woman, gray-haired and plump in a flowered housecoat, who'd been hurrying across the yard toward them and reached the edge of the stoop in time to hear what he'd said. She was holding out a key ring and fumbling to locate the right key. "Here it is. What's wrong? Is something wrong with Marsha?"

"You need to go home, Greta," Milton told her as another neighbor, a stoop-shouldered elderly man in a robe over what looked like pajama bottoms, reached them and started asking questions, too.

"Keep 'em out," Joe said over his shoulder to Milton. With the key, the door opened easily. Joe found himself looking directly into a dark living room. Nothing moved—nothing to see but shadows everywhere.

"Police officers," Joe yelled through the open door. "Anybody home?"

No response. At his signal, they started moving in, cautiously, weapons drawn. Just to be on the safe side, he yelled again. Nothing.

"Don't touch anything you don't have to," he cautioned his men. They were already fanning out, moving carefully around the perimeter of the room toward the two arches at either end, one of which presumably led to the kitchen and the other to the bedrooms. The living room itself was a typical setup: couch, two chairs, some tables, lamps, a TV. A peculiar buzzing sound caught Joe's attention as he neared the couch. It was not all that loud, but it was insistent, irritating—*familiar*. Frowning, he tried to place it as he paused to turn on the lamp beside the couch. The instant the light came on, he saw what it was.

There was a white princess phone on the end table at the other end of the couch. It was off the hook, the receiver dangling from its cord toward the floor, and was clearly the source of the annoying drone.

Was he looking at the phone from which the call to Nicky had been placed? Maybe. Probably.

"Shit," Joe said, at almost the same moment as Locke, who had moved into the hall that led to the bedrooms, started yelling, "Here! In here!"

Seconds later, Joe stood in the doorway of the house's single bathroom, staring down at the blood-soaked body of a petite woman lying sprawled on the gray tile floor. She was blonde and barefoot, wearing a long, pale-blue nylon nightgown that was hiked up past her knees. The small bathroom looked like a slaughterhouse. Blood was everywhere; on the floor, on the walls, on the sink and toilet and tub, splotching curtains and towels with gore. The woman lay facedown between the toilet and the bathtub in a still-growing pool of crimson that shone beneath the overhead light like wet red paint.

The smell was sickening. It reminded him of rotting meat. Breathing it in, Joe fought to keep his face impassive.

He knew that smell. He hated that smell.

"Oh, Jesus," somebody whispered behind him. "It's Marsha Browning."

Marsha Browning. That was the name that had come up on top on Nicky's phone log. The call Nicky had received on the beach had come from her phone. Once again, the killer had called Nicky from his victim's phone.

The thought made Joe's gut clench.

"I HAD A KEY to her house, and she had a key to mine, in case of emergencies or something, you know. We've lived next door to each other for nine years." Tears ran down Greta Frank's face as she looked into the camera that was balanced on Gordon's shoulder. "She was just a lovely person. I can't believe . . . Why would anybody do something like that?"

"When did you last see her alive?" Nicky asked softly. The true ramifications of the horror of what had happened in the house behind her was something that she refused to allow herself to think about just yet. For now, all she could do was operate on pure professionalism until the job was done. The cold little tendrils of fear that shivered around the edges of her consciousness were just going to have to wait.

The killer had called her from Marsha Browning's phone, probably after she was dead, just as he'd called her from Karen's phone after murdering her. He'd known she was on the beach. He might even—and the possibility was like an icy finger trailing down Nicky's spine—be watching her now.

As the thought occurred, only by exercising every ounce of self-control that she possessed did she manage to keep her eyes on Mrs. Frank.

"About seven," Mrs. Frank answered. "She was watering the flowers in her backyard. We waved at each other, and then I went inside. I don't know what she did after that."

They were standing in the small, well-tended front yard of Marsha

Browning's house just a few yards from the open front door. Through the barely-there veil of the screen, which was closed, Nicky—and the camera—had already gotten glimpses of the cops' methodical search of the premises, of the living room being dusted for fingerprints, and of various vivid images that she might or might not be able to use, such as a paramedic emerging from the nether regions of the house, peeling off his bloody surgical gloves, and the burly mayor cursing his head off as he pushed his way into the crime scene. Now, as she stood in front of it, interviewing Mrs. Frank, the entire house was ablaze with lights. Beyond that artificial brightness, darkness waited like a crouched predator. The moon was small and pale and distant overhead, sailing high in a black sky chockablock with tiny, cold stars. A stiff salt breeze blew in off the ocean, carrying the coconut scent of the pawpaw with it. It whipped Nicky's hair back away from her face so that it fluttered behind her like a banner. Still clad in the same outfit she'd been wearing for a good eighteen hours now, Nicky was just becoming conscious of a creeping exhaustion that was leaching away her concentration. Microphone in hand, she had angled herself and Mrs. Frank so that as much of the scene behind them as possible could be included in the shot. It was getting close to two A.M. on Sunday morning, and she and Gordon had been working the story since not long after the body had been discovered around eleven. They'd managed to get a lot of good shots and a few good interviews, all of which still had to be edited for use on that night's broadcast, which meant sleep remained a distant, theoretical concept rather than a concrete possibility. Fortunately, Nicky was getting the sense that things at the murder scene were starting to wrap up. The county coroner's van had arrived not long before, and was now parked at the curb. A stretcher had been taken inside. Police and various other official-looking types were moving out of the residence instead of the earlier pattern of arriving and disappearing inside. The crowd of neighbors still huddled on the lawn near the edge of the driveway, but the group was smaller now, as the less prurient—or more exhausted—had started to drift away. There was another TV news crew—WBTZ, a local channel—and a couple print reporters on the scene now as well.

There would be more as soon as word of what had happened got out, Nicky knew. The murder would lead the morning news locally—barring a catastrophe of some sort, of course—and that would alert the pack. Her own report on Marsha Browning's slaying would be included on that night's edition of *Twenty-four Hours Investigates*, which, she calculated, could be confidently expected to scoop the national scene by virtue of its timing if nothing else. However, she could probably count on having other news teams converging on Pawleys Island pretty shortly after it aired. The sensational aspects of the crime were sure to draw the competition like buzzards to roadkill.

"This, it is becoming increasingly clear, is the second of the three murders threatened by Lazarus508," Nicky said into the camera. "The newest victim, Marsha Browning, was a reporter for the local *Coastal Observer*. She was forty-six years old, recently divorced, childless, and lived alone. Like the previous victim, Karen Wise, Marsha was brutally slashed to death. The hair around her face was hacked off. And the killer called this reporter on . . ."

"What the hell do you think you're doing?" The question exploded behind Nicky without warning. She jumped, almost dropping the mike. The voice was male, loaded with suppressed anger, and familiar. *Way* familiar.

"Cut," Gordon said, disgusted, and lowered the camera as Nicky looked around to meet—no surprise—Joe's glare. Since he'd left her in her mother's kitchen, she hadn't seen him. As far as she was aware, he hadn't even known she was on the scene. Now, obviously, he did. He was standing behind her, fists on hips, his stance radiating aggression. In the garish glow of the lights that had been set up around the house, his face looked tense and drawn, and there were lines around his eyes and mouth that she hadn't seen there before. His jacket and tie were gone, the top couple buttons on his shirt were undone, his sleeves were rolled up, and his thick, black hair was wildly unruly, as if he'd been running his fingers through it.

All in all, he looked tired, grouchy—and still sexy as hell.

"You scared me." Nicky blew out a breath of relief. Despite the fact that he obviously didn't reciprocate the sentiment, she was glad to see him. Of its own accord, a smile quivered around the corners of her lips.

"I'm glad to know *something* can scare you." His tone was grim. His expression matched, as his eyes moved over her face.

"Oh, Chief Franconi, do you have any idea who did this?" Mrs. Frank quavered, touching the sleeve of Joe's jacket and distracting him.

"We're working on it." Joe's tone gentled as he spoke to her. "We're doing all we can to find out. Why don't you go on home now? And tell your neighbors, too: Everybody needs to go home."

"I'm just so afraid. . . ."

Behind Joe, Nicky saw that the body was at that moment being brought out of the house on a stretcher. The body: Even as the thought went through her head, the term jarred her. It was impersonal, objectifying what just a few hours before had been the living, breathing woman who had watered her flowers, waved at her neighbor, and then gone inside—the poufy-haired blonde in the miniskirt who had gushed over her mother in the hall of the Old Taylor Place last Sunday night, proclaiming herself a fan and asking for an interview. A reporter like herself. Nicky felt a chill prickle her skin.

It could have been me. . . .

But she refused to dwell on that now, refused to entertain thoughts about anything except doing her job the best way she knew how. Signaling to Gordon, she eased away from Joe, who was still reassuring Mrs. Frank, and got into position. As the camera started rolling again, she began describing what was happening behind her: the stretcher being trundled down the yard toward the waiting van, the body wrapped in a white sheet with, horribly, a slowly spreading crimson stain blossoming on it, paramedics opening the van's rear doors . . .

". . . autopsy will be performed first thing Monday morning," Nicky said as the body was loaded into the van and the doors were slammed shut behind it. "At this time, we are being told that the approximate time of death was between nine and ten P.M. Ms. Browning was apparently surprised in her house—"

"Can I talk to you?" Joe was beside her again, his hand sliding around her upper arm to grip it firmly, his tone almost too pleasant. Nicky broke off to glance up at him with some annoyance. Backlit by the house now, he loomed menacingly large, and the vibes he was giving off practically screamed extreme aggravation. Which was just too bad. He was interfering with her work, and despite the developing state of their relationship, she didn't like it. She was tired, she was sad, she was scared. At the moment, what she didn't need was Joe in his overprotective mode on her case.

"I'm a little busy right now." She gestured toward Gordon and the camera.

"It'll just take a minute." His eyes glinted down at her, their expression belying the politeness of his tone. His jaw was hard, his mouth unsmiling. He looked, in short, like a man in a snit. His gaze moved to Gordon. "You might want to turn off that camera."

Nicky took advantage of the fact that Joe wasn't looking at her to shake her head at Gordon. Instead, she pointed at herself, and the camera obligingly zoomed in.

"We have with us Pawleys Island Chief of Police Joe Franconi," Nicky said into the camera, and watched as the lens widened for a broader shot that included Joe standing beside her. Then she looked up at Joe. His eyes widened fractionally as she thrust the microphone toward him. "Chief, do you think we're dealing with a serial killer here?"

He smiled at her. It wasn't a nice smile.

"No comment," he said.

"We've been told that there was no sign of forced entry into the house. Would you say that indicates the victim knew her killer?"

The smile died. "No comment."

"We've also learned that the victim was stabbed to death multiple times, and that some of her hair was taken as, apparently, a trophy. Would you say that these details are enough to confirm a link, not only with the Karen Wise murder but with the slaying of Tara Mitchell fifteen years ago?"

His lips thinned. "No comment."

"At this point, do you have any suspects?"

"Damn it, Nicky——"

"Careful, Chief, you're on camera," she said, and smiled at him. Granted, her smile had a slightly taunting quality to it, and a man in a snit could not be expected to respond well to teasing. But the bright blaze of anger that suddenly flared in his eyes could absolutely be characterized as an overreaction.

"Okay, I've had enough of this." His eyes cut to Gordon. "If you don't turn that thing off, I'm going to shove it up your fucking ass."

Make that *extreme* overreaction.

"Shit. You can't say that on TV. We can't use that," Gordon complained, then broke off when he got a good look at Joe's face.

"Right," he muttered, and the light indicating that the camera was on went off.

"Thank you." Joe's tone was, if anything, even more controlled than before. His gaze shifted to Nicky, and his fingers tightened on her arm. "Now then——"

"You can't keep interfering with my work, you know," she said. "I'm a professional, and this is my job, and I intend to do it."

"Like I said before, I just need a minute of your time." His voice was still perfectly even, but it was clear that he was nearing the limits of his patience. The idea of Joe losing his temper was intriguing, but she was tired and she knew he was tired, and under the circumstances, this just didn't seem like the time or place to continue to provoke him.

"Oh, fine. I'll be right back," she said to Gordon, and allowed Joe to pull her away toward the far edge of the yard, where the fewest people had congregated. By the time he stopped, they'd been enveloped by shadows. Nicky was fairly confident that they were out of earshot, even if they weren't completely hidden from sight of the rest of the people milling around outside.

"What?" she said. She pulled her arm from his hold and, operating on the theory that a good offense was the best defense, made her tone belligerent. Of course, the truth was, she'd known what he was bent out of shape about from the start.

"What part of 'stay inside and keep the doors locked' did you not understand?"

Yep, she was right. She narrowed her eyes at him.

"The part where you get to give me orders."

"Oh, so is that what this is about? What are you, one of those people who has to do the opposite of whatever you're told just to prove you can?"

"I've got a newsflash for you, Mr. Police Chief: This isn't about you. This is about me doing my job."

"To hell with your job."

"You know, there are other reporters here. Go harass them."

" 'Harass—' " He broke off, seemed to struggle with himself, and started again in the tone of a determinedly reasonable man talking to a lunatic or a child. "I'm trying to keep you alive, for God's sake. I couldn't give a rat's ass about whether or not there are reporters on the scene. They're welcome to report all they want. You're welcome to report all you want. That's not the point, and if you had the sense of a gnat, you'd realize it."

"So what is the point, then?"

"The point is that for whatever reason, the killer is communicating with *you*. After both murders we know he committed, he's called you. Tonight he knew you were on the beach, which means he's watching you. I'm willing to bet that you'll be getting an e-mail or some other form of communication from him within the next few hours, if you haven't already. And in case it's missed your notice, both victims are media types, like you. If you need some help dotting the i's and crossing the t's here, then let me spell it out for you: It's very possible that you're right up there on the top of his hit list."

Nicky sucked in air. She'd reached the same conclusion herself, of course. But having Joe put it into words made it seem concrete and terrifying and *possible* in a way it hadn't quite been before.

"I realize that. I plan to be careful."

The look Joe gave her was so charged that it practically crackled.

"It doesn't look to me like you do *careful* very well," he said grimly. "If you did, you would have stayed the hell in Chicago."

"I'm being careful. Notice I'm not alone? Gordon picked me up, and when we're finished here, he'll take me home."

Joe's eyes left hers for a moment to find Gordon. He was approximately where they'd left him, and he seemed to be filming the coroner's van as it drove away.

"Oh, well, I didn't realize you had Gordon with you. *That* makes all the difference."

There he went with the sarcasm again. Nicky started to call him on it, but before she could say anything, his eyes widened.

"Is that your mother over there?"

Nicky didn't have to follow his gaze to know the answer: yes. Leonora and Livvy and Uncle Ham and Uncle John had insisted on following her and Gordon to the murder scene. She hadn't objected—not that it would have done any good if she had—and anyway, their assistance had proved invaluable. Nicky had been gone a long time, but most of these people were her family's longtime friends and neighbors, cops—except for newcomer Joe—included. Much of the information she planned to use on the air had come from sources they'd found for her.

"And your sister. That's your sister, isn't it? What did you do, turn this into a family outing?"

Okay, so having her family follow her out on a story was not exactly professional. In this case, it was one of those things, like death and taxes, that there was no doing anything about. They'd made up their minds to come, and they'd come. End of story. That, in a nutshell, was life with her family.

Nicky lifted her chin. "I told you I was being careful. They followed Gordon and me over here, and they'll follow us home. Then I'll go inside with them, and we'll all be together in the same house all night. How safe is that?"

"Christ." Joe took a breath, and when he spoke again, every last trace of sarcasm had left his voice. "Look, I'm not sure you're getting the drift here. This woman was *butchered*. As far as we can tell at this point, and it's preliminary but I'm pretty sure it's going to stick, there was no sexual assault, no robbery, no purpose in what he did except just to kill. Whoever this guy is, he's sick, and he's dangerous, and he's apparently formed some kind of attachment to you. When he comes for you, if he comes for you, he's going to come at you out of nowhere, Gordon and your family notwithstanding. By the time you realize what's happening, it might very well be too damned late."

At Joe's words, Nicky experienced a fresh clutch of fear. By this time, it was starting to feel almost normal.

"So what do you suggest I do? Run back to Chicago and hide in my apartment?"

"That's pretty much what I had in mind, yeah."

"So you can guarantee that if I go back to Chicago, he won't come after me?"

She had him there, she knew. For a moment, he simply looked at her without answering.

"You can't, can you?" she demanded triumphantly.

"You'll be safer," he said. "If for no other reason than he'll have to expend more effort in getting to you. If this is a serial killer, then he's not likely to want to travel outside his comfort zone."

"What if it's not a serial killer? Or what if he hasn't Googled serial killers lately and doesn't know that he's supposed to operate in a comfort zone?"

His eyes narrowed at her. "Funny." A beat passed. "So don't go back to Chicago. Go somewhere else. Take a vacation in the Bahamas or something, and don't let anybody know where you are until we catch this guy."

"Nobody's caught him in fifteen years. What makes you think you're going to do any better?"

"We don't know that this is the same perp."

"What makes you think it's not?"

He frowned thoughtfully, seemed to be about to say something, and then his gaze sharpened on her face. "Oh, no. Think I'm going to tell you? So I can see it all over TV? Not likely."

"Fine," Nicky said. "Don't tell me. I'll find out for myself. The show's called *Twenty-four Hours Investigates*, you know, and there's a reason: We investigate things. Like these murders. Which is what I'm here to do."

"Great," Joe said, with an unmistakable edge to his voice. "But maybe while you're doing that, your show ought to think about changing its name. Instead of *Twenty-four Hours Investigates*, how about calling it *The Amateur Hour?*"

Nicky's brows twitched together. She'd had it up to about here with the sarcasm, and she meant to let him know it.

"You—"

"Joe." Deputy Dave appeared out of the darkness before Nicky could give vent to her displeasure. Joe glanced around at him. "The mayor gave me a message for you: He wants you to"—his gaze touched on Nicky—"uh . . . umm . . ."

"What?" Joe snapped.

"Run all the reporters out of here," Dave concluded miserably. "Now."

"Now there," Joe said, his eyes returning to meet Nicky's, "is a man with a plan."

"He can't run us out," Nicky said instantly. "If he tries, he'll be looking at a lawsuit big enough to bankrupt the city, to say nothing of the public-relations fiasco it'll create when we start slamming the investigation on the air."

For a moment, the threat hung in the air between them.

"Great. Just great." Sounding thoroughly fed up, Joe glanced at the brightly lit house as he ran a hand through his hair. Nicky saw instantly how it had gotten so disheveled. His eyes cut back to her. "You would, too, wouldn't you?"

"In a heartbeat," she said, and smiled at him.

For a moment, their eyes remained locked as they silently took each other's measure. Then, as she had known he had no choice but to do, he caved.

"So-o." He drew the syllable out. "I guess I'll go try to explain the concept of a free press to Vince." His gaze shifted to Dave. "In the meantime, I want you to take Lois Lane here home, and I want you to stay there with her until I get there." He looked back at Nicky, who was already winding up for a protest. "And if she gives you any trouble, or tries to elude you in any way,

I want you to place her under arrest, take her downtown, lock her in a cell, and sit in front of it until I get there. Got it?"

Dave's eyes had grown wide. The glance he gave Nicky, who was swelling with ire, was full of alarm. "Uh . . . sure thing, Joe."

"Wait a minute," Nicky said. "You can't—"

"The hell I can't." Joe's voice was soft, perfectly pleasant, and deadly. A glance at his eyes told Nicky that this time he wasn't bluffing. "Honey, believe me, I not only can, I will. So deal with it. Or go to jail. Your call."

With that, he turned and started walking away toward the house.

Seething, Nicky started to yell something along the order of "screw you" after him, and never mind that he had a cute butt. But she remembered her dignity in the nick of time—and remembered, too, the saying about catching more flies with honey than with vinegar. With that in mind, she managed a rueful shrug and a smile for Dave, whose expression said as loudly as any words that he wished he was elsewhere.

"Looks like we're stuck with each other." Her tone was deliberately disarming. "Which is fine. I'm actually all finished here anyway. I just wish you'd tell me something first. . . ."

HE HAD SENT DAVE with Nicky because he couldn't go himself just then, and, Joe realized, Dave was the only one of his men he knew well enough to actually trust with her life. It was a sobering realization, but there it was. He was a stranger in a strange land here, and it was putting him at a grave disadvantage. As he'd warned Nicky earlier, being a cop didn't necessarily make a man honest, or trustworthy, or anything except a cop. Two women had been slaughtered on his watch in less than a week. He meant to make damn sure that Nicky wasn't the third.

If she wouldn't be careful on her own behalf, then he would be careful for her.

"Were you out there giving a fucking interview?" Vince roared at him as Joe stepped through the door. "We want to keep this quiet, not turn it into a media circus."

It was too hot inside the house now from the crowding together of too many bodies, too bright from all the lights that had been set up to facilitate the search for even the most minute bits of evidence, and claustrophobic as hell. Now that he knew what it was, even the tiny hint of the death smell that hung in the air was nausea-inducing. As soon as the screen door swung shut behind him, he was conscious of wanting to be back out in the fresh air again. Not that turning tail was an option, but still.

"We're going to have to deal with the media," Joe said in an even tone as he headed toward Vince. Still clad in the khaki slacks and forest-green jacket he'd been wearing earlier but minus the tie, Vince was standing over behind the couch, watching as Milton, under the supervision of a guy from the Georgetown County PD's CSI department, which Joe had insisted be called to the scene, painstakingly used an X-Acto knife to cut through a square of carpet in the corner of the living room that might or might not have a couple drops of the victim's blood on it. Bright flashes of light from the bathroom told Joe that pictures were still being taken of the death scene. The body was gone, but the pattern of blood spatter and smears could tell them a great deal about the attack, Joe knew. A blue glow from the bedroom told him that they were using luminol to search for more blood in there. "They're not going to go away, and we can't make them. What we're going to have to do is cooperate with them to a degree, feed them select bits of information while keeping what we want to keep quiet out of the loop, and try to manage the story as best we can that way."

"To hell with that." Vince was practically foaming at the mouth. He glared at Joe. "What, don't you have the balls to tell your girlfriend to take a hike? Oh, yeah, don't think I didn't hear about you two being all lovey-dovey over *dinner*, for chrissake. I own that damned hotel, you know. A place like this, word gets back."

Joe felt his stomach tighten.

"Vince," he said. "Let me give you some advice: Keep your nose the hell out of my personal life."

Their eyes met and held.

"I got no interest in your personal life," Vince said in a milder tone after a moment in which the issue hung in the balance. "But we got to contain this. It's going to ruin us if we don't. You think the guy what did this is the same guy what did the girl at the Old Taylor Place last Sunday?"

Joe shrugged. "Hard to be one hundred percent certain at this point, but I'd say so."

"Same guy who killed that fucking ghost girl fifteen years ago?"

"I don't know about that. Maybe. Maybe not."

"You don't think so," Vince translated. "Why not?"

"A lot of things," Joe said. "Number one, where's he been for fifteen years? Number two, he's cutting off the hair, but he's not mutilating the faces. Tara Mitchell's face was cut to ribbons. Karen Wise, this woman tonight—they were butchered, but their faces weren't touched. Number three, we got no record that the perp fifteen years ago ever contacted anyone. This guy called Nicky Sullivan from the victim's phone after both murders, sort of like he wanted her to know that he was out there. I'm putting protection on her, by the way. I think it's justified at this point."

Vince looked aghast. "Do you have any idea what that's going to cost?"

"Yeah," Joe said. "I do. A shitload. And I don't care. You can fire me if you want, but as long as I'm Chief of Police, she's getting protection."

A deep red stain started to creep over Vince's cheeks. It meant he wasn't happy, and Joe knew that. He also knew that he wasn't backing down. Since coming to Pawleys Island, he'd pretty much said "How high?" every time Vince said "Jump." But that had been because he hadn't cared. About anything.

Now he did.

"Shit," Vince said. "You want her to have protection? Fine. Give her protection. But we got to get this thing resolved. We can't have all this shit happening. Not now. Not anytime, but especially not now."

"What's so special about now, for Chrissake?"

Vince's eyes collided with his. "Tourist season is coming up."

BY THE TIME Nicky walked into the kitchen of Twybee Cottage, she was so exhausted that she felt practically boneless. The parade that had followed her home followed her inside, with the exception of Gordon, who'd taken off for his hotel room. Even Dave came in. The lights were on, the fan was turning overhead, and the scent of coffee hung in the air. Harry was standing at the counter, pouring himself a cup. He turned at their entry, surveying the seven of them—Nicky, Livvy, Leonora, Uncle Ham, Uncle John, Marisa, and Dave—with a frown.

"So, where'd all of you go haring off to? I was getting worried. I thought maybe Olivia—but I see she's still in one piece."

"You mean you haven't heard . . . ?" Leonora began, and then they all chimed in, filling Harry in on the details of Marsha Browning's murder. Nicky, meanwhile, left them to it and went upstairs to her bedroom, lugging her suitcase and laptop case, which she had retrieved from the trunk of her car, and turning on lights as she went. Her bedroom was one of four on the second floor, and it hadn't changed by so much as a shift in position of the framed picture of herself in her high-school graduation gown that still sat on the corner of her dresser from when she had left for college eleven years before. It was a large room, approximately fourteen by eighteen feet, with the same tall ceiling—nine feet upstairs, ten feet down—as the rest of the house. The walls were a deep, soft moss green, the curtains and trim were white, and the furniture was old—not quite old enough to qualify as antique, but old. The bed, a double four-poster nestled between the pair of tall windows; dresser; and desk were cherry. The rectangular mirror over the dresser was framed in shells, which Nicky had attached herself with a hot-glue gun in her young teenage artsy-craftsy phase, and, in the same corner it had always occupied, the armchair where she'd once spent hours reading was covered in a green-and-white fern-frond print that matched the bed-spread. There were two doors, one that led out into the hall and one that led into the bathroom that she shared with Livvy, whose identical room (except for the deep rose color scheme and white painted furniture) opened off the bathroom on the other side.

Nicky dropped the suitcase by the desk and unzipped her laptop from its case. Her pulse was already beginning to race as she set it up on the desk. Es-tablishing Internet contact took a moment—Twybee Cottage's roof was metal, which interfered with everything from TV reception to telephone calls—but she eventually got through. It took no time at all to scroll through her e-mail.

Her heart lurched when she saw it: a message from Lazarus514. May 14. Yesterday—the date of Marsha Browning's murder.

She'd been expecting it, fearing it, but still. . . . The cold reality of it made her stomach twist.

Drawing in a shuddering breath, she clicked on the message:

> *Dogs howling in the dark of night*
> *Howl for death before daylight.*
> *Cross my heart and hope to die*
> *Cut my throat if I tell a lie.*

She was still staring at it when, from the corner of her eye, she caught a glimpse of a man's tall shadow behind her.

16

———

NICKY WHIRLED WITH a squeak. It would have been a full-blown scream, but even before the sound came out of her throat, she realized who was in her bedroom with her.

"Joe." It was a sigh of relief. She might be mad at him, but she wasn't afraid of him. Leaning against the desk for support, she pressed a hand to her heart, which was still pounding double time. "What are you doing here?"

"I knocked on the door; your mother told me to come in and said you were upstairs. Then she said if I wanted to talk to you, I should go on up. So here I am. For one thing, I need a list of everyone who had access to your new phone number." His eyes were on her laptop by that time. "Anything?"

Reminded of her original fright, Nicky sucked in air. "Yes. Look."

Turning, she pointed at the screen. Joe moved, and she could feel him close behind her. Fear trumped anger, she was discovering, and the dread that had filled her upon finding that message was enough to wipe the slate clean between Joe and herself. Well, almost clean. The urge to lean back against his solid strength was almost overwhelming, but she resisted. She and Joe—*not a good idea*, she told herself firmly. There was definitely something between them—all right, maybe even something above and beyond simple chemistry—but they were on opposite sides of the fence. She was a reporter, he was a cop, and pursuing a personal relationship while they were both working the same investigation was a bad idea. It was, in fact, a conflict of interest waiting to happen, and she, now that she was out of the moonlight and off the beach, was enough of a professional to realize it. So there.

"I knew it," he said. She didn't have to glance around to know that he was reading the message that still showed on the screen.

"I told you I heard a dog howling." Her voice was uneven. "At the Old Taylor Place, not long after I saw Tara Mitchell in the window. And before, on the night Karen was killed."

Joe didn't say anything for a moment. Unable to stand the silence, Nicky turned to look at him. They were just inches apart, so close that she had to tilt her head back to see his face. His focus was still on the computer screen. He was frowning, and he looked even more tired than she felt. His eyes were bloodshot and surrounded by a web of tiny, fine lines, his mouth was hard and set, and his jaw was dark with five o'clock stubble.

He looked irritable and sleep-deprived, and even in that less-than-optimum state, he still managed to make her heart go pitter-pat.

Their eyes met.

"If you heard a dog howling earlier, then he probably did, too, or he wouldn't have sent this particular message. Which means he was probably lurking around the Old Taylor Place when you were there." His jaw hardened. "What time did you hear the dog howling?"

Nicky told him.

"We've got to assume that he saw you at the Old Taylor Place, too, then. We know he saw you later on the beach. Which makes it likely that he's actively following you. Jesus Christ, that's three times now you could have been killed. That we know about."

"Gordon was with me the whole time at the Old Taylor Place," Nicky said, striving for calm, although this new possibility made her stomach knot. "And by the time the dog started howling, I was in the back of a police car with two cops to protect me. And then, on the beach, there was you."

She couldn't help it. Her voice went soft on the last three words.

"Being way too careless." Joe's voice was anything but soft. Like his face, it was positively grim. His lips thinned, and he cupped her face and looked down into her eyes. His hands were big and strong and warm— quintessentially masculine hands. It would have been a seriously loverlike gesture—if he hadn't been scowling at her. "I need you to consider that vacation. You're scaring the life out of me here."

"Joe." Keeping the fact that they were on opposite sides of the fence firmly fixed in her mind wasn't going to be all that easy, Nicky discovered. What she really wanted to do at that moment was wrap her arms around his neck and press her mouth to his and have him kiss her until the fear that was slowly turning her blood to ice water was forgotten in an explosion of steam. But she still had some self-control left, and so she didn't. Instead, she grasped his forearms—they were hard with muscle and roughened by fine, black hair—and looked steadily up at him. "Don't you see? I'm your link with him. He's communicating with me. You can use that."

"I don't want to use that. I want you off somewhere, sipping margaritas on a beach about a thousand miles from here."

"I have to come back sometime. I have to come back *here* sometime. It's home." Nicky tried for a smile that she suspected fell sadly short. "The only way I'm going to be safe is if we work together to catch this guy."

"Work together?"

"Yeah, as in, you and me. A team."

"Not happening."

Her eyes narrowed at him. "Fine. You investigate, and I'll investigate, and we'll just end up duplicating each other's efforts and wasting a lot of time."

His hands dropped away from her face. "I've got a better idea. I investigate and you stay the hell out of the way."

"It looks to me like you can use all the help you can get."

"Not from you."

Nicky bristled. "What do you mean, not from me? For your information, I'm a damned good reporter. In fact, I'm willing to bet I can investigate you into the ground. I know how to find sources, and I know how to get information out of them. I know where—"

The corners of his mouth quirked up in the merest hint of a smile. "Wait. Whoa. There you go again, getting all huffy over nothing. I'm not questioning that you're good at what you do. I'm just telling you I don't want your help. And the reason I don't want your help is because I don't want you putting yourself in any more danger than you're in already. My worst nightmare is to get a call about a third victim and find out it's you."

There was a lot to object to in that speech, and Nicky caught every hackle-raising nuance as it was uttered. But what she also caught was the darkening of his eyes and the hard strength of his hands as they gripped either side of her waist. Her pulse speeded up.

"Oh," she said, because she was suddenly too busy sliding her hands up over his chest to think of anything better.

"What I'm trying to say here is that I like you better alive than dead."

"That's romantic," Nicky decided.

"Isn't it?"

His head lowered, and Nicky felt her breath catch in response. He was going to kiss her. . . . She *wanted* him to kiss her.

She could almost feel the steam.

"Nick," Livvy said from the general direction of the hall.

Joe's head lifted, his hands dropped, and he looked past Nicky toward the doorway.

Ever impatient, Nicky was stopped in the very act of going up on tiptoe to hurry the kiss along, all her carefully reasoned-out caution having been blown to smithereens by the flash of real tenderness for her that she was almost sure she had just seen in Joe's eyes. Thwarted, she glanced around at her sister with a "get lost or die" frown.

"Sorry." Livvy folded her arms on top of her swollen belly and made an apologetic little face at her. The thing was, though, that she showed no signs of leaving. "Marisa wants to head home, and Mama thought Joe might want to listen to the tape before she goes."

Joe's face suggested that he felt a distinct lack of interest in the tape right at that moment. In consequence, the look Nicky gave him was severe.

"Livvy! Nicky! Are you all coming down?" Uncle Ham yelled from the bottom of the stairs. "Bring Joe."

"We're coming," Livvy yelled back, and gave Nicky a pointed look.

"My mother can help you solve this thing if you let her," Nicky said to Joe, accepting the fact that there was even less privacy to be had in her childhood home than on the beach, and abandoning all thought of persuading Livvy to leave so that she and Joe could take up where they had left off. Instead, she gave him a little shove toward the door. "Go on, go downstairs. So you don't believe in ghosts. Fine. You don't have to. But the least you can do is listen to the tape with an open mind."

"You're lucky," Livvy said wistfully as Nicky walked past her. Joe was a few paces away, near the top of the stairs by this time, which placed him just out of earshot. "He's hot." Then her mouth twisted. "How did this happen? I was always the one who got the hunky guys, not you. And now look at me. And look at you."

"You're just going through a bad patch," Nicky said. "It will pass."

Livvy rolled her eyes. "You sound just like Mama. Come on, let's go down."

"HE'S BACK. He's back. It's him. He's here."

Once he knew what he was listening for, Joe could hear the voices distinctly. They were soft, feminine exclamations that popped up at various intervals throughout the audiotape, whispering over the primary action, repeating the same two-word phrases over and over. Unfortunately, that didn't necessarily make what he was hearing germane to the investigation: As far as he could tell, he could be listening to just about any whispering female on the planet. How this group could tell that the voices belonged to a ghost at all, much less the ghosts of the three girls in question, was beyond him, but he kept that thought to himself. He listened politely, doing his best to keep an open mind—which was vital, because Nicky kept glancing at him—while battling the bone-deep weariness that made concentrating on anything at all, much less ghost voices on tape, an effort. As the tape neared the end, his efforts were rewarded in a way he would never have foreseen, which, in his opinion, went a long way toward proving the old adage that being lucky was better than being good—sometimes much better.

Forget ghost voices. What he heard, distinct from all the hullabaloo that was the program itself, was a phone call being answered by a real, live human being.

The phone must have been on vibrate, because he didn't hear a ring, just a tiny click and then. . . .

"Hello?" a woman murmured.

A beat passed.

She said something that was unintelligible.

Another beat.

"I can't hear you," she said, a little louder. "You'll have to speak up."

Another beat.

"Oh. That's [unintelligible]." She sounded surprised, even nervous. "What? There's static . . . I can't really hear."

Another beat.

"Fine. That's good." A definite note of relief. "What? All right, I'm going to walk outside and see if that helps."

"Stop the tape," Joe said, as the action swept on without any repeat of the woman's voice.

Marisa, clearly surprised, stopped the tape. Everyone around the table—because that's where they were all seated, in a big, happy family group crowded in with the remains of homemade muffins and cups of coffee littering the tabletop in front of them—looked at him inquiringly. Joe suppressed a sigh. In the past, when he'd investigated a crime, he'd worked either alone or with a small, select cadre of seasoned law-enforcement types. Eight wide-eyed civilians, plus Dave, were not the people he would have chosen to share this type of sensitive material with.

But asking everyone except Nicky, whose help he needed, to leave the room was clearly a waste of time. Number one, they had all heard the tape, most of them before he had, as Marisa had apparently played it for Leonora and company while he and Nicky were on the beach. Number two, he'd seen enough of how Nicky worked to know that what she knew, her family would worm out of her soon afterward.

So he might as well forget from the outset any idea of keeping this particular detail secret to the investigation.

And chalk it up: Such were the hazards of conducting police work in paradise.

Several of the family members opened their mouths to speak as soon as the tape was switched off. A few whats and whys even made it out into the open air before he managed to shut them down. Reminding himself of a kindergarten teacher, Joe went "Shh!" with a finger pressed to his lips and a monitory glance around the table.

"I need a couple of minutes here," he said.

The group goggled at him but obediently fell silent.

"Could you replay the last part, please?" he asked Marisa. She nodded and reached toward the tape recorder. Then, to Nicky, Joe added, "I want you to listen to the phone call in the background and identify the voice for me, if you can."

At his signal, Marisa replayed the tape.

The dominant sound was a set of rapid footsteps and quickened breathing, echoed by a number of less distinct footsteps and some rustling, as if a whole group of people were moving in the same general direction at once.

Then, in the background, came the barely audible conversation that Joe had picked up on before.

It was short, only a few seconds, and when it ended, it was followed almost instantly by Nicky's voice.

"We're heading for the second floor now," Nicky said on the tape, her voice clear and easily recognizable.

Joe signaled to Marisa to turn off the tape. The whole time he'd been listening to it, he was watching Nicky's face. Even before he asked her who the speaker was, he was certain from her expression what her answer would be. As it happened, she didn't even wait for him to ask.

"That was Karen," she said to him, sounding as if her throat was suddenly tight.

He nodded his thanks to her.

"Could I have that tape, please?" he asked Marisa. Not that he needed her permission to take possession of it, just as he hadn't needed Nicky's permission to take her phone, her second phone, which he'd carried with him off the beach and which was now, hopefully, tagged and bagged down at the station along with the first. The tape, like the phones, was evidence and could be seized, but he always tried to be polite when possible. In Jersey, it hadn't always been possible, but down here in paradise, politeness tended to work like a charm.

As if to prove his point, Marisa nodded and pushed the tape recorder toward him.

"So what was that?" Livvy burst out, looking from Nicky to him and back.

"That call must have been the reason she went outside," Nicky replied, with the exact amount of concern for secrecy that he had expected her to show. Her eyes were on him rather than her sister. "There was static on her phone. Somebody called her and she couldn't hear what they were saying, so she went outside to see if she could get better reception."

Conscious that secrecy was a lost cause, Joe nodded confirmation at her. That was what he thought, too. He'd have to check the timing against the videotape to be sure, but what he'd just listened to had to have been the start of one of the last calls Karen had received.

That, to him, held more significance than the whispering of a hundred ghost voices.

None of the callers he'd interviewed had said anything to him about Karen going outside because of static.

BY THE TIME Joe left, after extracting a firm promise from Nicky that she wouldn't so much as step outside the house without one of his men by her side, it was after four A.M. and only the family remained. After a little more desultory conversation, everyone finally surrendered to exhaustion and went off to bed. Once there, Nicky snuggled beneath the covers and kept her eyes tightly closed and tried to focus on pleasant things—like the warm familiarity of her childhood bedroom, and the lulling roar of the waves coming in, and the knowledge that her family was all around her—so that she could fall asleep. But it didn't work. Nothing did. The terrifying thoughts and images would not be denied. Against her closed lids, she kept seeing the slick red shine of Karen's blood as the headlights hit it, and the lumpy, white-wrapped shape that was what remained of Marsha Browning as her body was taken away on a stretcher, and the glow of Nicky's own computer screen.

Dogs howling in the dark of night. . . .

The doggerel scrolled through her mind. She did her best to push it out, seeking desperately for something—anything—that might hold at bay the icy fear that raced along her nerve endings. Joe's face popped into her mind's eye: She could almost see his eyes darkening with tenderness for her. She could feel his arms around her, taste his kiss . . .

Warmth began to take the place of ice. If she could just keep on thinking of Joe . . .

"Nicky?"

Coming out of the darkness as it did, the whisper made Nicky start. Her eyes flew open as she realized that the voice was one she knew. If she hadn't been so jumpy, in fact, she would have recognized it instantly.

"Mama?" That was what both she and Livvy had called Leonora as they were growing up. Only after Nicky had left home for college had she switched to the more adult-sounding "Mother." Livvy never had. Now that she was home again, Nicky found herself reverting back—in lots of ways, including how she thought of her mother. Under the circumstances, "Mama" just felt right.

"You weren't asleep, were you." It was a statement rather than a question. Leonora was standing in the open doorway, hardly visible at all, a denser shadow in the darkness. "Are you all right?"

Nicky turned over onto her back, pulled the covers up under her chin, and said to the shadowy ceiling, "I saw Tara Mitchell's ghost today."

Leonora didn't reply for a moment. Then she made a sound, as of a sigh or a deeply indrawn breath, and moved into the room. Nicky could hear her slippers shuffling across the hardwood floor. She didn't have to see her mother to know what she was wearing: her zip-up terry-cloth robe over a nightgown. Seconds later, as Leonora sat on the edge of the bed, Nicky felt the mattress sink beneath her weight and smelled the pleasant lotiony aroma of her mother at bedtime. Though she could see the dark shape that was Leonora out of the corner of her eye and feel the warmth of her nearness, Nicky continued to look at the ceiling. To her surprise, she could feel her heart pumping faster. To talk to her mother about seeing a ghost was not easy, she was discovering. It felt uncomfortable, almost as if she was impinging on forbidden territory.

"Where?" Leonora asked. Her voice was quiet, in keeping with the hush of the sleeping house, but entirely matter-of-fact. Of course. For Leonora James, seeing a ghost—or multiple ghosts—was just another day at the office.

For Nicky, it was something else entirely.

Keeping her voice carefully even, Nicky told her mother about her experience.

"I'm not surprised," Leonora said when Nicky had finished. "Or, rather, I'm surprised it took so long."

"What?" Nicky's eyes cut to her mother's face, which she could now just barely—her eyes having adjusted to the gloom—discern. "What do you mean?"

"Have you really forgotten?" There was something in Leonora's voice that made Nicky frown.

"Forgotten what?"

"I always wondered, you know. If you did it deliberately, or if it was some kind of involuntary defense mechanism. I finally decided that it was a defense mechanism."

Nicky felt a cold niggle of apprehension and shivered. "What are you talking about?"

Leonora gave a rueful little chuckle. "Your father and I, we used to tease each other about how we'd produced two tiny clones. Olivia was—is—just like him. He was fair-haired and blue-eyed and so handsome and popular. A golden boy. Everybody loved Neal. Girls, boys, everybody. He was always, always the life of every party. You know what? I miss him still. *He* was my husband. These others—I guess I keep trying to replace what I had. But I'm finally realizing you only get to love like that once in a lifetime."

Nicky rarely thought about her father, because remembering the laughing man whose favorite she had been hurt terribly even after the passing of so many years. But her mother's words brought him sharply back, and for a moment, she had to grit her teeth against the pain.

"And you," Leonora continued softly. "My precious little red-haired baby. You were *my* clone. Sometimes I think that's why we've always sort of butted heads. From the moment you were born, I couldn't believe how much alike we were. And not just in looks. You had this wonderful, wild imagination like mine, and a fiery, spunky disposition"—Leonora's voice dropped to a near-whisper—"and, unlike Livvy, as a young child, you showed real signs of being psychic."

"What?" Nicky's hands clamped around the edges of the covers. Her eyes stayed fixed on her mother's face. The words hit her like a shock of cold water. Whatever she had expected, it was not that. But deep inside, in some barely comprehended atavistic place in her soul, she knew that what her mother was saying was true, *had been* true.

"You repressed it," Leonora said. "The gift. I'm positive you had it, but after your father died, you didn't want it anymore. You refused, *refused*, to acknowledge that you could see anything, or feel anything, or know anything that was not of this corporeal world."

Nicky sucked in air. The memories were rushing in, almost attacking her, agonizing memories of a smiling, blond-haired man standing at the helm of a twenty-eight-foot cabin cruiser he named the *Anticipation* because all week while he worked as a banker he anticipated the weekend, which he would spend on his boat with his family. But on this particular weekend, both Nicky and Livvy had been recovering from strep throat, and they and Leonora had stayed home, leaving him to go out alone. He'd kissed them good-bye and gone. Nicky's next vision of him had been on the deck of the boat, which was racing frantically toward shore as huge black clouds rolled across the sky toward it. The waves had picked up until the boat was being tossed around like a toy. There was a sharp *crack* as the hull smashed into rocks, and then the boat went down. She had seen it going under, seen the deck being swamped by torrents of cold, dark water. . . .

"Daddy." Not even aware that she was doing it, Nicky reached for her mother's hands, clutching them tightly, her eyes wide with horror. "I saw Daddy—"

Her voice broke, and she felt the sting of tears in her eyes.

"I know." Leonora's grip on her hands was firm and comforting. "I remember. The night your father died, before we knew anything was wrong, you woke up screaming. When I ran into your bedroom, you told me your daddy was drowned, and described everything that had happened, down to the color of the shirt he was wearing when he died. He'd changed after leaving home, you see, so you would have had no way of knowing. But you were right."

"It was yellow," Nicky breathed. Her throat ached, her heart pounded, and she felt a horrible, wrenching grief. It had happened so long ago—why did it still hurt so much?

"Yes." Her mother's hands tightened. "You didn't speak for days. Then, when you finally began to recover a little, you were angry—with yourself, and especially with me. Oh, for a long time. Don't you remember? It was as if you blamed yourself for not being able to do anything to save your father even though you saw what was happening, and blamed me for giving you the gift that allowed you to see it. And you would never, ever talk about what you'd seen that night again. You were so . . . closed to it that after a while I just let the whole thing slide, because it obviously disturbed you so much. From that day to this, as far as I know, you never had another psychic experience. I always wondered if the gift might resurface in you one day."

"I don't want it," Nicky said with difficulty around the lump in her throat.

"Sometimes," Leonora replied, "neither do I."

There was so much sadness in her mother's voice that even as she blinked back tears, Nicky sat up and hugged Leonora fiercely. Leonora hugged her back just as hard, and they stayed like that for a long time.

"So, THIS is where we are," Joe concluded his overview of the Marsha Browning investigation. He was standing in the police station's grimy squad room in front of an oversized dry-erase board on which he'd scribbled a crude timeline of the crimes, starting with Tara Mitchell and ending with Marsha Browning. The fifteen-year gap he'd marked with a huge question mark, which he stressed that they needed to answer. His remarks were addressed to his assembled police force minus Randy Brown, who, having had a strong enough alibi to convince Joe that he couldn't possibly be the killer, had been dispatched to babysit Nicky. It was Sunday evening, about six P.M., a time when ordinarily at least two-thirds of the force would have been off duty and he, personally, would have been kicking back with TV, some food, and maybe a brew. But under the circumstances, everybody was working basically around the clock, himself included. Given the small size of the force, the urgency of the situation, and Vince's insistence that the whole thing be kept as quiet and contained as possible, this was the way things were going to stay for the foreseeable future—or until they caught their perp. At the moment, the guys were nodding as they scarfed down the last of the pizza that a local franchise had sent over gratis as a kind of morale booster, and Joe was getting ready to give out the next day's assignments.

"Cohen and Locke, you're still working that list of recent parolees within the target area, trying to find them, checking their alibis; Milton and Parker, you're canvassing the neighborhood around the Old Taylor Place for any kind of word on suspicious persons who may have been in the area on either the eighth or the fourteenth; also, you are looking for a dog that might have been howling in that same vicinity on those same dates; Hefling and Roe, you're going door-to-door around Marsha Browning's house, asking about possible suspicious persons that may have been sighted within the last few days; Krakowski, you're compiling a list of female residents of the island who live alone, which we need ASAP; O'Neil, you're going over land and cell-phone records for both victims; and the rest of you are taking care of anything else in the way of normal police work that may come up. Any questions?"

There were a few, and Joe answered them to the best of his ability. As they finished up, his troops pushed back their plastic chairs and went their separate ways. Some of them returned to their desks while others exited the building.

Joe was headed home. He had a few phone calls to make that needed to be placed in private. After that, he meant to grab a shower and then probably start cross-checking the information they had put together on the Marsha Browning murder with what they had on the Karen Wise case and then the old Tara Mitchell file. It wasn't difficult work, but it was time-consuming, and you had to know what you were looking for, which was why he was reserving that task for himself.

"So, you think we should warn our lady citizens who live alone to start locking their doors?" Milton asked, falling into step beside Joe as they walked out the back door. The last shimmers of daylight were fading away, and the fronds of the palmettos that surrounded the parking lot rustled in the quickening breeze. A couple cruisers were already pulling out of the lot, and the smell of their exhaust hung in the air.

"That would probably be a good idea." As he headed toward his own car with Milton still keeping pace beside him, Joe tried to keep the dryness out of his voice, with indifferent success. In his opinion, any woman living alone who didn't lock her door needed to have her head examined, but he knew that given the relaxed culture of the island, there would be some who needed re-minding, even under the circumstances.

"And we should tell them that we're going to be doing regular drive-bys just to check on them," Milton said.

"Absolutely," Joe replied, and lifted a hand in farewell to Milton as he headed away toward his own car.

"Chief Franconi."

Hearing his name uttered in an unfamiliar near-shout, Joe glanced around sharply. There seemed to be at least three separate streams of people racing his way from the street in front of the building. A lightning survey identified a lone woman who was waving her hand at him while she yelled his name, a male-female team, and a male-male pair in which one of the men had a cam-era balanced on his shoulder.

Joe stopped and stared.

"Is it true that the Lazarus Killer claimed another victim last night?" Hav-ing outpaced the competition by a stride, the woman reached him first. She was carrying a tape recorder, but Joe didn't need to see it, or hear her panted question, to realize what he was dealing with: the press. He started walking again, fast. *Jesus Christ, how had word gotten out so fast?*

"No comment," he said.

"Is this the same guy who killed those girls fifteen years ago?" That ques-tion came from a man. Joe heard a faint whir and realized that the TV cam-era was pointed at his face.

"No comment."

Thankfully, by this time he had reached his car. Pressing the button on his key ring, he unlocked the door.

"Is it fair to say that there is definitely a serial killer stalking Pawleys Isand?"

"No comment," Joe repeated for the third time, wrenched open the door, and slid inside. They were still shouting questions as he peeled rubber out the back side of the lot, and he had a feeling that he should be thankful they had all apparently parked out front, on the street.

Vince was going to love this, Joe thought dryly as he drove home and picked up his phone to alert the mayor before he, too, could be ambushed.

"Jesus, Mary, and Joseph," Vince groaned. "This is all the fault of that damned show. I knew I should have stopped them filming that first night, but no-o-o, you wouldn't let me. Now look what's come of it. It's a goddamned disaster. Do something!"

Then he slammed down the phone.

Joe made it home unmolested, parked out front, and went inside, losing his coat and tie as soon as he got in the door. Just to make sure nobody was going to be taking pictures through the windows, he drew the curtains before he turned on the lights. Then he went into the kitchen, grabbed a Bud Light from the fridge, and settled down at the table to make some calls.

The first one, to the friend who was tracing the Lazarus508 e-mail for him, drew a blank. He left a message saying that he would be forwarding a second e-mail for the same treatment, and hung up.

The second call, to another old friend, fared better.

"I need you to enhance an audiotape for me," Joe said. "ASAP. It's not long—less than a minute. A few garbled words I need to be able to understand."

"You got it," his friend said. "Send it along."

"Will do."

Joe disconnected and started to place call number three. Out of the corner of his eye, he saw Brian saunter into the kitchen. Everything—from the sound of his boots on the vinyl floor to the texture of the blue jeans the guy was wearing to the too-long dark blond hair that kept falling over his forehead—looked real. Nothing blurry, nothing ethereal. No woo-woo at all. *Real.*

Joe paused in the act of punching in the number.

"Get the fuck out of my life," he said, and meant it.

Brian stopped walking and grinned at him.

"Ah-ah. That's not very nice," he said, and waggled an admonishing fore-finger at him.

That was so much like something the son-of-a-bitch would do that Joe felt his heartbeat speed up. Either he was talking to a ghost, who was talking back, or he was having the mother of all hallucinations. Neither possibility boded well for his long-term sanity.

"I'm nuts," Joe muttered, his eyes still locked on Brian. "I'm fucking nuts."

"I could've told you that," Brian said cheerfully, and resumed his amble toward the back door. "But you're making progress. At least we're speaking again."

"You're dead," Joe said, knowing even as he did it that he was going to hate himself later for violating the ignore-it-and-it-will-eventually-go-away strategy he'd been operating under for the past eighteen months or so. Blame it on Nicky and her ghost-happy family. Apparently, she was managing to get under his skin in more ways than one.

"So?"

"What do you mean, 'so'? *You're dead.* Go to heaven. Or hell. Or wher-ever. I don't give a shit. Just go."

"Careful. You're going to hurt my feelings."

Joe stared at him. Brian was looking wistfully at Joe's beer. Watching him, Joe picked up the bottle, put it to his lips, and took a long chug.

"Asshole," Brian said without malice as Joe swiped his lips with the back of his hand.

"Asshole"—God, how many times had he heard Brian call him that? In just exactly that tone, too.

"If you're really there," Joe said in a voice gone slightly hoarse all of a sudden, "then make yourself useful for once and tell me who the hell is killing these women."

"*What*, do I look like I have ESP? How the hell should I know?"

"So, what are you doing here?"

"Ah. I've been waiting for you to ask me that." Brian gave him one of his patented wide, shit-eating grins. "I'm your guardian angel, pal."

Joe's mind boggled. *Brian* as his guardian angel? The universe couldn't be that messed up.

"*Bullshit.*" He clapped his hands down flat against the tabletop and rose from his seat so abruptly that the chair fell over with a crash behind him. "This is all a bunch of *bullshit.* I've got some kind of weird brain damage. There's nobody here. *I am all alone in this damned kitchen.*"

A knock sounded at the back door. Joe, silenced mid-rant, looked past Brian to see Dave with his face pressed practically up against the glass, peering in through the window at him. Beyond Dave, it was full night now, which made Joe wonder with some alarm just how long he'd been ranting and raving in his kitchen. Maybe he'd suffered some kind of seizure or something.

Now there was a thought: Brian was the result of a periodic brain spasm.

"Hey, Joe." Dave waved at him. He was looking slightly worried, and Joe guessed that Dave must have heard him yelling and maybe even seen him slam his hands down on the tabletop, too.

God, Joe hoped Dave hadn't seen or heard any more than that. Watching his boss have a one-sided conversation with an unseen presence wasn't going to do anything for Dave's morale—to say nothing of the rest of the force's—if word of this got out.

Joe crossed to the door and pulled it open.

"I was on the phone," he began, feeling a little awkward as he attempted to explain away whatever Dave might have witnessed. A snuffling sound caused him to break off and look down in the general vicinity of Dave's knees. Cleo looked back at him, her velvety snout quivering, her round, black eyes shining in the reflected light from the kitchen.

He might be in the middle of having some kind of mental breakdown, but that didn't make him stupid.

"No," he said before Dave could say anything. "Like I said before, I don't do pigs."

"It's not just Cleo," Dave said forlornly. "It's me. Amy's kicked us both out. I need a place to stay the night, too."

A beat passed.

Let's see, Joe thought as his gaze moved from one refugee to the other, the last twenty-four hours had included a hot romantic interlude, a grisly murder, a whole lot of crap from a whole lot of people, a buttload of work, an ambush by a pack of reporters, a ghost or a mental breakdown (take your pick), and now a prospective new roomie who came complete with his own pig. In other words, just one more happening day in paradise.

" 'Like sands through the hourglass, these are the days of our lives,' " Brian said in his ear. The bastard was standing right behind him, and Joe didn't have to glance around to know that he was grinning like the Cheshire Cat. Clearly, Dave wasn't seeing or hearing a thing.

"Shit," Joe said in resignation, opening the door wider. "Come on in. Not you, pig."

17

JOE PICKED UP THE CHAIR, Dave raided the refrigerator, and they were just sitting down at the table with two cold ones and a couple bologna sandwiches when Joe noticed the pig up on its hind legs, looking through the window at them. He alerted Dave, who went out and fed it the rest of the brand-new package of bologna from Joe's refrigerator that Dave had just opened to make the sandwiches. It was beef bologna, so it was all right for the pig to eat it, at least in a karmic sense, but as Joe had had other plans for the lunch meat, he was feeling slightly disgruntled when Dave came back into the kitchen.

"You owe me a package of bologna," Joe said, looking up from the Marsha Browning file, which was one of several he'd brought home with him. On the plus side, at least the pig was no longer looking at him through the window.

"I'll stop by the store tomorrow," Dave promised. "You want me to pick anything else up while I'm there? Milk? Eggs? What do we need?"

That "we," coupled with the idea of Dave doing the grocery shopping for the both of them, had sort of a cozy sound to it—way too cozy for Joe. They were fifteen minutes into the whole roomie thing, and already it wasn't working for him.

That being the case, the thing to do was get his new roomie back home where he belonged without delay.

"Forget about the bologna," he said. "Tell me what happened with Amy."

That was all the encouragement Dave needed. He sat down with his beer and started giving Joe a play-by-play that soon fell under the category of Too Much Information. By the time Dave finished his tale of woe, Joe, who by then was listening with half an ear, had finished his beer and his sandwich and was halfway through his cross-check of the Karen Wise and Marsha Browning files. The reason he was able to listen and go over evidence at the same time was simple: There had been almost no doubt in his mind right from the beginning that those two murders had been committed by the same perp. Comparing either of them with Tara Mitchell required more concentration: There were many more areas of dissimilarity, enough so that he was almost ready to conclude with some certainty that the same perp was not involved. Of course, the Mitchell file was fifteen years old and compiled on somebody else's watch. It was always possible that it wasn't entirely accurate, or that things had been lost or left out.

Hell, that was always possible on his watch, too.

"I mean, I understand Amy's position," Dave concluded forlornly. "But Cleo was just hungry. That's all it was."

Joe looked up from his vital, potentially case-solving work to meet his Number Two's hangdog gaze. Under the circumstances, staying out of this had ceased to be an option. Just call him Dr. Phil.

"So, Amy brought home a pizza and the pig knocked it out of her hands and ate it." Joe summed up in a sentence the story it had taken Dave a good fifteen minutes to relate.

"Amy says Cleo attacked her again. Cleo didn't *attack* her. She's not that kind of pig. Amy just won't listen." Dave picked up his bottle of beer but set it back down before it even touched his lips. Apparently, this latest contretemps had upset him to the point where even beer had lost its appeal. "Anyway, it was my fault. Cleo is used to getting table scraps in the morning and at night. What with, you know, the murder and all, I've been working for pretty much the last twenty-four hours straight. I didn't get a chance to get home to give Cleo her treats. All she had was the food in her dispenser, and she doesn't much like that."

Joe considered various diplomatic approaches to what he had to say.

"You know, I may be missing the big picture here. But it seems to me that you were a lot happier before Amy moved in with you than you have been since."

Dave frowned. "So, what are you saying?"

"All I'm saying is that maybe Amy's not the woman for you."

"In what way?"

Joe sighed. Diplomacy clearly wasn't his thing. At any rate, Dave didn't seem to be getting the drift.

"You like pigs; she doesn't. Maybe you should give up on her and start looking for somebody you'd be more compatible with."

"Amy and I are compatible." Dave gave Joe a wounded look. Then his mouth twisted and he slumped a little. "Well, sort of. Except for her griping when I have to work overtime and weekends. And then when I am home, *she* works late. And there's always something going on with her ex-husband and the kids. And, um, then there's Cleo."

To hell with it, Joe thought. He was too tired for this. Let Dr. Phil be Dr. Phil.

"There you go, then. You two are clearly soul mates." Sick of the whole subject, he went back to work. "Did you get those phone records checked?"

"About a third. It's pretty time-consuming. Both those women spent a lot of time yakking on the phone. Then, when I call to verify what was said, a lot of time I get away messages. And some of the unknown-caller types take a while to track down."

"Yeah," Joe said. "I—"

A sudden explosion of sound in the living room made both him and Dave jump.

"What the hell?" Joe said, as the noise resolved itself into the TV, which was now blaring at top volume.

He and Dave were already on their way into the living room when it occurred to Joe that the set had been turned off the last time he'd looked. But it was definitely on now, he saw as he reached the living room. The volume was so loud that it made him wince as he hurried to grab the remote from the end table and turn it down.

"How'd that happen?" Dave said when they could make themselves heard again. He was frowning as he stared at the TV. "That was weird."

But Joe's attention was riveted on the screen. Once he saw what was on, the situation became all too clear. Brian again, or some kind of weird energy from a brain spasm that he hadn't even felt. Or something.

Whatever, he was looking at Nicky.

"Good evening. This is *Twenty-four Hours Investigates*, and I'm Nicole Sullivan," Nicky said into the camera. Her face filled the screen, and Joe missed a beat or two of what she was saying as he absorbed just how truly gorgeous she was. Shining red hair; big brown eyes; porcelain skin; full, pouty lips—watching her, he had a tantalizing flashback to how she had felt in his arms. He now knew that those lips were as soft and hot as they looked. . . .

"We found a bloody footprint in Marsha Browning's house that matched one at the site of Karen Wise's murder?" Dave asked, frowning. "I didn't know that."

Clearly he'd missed something, Joe realized. He mentally tuned back in to the program just in time to watch as a shot of Marsha Browning's body being rolled down her lawn to the coroner's van filled the screen. Then Nicky was back, saying, "Both times the Lazarus Killer called this reporter from the victim's own phone. In Marsha Browning's case, the call was placed from a landline in her house *before* the body was found. Police used that call to locate the victim. Afterwards, in the wee hours of this morning, the Lazarus Killer sent me another cryptic e-mail. This is what it said." A printout of the e-mail filled the screen. "Dogs howling in the dark of night . . ."

"Shit," Joe said, and sat down abruptly on the couch to watch with growing horror as every significant detail the investigation had turned up so far was aired on national TV.

"YOU LOOK GOOD ON TV," Elaine Ferrell said as she walked Nicky to her front door. "Maybe you might want to think about adding a little poof to your hair. If you do, just let me know, I can work you right in. Anyway, tell your mom I said hi."

"I will," Nicky promised as she stepped outside into the star-studded night. "And thanks."

Mrs. Ferrell waved and closed the door, which meant that Nicky was now alone, standing on the small front stoop with the dim glow of the porch light illuminating her for all to see. The idea creeped her out. With a long look around to make sure nothing lurked behind the well-trimmed bushes that hugged the front of the house, she moved off the stoop and headed quickly down the lawn. She'd been inside, talking to the bleached-blonde, sixty-year-old Mrs. Ferrell for almost an hour. It was a little after ten P.M., and except for the glimmers of lights spilling from the windows of the houses lining the street, the night was dark as a cave. The breeze was no more than a warm breath against her skin, but she felt chilly in her black T-shirt and white jeans. She could hear things—the whir of insects, the faint bass beat of a distant stereo, the muffled clang of metal against metal. She could feel things—like unseen eyes watching her through the darkness. The thought was fanciful, but it still made her shiver. If it hadn't been for the presence of Lieutenant Randy Brown, her police escort, now standing patiently beside his cruiser, which was parked at the curb a mere fifty feet away, she would have been as nervous as a turtle on the freeway as she hurried toward her car, which was parked in front of the cruiser. As it was, she couldn't escape the feeling that something was keeping pace with her just beyond her field of vision, scuttling along through the dark. She could almost feel the whisper of evil breathing down her neck.

It was, she was almost sure, her imagination, fueled by the horrific events of the past week. The memories her mother had unleashed last night seemed to have left her sensitized to atmosphere, and the disturbing dreams that had followed hadn't helped. Karen and Tara Mitchell had appeared, separately and together, whispering to her in voices so low that she couldn't quite understand what they were saying, no matter how hard she had strained to hear.

But she had formed the impression that they were trying to warn her.

They were only dreams, of course, and no wonder she was having them. Anyone would, under the circumstances. And Tara Mitchell's ghost had appeared to many people. It didn't mean—none of it meant—that she had some long-buried, slowly awakening psychic ability.

Did it?

Every time Nicky allowed herself to entertain it, the possibility made her shiver, which was why she needed to put it out of her mind, she told herself firmly. It would do no one any good to succumb to the eerie, unshakable sensation that no matter what she did or where she went, she was marking time until something terrible happened.

The key to keeping rooted in the here and now was to stay focused on her job, and that was what she intended to do. Her segment of *Twenty-four Hours Investigates* had looked and sounded great. She'd logged a number of congratulatory phone calls, most notably one from Sid Levin saying that he was now sure he'd made the right choice in sending her instead of Carl.

And then Mrs. Ferrell, who also had watched *Twenty-four Hours Investigates*, had phoned Leonora with some news to be passed along to Nicky. Mrs. Ferrell was Leonora's longtime hairdresser. She was also the island's biggest busybody, forever peeping out her windows and prying into other people's affairs. The pertinent thing about this was, Mrs. Ferrell lived across the street and two houses down from Marsha Browning.

Mrs. Ferrell reported that she was almost positive she'd seen a man close Marsha's living-room drapes on the night of the murder.

This bit of information, when relayed by her mother, had sent Nicky hightailing it over to Mrs. Ferrell's house for a little girl talk. Neighborly gossip was what Nicky had been after, and neighborly gossip was what she'd gotten. All kinds of good, juicy dirt that when sorted through just might provide a solid lead or two. All it took was the right one, and the monster would be caught.

Headlights lit up the night, causing Nicky to glance around. A white-paneled van drove past just as Nicky reached the street. As it drew even with

Marsha Browning's house, it stopped. The rear door slid open with a harsh metallic sound, somebody jumped to the pavement, and seconds later, an explosion of popping white lights lit up the night.

Nicky checked for a moment, watching wide-eyed. She knew those lights: They came from a professional photographer's camera. More press was on the scene. Marsha Browning's yard was ringed by crime-scene tape, and there was a cop car parked in the driveway, but as Nicky knew from her own experience, that had never stopped any reporter worth his or her salt.

The pack was closing in.

"Hey, get out of here," Brown yelled, waving his arms as if he was trying to shoo away a flock of pesky birds as he walked toward the van.

The lights kept popping. The interior light of the police car parked in Marsha Browning's driveway came on as that cop got out of his car. He was walking down the driveway in a purposeful way when the photographer jumped back in the van and the van took off.

As the red taillights receded into the distance, it occurred to Nicky that her police guard was staring after the van—which, as far as keeping a protective eye on her was concerned, was looking the wrong way.

Okay, so maybe she was a little on edge. This did not strike her as reassuring. Time to head for home.

Pressing the button to unlock the doors, Nicky opened the driver's-side door and started to slide inside. In fact, she already had one foot in the pale gray footwell and was lowering her backside into the cushy leather driver's seat when a sudden sound made her glance sideways. She was just in time to watch as the passenger-side door was jerked open. Her eyes widened with horror as a man dropped into the seat next to her.

Nicky let out a screech and almost fell sideways out of the car before she realized who it was.

"You really don't do careful well, do you?" Joe said, grabbing her arm just in time to prevent her from tumbling out onto the pavement. "I could have been—oh, I don't know—the Lazarus Killer."

"Well, you're not." Having been hauled upright again and then released, Nicky rested limply back against the seat. Her heart still pounded from fright, and she had to work to keep her voice steady. It took a moment for her to recover at least some semblance of equilibrium. When she did, she pulled her door shut and glanced over at him. With the interior light off, he was little more than a solid presence that seemed to take up an inordinate amount of space in the dark. She could hear him breathing, sense his restless energy, see the glint of his eyes as he looked over at her. For a moment, his profile was highlighted against the lighter darkness outside the window. It was masculine, handsome, sexy.

Nicky felt her strength returning.

"Then I'd say that's lucky for you, isn't it?" Joe stuck an unlit cigarette in his mouth. She could see the metallic flash of the lighter in his hand. "If you want to start the car, I'll roll down the window."

"Fine." Nicky took a deep breath and started the car. He rolled the window partway down. The flame on the lighter flared for a second as he lit his cigarette. "Hopefully, Lieutenant Brown back there would have stopped any strangers from getting into the car with me. Isn't that supposed to be why he's following me around?"

"In theory. Only, in case you didn't notice, he got distracted back there." The tip of his cigarette glowed bright red and the lighter disappeared into his pocket. "That's all it takes. One moment of distraction. Then, boom, you got a murderer in the car with you. Of course, if you lived through it, the story sure would make for must-see TV."

Call her slow, but it had taken this long for his tone to percolate through the fright residue. There was a definite edge to his voice. He was unsmiling, his jaw was set hard, and there was a kind of controlled forcefulness to his movements that told its own tale. Nicky knew him well enough by now to recognize the signs. Mr. Police Chief was in a snit again.

"Did you want something?" she asked. "Or were you just trying to make a point by scaring me half to death?"

"Oh, I want something. Suppose you start driving and I'll tell you all about it."

She could have objected to his presence, she supposed, and even ordered him out of her car, although the chances that he would listen and obey seemed slim, but there didn't seem to be much point in it. He might be mad about something, but he was still Joe. In a snit or not, he had the power to raise her heart rate and warm her blood and make her go all buttery inside.

And then, too, with him beside her, she felt absolutely safe—which, under the circumstances, was no small thing.

"I'm going home," she said, just to advise him of her destination as she buckled her seat belt and pulled away from the curb.

"Well, hallelujah."

O-kay. Somebody was definitely in a bad mood.

Except for the police cruiser following along behind, there were no other cars on the street now as Nicky headed toward Atlantic Avenue. Her headlights illuminated mailboxes, trash cans—right, tomorrow was garbage day—and a shining-eyed tabby cat slinking across the road. Beside her, Joe was talking to someone she presumed was Brown on a transistor-sized police radio he had produced from somewhere on his person. Since he was wearing jeans and a dark-colored T-shirt with a dark-colored jacket, she was guessing it had come from his pocket. Or maybe he had been wearing it clipped to his belt.

"You can go on home now," Joe said into the radio. "I've got things covered here."

"Good enough. See you tomorrow," Brown replied over a sharp crackle of static.

Then Joe pressed a button on the radio and it went silent. As he tucked it away out of sight, Nicky slowed the car at the stop sign at the end of the street and then turned right, toward home.

"So, who told you about a lock of Karen Wise's hair being found in Marsha Browning's house?" Joe asked, his voice deceptively casual. "That was something I was kind of hoping to keep secret."

Nicky sent a sidelong look his way. "You watched the show."

"Oh, yeah." He blew smoke out the window. "So, who told you?"

"As a reporter, I don't reveal my sources."

"You had to get that information from a cop, and it wasn't from me."

"Just so you know, there are no secrets on this island. Everybody pretty much knows everything."

"The thing is, your show is broadcast to an awful lot of people who don't live on this island. Do you realize how much harm you did to the investigation by putting all that stuff out there? Now the perp knows exactly what we know."

"If I hadn't put it out there, someone else would have. The interest in this is big, and I'm guessing it's only going to get bigger. You saw that photographer back there. Anyway, I did some good, too. Know where I was just now?"

"Where?"

"Elaine Ferrell's house. She's my mother's hairdresser. She watched the program, then called my mother to tell her she had a tip for me."

"And that was?"

"She saw a man closing Marsha Browning's curtains the night of the murder," Nicky said triumphantly.

A beat passed. Nicky could feel Joe looking at her. The cigarette came out of his mouth.

"You're telling me she came to you with that instead of the police?"

Nicky gave a delicate shrug and tried to keep the smile off her face. "Hey, she knows my mother."

The cigarette went back in Joe's mouth. The tip glowed red. "She get a good look at him?"

"Yep."

"You want to give me a description?"

"Caucasian, blond or fair hair, slender build, white dress shirt, looked fairly young."

"Excuse me a minute." Joe sounded like he had indigestion. His cigarette disappeared, presumably flicked out the window. Nicky said nothing while he fished out his cell phone and placed a call. When someone at the other end picked up, Joe said, "You interviewed an Elaine Ferrell yet? Lives across the street, a couple of doors down from Marsha Browning?"

There was a pause, as though whoever was on the other end was checking a list of names.

"Not yet," came the reply. It was faint, but Nicky could hear it. "We were planning to get to that side of the street tomorrow."

"Yeah, well, I just got word she saw a man closing Marsha Browning's curtains the night of the murder. Get somebody over there to get her statement." Joe's voice was tight.

"Will do. Uh, it's almost ten-thirty. Should we wait until tomorrow?"

"Do it now," Joe said, and disconnected. Dropping the phone back into his pocket, he cut his eyes toward Nicky. "You learn anything else?"

"Just gossip. If any of it turns out to be pertinent, I'll let you know."

"You do that."

"I told you, we should work together."

He made a sound that was a cross between a snort and a laugh. "And have everything we turn up wind up on TV? I don't think so. You know, keeping the fact that Karen Wise went outside because of static on her phone a secret could have been a big help to us in zeroing in on—what was it you called him?—the Lazarus Killer? Good name, that. Catchy. Bet it wows your audience. Hey, maybe you'll get an Emmy. But see, up until the point where you told the whole country, not many people knew why Karen went outside: a few cops, you and your family, and—maybe—the killer."

Nicky shot him a glance. He had passed the snit stage a while back. Now he was sounding downright mad.

"This is news, Joe. You're not going to be able to keep it off TV. Or out of the papers. Your best bet is to use the publicity to generate leads. Take Mrs. Ferrell, for example. She wouldn't have contacted me if she hadn't seen *Twenty-four Hours Investigates* tonight."

"We would have gotten to her tomorrow."

"Yes, but you have to ask yourself, how many Mrs. Ferrells are there out there you won't get to?"

"Sooner or later, we'll get to everybody we need to get to."

"I think the operative word there may be *later*." Nicky glanced at him. "Besides, there's a lot of other information I can get that you can't."

"Like what?"

"If my mother is able to contact Karen, or Marsha Browning—"

"Jesus Christ," Joe said. "No. I've had it up to here with the psychic stuff." He must have caught Nicky's sideways glare, because seconds later he added, "All right, fine. *If* your mother manages to make contact with Karen or Marsha, or anyone up there in Woo-Woo Land who knows Karen or Marsha, and if they feel like talking to us folks down here on Planet Earth and telling us something interesting like, I don't know, *who killed them*, I'd be happy to be let in on the secret. But so far, that doesn't seem to be happening, does it?"

Nicky's hands tightened on the wheel. "You know what, you need an attitude adjustment."

"What I *need* is for you to stay the hell off TV. I got two women dead and a killer who has promised to kill three. From the way the timetable is shaping up, he'll be trying again soon. He's contacting you, he's following you, we can probably assume he's getting all psyched up from the publicity you're giving him. You know how you're calling him the Lazarus Killer? If he's a classic serial killer, he's loving it. He's feeding off it. It's making him bolder. And I'm afraid what the upshot of it is, he's going to be coming after you. To him right now, you've got to be looking like the ultimate rush. You might as well be jumping up and down and yelling 'Come get me.' "

The thought was terrifying, but it wasn't anything Nicky hadn't already figured out for herself. "So we need to catch him first."

"Honey, there's no 'we' in this. The police department is investigating. What you're doing is providing entertainment for the bloodthirsty masses."

"Fine." They had reached Twybee Cottage by this time, and Nicky turned up the driveway a little faster than she normally would have. Pea gravel flew out from under the tires, peppering the sides of the Maxima. Lights were on in the upstairs windows, spilling golden rectangles of light over the roof of the garage. As Nicky pulled into the parking area, she saw that the lights were on downstairs, too. "You conduct your investigation, I'll conduct mine."

She parked beside Livvy's Jaguar, turned off the car, and got out. Joe got out, too. Stalking toward the house, she was aware of him right behind her. At the bottom of the steps, she turned to glare at him.

"All right, I'm home, I'm safe, and you can go now."

He smiled at her. It was a slow, mocking smile that as far as she was concerned put him firmly back in nasty-cop territory.

"You know, I would, but since all my men are working flat out and I can't spare anybody to sit out in front of your house all night, I'm going to be spending the night on your couch. I've already worked it out with your mom. See, she doesn't want you getting turned into sushi any more than I do."

Nicky stared at him, aghast. Then, knowing that that sounded exactly like something her mother would agree to, she turned around again and stomped up the steps. She could feel Joe right behind her every step of the way.

JOE OPENED HIS EYES to the smell of coffee. He was groggy, disoriented, and for a moment had trouble remembering where he was. An uncomprehending glance around revealed dark paneled walls enlivened by paintings of Civil War battle scenes, closed gold curtains, a desk, and a pair of big leather chairs on either side of a fireplace. He was lying on a couch opposite them, with a sheet tucked up around his armpits and a pillow bunched beneath his head. Realization struck with a flash: The pillow and sheets were courtesy of Leonora, and he was stretched out on the couch in the study at Twybee Cottage. A glance at his watch told him that it was nearing seven A.M. Until shortly after four, he'd been awake, going over the details of the murders in his mind, cross-checking the files that he'd had Dave—who he'd left in possession of his house—drop off for him. At seven, Bill Milton was supposed to arrive at Twybee Cottage. His alibi had been checked and found good, too, and he had drawn Nicky duty for the day.

Joe, meanwhile, meant to go home, grab a shower and change clothes, and head over to the Georgetown County morgue. Marsha Browning's autopsy was scheduled for nine A.M.

He'd slept in his jeans. Pulling on his shirt and socks and shoes, strapping on ankle and shoulder holsters, he secured his Chief and his Glock and then topped the whole thing off with his jacket so nary a trace of a weapon could be seen. Then he headed for the kitchen.

The back door was open to let the early-morning breeze waft in through the screen, and the paddle fan was doing lazy rotations overhead. And Nicky was sitting at the kitchen table, talking to her mother.

Joe checked on the threshold.

"Good morning, Joe. Want coffee?" Leonora greeted him with a thin smile. She was wearing a zip-up robe in pale green, her hair was slightly squashed on one side, and her face was pale and devoid of makeup. Still, except for the difference in age and weight, she looked enough like Nicky that Joe realized that he could have picked her out anywhere as Nicky's mother.

Nicky, on the other hand, was fully dressed. Her bright hair gleamed in the early-morning light that poured in through the windows, and she was wearing makeup and a sunny yellow blouse. What she wasn't wearing was a smile. In fact, she looked him over with fairly obvious dislike.

"Thanks, yeah, I'd like some," Joe said.

"Pot's on the counter. Help yourself." Nicky's first words to him of the morning were uttered in a clipped voice that told him they were still on the outs. Well, fair enough. He headed toward the counter where the coffeemaker waited.

"*Nicky.*" Leonora started to rise, her tone making her daughter's name a reproof. Joe had been around the South for long enough to know that a polite hostess never just told a guest to help himself, especially not in a snippy tone.

"I got it," Joe said, and since he was already at the counter, Leonora sank back in her seat, although not without a censorious glance at Nicky.

"I've been trying to convince my pigheaded daughter that she needs to get away from here," Leonora said as Joe filled an earthenware mug with coffee, returned the coffeepot to its spot, then took a sip of the strong, hot brew. *Great coffee*, he thought appreciatively—and, more important, he needed the caffeine. Badly. "Maybe you can add your thoughts to mine."

"He already did, mother."

Joe turned around, mug in hand, and met Nicky's eyes. "For all the good it did, right? But I'll say it again, just for the record: I think you ought to take a vacation somewhere until this guy is caught."

"Oh, me, too," Leonora seconded eagerly.

Nicky gave them both an impatient look.

"No," she said. "I know you both think I'm in danger, and I may be. But if this guy wants to kill me, there's no guarantee he won't turn up wherever I go, where I won't be expecting him, so I won't be on guard. At least here I've got twenty-four-hour police protection. And I can help catch him, which is the only way I'll ever be truly safe."

"But Nicky . . ." her mother said in a piteous tone.

"I'll be all right, Mama." Nicky stood up, dropped a quick kiss on her mother's cheek, and headed for the door. As she reached it, she looked back over her shoulder at Joe. "I wrote out a list of everyone I know who had my new phone number, by the way. Check your e-mail. It's there."

"Wait a minute," Joe said, putting his cup down on the counter. "Where are you going?"

"It's after seven, and my bodyguard should be here. I'd offer you a ride but"—she smiled caustically at him—"remember the rules: You conduct your investigation, and I'll conduct mine."

With that, she went out the door.

"Oh, dear," Leonora said with an unmistakable smidgen of pride, as Joe cast a quick look out the window behind him. Sure enough, there was Bill Milton in his cruiser. "When she gets her dander up like this, there's just no doing anything with her."

Joe watched her greet Milton, then get into her car. It was a beautiful morning, all sunshiny and bright, and so far as he knew the killer hadn't attacked anyone in broad daylight yet. And she would have a police escort throughout the day. . . .

"She's safe enough." He turned back to look at Leonora. "For today, at least."

"It's just . . . I worry," Leonora's face was troubled. "I have this *feeling*. And I'm blocked, which I've never been before in my life. I hate to think what it might mean." She met his gaze. "The truth is, I'm afraid for Nicky."

So am I, Joe thought, but he didn't say it aloud. Instead, he carried his coffee cup over to the table and sat down. A thought occurred: Maybe he could get more information out of Nicky's mother than he could out of Nicky herself.

"You know," he said, smiling at Leonora, "one thing's been puzzling me. Ever since Sunday's show, I've been trying to come up with a source for those screams. . . ."

JUST AS NICKY had expected, the press descended on Pawleys Island like flies on a corpse. By midweek, practically every entertainment tabloid in the business had sent a team. In what was apparently a slow news cycle, the Lazarus Killer seemed to have captured the public's imagination. Print reporters, radio reporters, and TV reporters all vied with each other to be the first to come up with a new angle on what *The National Enquirer* called "a real-life horror story." The linking of a fifteen-year-old triple murder with two new murders, plus ghosts and poetic communications from the killer, proved especially irresistible to the TV group, all of whom were after the same thing Nicky was herself: a sweeps victory for their show.

Fortunately, with Nicky's local connections, she continued to have the inside track. She and Gordon filmed everywhere. Neighborhood gossip yielded so many leads that it was going to take weeks to follow up on them all. Nicky personally worked only the most promising. The rest were turned over to the police department, which was swamped to the point that the entire team, not just Joe, looked as though they were running on caffeine fumes and desperation. Another advantage Nicky had was that none of the other reporters had a psychic medium for a mother. Leonora, whose performance in the first show was still airing in the promos for upcoming segments, was a smash hit.

"This is *great*," Sarah Greenberg enthused to Nicky in an excited phone call. "The numbers are really going up. And we're getting lots of e-mail about your mother. We definitely want her in the final segment. Sid even said something about offering her her own show for next fall."

That was one of those good news/bad news situations. Leonora was pleased that she'd managed to reconnect with her audience, as she put it, intrigued by the possibility of a fall show—but she was still blocked. But she was nonetheless willing to help with the case. With the assistance of friends and neighbors, Nicky was gathering items belonging to the victims. Besides Karen's blazer, she had a watch of Marsha Browning's that had been left at the Seaside Resort Jewelry Shoppe for repair, and a blouse of Lauren Schultz's, donated by her parents. She had contacted Becky Iverson's mother, who was now divorced from her father and living in Colorado, and had agreed to send an article of Becky's clothing. So far, Nicky hadn't gotten a response from Tara Mitchell's family, and if she didn't hear from them soon, it would be too late for something of Tara's to be included in the spot. Leonora was going to use the items to try to channel the victims as soon as the package from Becky's mother arrived, and Gordon was going to film it. If it turned out well, Nicky would put the bit on the show.

How cool would it be if one of the victims came through and identified the killer on TV?

"Don't count on it," Leonora warned her dryly. "Even under the best of conditions, spirits aren't usually that direct. And as far as I'm concerned, these definitely aren't the best of conditions."

The weather was increasingly hot and dry as May raced toward June. The tropical ambience of the island grew more pronounced as vines and flowers and trees burst into glorious bloom. Yards turned emerald green. Swimming pools sparkled under the sun. The sky was bluer, the ocean was smoother, and the mood of the island was as jittery as a kid in a dentist's chair.

Everybody, including Nicky, seemed to be looking over their shoulders, waiting for something to happen. When nothing did, the sense of dread grew until it was as palpable as the increasing humidity.

Tension hung in the air right along with the smell of the sea. With each day that passed, Nicky could feel it tightening like a rubber band being slowly stretched. All anybody wanted to talk about was the murders. Everywhere she went—grocery store, gas station, post office—people would gather round her, asking her for the latest news. Joe was apparently subject to the same treatment, with the added stress of having a pack of reporters liable to descend on him without warning.

"Get the hell out of here!" he bellowed at a team from Court TV that invaded the police station on Wednesday afternoon. Nicky knew this because she, like much of the rest of the country, saw the outburst on TV.

"You want to be nice," she warned him that night. It was just after eleven P.M., and he walked into the kitchen at Twybee Cottage, looking haggard and exhausted and spoiling for a fight. As he was continuing to spend his nights in their study—although, from the look of him, he wasn't getting much sleep—Nicky saw him pretty much every morning and every night, as well as occasionally during the day when their paths crossed while they were conducting their pointedly separate investigations. They were still very much on the outs, and from the look he gave her as she offered him her advice on handling the press, they were going to stay that way.

"Screw being nice," he said. Then, as Leonora walked into the kitchen, he responded to her offer of a cup of soup and a sandwich with a tired smile that had been nowhere in evidence when he had addressed Nicky, and a perfectly pleasant "No, thanks." Following Nicky from the room, he added, in the same low, growly tone as before, "I tried being nice. It didn't work. Now they're everywhere I turn. They're hounding me, they're hounding my men, they're hounding the whole damned community. I can't make a move without somebody shoving a camera in my face. They don't deserve nice."

"Your call," Nicky said with a shrug and headed for bed, the glass of juice for which she'd entered the kitchen in hand, leaving him to the tender mercies of her mother, who seemed to be developing a completely misplaced fondness for him. At the foot of the stairs, though, she paused to glance back over her shoulder at him. "But if you're not nice to them, they'll keep playing gotcha with you until they've, um, got you."

"I'll take my chances."

The next time Nicky saw him was on TV. She was in Linney's Bar down on the waterfront, talking to a waitress about a man who had ordered a martini some fifteen minutes before Nicky had gotten the call from the Lazarus Killer while she'd been with Joe on the beach. As the big front window of Linney's Bar overlooked the stretch of sand leading up to the hotel complex, and the man was unknown to anyone in the bar, it seemed like a decent tip. The waitress was in the midst of describing how suspiciously the man had behaved, when something—a familiar voice, a sixth sense, something—caused Nicky to glance at the small TV behind the bar and get an eyeful of Joe, shirtless and bleary-eyed, framed by the back door of a small blue bungalow, a heaping plate of food in hand as he talked to a *pig*.

18

CLEARLY, the shot had been filmed around twilight, probably the previous day. Stripped to the waist as he opened his glass back door and stepped outside, Joe was all ripped muscles and bronzed skin, with a nice wedge of black hair in the center of his chest. He was lean, sinewy, without an ounce of extra flesh, but his bones ensured that he was still a big man, tall, with broad shoulders and a wide chest that tapered to narrow hips. His jeans rode low, revealing an impressive six-pack and a nice inny navel.

Yum, Nicky thought appreciatively, picturing the shot being freeze-framed and mounted on the walls of countless schoolgirls.

Of course, that was before he started talking to the pig. The camera pulled back, and there it was beside him on the wooden deck, practically dancing on its four little hooves, staring up at the plate in Joe's hand. It was attractive, she supposed, at least as attractive as pigs got, black, a little taller and a whole lot fatter than a basset hound, with floppy ears; a cute, round snout; and a little corkscrew of a tail that wagged madly. But it was still a pig.

"All right," Joe said to it, sounding bad-tempered. "You want this? Fine. Here you go. Think I can eat it with you watching me? Hell, no. What kind of pig eats ham sandwiches and pork and beans anyway?"

And he set the plate down in front of the pig.

Watching, you had to balance the hunkiness quotient, which was mouth-wateringly high, against the looking-ridiculous quotient, which was also high.

As the issue hung in the balance, Joe straightened and seemed to see the camera for the first time. His face changed in an instant from merely irritated to downright livid.

"What? Who the . . . ? Get that camera out of here! Get off my property!"

Charging across the deck, presumably to confront the still-filming crew, he almost tripped over the scuttling-to-get-out-of-the-way pig.

Nicky had to laugh and groan at the same time.

But as the accompanying story focused on the ineptness of the police department's investigation, it really wasn't that funny. At least, she was sure that from Joe's perspective it wasn't.

Later, as they once again did their ships-that-pass-in-the-night thing in the hall of Twybee Cottage, Nicky couldn't resist saying, "I saw you on TV today. I didn't know you had a pet pig."

Joe's mouth twisted sardonically. "Honey, there's a lot you don't know about me."

That, Nicky reflected as she sat upstairs at her desk, working into the wee hours because now only exhaustion allowed her to sleep without terrible dreams, was undoubtedly true. But she knew enough about him not to worry about the Lazarus Killer somehow getting to her while he was spending the nights in her house.

And that, she decided, was a whole lot.

The thing was, with all the news crews that were now on the island, they all constantly ran into each other everywhere they went. Some of her fellow reporters Nicky already knew, some of them she didn't, but a camaraderie of sorts developed among them, along with a fierce sense of competition. Two of the teams resorted to bringing in their own psychics, who, while Nicky hadn't heard anything about them being blocked, didn't seem to be having any more luck in identifying the killer than Leonora was having. Most, though, continued to follow various police officers and public officials around, doing what they called "guerrilla filming" as the cops went about their jobs of interviewing witnesses and tracking down leads, and the officials went around talking about things like how the killings were likely to affect the upcoming high season. Still, with so many teams rehashing the same information, producers started screaming at their reporters to bring them something fresh. Friday passed, then Saturday, then Sunday with its broadcast of *Twenty-four Hours Investigates*. The ratings were up again:

they were at 32 now. The powers-that-be were excited, calling to offer congratulations, sending flowers, cheering Nicky on. Meanwhile, the island held its collective breath. Just six days had separated the murders of Karen Wise and Marsha Browning, and yet ten days had passed in which the killer had done nothing. As the new week began, much of the reporting, therefore, started to focus on the island itself and the personalities of the people involved in the case.

A CNN team decided to do a piece on the competency of the investigators, which quickly boiled down to a piece about Joe. When Nicky heard some of the rumors about what they were planning to air, she was appalled. And angry. And disbelieving.

She immediately phoned Sarah Greenberg and had their fact-checking department run a background check on Joe, just to be sure.

Sarah called back with the results at about seven o'clock Wednesday night, moments after Nicky had wrapped up an interview with Marsha Browning's nephew, who, disappointingly, turned out to have been the man Mrs. Ferrell had identified as having closed Marsha's curtains on the night of the murder. The nephew had been at her house to drop off some family photos. He'd left at about nine, which meant that if he wasn't the killer (and Nicky didn't think he was, although Joe refused to remove him from the suspect list until certain DNA tests came back), he was the last person to see Marsha Browning alive, which meant he was still a viable interview.

But Nicky forgot all about Marsha Browning's nephew when she heard what Sarah had to say.

"It's true," Sarah said. "Every bit of it."

"It can't be." Nicky was so shocked that she was surprised she could speak at all.

"It is." Sarah was brisk and certain. "You have good instincts, Nicky. This definitely has all the elements of a huge spin-off story. Go get it, girl."

"Yeah, I will. Thanks, Sarah." Nicky felt sick to her stomach as she disconnected. She was sitting in the front seat of her Maxima, which was still parked in front of the nephew's house, and for a minute she couldn't do anything but stare out her windshield at the last crimson feelers of the sun as they streaked across the darkening sky. Gordon, who'd captured the interview on camera, honked as he drove past. Since that was the last interview that Nicky had scheduled for the day, he was heading out to get some shots of the beach and the sea as night fell. Yanked from her reverie by the sound of the horn, Nicky waved, checked her rearview mirror to ascertain that her police escort was still with her—he was—then started her car and pulled away from the curb.

It was only as she reached the end of the street that she realized what she had to do.

She had to warn Joe.

IN THE MIDST of chaos, he had managed to develop a routine, Joe reflected as he stepped out of the shower. Around suppertime each day, he stopped by his house, made some phone calls, fixed himself a quick meal, and fed the pig. Feeding the pig wasn't something he had to do, really. Dave kept its dispenser topped off with pig chow, so the animal wasn't going to miss a meal if Joe didn't come home. The thing was, though, Joe liked to grab supper while he was at the house, and he found it impossible to eat with the pig staring through the back window at him unless he fed it something, too. Although Dave had gone back to his own house after spending only one night at Joe's, the pig remained on a strictly temporary basis. Amy refused to have it back, and Joe was too eager to have his house to himself again to insist that Dave take it with him. Besides, as he had reasoned at the time he'd agreed to the arrangement, since he wasn't going to be at home much in the foreseeable future, what harm could it do?

He had discovered the answer to that when he'd watched that little clip of himself and the pig on TV.

If his pals back in Jersey had seen that—and he hadn't heard anything to suggest that they had—they'd be laughing still.

The good news was that he hadn't seen Brian since he had told him to get the fuck out of his life. If he'd known getting rid of the bastard was that easy, he would have done it a whole lot sooner.

The bad news was that he had so many other problems that Brian was the least of them.

Today, because he was hot and sweaty and dead on his feet when he stepped through the door of his house, a shower had been added to his usual routine. Joe was toweling off when his cell phone began to ring.

Hitching the towel around his waist and hotfooting it toward the living room, where the TV was turned to ESPN and his phone rested on the coffee table, he picked it up and answered.

"Joe?"

He would know her voice anywhere: Nicky.

"Yes. What's up?" He was immediately alert, since she only ever called him to report bad things.

"I need to talk to you."

"So talk."

A beat passed. He frowned a little as he registered the quality of her silence.

"In person," she said. "In private."

"Are you okay?" There was something bothering her, that was for sure. He'd never heard that particular tone from her before. He didn't think she was in danger, there wasn't enough urgency in her voice for that, but . . .

"I'm fine. Can we meet somewhere? Now?"

"I'm over at my house. We can talk here. Do you know where it is? 264—"

"I know where it is," she interrupted. "I'll be there in a few minutes."

Then she hung up.

By the time Joe got dressed, her car was pulling up out front. He saw it through the big front window, went to the door, opened it, and stepped out onto the stoop, waiting for her. It was almost—but not quite—full dark, and lights were on in the houses up and down the street. The air was heavy with a humidity that was new to him, and it smelled more of overabundant plant life than of the sea. Kids playing a few yards over were loud enough to drown out every other sound. As Nicky walked toward him across his front yard, which badly needed cutting, he was struck by how much he liked watching her move. In deference to the heat—the temperature hovered around eighty degrees but had been much higher earlier in the day—she was wearing some kind of slim, sleeveless dress that ended above her knees. It was a kind of acidy yellow-green, a color that was unwearable by anyone except a true red-head, and her legs flashed long and slim and pale below it. Bill Milton, her cop escort, who had pulled up behind her, waited in his cruiser, presumably watching her cross the lawn, too. Joe waved acknowledgment at him. Then Nicky was on the stoop, looking at him, her expression almost fierce in the shadows, and he smiled at her because he couldn't help himself.

On her, fierce looked good.

She didn't smile back.

"CNN is getting ready to air a story I think you should know about," she said without preamble as she walked past him into the living room.

Must be bad if she was coming to warn him, Joe thought with resignation as he closed the door behind her and immediately felt dog tired all over again. It was one more thing to deal with, and he was fresh out of both patience and time.

"About what?"

She turned to look at him. "You."

HE WAS WEARING a dark gray T-shirt with a Miami Heat logo and worn jeans, Nicky saw with a sweep of her eyes. His hair was unruly and faintly damp, and his feet were bare. The faintest suggestion of soap and steam hung in the air, although they were standing in the living room, with nary a bathroom in sight—but then, it was a small house.

She was watching him for a reaction, but the one she got wasn't what she expected. He gave her a small smile.

"If it's the pig again, Dave's going to be directing traffic for the rest of his life."

"It isn't the pig." As she spoke, he was moving, closing the curtains, stepping past her to pick up the remote from an end table by the couch and turn off the TV; she had to turn to keep him in sight. "It's you."

"Me." He blew out a sigh, turned to look at her, and gestured toward the couch. A single lamp lit the living room, which seemed to lack any ornaments or pictures, even on the walls, but it was neat and clean, with functional if not especially well-coordinated furniture. "Want to sit down while you tell me all about it?"

She didn't move. Her pulse was elevated. Her stomach was in a tight knot. Her hands were clenched into fists at her sides. She became aware of all these things only as she looked at Joe and tried to reconcile this man who now loomed large in her life with what she had just learned.

"You were a dirty cop," she said.

He went very still. Then his face changed. It tightened, hardened, and his eyes went flat and black.

He didn't say anything.

"You took payoffs in exchange for providing protection for a drug ring you were supposed to be investigating."

His hands flexed at his sides. Except for that, he stood motionless, as if he was waiting. She knew what he was waiting for: the rest of the story.

"Unfortunately for you, the DEA was investigating this particular drug ring, too, and they set up a sting. They got you on tape accepting cash, ten thousand dollars at a time. Several times. You were caught red-handed, along with three other cops. When the feds sprang the trap, you were all in a warehouse with the drug traffickers. Somebody started shooting, and when it was over, nine people were dead, including the other cops. You were critically wounded, shot twice in the head. They expected you to die. When you didn't, they arrested you in the hospital, charged you with multiple offenses, including murder, and sent you off to a prison hospital to await trial. You were still there when the charges were dropped on a technicality. Only you couldn't get your job back. No way. So you wound up here."

A beat passed in which they stared at each other. Then his eyes flickered.

"Now you know my secret," he said lightly, mockingly.

Her heart plummeted right along with her stomach. She sucked in her breath as the pain of it went through her like a knife. He was still Joe—still tall, dark, and sexy, with the power to make her go weak in the knees; still a man she would unhesitatingly trust with her life. But she had sensed before that there was another side to him, a dangerous side, a side she hadn't met and didn't want to, although she now knew irrefutably that it was there.

"It's true." Her tone made it a statement rather than a question.

He moved then, heading, she thought, for the doorway that led into the kitchen. "Want something to drink?" he asked. "I know I do."

She caught his arm, stopping him as he walked past her. His biceps felt warm and hard with muscle beneath her hand.

"Is it true?" She had to ask even though she knew that it was, even though CNN was going to do a feature on it, even though Sarah Greenberg had confirmed it for her.

He looked down at her. His mouth curved into the smallest of sardonic smiles, but his eyes, dark and unreadable, didn't match.

"What do you care?"

Nicky looked deep inside herself and realized something.

"I care," she said.

Then he moved his head, and the way the lamplight hit his face changed. She saw two pale, ragged scars gouged out of the bronzed skin of his temple that disappeared into the unruly thicket of his black hair.

Her gaze fastened on them. She caught her breath.

"Is that where you were shot?" Even as she asked it, her hand was rising of its own accord to gently touch the puckered flesh.

He caught her hand just as her fingers slid over the roughened skin, his grip hard, his expression savage, and for a moment, as their eyes met and held, she thought he was going to fling her hand away from him, utterly rejecting her instinctive soothing of the terrible marks.

But instead his eyes flared and his hold gentled.

"Yeah, that's where I was shot," he said, his voice husky, and, still holding her gaze, he carried her hand to his mouth. He kissed the back of it, then her fingertips, one by one. Nicky felt the touch of his lips against her skin like a brand. Her breathing suspended, her heart lurched, and when he lowered her hand and his head dipped toward her mouth instead, she closed her eyes and tilted her head and kissed him back, their mouths soft and hot.

Then he pulled her into his arms and kissed her harder and her brain went a little fuzzy. She wrapped her arms around his neck and went up on tiptoe and kissed him with all the pent-up emotion that had been locked inside her since she had spoken to Sarah Greenberg on the phone.

It was a soul-shattering kiss, electric with desire. He felt so warm, so solid against her, and he smelled just faintly of soap and tasted just faintly of cigarettes, which was another way she knew it was Joe, and she wanted him so much that her heart pounded and her stomach clenched and, deep inside, her body tightened and began to throb.

When he lifted his head and broke the kiss, she made a tiny sound of protest as she opened her eyes to see what he was doing. He was looking at her, his face just inches away, his eyes heavy-lidded and gleaming, a faint flush high on his cheekbones. She could feel the solid bands of his arms around her, feel the rise and fall of his chest against her breasts, feel the unmistakable proof of his desire for her against her stomach.

"Joe." Her heart was in her voice.

"I'm a dirty cop, remember? You should go."

"I don't want to go."

To stop him from talking—and to stop herself from thinking—she closed her eyes and kissed him again, pressing her mouth to his, sliding her tongue inside his mouth, rocking into him. He let her kiss him for a moment, his mouth pliant and responsive but no more, but then his arms tightened around her and suddenly he was kissing her like she wanted to be kissed, like she needed to be kissed, like a man kisses a woman whom he's crazy about. His mouth was hot and wet and hungry, insistent, and his tongue moved against hers, stroking it, coaxing it, staking its claim to her mouth. She returned the kiss with wild abandon and felt fire shoot clear down to her toes.

Then his hand found her breast, covered it, and caressed it through the thin layers of her dress and bra. Nicky felt the heat of that hand, the weight of it, and her legs turned to Jell-O. Her breast swelled into his palm. Her nipple went rigid. She clung to him, suddenly dizzy, as he lifted his mouth from hers.

"We're not on the beach now," he said in a low, thick voice as his mouth slid across her cheek to her throat. The whisper of his breath feathered across her skin. The hot, wet glide of his mouth over the sensitive cord at the side of her neck made her shiver. She knew what he was asking, and just the thought of it made her heart thud and her insides melt.

"I know." There was, quite simply, no other answer she could give.

His hand left her breast to slide around her back. When she felt the slight tug at her nape and heard the unmistakable sound of her zipper being lowered, she shivered. Cool air caressed her spine. She could feel his knuckles pressing against the first tender curve of her butt, just below where the zipper ended. The zipper gaped, and his hand slipped inside to glide warm and flat up her bare back. The sensation made her breath catch. In deference to the heat, she was wearing a simple linen shift—easy on, easy off—with little kitten-heeled slides and no hose. His mouth crawled around the base of her throat, his hand stroked down her spine—and she opened her eyes and gave a little shake of her head in an effort to clear it and stepped back, away from him. For a moment, as her hands lingered on his broad shoulders, on his strong arms, she was conscious of a tiny sliver of uncertainty about what she was doing.

This was Joe—but the truth was, she reminded herself, she didn't really know this man at all.

"Nicky." His voice was husky, his face hard and dark with desire. But he wasn't trying to keep her. If she wanted to go, he would let her go. Whatever else he was, whatever he might have done or been, he had never been less than protective of her. The knowledge chased away her last lingering doubt. The look in his eyes—it made her dizzy. Heat shimmered in the air between them, pure chemistry, but something more, too. Something that she'd been edging toward but now, under the circumstances, didn't want to face. Not yet.

She dropped her arms, gave a delicate shrug, and let her dress slither down her body to her ankles. His eyes blazed at her, heavy-lidded no longer. They seemed to scorch her as they followed the path of the dress in a quick, comprehensive sweep. Her undies were pretty, delicate things, thin coffee-colored nylon and lace. She looked good in them, she knew, and she could tell he thought so, too.

"You're beautiful," he said, and reached for her. Stepping out of the puddle of citrine linen around her feet, she slid her hands up under his shirt as he pulled her close. His waist felt warm and smooth. The muscles beneath were taut and sleek, resilient, contracting when she stroked them. Her hands moved up over his chest, over a wide, firm expanse of hair-roughened skin. She was still reveling in the feel of him when he made a slight choked sound that caused her to look up.

For a second, no longer, as her hands stroked over the honed contours of his chest, his eyes gleamed hotly at her. Then he kissed her. He let go of her once more to pull his T-shirt over his head. Nicky had just a moment to absorb the splendor of his wide shoulders, his muscled arms and chest, the triangle of black hair that tapered down over washboard abs to disappear beneath the waistband of his jeans, before he scooped her up into his arms and started walking and kissing her at the same time.

Twining her arms around his neck, dazzled by the easy strength with which he carried her, she let her head fall against the firm pillow of his shoulder and kissed him as if kissing him was the one thing she most wanted to do in life.

Her shoes fell off, one at a time. They each hit the hardwood floor with a small clatter. She didn't hear, or notice that they were gone.

She was so bedazzled that she didn't even notice that they were in his bedroom until he kicked the door shut behind them.

That sound was loud enough to get her attention. Her eyes opened in reaction.

The living room had been well and warmly lit. The bedroom was dark and cool. Mini-blinds over a single window were striped with slivers of moonlight. A small air conditioner purred busily. Her eyes found an easy chair in the far corner, and then, as Joe lifted his mouth from hers and rested a knee on something, she realized that they had reached his bed. He hadn't actually slept in it for a while, she remembered, as she realized that the bed was made. At least, she felt the soft, smooth thickness of what appeared to be a light-colored comforter beneath her back, and as far as she could see, the pillows looked tidy, so she assumed it was made. Then he came down beside her. The mattress sank beneath his weight, tipping her toward him, and she lost all awareness of everything except him.

His mouth was hard and hot and urgent as it found hers, and his hands were, too, sliding over her body, stroking her, finding and caressing her breasts, her belly, her thighs. She quivered, trembled, pressed herself close, her hands and mouth as greedy for him as he was for her. They were in a hurry, both of them, pulling at each other's clothes until they were naked. She felt the moist heat of his mouth on her breasts, on her nipples, and moaned. His hand slid between her thighs, working its magic until she gasped and squirmed with pleasure and came arching up off the bed. Just as she thought she was going to climax, had to climax, he stopped what he was doing and kissed her mouth again, leaving her trembling and dizzy and empty, and she slid her hands down his warm back, over the firm, round contours of his butt, lightly scoring his skin with her nails, as a kind of tender punishment.

"Jesus," he said, his voice so low and hoarse that it was almost a groan. His thighs, rough with hair and warm and strong, slid between hers. Then he pushed inside her, and he was huge and hot and she was on fire, burning up, melting as he moved in and out, thrusting deep and fast, taking her with him on a wild, hot ride that had her clinging to him and crying out and climaxing at last in a shattering series of fast, furious explosions that sent her rocketing away to some mysterious Technicolor universe where she had never been before.

"Nicky," he groaned against her neck, then drove into her quivering body with a fierce, deep thrust that sent her over the edge one more time as he found his own release. "Oh, God, *Nicky*."

Afterward, all she could do was breathe. She was limp with exhaustion and sated with pleasure and totally mindless.

But not for long. The thing about reality is that there's no escaping it, even after some truly mind-blowing sex. So after her mind returned from orbit and her body calmed down a little, she was left to face the situation she had put herself in—which was, in a nutshell, the fact that she was naked in bed with Joe.

Her eyes were accustomed to the dark by this time, and the tiny slices of moonlight filtering through the mini-blinds helped, too. She could see him fairly well. He was lying flat on his back beside her, staring up at the ceiling, one arm tucked beneath his head. The set of his jaw looked grim. The hard line of his mouth looked grim. In fact, everything about his expression looked grim, and she realized once again that she didn't know this man at all.

Which was not an especially comforting thought to have when she was curled naked against his side with a hand splayed across his chest, a thigh curved over his thigh, and his arm around her shoulders.

To say nothing of the fact that just beyond him, on the night table, rested his shiny black gun.

He was a dirty cop, an accused murderer, who had been involved in drug deals.

As far as new boyfriends went, none of the above was particularly promising. Taken as a whole, it was downright scary. She'd always made safe choices before: doctors, lawyers, accountants.

Boring maybe, but safe.

Never in her wildest dreams had she ever pictured herself getting naked and horizontal with someone who was not certifiably one of the good guys.

But here she was.

His eyes cut her way. Nicky almost jumped.

"If your eyes get any bigger, they're going to pop right out of your head." His voice was dry. He pulled his arm from beneath her and rolled out of bed. Nicky got an eyeful of tight, round butt and a lean, muscular back, and then he turned to face her and she got the full Monty. Of course, everything was veiled by shadow, but even without a clear view, it was obvious that what she was looking at was a very impressive package.

Then she realized that he was looking at her, too. The set of his jaw and mouth was still grim, but there was something about his eyes. . . .

Clearly, grim or not, he liked what he saw.

"So-o," she said, because he wasn't talking and it seemed somebody should. She sat up, tucking her legs beneath her as gracefully as she could and resisting the urge to wrap up in the tangled sheet—the comforter and pillows had hit the floor long since—only by reminding herself that such a display of modesty might make her look less than in control of herself, him, and the situation, which, since she wasn't, was an excellent illusion to maintain. Besides, it was dark. Reasonably dark. "What happens now?"

Without answering, he reached over to turn on the lamp beside the bed. Nicky barely swallowed a squeak as the action threw a soft circle of light over the place where she was sitting. His eyes moved over her, touching on all pertinent areas, and she watched them darken and heat. He stood there, casually naked, and she couldn't help but look, too. He was lean and muscular, and so hot that her heartbeat speeded up even though seconds before she would have sworn that she was so sated that there was no possible way she could ever be in the mood again, and she realized that whatever she might now know about him, the physical attraction between them was so strong that she wasn't just going to be able to turn her back on him and walk away.

And, while she was being honest, she might as well admit that the attraction went deeper than the mere physical—which left her exactly where?

"So, what happens now?" she asked again.

His lips compressed and his eyes narrowed. "We get dressed and get on with our lives." He was already on the move, rounding the foot of the bed, scooping up his jeans as he went. "The bathroom's down the hall."

"That's not what I meant and you know it," she said, but he was out the door by that time. If he heard, he didn't reply.

Nicky scowled after him, scooted off the bed, and grabbed the sheet to twine around herself. Under the circumstances, she didn't need his attitude. And she didn't understand. *She* was the one who should be doing the whole hate-yourself-in-the-morning thing, not him.

Unless. . . .

He *wasn't* guilty, and was just too damned stupid, stubborn, or macho (which was basically the same thing as the first two options combined) to tell her so.

The thing was, he had always made her feel safe.

Nicky paused in the act of stomping after him to consider. Her gaze touched on her panties, peeking out from under the comforter, which was now on the floor. Glancing around, she discovered her bra crumpled near the night stand. The position of both was silent testimony to the urgency with which they had been discarded. She and Joe had been so hot for each other that they'd come together in what was practically a fever. For him to be so prickly and standoffish after such really great sex was a definite red flag. The question was, a red flag indicating what? Picking up her undies, she headed for the bathroom. They were going to talk this out, whether he liked it or not. That being the case, she preferred not to initiate the conversation while she was wrapped in a sheet and still all flushed and sweaty with sex.

Grimacing at the giant daisies on the glass doors of the tub enclosure, Nicky took the fastest shower on record, toweled herself dry, put on her bra and panties, brushed her hair, and, with an encouraging grimace at her own reflection, left the bathroom. He wasn't in the living room, she was glad to see as she reached it, so she was able to step into her dress without an audience.

Zipping it up in a hurry, she walked barefoot into the only other place he could possibly be: the kitchen.

Sure enough, he was leaning against the counter at the far end of the small, galley-style kitchen, smoking a cigarette. Just beyond him, beady little black eyes glinted at her through the glass in the back door, and after an instant's surprise, Nicky realized that she must be looking at the pig she'd seen Joe with on TV. Since, at the moment, she was far more interested in the man himself, she ignored the pet in favor of focusing on Joe. He was fully dressed in the same jeans and T-shirt he had discarded earlier, and like her, he was barefoot. His jaw was dark with five o'clock shadow, his hair was tousled, and he radiated attitude.

Now she was prepared to deal with it.

"Okay," she said, skirting the table that seemed to serve as both desk and eating area. "Now we talk."

He pulled the cigarette from his mouth.

"Hell, yeah, it was good for me." The falsely hearty tone grated. "How about you?" Then his mouth twisted and his voice returned to normal. "That what you had in mind?"

Nicky ignored what she recognized as a blatant attempt at provocation. Stopping in front of him, she crossed her arms over her chest and gave him the same direct look she would give any potentially difficult interview subject.

"This is where you tell me *your* side of the story."

Joe stuck the cigarette back in his mouth and took a long drag. He exhaled before answering, and the smoke curled around his head.

"What makes you think there is a *my side of the story*?"

"Isn't there?" The smell of smoke tickled Nicky's nostrils. Ordinarily, she hated the smell—but this was Joe.

"No, Pollyanna, there isn't."

Her eyes challenged him. "So all that stuff is true."

"Hey, I'm not admitting to a thing. The charges were dropped, remember? I sure don't want to get them reinstated."

"They were dropped due to a technicality."

He shrugged. "Worked for me."

"Don't you want to clear your name?"

"Not particularly."

"CNN is going to say that you took bribes from drug dealers to let them stay in business."

"I have no control over CNN. It can say whatever it wants."

"If it's not true, we can stop them. Or at least run a story giving your version of events."

"There is no *my version of events.* I've got nothing to say."

"That's ridiculous."

"Is it? What if I don't have a different version of events? What if their version of events is the only one there is?"

She narrowed her eyes at him. "I don't believe it."

"Don't believe what?"

"Any of it. That you were a dirty cop. It just doesn't ring true."

He stared at her for a moment, sighed, and ground his cigarette out in the ashtray beside him before looking at her again.

"I think what you've got here is a bad case of afterglow. Just because you slept with me doesn't make me a saint."

A beat passed. Nicky could feel herself starting to simmer. His attitude, she realized, was beginning to get to her—big-time.

"Fine." She turned on her heel and left the kitchen. "I don't need you to tell me anything. I'll find out on my own."

"Wait a minute." He followed, as she had fully expected him to do. She was already picking up her shoes as he walked into the living room and stopped, frowning at her. "Where are you going?"

"I have work to do." Balancing on one foot, she slipped the other foot into her shoe. "Oh, by the way, the sex was great for me, too."

"Nicky." There was an underlying harshness to his tone that made her glance up at him as she stood on one leg like a flamingo and put on her second shoe. "You leave my past alone. It's none of your business."

"It is if we're going to have a relationship."

His brows snapped together. He folded his arms over his chest. "Who said we're going to have a relationship? Honey, just for the record, I don't do relationships."

Her lips compressed and, feet firmly in her shoes now, she headed for the door. "We're in one. You're in denial. Get out of my way. I'm leaving."

"Hold on." He caught her arm as she went past him, turned her around, and zipped her dress the rest of the way up before she could protest. "And by the way, I damn well am not in denial. Having sex once does not equal a relationship."

The words stung. Stiffening, she pulled away, opened the door, and glared back at him.

"Good to know," she said with bite, and stepped out into the still-steamy night.

19

JOE STOOD ON his front stoop, watching Nicky stalk (there was no other word for it) down his poor, neglected lawn toward her car and had to stop himself from going after her. There wasn't any need for it. Milton was still waiting patiently in his cruiser—a glance at his watch told Joe she'd been inside for maybe an hour and a half—and Joe saw him quite clearly as he opened his door and stepped out onto the street for a moment to say something to Nicky. Then he saw the light come on in her car as she opened the driver's door, saw her glance prudently into the backseat, and saw her close the door, turn the lights on, and drive away, with Milton in patient pursuit.

She was safe.

Only then did Joe go back inside his house, feeling more on edge than he had in a long time. Introspection wasn't his thing—he wasn't much into exploring his inner landscape, as one of the shrinks they'd sent him to had put it—but he had experienced this particular sensation a time or two before, so he knew it for what it was: the deep, soul-wrenching loneliness that came from realizing that in this world of couples and families and webs of connected hearts, there was nobody, not one single solitary soul, he could truly call his own.

We're in one, Nicky had said, meaning a relationship. The idea spooked him. As he'd told her, he didn't do relationships. He wasn't good at them. He'd been a one-man show for so long that the idea of linking up with someone else gave him the heebie-jeebies. To use shrink-speak again: Call him a commitment-phobe.

If you cared for somebody, then you were vulnerable. You could be ten feet tall and bulletproof. The other person is your Achilles heel, your exposed backside, your weak point—the thing that could destroy you.

He'd gone that route before. He wasn't going there a second time. The thought of being that vulnerable again made his gut clench.

That meant that this thing with Nicky—this "relationship," as she called it—needed to be put in the deep freeze fast, before it had a chance to spiral totally out of control.

In other words, smart guy, you need to stay out of her pants.

And this bummer of a realization, he thought with disgust, was coming right on the heels of the best sex he'd had in two years. Okay, make that the only sex he'd had in two years. Still, even without the burnish of months of damped-down desire, the sex had been phenomenal.

The thing was, the girl was phenomenal, too: gorgeous, smart, feisty, funny, and capable of turning him on with nothing more than a single glance from those come-hither brown eyes—the kind of girl a guy like him could go a lifetime without finding.

The kicker was that she believed in him. That was what got to him, hit him right in his wary, battle-scarred heart like a bullet with his name scratched on it.

Guys he'd worked with for years, girlfriends, ex-girlfriends, neighbors, you name it, none of them had questioned whether or not he'd actually been guilty of the deeds that had been laid at his door. As far as he could tell, they'd just accepted the official version as the truth and gotten on with the program, not shunning him or anything, not denouncing him, just treating him like they always had, which probably said more about him than about them, really. He'd been a cocky son of a bitch, sure of the world and his place in it, sure that there was nothing life could throw at Joe Franconi that he couldn't handle, because he'd already handled everything. Or so he'd thought.

He'd been wrong. Superman had found his kryptonite. The mighty had fallen.

And Joe Franconi had found something that he couldn't handle after all. It had nearly killed him. But he had survived, and even managed to almost get himself put back together again.

No way was he going there again.

But now, in a turn of events that was as disconcerting as it was surprising, on no evidence at all, Nicky believed in him.

This was a woman to grab hold of and never let go.

The idea scared him silly.

"Women," Brian said. "They'll get you every time."

Joe glanced around sharply and discovered Brian, solid-looking as ever, disappearing into the kitchen.

Shit.

"Shut up, you," Joe snarled after him. "And stay the hell out of my bed-room."

"Hey." Brian's voice drifted back. "I know what you're thinking, but you're off base there, pal. I've got *some* standards."

None that Joe had ever been aware of, but then . . .

His cell phone began to ring.

"Chief, we got a confession," Cohen, the officer on duty at the station tonight, said through the phone. "I think you ought to come down here and listen to this."

ABOUT AN HOUR and a half later, when Nicky pulled up Twybee Cottage's driveway, she was still mad. If she'd been suffering from afterglow, as Joe had put it, he'd done a fine job of curing her of it. Only the thought that there might be a reason for his less-than-loverlike-après-sex behavior, that maybe he'd been copping the attitude in a deliberate effort to push her away, kept her from mentally washing her hands of him then and there.

That and the sad fact that she was actually kind of crazy about the guy, attitude or not.

The more she thought about it, the more certain she was that the story CNN was getting ready to air was wrong. Joe's romantic side might need some tweaking, but every instinct she possessed told her that this was a stand-up guy. He was hard-working and decent, and actually kind of sweet beneath his macho cop exterior, and the idea that he took bribes or even looked the other way while drug deals were going down around him was impossible for her to believe. But she'd given him every chance, and he hadn't proclaimed his innocence, which, when she considered it, was one more tell-tale thing in his favor right there. In her experience, the guilty *always* proclaimed their innocence. It was the innocent who sometimes clung to the mantle of guilt, for a variety of reasons. Whatever the truth was, she was as sure as it was possible to be that she hadn't heard it yet. Joe obviously wasn't going to tell, so she would find out for herself, his "stay out of my business" be damned. She'd already put the wheels in motion to start digging deeper into his background. The great thing about having been a reporter for so many years was that she had friends in all kinds of places, and she knew all kinds of ways to get the dirt. If she couldn't get the inside scoop, nobody could.

In the meantime, she meant to put the fear of God into CNN in hopes of getting them to hold off on airing that story. She was going to see to it that word got to the company brass that there were serious problems with the factuality of the report. As for the reporter, she was pretty sure that backing him down would require no more than two little words: Dan Rather.

She meant to make sure that he heard them first thing the next morning.

For tonight, though, she was concentrating on Tara Mitchell. The ghostly image she'd seen in the window at the Old Taylor Place was permanently emblazoned in her mind, no matter how assiduously she tried to avoid thinking about it. Tara's ghost was the one most often seen; Tara had been channeled by Leonora, had come through in Nicky's own dreams, and her murder had been the catalyst for the nightmare of Karen and Marsha Browning's murders. Tara, Nicky was beginning to feel, was the linchpin to the case. In her quest to obtain a personal possession of Tara's for Leonora's use, she had been trying to contact Tara's family. So far, she couldn't find them. It was as if, when they'd left Pawleys Island, they had dropped off the face of the earth.

Of course, having their daughter murdered was bound to have caused all kinds of trauma to the family. Maybe the parents had split up. Maybe they'd left the country. There were a hundred and one good explanations for why they seemed to have disappeared.

But now she was curious. She needed to know what had become of them. She needed to find them in order to patch what was beginning to feel like a glaring hole in the fabric of the investigation.

After leaving Joe, she had gone to talk to a couple longtime residents who had known the Mitchells when they had lived on the island. She hadn't gotten a lot of information, but she'd gotten enough to give her a few fresh leads and make her curious to know the rest.

As soon as she got inside the house, she was going to follow up on those leads via computer.

With that intention in mind, Nicky parked in her usual spot beside Livvy's Jaguar and got out of the car, anxious to get inside and online while the interview she'd just completed was fresh in her mind. Her escort was right behind her; he would be pulling up the driveway any second. She didn't actually need to wait for his arrival to get out of her car, not when her family was clearly home and her back door was just a few yards away. Still, she walked quickly toward the steps. Her heels sank into the gravel, and she could hear the faint crunch of her own footsteps. She could hear, too, the roar of the sea

and the inevitable chorus of insects. Lights were on in the house, as usual—
she didn't think there was ever a time when *someone* wasn't home—and the
porch light was on, too. Its yellow glow made the night beyond the light seem
very dark.

As she rounded the front of Livvy's car, it occurred to Nicky that the
night *was* dark. A glance skyward told her why: A heavy cloud cover obscured both moon and stars. She registered the absence of a breeze, the
steamroom-like humidity, the sense of expectancy in the air. There would be
a storm before morning.

She had almost reached the back steps when an object just at the edge of
the circle of light caught her eye. Frowning, she looked closer and discerned
that the object was pink and about the size of a shoebox. Livvy must have
dropped something on her way into the house. . . .

Nicky walked over to it and bent to pick it up. Her hand was almost on it
when she saw what it was: Livvy's purse.

Livvy would never in a million years have dropped her purse in the driveway and just left it there.

"Liv?" Nicky picked up the purse and looked around uncertainly. She was
at the corner of the house now, and the magnolia tree loomed, wide and fra-
grant with waxy, white blossoms, to her left. Just beyond the magnolia, the
crepe myrtles running along the far side of the house added their distinctive
spicy scent to the night. There, near the bushes, about thirty feet away in the
dark, alley-like side yard, something moved.

"Livvy?"

The movement stopped. There was a moment—an instant, really—in
which everything was captured by the camera of her mind's eye as if in a
freeze-frame. During that moment, Nicky stared, uncomprehending. It was
dark as a cave there, in that corridor between the bushes and the house. She
could just barely discern a shape, hunched and vaguely triangular, rising from
the ground. She had the impression that it was a person and that it had turned
to look at her. Then the smell struck her. It had been there all along, an
earthy, musky aroma floating beneath the scent of crepe myrtles and magnolia and the sea, but she only realized what it was, and where she had smelled
it before, when something glinted silver in the darkness.

Then it hit her like a baseball bat to the stomach: The silver glint was a
knife. The scent, which she had smelled before on that nightmarish night under the pine trees, was blood.

Livvy's purse had been left on the ground. Now Nicky was holding it in
her hands.

Her heart lurched.

"Livvy!" Nicky screamed, hefting the purse like a weapon and charging toward the hunched figure as what she was looking at became all too hideously clear. Her sister—*her sister*—was being butchered before her eyes. *"No! Get away from her! Help! Help!"*

The figure leaped up and fled. It was a man—that was the one thing she was positive of. He seemed to be running hunched over, but from what she could discern through the darkness, he was unnaturally broad and bulky—and surprisingly fast. She could hear the dull thud of his feet on the grass.

"Help! Somebody help!"

"Police! Freeze!" bellowed a man's voice behind her, and Nicky realized that the cavalry had arrived in the form of her police escort as she dropped to her knees beside Livvy's motionless form lying curled in the fetal position in the cool, thick grass.

"Livvy," Nicky said urgently. Leaning over her sister, Nicky saw the still curve of her cheek, the slack mouth, the closed eyes, and felt time stop. Her heart pounded like a piston. Her blood turned to ice. Fear tasted sour in her mouth.

Oh, God, please, please, please . . .

As the silent prayer formed in her head, Nicky heard footsteps pounding toward her, felt the rush of someone running up behind her.

"Freeze!" the cop—Officer Milton—boomed over her head. She sensed more than saw that he had his weapon out and was in firing position above her, but it was too late: The killer had been swallowed up by the night.

Officer Milton said something that was directed at her, Nicky thought, but by then she was beyond making sense of mere words. Gasping with fear, she touched Livvy's shoulder, her neck, feeling for a pulse.

"Livvy."

If there was one, her shaking fingers couldn't find it. Livvy was still warm, though. She couldn't be dead.

Please, God, don't let her be dead. . . .

"Call an ambulance," Nicky screamed over her shoulder at the cop. He was already on his radio, shouting something into it. She could hear noises from the house, the bang of the screen door, the babble of voices, shouts. Her mother—her family—was running around the corner of the house toward them.

Oh, God, Livvy's baby . . .

"Livvy." Nicky gently placed a hand on her sister's swollen belly, then drew it back sharply as she encountered the warm stickiness of welling blood.

JOE DROVE TO THE SCENE faster than a fire truck on its way to a four-alarm. Pea gravel sprayed his cruiser as he fishtailed up the driveway. An ambulance blocked access to the parking area, its strobes lighting up the night. Beyond it, he could see a bustle of activity. Heart pounding, breathing like a runner on the last leg of a marathon, he flung himself out of his car and sprinted around the ambulance and toward the side of the house, which seemed to be the focus of activity. Fear drove his every step.

He'd been at the police station, talking to the local crazy who had walked in and confessed to the Karen Wise and Marsha Browning murders, when the call had come in that the Lazarus Killer had claimed a third victim at Twybee Cottage.

His blood had run cold. Terror had juiced his heart, knotted his stomach. He'd practically broken land-speed records getting here. Half the department was racing behind him, and they were still eating his dust.

"Chief . . ." A harried-looking Milton turned toward him as he rounded the corner of the house. A crowd of people milled around just ahead, talking, crying, praying, doing God knew what as they hovered in a loose semicircle around the body that was at that very moment being loaded onto a stretcher.

Horror was as palpable as the scent of blood in the air.

"You were supposed to be protecting her," Joe roared at Milton without ever breaking stride. Milton said something that Joe didn't catch. More people turned to look at him, to say something to him. He barely noticed, didn't hear. There was John, Ham, Leonora—oh, God, Ham had his arm around Leonora and she was crying like her heart would break. Harry was there, on the periphery as ever. . . .

"Nicky," Joe said hoarsely, coming to a stop beside the stretcher. There was a floodlight on the scene, illuminating excruciating details like the blood blooming on the blanket covering the victim and the pale limpness of one visible hand. Joe's eyes riveted on that hand as the paramedics secured the straps that would hold her in place.

His life seemed to pass before his eyes in those few seconds.

Then he saw that the hair of the woman on the stretcher was blond, not red.

Shocked, confused, suddenly too numb even to register relief, he saw another hand clasp the poor, limp hand on the stretcher. This hand was slender and lovely and pale. . . .

He followed the hand to its owner and found Nicky. She bent over the blonde on the stretcher, murmuring something, stroking her arm. Her eyes were huge and dark with grief; her mouth shook. Tears streamed down her cheeks, and her face was so white it could have been carved from alabaster. Blood smeared the front of her pretty green dress.

Finally he realized: The victim was Olivia.

And for one of the few times in his life, he had a moment when he thought he might pass out.

LIVVY WASN'T DEAD. As Nicky and Leonora rode to the hospital in the back of the speeding ambulance with Livvy, those were the words that pounded through Nicky's mind. Livvy was badly wounded, but she wasn't dead.

IV bags swayed, monitors glowed, and the smell of alcohol and blood filled the cramped space. Outside, the siren screamed and the night flying past the windows was a blur of black.

"I can't believe I didn't see it, I can't believe it, what good is this damned useless gift if I can't even see something like this happening to my own daughter?" Leonora wailed. Face awash in tears, she had one of Livvy's hands clutched in hers as she looked across the stretcher at Nicky. Nicky, who held Livvy's other hand, just shook her head. What good indeed.

Livvy, who had been as still and unresponsive as a mannequin since being loaded onto the stretcher, suddenly tensed and seemed to shiver. A low moan issued from beneath the oxygen mask strapped to her face.

"What's happening?" Nicky asked one of the two paramedics riding with them. The hollow rumble of the Causeway Bridge beneath them as the ambulance raced across it told her that they were still a good ten minutes from Georgetown County Hospital, which was their destination. The knowledge terrified her.

One of the paramedics checked his monitors and shook his head.

Livvy moaned again. Her head thrashed.

"Livvy," Nicky and her mother leaned close and said as one. Nicky's hand tightened on her sister's. On the other side, she was sure Leonora's grip had tightened, too.

"She may be going into labor," the paramedic said. "How far along is she?"

"Eight months," Nicky answered.

"Livvy, we're right here," Leonora said, stroking her daughter's limp hand. Then she began to pray: "Dear Lord, protect my baby. . . ."

Minutes later, the ambulance screeched to a halt. The doors opened, and the stretcher was rolled out. As Nicky helped Leonora to the ground, Livvy, now surrounded by medical personnel, was rushed through the doors of the hospital emergency room, which had been opened wide to receive her.

JOE WASN'T ABLE TO spend that night at the hospital with the group that gathered to wait for news of Livvy. He was, after all, a cop, and the top cop to boot, and it was his job to direct the investigation. An immediate search was launched for the attacker. Roadblocks were set up, the yards and dunes and beach near Twybee Cottage were searched, and a BOLO (Be On the Look Out) was issued for a suspicious person. Word of what had happened spread around the island like wildfire, and a crowd soon gathered around Twybee Cottage to gape. All kinds of media were on the scene, and Joe got to the point that he pretty much ignored them as long as they stayed outside the crime-scene tape.

Which, of course, they didn't do.

By morning, he and everyone else in the department were practically dead on their feet. He was running on pure adrenaline. By the time he reached the hospital, it was almost eight A.M. The storm that had threatened the previous night had passed over harmlessly, which was good news for the investigation. It meant that they were able to search the area where Livvy had been attacked by daylight for clues that might have been missed in the darkness; in the case of Karen Wise's murder, that opportunity had been lost because of rain.

Livvy was in the ICU on the fourth floor. Officer Andy Cohen was, as ordered, standing guard outside the door. Joe acknowledged him with a nod. A small crowd of relatives and friends were gathered in the waiting room beside the unit. Joe stepped inside and looked around. Ham, haggard and bleary-eyed like everyone else, got up from his chair and came over to him.

"Any idea who did it?" Ham asked quietly. But he was enough like Nicky that by now Joe could recognize certain signs: Ham had bloodlust in his eyes.

"No." Joe shook his head. "Where's Nicky?"

"In there with Leonora. Only two visitors allowed in ICU at a time."

"Think you could take her place for a while? I need her."

Ham nodded and accompanied him into the unit.

The hospital smell was stronger once they went through the swinging door. The color scheme remained the same: gray, gray, and more gray. Nicky was sitting in a molded plastic chair pulled up beside Livvy's bed. Leonora was in a similar chair beside her. Both women looked limp and drained. Livvy was motionless under a institutional gray blanket. Liquid dripped steadily from an IV unit into her arm, and the monitors surrounding the bed emitted steady droning sounds. Joe assumed that this was a good sign, because if it hadn't been, he knew Nicky and Leonora would have been giving off panicked vibes. Instead, they were just sitting quietly, not even talking, just staring at the bundled shape that was Livvy.

A nurse started toward him as he entered. He flashed his badge without breaking stride, and then Nicky looked around and saw him. Her eyes lit up, and a faint smile curved her lips. She said something to Leonora, who looked around and saw him, too. Then Nicky stood up and moved toward him, all slender, tragic grace.

Joe saw that she was still wearing the bloodstained green dress.

And in that moment, he acknowledged something that he'd been trying to avoid facing for the past ten hours.

For the second time in his life, he had a weak spot. Nicky had made him vulnerable again.

"YOU DID *WHAT*?" Joe yelped, hitting the brakes a little harder than the action called for. Pea gravel crunched. In the passenger seat beside him, Nicky clutched the armrest instinctively. As his cruiser slid to a stop, his head slewed around so that he was staring at her in disbelief. They had just pulled up into the parking area at Twybee Cottage. At Joe's request, Nicky, who had already given an official statement, was telling him about what had happened after she had found Livvy's purse the previous night.

"I started yelling for help and ran toward them." Nicky unbuckled her seat belt and reached for the door handle.

"Jesus Christ." Joe closed his eyes briefly, then opened them again to look at her. "Let me get this straight: You saw the killer, you saw the knife. You knew he was there. And you *ran toward him*? Do you have a death wish or what?"

"He was murdering my sister." Nicky opened the door and got out. She was so tired that her legs were wobbly. There was a funny little buzzing in her ears. Her head hurt. Even so early in the morning, it was already close to eighty degrees, with no breeze to speak of. The heat felt good, though. She realized that she hadn't felt warm since finding Livvy last night.

"Milton was right behind you. The smart thing to do would have been wait for him. I mean, consider the difference. You're a hundred-twenty-pound girl armed with a purse. He's a two-hundred-fifty-pound cop armed with a gun."

Joe fell in beside her as she skirted around the assortment of official-type vehicles with which the parking area was jammed to head for the back steps.

"If I hadn't gotten there when I did, he would have killed her. As it was, he almost did."

Nicky remembered the warm rush of Livvy's blood against her hand and felt cold all over again. Joe must have seen something of her emotions in her face, because he grimaced and shut up. Just beyond the magnolia, yellow crime-scene tape blocked access to the side yard. Cops and other official types were moving around inside it.

"Joe," somebody called, and Nicky looked over to see Dave ducking under the barrier.

"Yeah." Joe caught her hand, preventing her from going up the steps without him as he turned to wait for Dave.

"How's Livvy doing?" Dave asked, directing his question to Nicky. His round face was pale beneath its perpetual tan, and there were bags under his eyes. Like the rest of them, he clearly was operating on no sleep.

"She's holding her own. The doctors said that if she makes it through the first twenty-four hours, she has a good chance."

"We're all praying for her."

Nicky smiled at him. "Thanks."

"Did you want me for something?" Joe asked him pointedly.

"We got a neighbor on the next street over who says she was driving along when she saw a man jump in a car parked on the side of the street and take off like he needed to be somewhere in a hurry. It was about the right time. I think this may be our guy."

"She get a description?" Joe asked. His hand was warm and strong around hers, keeping her firmly at his side.

"Nah. It was too dark. But. . . ." He paused, and a triumphant smile lit his tired face. "She got a partial license-plate number."

"Way to go, lady." Joe's hand tightened on Nicky's, and his mouth quirked into a half smile. "Track it down."

"Will do." Dave fell back, and Joe followed Nicky into the house. For the first time since she could remember, it was empty. Everyone was at the hospital. The vast echoing silence of the place was almost eerie.

Upstairs in her bedroom, Nicky's heart started to pound as she turned on her laptop. It was for this that Joe had pulled her away from the hospital. She was very conscious of him behind her as the screen glowed blue, and she hit the icon to check her e-mail.

There it was.

> *This lesson well you should learn*
> *You only get back what you earn.*
> *Watching, waiting, always out of sight*
> *Death has sent his chosen into that long eternal night.*

It was signed Lazarus525.

Last night, the date Livvy had been attacked.

Tears stung Nicky's eyes. Her head throbbed. Her stomach roiled. She curled both hands around the top slat of the ladderback desk chair and squeezed hard.

I won't cry. . . .

"Nicky." Clearly moved by her distress, Joe gently gripped her bare upper arms. His voice was low and deep. "Nick."

Nicky's hands tightened around the chair as a hot, blinding tide of anger flooded her veins. The image of Livvy lying helpless and bleeding on the ground rose in her mind's eye. It made her want to jump through that computer screen and find the animal who had hurt her and rip him apart with her bare hands.

"I'm going to find you," she said softly to Lazarus525. "I don't care what I have to do, or how long it takes. I'll get you, I swear."

"Nicky." Joe's hands tightened on her arms and he gently tugged her back a pace, away from the computer screen. She obediently let go of the chair, clenching her hands into fists instead as he turned her around to face him. Still so angry that she was trembling with it, she looked up to meet his gaze. His mouth tightened at what he saw in her face, and his eyes turned dark with compassion for her.

"I'm so sorry, honey," he said, and wrapped his arms around her. For the briefest of moments, she stayed stiff with anger in his embrace, but then she slowly relaxed. Bit by incremental bit, she allowed his warmth, his strength, the mere fact that he was there with her, *for* her, to soothe her. Resting against him, she slid her arms around his waist. Letting her head drop to his chest, she closed her eyes.

"So sorry," he murmured again. Nicky felt what she thought was the brush of his mouth against her hair.

"We need to catch him," she said.

"We'll catch him." Joe's tone was soothing. "It's just a matter of when. He won't get away with this."

Her trembling had almost stopped. Nicky stayed where she was for a moment longer, absorbing his heat, absorbing his comfort, then took a deep, steadying breath and opened her eyes.

"We have to work fast." Her voice was surprisingly calm and strong. "He may disappear again. Notice he says 'Death *has* sent his chosen.' He's got his three."

"Maybe. Maybe not. Your sister isn't dead."

"No." Nicky drew strength from that thought. "She's not."

Okay, enough of the pity party. Letting her emotions take over did no one any good, least of all Livvy. Pulling out of Joe's arms, Nicky managed a brief smile for him.

"I want to take a quick shower and change clothes, and maybe grab a few things for my mother. Then I need to head back to the hospital. Will you wait for me?"

Joe's mouth quirked, and his eyes met hers.

"Count on it," he said.

WHILE NICKY SHOWERED and changed, Joe did a quick search of the upstairs rooms and then headed downstairs, where he also did a quick search of the premises. It didn't take long to make sure that except for Nicky and himself, the house was empty. Even though it was broad daylight and about a dozen cops were walking around outside while he was in the house, he was taking no chances. Relying on what he thought he knew just might be enough to get Nicky killed.

His blood ran cold at the thought.

He hadn't seen it coming, it was the last thing he wanted, but it was also too late to do anything about it: Good old Achilles had grown another heel, and it was showering upstairs. That being the case, he meant to make damned sure she stayed alive.

He hadn't seen what had happened to Livvy coming, either. Livvy didn't fit the profile of the other victims. She wasn't single, she didn't live alone, and she wasn't involved with the media. She'd been attacked on a Wednesday night. The other two had been attacked over the weekend. She was hugely pregnant. Of course, the soon-to-be-ex-husband, trying to pull off a copycat attack, was a possibility as a suspect. According to Dave, the man had made a complaint about Livvy assaulting him on the night of Marsha Browning's murder, which had never gotten followed up on because (a) the witnesses, all Livvy's family members, swore a blue streak that he'd been hit by a falling tree branch, and (b) the police were simply too busy. But Joe didn't think the ex had anything to do with it. He was virtually certain the attack was the work of the Lazarus Killer (hell, now Nicky had him calling the perp that, too), and he also thought it was very possible that Livvy hadn't been the intended target: It seemed more likely that the perp had been after Nicky.

Perhaps Livvy had seen him skulking in the shadows, and the perp had been forced to act sooner than he had planned.

That would explain certain things, like the dropped purse on the parking area, the midweek timing, and the fact that the attack had a hurried, almost improvised, feel to it—the most glaring evidence of which was the fact that it had not succeeded.

Joe's phone started to ring. He pulled it out, glanced down at the incoming number, and felt his pulse quicken.

He'd been waiting for this call.

"Yo," Joe answered.

"I got that tape enhanced for you."

"Yeah?"

"The girl starts off with 'Hello,' and then she listens. Then she says, 'I meant every word I said. And I'm not backing down.' She listens, says, 'I can't hear you; you'll have to speak up.' She listens again, says, 'Oh, that's what I was hoping you'd say. What? There's static—I can't really hear.' And then she listens one more time and says, 'Fine. That's good. What? All right, I'm going to walk outside and see if that helps.' And that's it."

Not much. Definitely no smoking gun, of course. When was life ever that easy?

"That help?"

"Maybe," Joe said. "Can you overnight me a copy of that?"

"You got it."

"I appreciate your help. Thanks."

"No problem."

Joe disconnected, thought for a second, then walked over to the back door—his perambulations had taken him into the kitchen by the time the phone rang—and opened it. Then he yelled for Dave. Going to find him wasn't an option. No way was he stepping outside the house while Nicky was alone in it.

"You finished checking those phone records yet?" he asked Dave without preamble as soon as he stepped into the kitchen.

"Almost. The last three people I spoke to mentioned hearing static, by the way. The funny thing about it is, one of them was on Marsha Browning's call list, and there was never any suggestion of static in the Browning case."

Joe felt a spurt of disgust. "I'm not surprised." He could thank Nicky and her show for that. Put an idea like that out into the collective consciousness, and it stuck like a burr in every mind that heard it. "Okay, I know we're swamped here, but that needs to be finished ASAP. And we need to start rechecking alibis."

Dave looked troubled. "You really think we're going to catch this guy?"

"Yeah," Joe said. Then his phone started to ring again. He glanced at the number, frowned, and answered.

Nicky walked into the kitchen just as he disconnected. She was still pale and drawn-looking but clean, with her beautiful hair all smooth and shiny and a touch of lipstick on her mouth. She was wearing a chocolate-colored tank top and matching pants and looked, literally, good enough to eat.

Joe hated what he had to tell her.

"That was your mother," he said, knowing that there was no way to make hearing this any easier for her. "We need to get you back to the hospital right away. There's a crisis with Livvy."

20

LIVVY'S DAUGHTER WAS BORN by Caesarean section at 5:18 p.m. With Livvy battling for her life, the doctors felt that taking the baby was the only option. The newborn was immediately whisked away to the neonatal ICU, more as a precaution than anything, as her life wasn't felt to be in danger. Livvy's soon-to-be-ex, Ben, who had shown up at the hospital several hours before, followed to stand watch over the infant, and a group—which apparently didn't include the bimbo, as neither Leonora nor Uncle Ham went ballistic—arrived to stay with him. Almost beside herself with anxiety, Leonora went back and forth between her daughter and granddaughter, and Nicky stayed with Livvy.

All through the night, she sat beside her sister's bed, holding her hand, listening to the beep and whir of the monitors, and praying like she had never prayed before.

Around four A.M., Livvy moved and made a small guttural sound. Alarmed, Nicky stood up and leaned over her.

"Liv?"

To Nicky's surprise, Livvy opened her eyes. Their gazes met.

"My baby?" It was a reedy whisper, sounding nothing at all like Livvy's usual voice.

"She's fine. You don't have to worry."

Livvy's hold on Nicky's hand tightened.

"Pinky swear?"

Nicky felt her throat start to close up. "Pinky swear."

The faintest of smiles just touched Livvy's mouth. Then she closed her eyes.

THE OTHER CALL Joe had been waiting for came in about eight A.M. Friday morning.

"Want the good news or the bad news?" his caller asked.

Joe grunted. "You mean there's actually some good news? You're already making my day."

"That untraceable e-mail address? Traced it."

"Yee-haw." Despite the complete and utter exhaustion that went hand-in-hand with having had almost no sleep for two and a half days, Joe felt a welling of excitement. "So, where'd it come from?"

"It started out with a free Bigfoot account, got encrypted, bounced around Asia a little bit, got encrypted again—"

"Can we cut to the chase?" Joe asked. "Things are kind of hopping here."

"Cutting to the chase brings us to the bad-news part."

"Shit."

"Yeah. Bottom line is, your e-mails originated from the Free Public Library in Charleston. Main branch. Original sender name was Mr. Potato Head. I could probably break it down to a specific computer for each e-mail for you, but I don't think it would do you much good. You know how many people use the computers in there each day?"

"Too damn many," Joe said glumly. "But at least it's a place to start."

He hung up and placed a call to the Charleston police.

NICKY AND LEONORA and Uncle Ham and Uncle John and Harry and Marisa and the police guards Joe had assigned to stand watch and God knew who else all stayed at the hospital until about three P.M. Friday, when Livvy's doctors said that it looked as though she was going to make it. By then, the strain was showing on everyone. Leonora broke down and cried. Nicky insisted that her mother go home and rest, and Leonora agreed to do so as long as Nicky promised to go home and sleep when she came back. This Nicky agreed to, and they, along with Uncle Ham and Uncle John and a few others, quickly worked out a loose schedule so that Livvy and the baby would not be left alone. Then Leonora left. By the time she came back, accompanied by

Uncle Ham and Joe, Nicky was so tired that she could hardly get up out of her chair.

"How is she?" Leonora asked.

"Better," Nicky answered. "She asked for water twice, and the baby once, so I think she's doing pretty well, considering."

"They've got her heavily sedated, you know," Uncle Ham said. "The doctor said they were going to start weaning her off it tomorrow."

"Come on." Joe slid a hand around Nicky's elbow. "You look like you're about to fall down. You need sleep."

Coming from a man whose face was gray with fatigue, this was something like the pot calling the kettle black, but Nicky was too tired to point it out. Anyway, she did need sleep—desperately. It was kind of touch and go as to whether her legs would support her all the way to Joe's car.

On the way to the elevators, they passed by the newborn nursery. Tired as she was, Nicky stopped for a moment to look through the glass. Hayley Rose—that was the name Livvy had chosen weeks before—appeared peacefully asleep in her incubator. She was tiny, red-faced, and wrinkled, with a little pink knit cap pulled down low over her brow. Livvy hadn't seen her yet. *Your mommy is going to love you*, Nicky told her new niece silently. Then, as the nurse inside the baby ward frowned at her through the glass and Joe tugged at her arm, she moved on.

The warm, sweet rush of fresh air that greeted her as she stepped outside the hospital for the first time in almost thirty-six hours revived Nicky to some degree. It was just after eleven P.M., and beyond the frosty halogens that lit up the parking lot, the night was still and dark. *Still and dark* had the power to spook Nicky now, so she held on to Joe's hand tightly and stayed close by his side all the way to his cruiser. It was possible that the Lazarus Killer had fulfilled whatever mission he was on and was even now in the process of fading away into the shadows for another fifteen years, but she wasn't ready to bet her life on it. Anyway, as Joe had pointed out, he had promised to kill three, and only two were dead. That knowledge gave her the shivers.

They reached the car, and Joe opened her door for her, then closed it as she settled in. By the time he slid into the driver's seat, Nicky had her seat belt on and her head was resting back against the smooth, faux-leather seat. Yawning, she inhaled the scent of plastic and coffee and cigarette smoke, which was what the inside of Joe's police car smelled like.

She was *so* tired. She couldn't remember ever being this tired.

"So, did anybody ever track down that partial license-plate number Dave was so excited about?" Nicky asked as Joe started the car.

Joe grimaced. "It was a rental. The guy was a tourist who was rushing off to a pharmacy to pick up a prescription for his kid's ear infection. Everything checked out."

"Oh," Nicky said, disappointed. "What about—"

"Wait." Joe pulled out of the lot. "Whoa. I'm not talking about this anymore tonight. I need a break, and so do you. You hungry?"

"A little. Mostly I'm just tired."

"Yeah, me, too."

He definitely looked it, she thought, taking in the lines of fatigue around his mouth and eyes and the unshaven stubble darkening his chin. His red power tie was loose, his white shirt unbuttoned at the throat, and his navy jacket and khaki slacks were badly creased.

"Did you sleep last night?" she asked.

"Some." He glanced her way with a half-smile. "How about you?"

"Some." It was by accidentally falling asleep in her chair at Livvy's bedside, which had resulted in a series of ten- or fifteen-minute catnaps interrupted by nurses, monitors, or wandering relatives. "I was kind of afraid to close my eyes. I kept thinking that if I quit watching Livvy, she might slip away."

"The doctors say she's going to make it."

"I know."

"By the way, in case I forgot to mention it while I was yelling at you for it, I think that was a hell of a brave thing you did, charging Livvy's attacker like that," Joe said. He glanced at her. "Stupid, but brave."

Nicky's eyelids were growing heavy. Lulled by the motion of the car, she blinked owlishly at him. "Hey, she's my sister. And if that was supposed to be a compliment, it kind of sucked."

His smile widened. "Yeah, well, bravery's a fine thing, but so is good sense."

Nicky made a face at him. She was simply too tired to argue.

They were driving over the South Causeway Bridge now, and the hollow rumble was oddly comforting. It was a sound she associated with going home. Below the bridge, Salt Marsh Creek gleamed like oil in the moonlight. Overhead, the sky was a softer black, ablaze with stars. She was just admiring the beauty of the pale sickle moon when she realized that they were turning the wrong way.

She frowned. "Where are you going?"

He glanced at her. "My house. You're spending the night. Probably several nights. With everybody running back and forth to the hospital and all the investigative work still going on at Twybee Cottage, I figure it's safer for you to stay with me than me to stay with you."

Nicky considered. "All my clothes and things are at Twybee Cottage."

"No, they're not. Your mother packed you a bag. It's in the trunk."

"You got my mother's permission for me to sleep at your house?" For some reason, Nicky found this amusing. Tired as she was, she had to smile.

"She thought it was a good idea."

"My mother likes you."

"I like your mother." He pulled over to the curb and parked, and Nicky saw that they were in front of his house. He got out, and she got out, too, waiting while he got her suitcase from the trunk. Then they went inside.

Joe shut the door, dropped her case on the floor, and flipped on the living-room light.

Nicky suddenly felt a little awkward. The house had two bedrooms, she knew. She wanted to sleep with Joe, but she remembered that they had been on the outs before Livvy had been attacked. Maybe she should opt for the spare bedroom. . . .

She could clearly hear Joe saying it: I don't do relationships.

She was too tired to get mad, too tired to do anything at all, so she sank down on the couch, which was tan corduroy, a little worn, a little lumpy, definitely well used. On one side of it was a navy plaid recliner, on the other an orange tweed rocker, neither one of them new. Joe headed for the kitchen, taking off his jacket as he went. Beneath it, she saw that he was wearing a black nylon shoulder holster over his white shirt. It made him look tough and capable and very masculine. And sexy. Way sexy.

"Want some eggs?" He called over his shoulder as he walked into the kitchen, turning on the light as he went. "Or a bologna sandwich?"

"You cook?" She settled deeper into the couch.

"Mostly just when I want to eat." His voice floated back to her. "You like 'em scrambled?"

"Sounds good." Nicky thought about going into the kitchen to help him, but she was just too tired to move. She thought about picking up the remote on the coffee table and turning on the TV, but she was too tired for that, too. In the kitchen, she could hear him moving around, opening the refrigerator, rattling cutlery . . .

HIS COOKING WAS a poor, pitiful thing compared to the delicacies Nicky was probably used to, staying in the same house as her Uncle Ham, but food was food and Joe was hungry. When the eggs were done—he'd made toast, too, although with the pig looking through the window at him every time he cooked, he'd quit with the bacon a couple days ago—he called Nicky. When she didn't answer, he went into the living room to get her.

She was asleep on his couch. Sitting up, head resting back against the cushions so that her glorious hair fanned out around her face, lashes forming thick, black crescents against milky skin, luscious lips slightly parted—and gentle snores issuing from between them.

Joe grinned. He walked over to the couch. For a long moment, he simply stood looking down at her, enjoying her beauty, enjoying the slightly ridiculous, wholly endearing picture she made. Then it occurred to him that he was feeling all warm and fuzzy inside, which wasn't a state he was either used to or comfortable with, and the reason was zonked out on his couch. His grin faded. He was in trouble here, already way too entangled with this girl, and his best course of action would be to cut and run before he got sucked in any further.

Unfortunately, cutting and running was impossible. She was in his house, asleep on his couch, and the reason she was there was because it was his job to keep her alive.

That being the case, he was left with three options: He could wake her and see if she was still hungry for eggs, he could leave her where she was, or he could carry her off to bed.

He chose the last one, picking her up carefully so as not to wake her. Not that there was much fear of that. She was a dead weight in his arms—surprising how heavy a hundred twenty pounds could feel—and she didn't so much as miss a snore while he maneuvered her through his open bedroom door and put her down on the bed. She was wearing white jeans and a pale yellow T-shirt and sandals with little bitty heels. The bedroom light was off, but he could see her well enough because of the light spilling in through the open bedroom door. He cast a quick look around—no Brian anywhere in sight—and considered.

He could let her sleep in her clothes. On the other hand, she would be far more comfortable without them.

Slipping off her shoes, he set them on the floor beside the bed. Then he unbuttoned and unzipped her jeans and pulled them down her legs. She wore tiny, deep-red panties, he was interested to see, that made the curve of her hips and the slender length of her legs look sexy as hell. His body's reaction was instant and automatic, and he grimaced as he tossed her jeans over the chair in the corner. That left her T-shirt. Getting that off was more of a struggle, but he managed and was rewarded by the sight of her gorgeous, creamy breasts in an itty-bitty bra. The deep-red color looked fantastic against her pale skin. Something—either the laboring breath of the air conditioner blowing across the bed or her subconscious reaction to his touch (he preferred to think)—made her nipples jut visibly through the flimsy fabric of her bra. She was smiling faintly in her sleep, and the temptation was almost overwhelming. More than he had ever wanted to do just about anything in his life, he wanted to crawl into bed with her and kiss her awake and . . .

She'd been through a terrible trauma, and she was dead tired. Sleep was what she needed, not sex.

That being the case, and also because he was a really good guy and a true credit to the fortitude and willpower of the red-blooded American male, he bundled her under the covers and left her to sleep.

And he went back into the kitchen to feed the pig a plateful of cold, greasy eggs.

NICKY SLEPT DREAMLESSLY until the sensation of a warm, firm mouth pressing down on hers woke her with a start.

She stiffened, and her eyes flew open.

"Hey, sweet thing, it's eight o'clock." Joe straightened away from her. For a moment she goggled at him, disoriented. He was fully dressed except for his jacket, and was in the process of sliding his knotted tie up to his shirt collar. He smelled good—like soap and toothpaste. He looked good, fresh out of the shower, clean shaven, with his hair brushed and his clothes pressed. He looked, in fact, like a man who had enjoyed a good night's sleep, and as Nicky cast an eye around the room, she realized that they were in his bedroom and he had, in fact, slept with her.

And she didn't remember a thing.

Oh, wait, she did remember something. She had told her mother that she would be back at the hospital by nine.

She groaned.

She was still wearing her bra and panties, she discovered as she scooted a little higher against the pillows while still keeping the covers she'd been burrowed under more or less in place across her chest. Which meant that Joe must have undressed her—but not all the way.

So he was a gentleman, was he? A slight smile curved her mouth. He could cop an attitude all he wanted; she was going to get to the truth about her big, bad cop anyway.

"I've got to go to work." Joe was strapping on his shoulder holster, which he had retrieved from the night table. "Dave's in the kitchen. He's going to drive you to the hospital and stay with you until three. Then Andy Cohen is going to take over until eleven, by which time I'll be back here and, presumably, you will be, too. I want you to promise me that no matter what, you won't go anywhere without one of them with you."

"Don't worry," Nicky said fervently, watching with interest as he checked his gun before tucking it securely in the holster.

"I do worry. And I want you to keep in mind that this Lazarus guy still doesn't have his number three." Joe picked up his jacket from the armchair in the corner and shrugged into it. There was something extremely intimate about lying in his bed and watching him dress, Nicky realized as her body tightened and a little tingle ran down the insides of her thighs. Then she remembered him saying "I don't do relationships" and clamped down on her way-too-forgetful body. "I'm going to give you a key so you can come and go as you please."

Joe picked up his keys from the night table and extracted a key from the ring. He held it up so that she could see it, then put it back down beside the lamp.

"Try to be careful, would you, please?" There was a wryness to his tone and an almost regretful gleam in his eyes as they ran over her. Then he was gone.

Nicky lay there for a moment longer, savoring the feeling of being rested, of being relatively free of worry about Livvy, of being warm and comfortable in Joe's bed. She could see the indentation from his head in the pillow beside hers and could tell from its position and her own that they had slept snuggled together. Her body had probably been attracted to his during the night like metal to a magnet.

Just the thought of it was turning her on, so she quit thinking about it and got out of bed. Her suitcase was leaning against the wall near the door, and Nicky felt another little glimmer of warmth for him as she registered that he had very thoughtfully put it where it was most convenient for her, especially considering that Dave was somewhere in the house. Chalking up one more sliver of evidence that the Joe she had come to know was not the Joe that Sarah Greenberg had described, she extracted some clothes and toiletries from the suitcase and headed for the shower. Fifteen minutes later, following the smell of coffee, she walked into the kitchen.

The back door was open, and Dave, in full uniform, was crouched just outside on the deck, apparently in earnest conversation with the pig. They were just about eye level, almost nose to snout, and Dave seemed to be chatting away.

Curiosity trumped even the lure of coffee. Nicky stepped out on the deck. It was a beautiful late-spring morning, she saw, sunny and just hot enough to be pleasant. The backyard was small, fenced, and dominated by a large black gum tree and a gorgeous stand of sunflowers. The deck was smaller still, maybe eight by twelve feet, with an octagon-shaped wooden table and benches and a pair of deck chairs—and Dave and a pig.

"Good morning." Dave glanced up at her with a quick smile and got to his feet. He, too, looked much more rested than the last time she had seen him. Last night must have provided a lull in which they had all gotten some much-needed sleep.

"H-hi." The stutter was because of the pig, which came snuffling around her legs. As she was wearing a short tangerine sundress and sandals, she could feel the animal's warm, moist breath against her skin. The sensation was disconcerting.

Her experience of pets had been pretty much limited to dogs and cats. She knew nothing about pigs.

"Have you met Cleo?" Dave regarded the animal fondly as it checked out the brightly colored beads that decorated Nicky's shoes. Since she wasn't quite sure what its intentions were toward the beads, and it clearly seemed to like shiny colored things, she curled her manicured toes as close to the soles of her shoes as they would go and gave it a clumsy pat on the head. Its black hair felt wiry and smooth. Its ears twitched in acknowledgment, and its little corkscrew tail gave a wag.

Think dog, Nicky told herself, *with hooves and the snuffles.*

"Not formally. I've seen her through the window. And on TV." Even with the pig still eyeing her beaded feet, Nicky had to smile at the memory.

Dave grinned, too. "Joe took some heat for that, didn't he? I felt bad."

"You felt bad?"

"Yeah. He was kind of doing me a favor to let her stay here."

Understanding dawned in a flash. "You mean it's *your* pig?"

"Yeah, she's mine. But my girlfriend doesn't really like her and, well, what with one thing and another, Joe said she could stay here."

"How . . . nice of him." Nicky thought of all the grief Joe had endured at the hands of the media because of the whole police-chief-with-pet-pig thing and shook her head. He had never once, not even to her, said that the animal wasn't his. That, she was coming to realize, was typical Joe: never complain, never explain.

"He's a good guy." Dave reached for something on the table. "Here, give her some bologna. She'll be your friend for life."

He thrust a slice of bologna at her, and Nicky, a little slow on the uptake that morning, took it. She had just begun to register the cold, slimy feel of the meat in her hand when the sensation was replaced by the insistent thrust of a warm, velvety muzzle. Nicky glanced down at the pig, who was going for the lunch meat with gusto, and realized it was eating out of her hand.

She dropped the bologna like it was on fire.

"See, she likes you," Dave said, as Cleo, having swallowed the last morsel, snuffled at Nicky's fingers for more.

"Good pig," Nicky said, curling her hands into fists. Cleo, disappointed, turned her attention back to the beads. Nicky patted the animal on the head again and escaped indoors.

INSIDE THE POLICE STATION, Joe felt as though he was in the center of a wagon train being circled by marauding Indians. Like mushrooms after a rain, the number of media on the scene had exploded after word of the attack on a third victim—Livvy—got out. Through the squad room's pair of grimy windows, he could see white tents being pitched on the lawn of the courthouse across the street. Blue beach umbrellas sheltered other teams of reporters from the sun. Trucks with satellite dishes roamed the streets. He'd already fielded one call from a local citizen that morning, who'd asked if accepting the payment the tabloids were offering for stories about the victims was legal. Just a few minutes before, a reporter from *The National Enquirer* had walked into the police station and started asking questions. The cop on duty at the desk, Laura Cramer, a rookie, had even given him some answers in sheer surprise before recovering her wits and escorting him outside.

"I don't believe this," Vince moaned. He was on the other end of the phone call that Joe was trying to end. "I got reporters on my front steps. They want a statement. What am I supposed to say, we got no fucking clue?"

"Try 'no comment,'" Joe advised. "It works for me."

When his cell phone had rung, he'd been seated at his desk, going over the lab results that had just come back. Now as he talked he was prowling through the station, looking out the windows, trying to decide the best route to take to escape to his car without being ambushed by a mob of reporters the moment he stepped out the door. The good news was that they had DNA from both the Karen Wise and Marsha Browning crime scenes, and it matched. The bad news was that it didn't match anything else in the system. If they got the guy, they were in business: The DNA profile could nail his ass to the wall. But until they got him, it was useless.

And the further bad news was that there was no DNA from the Tara Mitchell case to compare it with. If there had ever been any evidence that they might have extracted DNA from, it had long since been lost.

Vince was still bitching in his ear. "You're not an elected official. The town council *hired* you. And just remember, the thing about being hired is you can be fired again pretty damn quick."

"You trying to tell me my job's in jeopardy here, Vince?"

Vince snorted. "It would be, except then I'd have to get another police chief in here to handle this thing. By the time he got up to speed, the tourist season would be damn well over."

"Thanks for the vote of confidence." Joe's voice was dry.

"Yeah, well—"

The blip that signaled that he had another call trying to get through interrupted. A glance at the number told Joe that this was a call he needed to take.

"I gotta go, Vince. I've got another call coming in. It's important." Joe hung up on Vince and connected with the new caller. It was Detective Charlie Bugliosi with the Charleston PD.

"You're in luck: There's a bank across the street from the library, and they've got surveillance cameras on the ATMs twenty-four-seven. And guess what else it catches?"

"You tell me." Joe felt his pulse quicken with anticipation.

"The library's front entrance. There's a back entrance, but not a whole lot of people use it. And the bank recycles the tapes once a week, but . . ."

The meaning was clear: Livvy's attacker might very well have been caught on tape as he had entered the library to send the e-mail.

Once again, this proved that being lucky was sometimes much better than being good.

"I'll be there in an hour," Joe said, and disconnected.

ONCE AT THE HOSPITAL, where she found Livvy was much improved, Nicky realized to her shock that it was Saturday, May 28. The last *Twenty-four Hours Investigates* before the May sweeps ended was on Sunday night at eight. The rest of her team—Tina, Cassandra, Mario, and Bob—should already be en route, having learned from the previous traveling-to-Pawleys-Island fiasco not to press their luck as far as the airlines were concerned. So far, Nicky was about as unready to go on the air as she had ever been for any broadcast in her life. The taped segment for the regular show—which was really no more than a promo for the live program to follow—as yet included no mention of the attack on her sister. Her live show in which she was supposed to wrap up the investigation—which she had pretty much forgotten all about since the attack on Livvy—was scheduled to air at nine P.M., complete with, at Sid Levin's special request, her mother the blocked psychic contacting the newest victims—okay, any she could get.

In Livvy's hospital room, Uncle Ham held the new baby while Uncle John clicked his digital camera at them from a few feet away. Livvy smiled beatifically at her infant. And Nicky had a mental newsflash: She had approximately thirty-six hours to pull together a live program that was supposed to be the climax of her show's season.

Could anybody say "nervous breakdown"?

Livvy, thank God, was now awake and aware enough to talk to the police, to talk to Nicky and her mother, and to coo over her baby. She remembered nothing whatsoever of the attack. Her last memory of that evening was getting out of her car in the parking area. The one good thing about Livvy's memory gap was that Nicky didn't have to agonize over whether or not to use an interview with her sister in Sunday night's program. There was, simply, nothing of value that Livvy could add.

That was one ethical dilemma resolved.

Her other ethical dilemma revolved around exactly how much of what she was uncovering to reveal on the air. What had happened to Livvy had changed her focus from reporting the case to solving it. She wanted to catch the bastard who had done his best to murder her sister, in the worst way. From her sources within the police department—not Joe, who remained maddeningly close-mouthed, but Dave and her round-robin of police escorts were regular chatterboxes—she knew that they had lots of leads and so far no breakthroughs. But she herself had received information on Tara Mitchell that she found very interesting. It was interesting enough, in fact, to prompt her to visit the hospital ladies' room—which she was pretty much using as an impromptu office—to call Joe and pass it on.

He was once again maddeningly close-mouthed about where he was and what he was doing. But she told him her news anyway.

"Tara Mitchell's father was murdered the year after she was. Shot twice at close range in his car, which was parked outside a nightclub in Myrtle Beach. His murder was never solved, either."

"Oh, yeah?" Joe sounded slightly distracted.

"Don't you see?" Nicky was in no mood for distracted. "It means that maybe we're not looking for a deranged serial killer after all. Maybe there was a reason for Tara Mitchell's murder; maybe it was the same reason that her father was murdered."

"*Mmm,*" Joe said.

"Are you listening to me?" Nicky asked, outraged. "*This is important.*"

"I heard you. You're right, it is important. We'll follow up on it as soon as we get the chance."

"I suppose you've got better leads?"

Joe laughed. "Oh, no, you don't. I'm not talking to you about this case. Keep up the good work, Nancy Drew. See you tonight."

"*Nancy Drew?*"

Too late. He disconnected. Nicky shot the phone a blistering look and left the stall.

When Leonora arrived to take over Livvy-sitting, Nicky reminded her about her upcoming appearance on the next day's edition of *Twenty-four Hours Investigates,* which Leonora had, after a personal phone call from Sid Levin and the receipt of a sizable check, agreed to participate in. After listening to her mother moan about being blocked and not being able to connect and the stress of it all, especially under the circumstances, for fifteen minutes, Nicky got fed up and pointed out to her that if she didn't want to do it, she shouldn't have cashed the check.

Which earned her a sharp reply from Leonora.

"Guys, I almost died here," Livvy snapped, opening her eyes and glaring at the two of them impartially. "Could you two please quit bickering over my hospital bed?"

That sounded so much like Livvy-as-usual that Nicky and Leonora both stopped and looked at each other. Then they laughed and hugged Livvy, who protested that she was trying to sleep even as she hugged them back. By the time the family harmony-fest was over, Nicky had thought of a compromise. If Leonora would do a live walk-through of the Old Taylor Place in an effort to contact anyone who might choose to appear (Nicky planned to use her new information about Tara's father in this bit), then earlier that day, they could film a segment in which Leonora would use Karen's blazer, Marsha Browning's watch, Lauren Schultz's blouse, and Becky Iverson's newly arrived sweater to channel the dearly departed. They would feature it as live, although it would really be live-on-tape, which meant that it had been filmed live earlier and edited for boo-boos, which was a common practice in the TV newsmagazine industry.

After leaving the hospital, Nicky met Gordon at his hotel and spent the rest of the day in a mad rush. The short taped piece for the regular program had to be finalized, and mention of the attack on Livvy had to be added. Nicky chose to leave her sister's fate hanging in the promo piece, meaning to conclude the live broadcast on the hopeful note of Livvy's survival and the baby's safe arrival. She and Gordon went over how Leonora's live-on-tape channeling bit was supposed to work, and then filmed a live-on-tape tour of the various locations that would be mentioned in the broadcast.

By the time all that was finished, it was getting on toward nine o'clock. A call from the rest of the team confirmed that they had arrived at their hotel, and instead of getting together then, they agreed to meet at Twybee Cottage at two P.M. the following day for Leonora's live-on-tape filming. Then they would go over what they hoped would happen at the live filming at the Old Taylor Place Sunday night. Nicky had the beginning segment—a shot of the place under the pines where Karen had died—and the ending bit—she would say "He's still out there" in close-up—planned. After the opening, they would air the tour, then Leonora's channeling session. The rest of the hour was left up to the vagaries of Leonora's gift, the spirit world, and live TV.

One of these days, Nicky told herself wearily as she waved good-bye to Gordon and drove back to Joe's house, she might want to think about getting a less stressful job.

Since the house was dark and empty when they got there, Officer Andy Cohen walked her inside, did a quick search of the premises, checked the lock on the back door, and planted himself in front of the TV. He had instructions, he said, not to leave the house until the Chief got there. He was nice but taciturn, a middle-aged guy with the narrow shoulders and big butt that came from long days spent sitting in a patrol car, and it was clear that he was tired. After a little desultory conversation, Nicky retreated down the hall to the bedrooms. It had been a long day, and she wanted to take a bath and get into something more comfortable (at the moment, she was torn between sweats and sexy lingerie) before Joe got home.

She was just heading for the bathroom when her cell phone rang. A glance at the ID window told her that it was Lisa Moriarty, an old friend who was now a private detective in New Jersey.

"I've got some information for you," she said after Nicky said hello. "About that Franconi guy."

21

IT WAS ALMOST MIDNIGHT by the time Joe got home. He was tired, but tired was a relative thing, made better because it had been a productive day. The surveillance tapes were of poor quality and grainy to begin with, and the system had not been designed to monitor people entering and leaving the library, but they had captured enough to pique Joe's interest. He had sent them off to have certain frames enhanced, and had been promised the results by Monday. Then he would know whether or not they had anything. After that, he'd gotten back to the grunt work of good police investigations: reviewing files, verifying facts, cross-checking information. A few interesting things had popped up there, too. Then, driving home, he'd remembered that the day had even had a promising start: He'd woken up with Nicky entwined around him like spaghetti around a fork. She had been nearly naked and so silky soft and warm that he'd been aroused before he had even gotten his eyes open properly. The temptation to do something about it had been almost overwhelming, but he'd had an appointment at eight-fifteen and there simply hadn't been time. Besides, having sex with her a second time was probably going to get the whole relationship discussion cranked up again, which was a point he probably wanted to keep at the forefront of his mind while she was staying with him.

Women: Why did they always have to label everything?

But whatever the state of their acquaintance, it felt surprisingly good to walk into his house and know that she was there. Cohen—a sad substitute— was on the couch, and Nicky wasn't anywhere in sight, but the signs of her presence were unmistakable. Her shoes, sexy beaded sandals, were near the door, with one of them having fallen over on its side like she'd just kind of carelessly kicked them off. Her purse was on an end table. And there was an almost undetectable scent in the air—something flowery, some kind of soap, maybe, or shampoo—that had never been there before.

A woman's scent.

Breathing it in, Joe realized for the first time just how much he'd missed having a woman in his life.

He talked to Cohen briefly, and then the officer left. Joe went in search of Nicky.

The kitchen was empty and the bathroom and spare-bedroom doors were open, so that left just one place she could be: his bedroom. Just the thought made him hot. The room was dark, so she was probably already asleep. He would strip down and slide under the covers next to her. . . .

Tugging off his tie, he was already starting to unbutton his shirt as he opened the door. Walking into the room, careful not to make any more noise than he had to so as not to wake her, he unfastened his shoulder holster and took it off. There was just enough moonlight filtering in through the mini-blinds so that he could see the slender shape of her curled on her side beneath the covers. With one eye on the bed—he could hear the steady rhythm of her breathing and smell the soft floral scent he'd noticed earlier, both of which were playing hell with his pulse rate—he stripped down to his boxers and padded over to his side of the bed.

Wait a minute: The whole damn thing was his bed. Since when did he have a *side?*

Joe was pondering the ramifications of that as he climbed under the covers. His leg brushed hers—the smooth slide of her skin against his was enough to make his groin tighten—and then his arm brushed the silky thing she was wearing and he registered the soft curves beneath. He turned onto his back and stared up at the ceiling in an effort to combat the urge to wake her with a kiss and take it from there. But then the whole sweet-smelling warmth of her kind of crept over him like a fog and he could feel himself weakening, losing the power to resist. . . .

Who was kidding whom here? There was no way in hell he was going to be able to sleep in this bed with her tonight and not rock both their worlds.

He turned his head to look at her. To his surprise, he could see the gleam of her eyes looking back at him through the darkness. The smallest of smiles curved his mouth. So she had been awake after all.

"Hey." His voice was husky. "I thought you were asleep."

"Joe," she said, "who is Brian?"

He suddenly went as immobile as if he'd been turned to stone. For a minute there, Nicky wasn't even sure he was breathing. She had heard him come through the door, heard the rustle of clothing as he got undressed, watched the lean, muscular grace of him as he walked between the bed and the windows in his boxers, putting his gun and keys on the night table. Then he slid in next to her, stretching out on his back on the smooth, clean sheets, and she had felt his heat, felt the vibes he was giving off, and knew instantly what was on his mind: sex. She had a pretty nice buzz going on in that department herself, and at any other time, under these same conditions, she would already have been reaching for him.

But she needed a few questions answered first. His reaction by itself told her a lot. No doubt about it, he definitely knew who she was talking about.

"What do you know about Brian?" There was no intonation in his voice at all.

"I met him tonight in the kitchen."

"*What?*" Joe shot into a sitting position. The covers pooled around his waist. His chest and arms looked muscular and strong in the filtered moonlight as he turned around to stare down at her. "You met him . . ."

His voice trailed off. He sounded like he'd simply run out of air.

"I was getting the milk out of the refrigerator, and I turned around, and there was this blond guy standing at the end of the table, bending over your computer. I must have gasped or something—I know I nearly dropped the milk—because he looked up at me. I said, 'Who are you?' and he said, 'I'm Brian,' and I said, 'What are you doing in here?' and he said, 'Ask Joe.' Then he vanished. Poof! Just like that."

"Shit." Joe flopped back down on his back beside her and ran his hands through his hair. "I thought I was the only one who could see him. I thought I was nuts."

"Joe, is Brian . . . dead?" Nicky asked in a careful tone. She was pretty sure of the answer, but she wanted to make absolutely certain.

"Yeah." His arms dropped, and his eyes cut her way. "By the way, what was Cohen doing during this little comedy?"

"Watching TV. He never heard a thing. After I got over the shock of it, I was actually kind of glad the strange guy in the kitchen was dead instead of alive."

"Yeah." Joe took a deep breath. "That was definitely a good thing."

Watching him, a thought struck her, and she stiffened. "Wait a minute.

Let me get this straight: This whole time when you've been making fun of my mother because she can talk to the dead, when you acted like you thought I was imagining things when I saw Tara Mitchell in a window, you've been hanging out with a dead guy?"

"We don't hang out. He pops in whenever the hell he feels like it. And I thought he was a hallucination, maybe. Or that I had just frickin' lost my mind. After your mother didn't see him that night at the Old Taylor Place—"

"He was there?" Nicky asked, aghast.

"Big-time. Having a ball, too. Walking right beside her during most of the show. But she didn't see him. So I thought, there's one of two possibilities here: Either's she's a fake or I really am insane."

"She's *blocked*. She can't see dead people right now—at least, not in the way she usually does. I keep telling you that."

"Yeah." It was clear from his tone that he still didn't get it and wasn't that interested. "So you saw him, too. That puts a whole different spin on things. How likely is it that we would both have the same hallucination?"

"I definitely don't think he's a hallucination."

"No." There was a wealth of what sounded like relief in the syllable. He blew out a sigh, stuffed a pillow beneath his head, hooked an arm around her, and pulled her close. "Christ, I'm *not* nuts. Do you have any idea how good that feels?"

"*Umm,*" Nicky said. Just at that moment, the overwhelming rush of sensations that went along with having herself in her slinky nightie pulled tightly against his warm, muscular side left her too distracted for intelligent conversation. But as her mother had always told her, the James women bloom where they're planted, and in that spirit, she settled in with her head on his shoulder and a hand resting on his chest and a thigh curving over his. Breathing in, she smelled the faint scent of cigarettes and man that equaled Joe to her, and felt her toes curl.

"Hey." He slanted a glance down at her. "Does this mean you take after your mother in more ways than just the red hair?"

"No," she said firmly. "The only dead people I ever saw are Tara Mitchell in that window, I think, and Brian—definitely—in the kitchen."

"Good." He sounded relieved. His gaze switched to the ceiling. Staring up at it, he seemed deep in thought. Of their own volition, Nicky's fingers made little twisty curls out of his chest hair. The hair was fine and crisp, the skin beneath smooth and hot. . . .

"So, if we can both see him, that's a pretty good indication that he's really there. A ghost." Joe's voice was thoughtful. She glanced up from twisty-curl city to find that he was looking at her again. "Christ. I don't believe it. What do you think he wants?"

"Hard to say." He really had great pecs, she thought, as her fingers, tiring of the twisty-curl thing, surreptitiously stroked the firm muscles beneath. "He must have some unfinished business with you. Did you ever ask him? Um, do you guys talk?"

"Talk?" Joe grimaced. "Me? To a dead guy? No. Well, not much. I mean, there was only so crazy I was going to let myself be. But I did ask him why he was here once, and he said he was my guardian angel." He drew in an audible breath and shook his head. "God, I've got to get used to this. Just talking about it makes me feel nuts."

Nicky ignored the side issue. It took lots of people a little time to accept that they'd seen a ghost. As a case in point, she'd been around ghosts her whole life, but seeing Tara Mitchell had still knocked her back a little.

"So there you go, then. If he said he's your guardian angel, then he probably is."

Joe laughed. It was a harsh sound, unamused. "If you knew this guy, you'd know how funny that is."

"So who is—*was*—he? A friend of yours?"

"He's the guy who shot me."

Nicky's hand stilled. For a long moment, she simply lay there, looking up at him through the darkness. Then she moved, reaching up to press gentle fingers against the scars she knew were there but couldn't see.

"He gave you *these?*" she asked in a voice that was really more of a croak.

"Yep." He caught her hand, pressing his mouth to her palm. His lips were warm and firm, and she could feel the prickle of his stubbly chin against her skin. Ordinarily, the gesture would have made her blood heat, but she was so shocked by what she had just learned that getting turned on was beyond her for the moment.

"Okay," she said. "I think you better tell me the whole story."

"*Mm.*" He slanted a glance down at her. He kissed her palm again, letting his tongue touch it this time. It was warm and wet and . . . *Wait. Stop.* She wasn't going there, not yet.

She had a strong suspicion that he was trying to distract her.

"And you might as well make it the *truth.*" She narrowed her eyes at him and pulled her hand away from his mouth. It ended up back on his chest, with his resting lightly on top of it. At the look in his eyes—a gleam of pure calculation came into them at her words—she sighed.

"Maybe, just to save time and aggravation here, I should get you started. To begin with, the night you got shot, you were a vice cop who was also working undercover for the DEA, helping to set up a bust. The plan was to arrest the local drug kingpin and his gang as they accepted delivery of about five million dollars' worth of cocaine, and at the same time bust the cops who were protecting them—you were pretending to be one of those cops—*and* the out-of-town guys bringing in the drugs. But somebody found out you were an undercover agent, and the whole thing went wrong."

His arm had hardened around her in incremental degrees as she spoke. By the time she finished, it was like an iron band. His hand pressed hers into his chest. He was motionless as a rock, staring down at her through narrowed eyes.

"Where in hell did you come up with that?"

"It's the truth, and you know it."

He stared at her for a moment longer, still radiating tension. "Nobody knows that. Nobody's supposed to know that. They're still working leads from that bust."

With her head still pillowed on his shoulder, Nicky tilted her chin and gave him a saucy half smile. "Hey, like I keep telling you, I'm a reporter. A good one. Finding out secret stuff is what us good reporters do."

"Tell me you didn't go poking around in that mess up in Jersey."

"I had some people check some things out, is all. Don't worry, it was done very discreetly."

"You are a *menace.*" Despite her assurance, he sounded appalled. "Those are dangerous people. You don't want to mess with them."

Since she didn't feel like listening to him bitch at her about being careful for half an hour, it was her turn to distract him. She tweaked his chest hair, and he said "Ow!" and flattened his hand over hers again.

"So now that we've got the whole dirty-cop fiction out of the way, you want to tell me about Brian? Who he was, and how he came to shoot you?"

A beat passed in which he merely looked at her without saying anything. Nicky got the impression that something important hung in the balance: trust.

"Strictly off the record," she encouraged him. "No reporter, no cop. Just me and you."

"Exactly how much digging into my background did you do?"

"What I told you, basically. Why?"

"Because in order for you to understand who Brian is—*was*—I'd have to tell you the story of my life, which is something I don't go into with people. Ever."

"Maybe you could make me an exception." Acting on instinct, she turned her head and pressed her lips against his warm, bare shoulder in a soft, sweet, coaxing kiss. "I mean, I know you were an undercover DEA agent, and I know you have a ghost paying you drop-in visits. What's the story of your life after that?"

"Good point." The slightest glimmer of a smile touched his lips as his eyes met hers. It was a sign of trust being extended, and she tucked the knowledge away somewhere close to her heart. He blew out a sigh. "Okay, here goes. Bare bones." His tone was brisk, unemotional. "My dad left the family when I was three. My mother took off when I was six. We—my little sister, Gina, and I—were put into a foster home. Not long afterwards, they split us up. I found out later that my sister had been adopted. I wasn't. I guess I was too old, too bad—I've got to admit, I wasn't the best-behaved kid in the world—something. Anyway, I stayed in the foster system, bounced around from home to home—some good, some not so good. By the time I was fourteen, I was considered kind of incorrigible, and I wound up in a group home for teenage boys nobody had the time or patience to deal with. Brian was living there, too. We shared a cottage—one of ten in the complex—with four other bad-news kids and a pair of foster parents who didn't have the slightest idea how to deal with us. We got in trouble—of course we got in trouble, trouble was what we lived for—and Brian and I finally got arrested for bashing in car windows with a baseball bat and stealing whatever happened to be in the cars. We were in jail for a week before somebody came to get us out, and it scared me straight. I never in my life wanted to go back to jail. It had a different effect on Brian."

Nicky had been listening in silence, her heart aching for the lonely, scared little boy and just as lonely, just as scared, but determinedly macho teenager he must have been. Now, as he paused, she snuggled closer, stroking his chest with her fingertips, brushing a kiss against the side of his neck, encouraging him to go on with body language rather than words. Words, she feared, might remind him that he was giving her a glimpse into what she had already divined was a very private, very guarded heart.

He must have gotten the message, because after a moment, he continued. His arm stayed securely around her, but he was looking up at the ceiling now as he spoke.

"They kick you out of the system when you're eighteen. Brian is—*was*—about a year older than I am, so he left first. His birthday came and *boom*, he was gone. When it was my turn to leave, I floundered for a few months, then got my act more or less together, worked, and borrowed my way through college, became a cop. I was working vice in Trenton when I ran across Brian again. He knew I was a cop, of course. Since he was involved in just about every illegal thing you can think of, running scams right and left, you can understand why we didn't exactly renew our childhood friendship. But we kept in touch, kind of indirectly. Then I got approached by some DEA guys I knew. They wanted me to help them take down some cops who were getting paid big bucks to look the other way while this major drug ring set up operations in our area, and I agreed. Not long after that, Brian got busted for felony drug possession. Since he was looking at some major time, he sent for me, thought maybe he could trade on our old friendship and get me to help him out with that. Bingo. I had my way in. I made a deal with Brian. He would bring me into his circle, introduce me around as a cop who wanted to make some money on the side, and if things went right when it was all over, I would see to it that the charges against him were dropped. Then, while all this was going on, Gina—remember my little sister?—found me through some damned Internet group that helps kids who've been adopted locate their birth families. I couldn't believe it. All those years without a word, and with the worst timing in the world, there she was, divorced with a kid of her own, just barely making it as a waitress up in Newark."

"Were you glad to see her?" Nicky prompted when he hesitated just long enough to make her wonder if he intended to stop right there.

"Yeah." His voice was soft. "Hell, yeah. My *sister*, you know? When you don't have any, family means a lot. Anyway, she was having a hard time of it financially, so I helped her out a little, went by and played with the kid. A boy, Jeff. Ten years old. Then I started thinking that maybe it wasn't too safe for them to have me hanging around, what with everything that was going down with the drug ring, so I kind of backed off, figuring I'd pretty much stay away until it was all over. But by then, from stopping by my place, she'd already met Brian. Brian, being Brian, immediately started playing the angles. He thought he could use her to his advantage in his dealings with me. He started calling her up, taking her out. By the time I'd found out what was going on, the damage had been done. Brian, the damned fool, had been showing her off to his scumbag associates, telling them she was my sister."

He paused, and Nicky realized that all of a sudden she could feel his heart beating beneath her hand. A long moment passed before he went on.

"Anyway, like you said, the bust was all set up. We were going to take down the cops who were taking the payoffs and the drug traffickers all at the same time, and confiscate five million dollars in drug money and five million dollars' worth of cocaine to boot. It was going to be sweet, we thought. And it should have been. Only Brian, the son of a bitch, sold me out. He told Lee Martinez—he was the local drug kingpin we were getting ready to bust—that I was undercover DEA. We were all in the warehouse with these trucks loaded with coke, waiting for the guys with the money to get there. Agents were outside, watching for the money guys to come, because that's when they were going to make the bust. We had just found out the location that day, so there was no time to set up any internal surveillance. The arrival of the money guys was supposed to be the signal. So we were all just waiting, there inside the warehouse, all kind of antsy, when I got the word that Martinez wanted to see me in his little office at the back. Soon as I got in there and saw that Brian was in there with this stupid little smirk he always got when he thought he'd outsmarted somebody, I knew I had trouble, and sure enough, Martinez's thugs jumped me. Searched me for a wire, which I wasn't wearing because Martinez was such a paranoid son of a bitch, you never could tell when he was going to get suspicious of somebody and have them searched. So there I was, on my knees, cuffed, with a gun to my head, when they brought in Gina. She was tied to one of those rolling chairs, and there was duct tape over her mouth. She was crying, no sound but big tears running down her cheeks."

He broke off. His heart was thudding beneath her hand now. Nicky could feel it beating like a piston. His body was rigid against her, with tension emanating from him as palpably as body heat. He took a deep breath, blew it out, and went on.

"I'll give Brian this. He looked surprised, like he hadn't known Gina was there. See, that was the thing about Brian. The piece of shit had this positive genius for getting stuff started that in the end blew up in his face. Brian didn't know any details about the operation we were running, 'cause I hadn't told him. He didn't know, for example, that the bust was going down that very night. All he was able to tell them was that I was working undercover for the DEA. So Martinez and his goons thought that they would use Gina as leverage to get the lowdown on what the feds were up to out of me. And it worked. They started making little cuts on her face with a knife, and she was just bucking and crying in that chair, and you better believe I sang like a bird. Of course, it was all lies. I was lying, and praying the whole time that the money guys would get there, that the bust would go down in time. It didn't happen. Martinez must have gotten tired of hearing me talk, or else time just ran out for some reason, because he kicked me in the stomach to shut me up, and then somebody else hit me over the head with something that knocked me for a loop. I was down on the ground, not quite unconscious, trying to hang on, knowing that any minute the feds would be busting down the doors. Then I heard Martinez say to Brian, 'You brought him in here, you fuck-up, you whack him,' and I felt a gun against my temple. I kind of got one eye open and looked up, and there was Brian, standing over me, getting ready to pull the trigger. He was sweating bullets, looking scared enough to piss himself, and I remember thinking, *You asshole, you don't have the balls.* Then, damn, he did it."

Joe's voice broke off and he closed his eyes. Nicky lay frozen with horror, unable to speak, unable to move. After a moment, opening his eyes again, he continued in a voice so soft that she had to strain to hear it.

"I should have been dead. I was probably about as close as you can get and not go on and die. I know Martinez and his goons must have thought I was dead. The funny thing is, after the bust was over, when the paramedics came in and were working on me, I sort of came to or something for a couple of minutes and saw everything that was going on in that office. It was like I was looking down on the action from the ceiling, and I could just see it all real clearly. Everybody in there was dead. Martinez and his thugs, Brian, Gina."

He paused, took a breath, and Nicky realized that her own heart was pounding right along with his.

"Gina, still tied to that chair. Covered in blood, bullet through the head." His voice was raw, and Nicky's heart ached for him. "I learned later that the money guys had arrived and the feds had come roaring in right after Brian had shot me, and Martinez and his thugs had started shooting. Nine people ended up dead." He took a breath. "Out of everyone in that office, I was the only one to come out alive."

He quit talking and sucked in air. He lay there, one arm tucked behind his head, the other wrapped around her. His eyes were fixed on the ceiling. She could feel his racing heart, feel how hard he was trying to control his emotions by the unyielding rigidity of his body. He was breathing in a slow, steady rhythm, and she realized that he was deliberately controlling that, too.

"As soon as I could, I flew to California to check on Jeff, who was living with his dad. Just to make sure, you know, that he was okay. He was playing out in the front yard of this two-story brick house when I got there, everything looking good, so I walked across the grass to say hi. He looked up at me and got this really scared look on his face and said, 'You got my mom killed. Go away!' and ran inside the house. I don't blame the kid: He was right. His dad came rushing out, and I could see Jeff was fine, so I left. Went back to Trenton, found out that I was stuck with being labeled a 'dirty cop' until the feds finished their investigation up there, which at this point is looking like it's going to take years, and got some strings pulled on my behalf so that I could get this job down here." He paused and took a breath. "So there you have it: the story of how a Jersey vice cop wound up as a police chief in paradise."

The slightly mocking tone in which he said that last sentence couldn't disguise his underlying pain. Nicky could feel it in his knocking heart, in the tension in his muscles, in the hardness of the arm around her. She could see it in the taut line of his jaw and the way he continued to focus on the ceiling instead of looking at her.

He didn't want to look at her because he didn't want her to be able to read the emotion in his eyes. And she realized that underneath the calm, capable exterior of this very adult man still lurked that lonely, scared but determinedly macho boy.

She realized, too, that tears were stinging her eyes—that she *cared*.

"Joe." She slithered on top of him, propped herself on her forearms, and framed his face with her hands. He met her gaze then. His hands slid down her back to rest lightly at her waist. The pillow beneath his head meant that their eyes were almost level. His cheeks were warm and faintly prickly beneath her palms. His body felt very solid and strong beneath her, and she could feel the hard wall of his chest beneath her breasts, rising and falling as he breathed. Below his boxers, his legs were hard with muscle and rough with hair.

She stroked his cheek. "It wasn't your fault, what happened to Gina."

"Yeah," he said, and his voice was raw and thick. "It was."

The moonlight filtering over the bed allowed her to see what she had already known would be there in his eyes: a deep, atavistic suffering that no words had the power to soothe. The guilt and grief were a burden he would carry with him as long as he lived, she knew.

Her throat constricted. The knowledge that he was hurting hurt her.

"Hey," he said, in a near approximation of his normal voice. "Are those tears? Tell me you're not crying."

Nicky swallowed. Clearly no sympathy was going to be allowed. Of course, big, bad cops didn't wallow in emotion. They sucked it up and got on with life.

"No, of course not." Nicky's hands retreated from his face to his broad, bare shoulders. She resisted the urge to sniffle or try to blink back the tears that she knew were on the brink of spilling from her eyes for fear that doing either would make them even more obvious. The thing was, she discovered, she just couldn't stand to think of him in such emotional pain, whether he wanted her sympathy or not.

"Liar." His eyes glinted at her. She thought she detected something like tenderness in his voice.

"So what if I am?" she said, goaded into glaring at him through the film of tears that she couldn't hide. "I feel bad for you, okay?"

"The thing is"—he smiled at her, a sweet and charming smile the likes of which she'd never seen on his face before—"I don't think anybody's ever cried over me before. And you know what?" He rolled with her, pinning her beneath him in a tangle of limbs and covers. "I like it."

Then he kissed her, licking into her mouth, and heat exploded inside her like a supernova.

His mouth was hot and wet and his body was hot and hard, and Nicky wrapped her arms around his neck and closed her eyes and kissed him back with an intensity that made her dizzy. Her flimsy nightgown was rucked up around the tops of her thighs, and she had nothing on beneath, which meant that she was all but naked. His weight pressed her down into the mattress. His body heat seeped into her pores. One of his legs was wedged between hers, and the steely muscles of his thigh pressing against her most intimate flesh made her body quake and burn. His hand slid between their bodies. It felt big and warm through her thin nightgown, and when it closed over her breast, she shivered a little. He caressed her through the silky cloth, running his thumb over her nipple, and she arched up against his hand and pressed her nails into his shoulders and squeezed his thigh with hers, suddenly so turned on that she felt as though she was melting inside.

He broke off the kiss, lifting his head.

"Joe." It was a murmur of protest. Breathing way too fast, Nicky opened her eyes and looked up at him. He was looming over her, the hard, handsome planes of his face and the broad outline of his shoulders silvered by moonlight, and she could see the hot, dark gleam of his eyes, the sensuous curve of his mouth. His hand looked very big and dark against her ivory gown. The fact that it was curved over her breast made her mouth go dry.

"Remember how I said I don't do relationships?" His voice sounded surprisingly normal, especially given the fact that she was practically breathless with desire. Then she remembered: This was a man who kept his emotions under control.

"Vividly," she answered, striving for a light note, although she was on fire for him, burning for him, wanting him with a passion that was making her heart pound and her toes curl and her body throb. His leg moved so that his hard, hot thigh was pressing even tighter against her, and it was all she could do not to squirm with pleasure.

"I was wrong," he said, his voice a little huskier now, and slid his mouth down her throat. Her skin, she discovered, was sensitive, so incredibly sensitive that the hot, wet glide of Joe's mouth moving over it made her shiver with delight. "I want a relationship. With you."

"You sure you're ready for this?" It was hard to inject a dry note into her voice when he was tracing the lacy neckline of her nightgown with hot little kisses pressed into her exquisitely receptive skin and rubbing his thigh against her and caressing her breast all at the same time, but she managed. He wasn't the only one who could be cool under pressure. "Pardon me if I'm wrong, but aren't you the guy who said, 'Having sex once does not make a relationship'?"

"I figured you'd still be huffy about that. It's that red hair." Joe lifted his head and smiled at her. If it hadn't been for the hot, dark glitter of his eyes and the unmistakable evidence of his desire that she could feel pressing hard and urgent against her, she might have been fooled into thinking he was as unruffled as he sounded. "Anyway, this will be twice."

Then his head dipped and his mouth found her breast, her nipple. It was wet and scalding hot through the thin cloth as he suckled first one breast, then the other. Nicky caught her breath. Her body surged against that sinewy thigh, sending shock waves of pleasure through her system.

"What if *I* don't want a relationship?" It was difficult to talk, much less make sense, when her heart was pounding and her blood was racing and her body was quivering with sensation. She slid her hands down over the warm, damp skin of his back, loving the blatant masculinity of it, the feel of strong muscles flexing beneath sleek skin. Her fingertips encountered the waistband of his shorts and slipped inside.

He lifted his head from the exquisite torture he was inflicting on her breasts to look at her. "You'd break my heart."

She would have been fooled by the almost whimsical tone of that statement if his eyes hadn't been fierce and black.

"Joe," she said, which he clearly took to mean *yes* to a relationship because he kissed her, gently at first and then with ferocious need. Nicky kissed him back, wildly, passionately, bursting into flames as his hands slid over her, pulling her slinky nightgown over her head, leaving her naked and vulnerable as he caressed her everywhere, kissing and touching until finally, because patience had never been her strong suit and she was really tired of waiting, she pushed his boxers down his legs and closed her mouth around him and did to him what he had been doing to her.

"Christ," he said. Then, *"Nicky."*

Then he rolled her over and came into her, just like that, enormous and hot, plunging deep inside her so that she gasped and clung to him, moving with him as he loved her with a torrid eroticism that made her shiver and burn and cry out again and again and again. Finally, he drove inside her with a series of fierce, deep thrusts and she came, just like that, exploding in fiery starbursts of passion, digging her nails into his back and wrapping her legs around his waist and gasping out his name.

"Joe, Joe, Joe, Joe, *Joe.*"

"Nicky," he groaned in answer, holding himself deep inside her shaking body, shuddering as he found his own release.

Afterward, she lay spent in his arms, warm and relaxed and sleepy, and listened to the deep, steady rhythm of his breathing. He felt hot and faintly sweaty and big and solid and altogether good against her. Her head was on his shoulder, and she tilted her chin so that she could look up at him. What she saw was the lean angle of a stubbled jaw, the sensuous curve of slightly parted lips, the sweep of dark lashes against his cheeks, the hard curve of his cheekbones—and, above, bisecting his temple, the pale, puckered lines of the scars where he'd been shot.

And her gut clenched like a giant hand had reached right inside her body and grabbed it and twisted.

22

A T ABOUT FIVE A.M., Nicky was so tired that she actually fell asleep—deeply, dreamlessly asleep, not the little twenty-minute dozes she'd been drifting into between lovemaking sessions all night. By the time she zonked out, Joe's twice had been long since left in the dust. If his standard of measurement was any indication, they now definitely had a relationship going on.

And she still hadn't told him that she was in love with him. That was a secret she meant to guard until she was sure the words wouldn't send him racing for the nearest exit. At the moment, she sensed that just committing to an ambiguously defined "relationship" was as far as he was prepared to go.

Not that she was particularly unhappy about it. She recognized that he saw an enormous risk when he thought about letting someone into his heart. She was willing to give him some time—and anyway, she needed time herself to make sure that this wasn't just some stress- and lust-induced aberration.

But she didn't think it was. It felt like—*gulp*—the real thing.

Which was a scary thought all by itself. Making things worse was the fact that the last *Twenty-four Hours Investigates* broadcast would be over soon, which meant that soon—not immediately, because she wanted to stay around until Livvy was out of the hospital at least, but soon—she would be leaving Pawleys Island. Whatever happened with the show, or with *Live in the Morn-*

ing or any other gig she might be offered, her work was elsewhere. She simply couldn't stay.

She could visit, though, and she would, frequently, because she meant to keep looking for the bastard who had attacked Livvy until he was caught or she died, plain and simple. And also—she would visit for Joe.

She wondered how he felt about commuter relationships. One thing she could be sure of was that as soon as it occurred to him that she would be leaving soon, she was going to find out.

By the time she woke up, it was nine A.M. and she was alone. She glanced around the bedroom, a little warily because she was just then remembering Brian, but there was no ghost in sight. No Joe, either. That being the case, and since the day in front of her was jam-packed with things she absolutely had to do, she rolled out of bed.

In the bathroom, she took one look in the mirror and nearly shrieked. Forget about love's rosy glow. She had bags under her eyes from lack of sleep, and there was whisker burn—yes, definitely whisker burn—on her cheeks. And was that a hickey at the base of her throat? *Ohmigod,* it was. And she had to be on live TV *tonight.*

Mario and Cassandra and Tina would have their work cut out for them, Nicky thought, patting the puffiness under her eyes with her pinkies with horror. Maybe things would improve during the day, but right now she was looking like the poster girl for the morning after the night before.

A cold shower helped with the bags, if nothing else. She put a little lotion on the whisker burn, and added a peach-colored T-shirt that fit close around her throat in hopes that it would cast a flattering glow over her face and hide the hickey at the same time, and she realized that she had done the best she could without professional help.

She would grab a cup of coffee and head out. Next stop, the hospital and Livvy. Then she had to do a little more digging into Tara Mitchell's father. . . .

The funny thing was, she reflected as she crossed the living room and glanced out through the big front window to see that Joe's cruiser was no longer parked in front of the house, she'd known that Joe wasn't in the house almost from the time she'd woken up. The place had felt empty in a curious kind of way, as if its energy had gone. If she was that attuned to him, she had it bad, Nicky thought, as she walked into the kitchen to find Dave sitting at the table, holding a pencil and checking off data on a computer printout that lay on top of a stack of papers scattered across an open folder. A cup of coffee was sitting beside him. A glance told her that Cleo was, as expected, looking in through the back door. A further glance told her that the day was cloudy and overcast—not a ray of sunshine in sight.

Great.

"Hey," Dave greeted her when she said a cheery good-morning and started pouring coffee into a cup. "Joe had to leave. He said to tell you he'd call you later."

If Nicky had thought she looked bad, it was nothing compared to how awful Dave looked. His eyes were bloodshot, his normally ruddy cheeks were pale, and every muscle in his face drooped.

Nicky felt a little thrill of alarm.

"Is anything wrong?" she asked, her coffee cup suspended halfway to her mouth. Her first thought was that something had happened with the Lazarus Killer.

Dave grimaced. "Amy moved out last night. She took the kids and went back to her ex-husband."

"Oh," Nicky said softly, having heard all about Dave's girlfriend during the long hours he'd spent babysitting her. She sat down at the table and looked at him sympathetically. "I'm sorry. Are you all right?"

"Yeah, sure. Like Joe said, it just wasn't meant to be."

"Joe said that?"

Dave nodded. "He had her pegged right from the start, I guess. Cleo, too. Neither one of them ever liked Amy. I guess I should have listened."

Nicky reached across the table and put her hand over his.

"There's somebody out there who *is* right for you, Dave. You'll find her. You'll see."

"I guess." He made a face and took a sip of coffee. "At least I get to take Cleo home again. I know Joe's ready to see her go. I'll pick her up later today, I guess." He finished his coffee and started putting the papers he'd been working on back into the folder. "You ready to go?"

Nicky nodded, finished her coffee, and stood up.

"This place has turned into a damned freak show," Vince growled, glaring out the window of the squad room at the dozen or so men in Civil War–era uniforms marching across the courthouse square. A TV camera crew rode alongside them on a mobile camera unit, taping the whole thing. The white tents and blue beach umbrellas of the press occupation had been joined by a full contingent of vendors hawking everything from lemonade to "I survived the Lazarus Killer" T-shirts. "What the hell do you suppose they're doing now?"

"At a guess, I'd say something about the history of the island." Joe glanced out the window without much interest and then turned back to the dry-erase board where pictures of Karen Wise, Marsha Browning, and Livvy Hollis—who was considered a victim although she had survived—were taped to the top right, while pictures of the three earlier victims were taped to the top left. Everything the most recent set of victims had in common was listed beneath their pictures, while everything those three women had in common with Tara Mitchell, Lauren Schultz, and Becky Iverson was listed beneath the girls' pictures. Acquaintances, places they had frequented, hobbies they had enjoyed, things like that. There was a surprising amount of overlap between all of them except Karen Wise, Joe thought, going over the list. But then, the other five had all been residents of Pawleys Island, which was small, and which meant, necessarily, that their lives would overlap. Even fifteen years apart. So far, Karen Wise's link was that she had spent approximately two hours on the island before being killed.

Not a lot of time to meet a murderer.

"Are you ever going to solve this?" Vince turned to glare at him. "I'm guessing no, right? You know what? From start to finish, this is all the fault of your girlfriend's damned TV show."

His girlfriend. Joe instantly pictured Nicky and felt something that was ridiculously akin to a warm-and-fuzzy glow right in the region of his heart. Vince had called her that before, and it had annoyed the hell out of him at the time. Now the description felt right.

He hadn't meant for it to happen, but somehow or another, Nicky managed to get through the flak vest he'd zipped around his heart. The thing about this case was that the killer seemed to be focused on her. That not only scared the hell out of him, it also made him want to catch this guy in the worst way and stomp his ass into the ground before he could come after Nicky again—which Joe had a real bad feeling that before this was all over, he was going to do.

"Working on it," Joe said mildly to Vince, and went back to studying his chart.

BEN HOLLIS WAS with Livvy in her hospital room when Nicky walked in. Leonora had just arrived, too, and Uncle Ham, who had spent the night, was just leaving. Uncle John, who had come to fetch Uncle Ham, was standing right inside the door, arms crossed over his chest, glaring at Ben. And Hayley was there, too, bawling her head off in the arms of a uniformed nurse who was carrying her from the room.

The tension in the air was so thick that Nicky, who was carrying a vase of Livvy's favorite daisies, nearly turned around on the threshold.

Then she sighed, cooed at Hayley in passing, and kept going to plunk her daisies down on the table by Livvy's bed. *Look at it this way,* she told herself:

The good news is that Livvy is well enough for the family to have sunk into chaos as usual.

Back to his usual *GQ* self, Ben greeted Nicky with a curt nod, which she returned with disinterest. If this was war, and it seemed it was, she was squarely on Livvy's side.

"You think about it," Ben said to Livvy, and to Nicky's surprise—and in the teeth of the concentrated glares of everyone else in the room—he bent down to brush his mouth against her cheek.

Which Livvy averted.

Then he walked out of the room as everyone practically hissed at his back.

"What was that?" Nicky was wide-eyed as she looked at Livvy.

"He wants to get back together." Livvy didn't look as happy about that as she presumably should.

"The bimbo dumped him." Uncle Ham's voice seethed with vicious satisfaction.

"And I'm guessing that he's figured out just how much he stands to lose in a divorce," the ever-practical Uncle John added in a dry tone.

"It's possible that he's finally realized just what he's throwing away," Leonora said to Livvy. "Sometimes it takes a crisis for men to get a clue."

"So, what are you going to do?" Nicky asked her sister, awed by this latest one-eighty-degree turn in Livvy's once-Stepford-perfect life.

Livvy met her gaze. Her blue eyes looked troubled.

"I don't know," she said. "I'm thinking." Then her gaze shifted and dropped, focusing like a laser on something about a foot lower than Nicky's eyes. "Is that a hickey on your neck?"

"DEPENDING ON HOW you look at it, the list of possible suspects ranges from practically limitless right down to zero," Joe said. He was talking to select members of what Vince, from the steps of the police station, which he had exited an hour before, had described to the media as the Lazarus Killer Task Force, which, also according to Vince, was working under the mayor's direct supervision 24/7 and was well on the way to solving the case. In actual fact, the Lazarus Killer Task Force was the entire police department, which really was working as close to 24/7 as it was humanly possible to do but wasn't a whole lot closer to solving the case than they had been on the night of Karen Wise's murder. They were all on a steep learning curve, and there was a mountain of information to wade through, but at some point, Joe was hopeful that somebody was going to dig up the kernel of evidence that would lead to the truth.

Of course, unless they got lucky, he might be a grandpa by then.

"We've got these guys here." He tapped a list of fifteen men, all violent criminals who lived within a two-hundred-mile radius of the island, who'd been convicted of a violent crime and had spent the last twelve to fifteen years in prison. He was seated at the long table in the police station's grungy beige conference room, with Bill Milton, George Locke, Randy Brown, and Laura Cramer—or, in other words, Sunday morning's edition of the Lazarus Killer Task Force—around him. "I want pictures and a physical description—height, weight—on them by tomorrow."

"I already checked them out," Milton objected. "They've all got alibis for at least one of the attacks."

"Yeah, and I checked out this group." Brown was looking at another computer-generated list of the people who had called Karen Wise's cell phone in the last half hour of her life. Joe's gut feeling about the call with the static hadn't borne fruit, but that scenario still tugged at his mind. "Nobody on it is even a possibility. Most of those calls came from Chicago. One was from Kansas City. None of them could have done it, because they were hundreds of miles away from Pawleys Island at the time."

Which was why the scenario of Karen Wise being lured from the house to her death by a phone call with fake static on it was running into trouble.

"I still want pictures and a physical description," Joe said. "By tomorrow."

Tomorrow was when he expected his former good buddy from the DEA to come through with the enhanced pictures of certain interesting library patrons. With those in hand, he meant to start making comparisons.

"I don't suppose it's going to do any good to tell you I went over this group with a fine-tooth comb?" Locke picked up the third sheet, which contained the names of everyone who had been at the Old Taylor Place on the night of Karen Wise's murder. "Not only did I check them out, I cross-checked to see what they were doing when Marsha Browning was killed *and* when Olivia Hollis was attacked. There's not one person there who doesn't have an iron-clad alibi for at least one of those times."

"Yeah," Joe said. "I know. I want their pictures and descriptions anyway."

BY THE TIME Nicky pulled up Twybee Cottage's driveway for Leonora's live-on-tape channeling session, the day's gloomy start had degenerated into a full-fledged thunderstorm. Lightning flashed. Thunder boomed. Torrents of rain pelted down, cutting tiny rivers through the pea gravel. The dull roar of the rain drowned out even the ubiquitous sound of the sea. Nicky got out and ran for the back steps with an umbrella over her head as Andy Cohen, who was babysitting her for the afternoon, pulled into the parking area behind her. On the back porch, Gordon stood with his camera focused on the sky.

"This is great," he said to her as she shook her umbrella and folded it before heading inside the kitchen. His face was positively gleeful. "What a backdrop. Talk about your vintage haunted-house shots."

Glad Gordon was so well entertained, Nicky went inside and found herself immediately swept up in an embrace by first Tina, then Cassandra, then Mario, who were all in the kitchen with the tools of their trade spread out on the table and counters.

"I'm so glad you're doing okay," Tina said as the hug-fest ended. "You look *wonderful*."

"She does *not*." Cassandra had been studying her with her head cocked to one side. "You got bags under your eyes. I'm going to have to break out the Preparation H for that. And what's that on your neck?"

"A hickey," Tina squealed, looking closer. Her eyes flew to Nicky's. *"Ohmigod,* who's the guy?"

With the best will in the world not to, Nicky could feel herself blushing. It was, as she'd known all her life, the curse of the fair-skinned.

" 'Dickey' I know," Mario said thoughtfully. "A false shirt. But what's this *hickey?*"

"You know, a love bite," Cassandra told him. She pursed her lips. "Kissy-kissy."

"Can we just get on with this, please?" Nicky picked up a lip brush and thrust it at Tina. "Or I'm going to do it myself."

JOE DROVE ACROSS the South Causeway Bridge toward the mainland more slowly than usual because of the downpour. The rain was pelting down so heavily that he and the other drivers had their headlights on. The cruiser's windshield wipers were in continuous motion with a rhythmic swishing sound that, combined with the dull roar of the rain itself, was almost soporific in its effect, especially since he'd gotten something like two hours of sleep the night before. Not that he was complaining. At least the way he'd spent the previous night was a good way not to sleep. The best, in fact. As a cure-all, hot sex beat every other treatment he'd tried, hands down. Today he was feeling like himself again. Like the Joe Franconi he'd been before. A kinder, gentler version, maybe, but at least the same guy. Knowing that he was not totally nuts helped, of course—the fact that Nicky had actually seen

Brian, too, blew his mind almost as much as the knowledge that he was being haunted by his own personal ghost—but most of the credit went to Nicky.

She'd healed something inside him. Taken something that was broken and made it whole again.

Like his heart.

That was the good news. The bad news was that he had this horrible sneaking suspicion that she now owned it, which was something to worry about another day. For now, he meant to just savor the fact that she was part of his world for as long as he could.

Lightning flickered across the sky, lighting up the roiling gray clouds above and the ink-black waters of Salt Marsh Creek below the bridge. He was on his way to Georgetown County Hospital to ask Livvy a couple more questions. It had come to his attention that she and her husband might have employed as a gardener one of the men on the list of violent offenders who were recently released from prison.

As a solution, how easy and neat would that be? Vince would practically kiss his feet.

But something about it just didn't feel right.

In fact, as he left the bridge and turned onto Highway 17 toward the hospital, Joe realized that he'd had the equivalent of a brain thorn all day. It had been poking him, irritating him, refusing to allow him to forget about it. Now he realized what it was—something Vince had said: "From start to finish, this is all the fault of your girlfriend's damned TV show."

Vince was right. It was.

Tara Mitchell, Lauren Schultz, and Becky Iverson had suffered their fates fifteen years before. Nothing had happened since. The case had gone dormant. Most people had forgotten—until Nicky's show had come to town and stirred things up again.

This rash of murders—the whole Lazarus Killer thing—had begun with that TV show.

Joe thought about that for a moment longer, then picked up his cell phone.

THE FRONT PARLOR (which was really old-house-speak for living room) at Twybee Cottage was basically reserved for guests—or Leonora's private clients. The family rarely used it. The walls were painted deep gold, the floor was covered with an ancient (read "old and threadbare" rather than "antique") Oriental carpet, and the furnishings were Victorian-era couches and chairs, some with the original horsehair stuffing. There was a fireplace with a beautiful mahogany mantel and two windows, one looking out onto the side yard where Livvy had been attacked, and a larger one facing the sea. The curtains—the same gold brocade that was in the study—were closed on both windows at the moment, in an effort to improve the lighting. On such a dark day, Gordon and Bob were having to work extra-hard to properly light the shot.

Leonora, in her full psychic-medium garb of purple caftan and lots of makeup, was seated on the red velvet–covered sofa, with Karen's black blazer in her hand. Her eyes were wide, her lips were tight, and every time Nicky looked around, she got a glare.

"I'm not getting anything," she hissed at Nicky after calling for a break. The cameras had already been on her for a full five minutes, during which nothing happened.

Nicky suppressed a sigh. The diva was back, the block had not lifted, and the timetable was tight. Welcome to her life.

"Just take your time," she said. "We'll keep the cameras rolling, and you just sit there and do what you do."

Leonora gave her an evil look.

"How can I do what I do if I'm *blocked?*"

Nicky took a calculated risk. "He almost killed Livvy, mother. And if you can't help us, he may come after her again—or come after me instead."

Leonora stared at her. Then she closed her eyes and ran her hands over the blazer again.

Nicky motioned urgently to Gordon and Bob, who were filming from two different angles because the size of the room didn't permit much camera movement. The cameras came back on.

Leonora sat silently on the couch, fingering Marsha Browning's watch. She touched the other items—her eyes were still closed—and went back to Karen's blazer.

"I feel . . . I feel . . ."

Nicky held her breath.

The group crowding the hallway went totally silent. Isabelle Copeland, a slim, blonde, twentysomething production assistant who had flown in with the team to fulfill Karen's duties for this final segment, had been on her cell phone to Chicago, reporting on the progress of the filming almost continually since Nicky had arrived. Her phone—now hopefully set on vibrate—was clutched against her breast in both hands as she watched with total absorption. Mario, Tina, and Cassandra, having encountered Leonora in diva mode before, were wide-eyed and as silent as the grave. Marisa hovered just out of camera range, tape recording away. Uncle Ham (Uncle John was at the hospital with Livvy) had his arms folded across his chest, leaning back against a wall as he watched. Harry lurked near the back of the hall, looking resigned.

Andy Cohen, driven from his car by either curiosity or the storm, stood near Harry.

Go Mother, Nicky urged silently. Her mother pulled the blazer through her hands like a scarf.

"I feel . . . something in the pocket," Leonora said grimly as her eyes popped open.

It was all Nicky could do not to groan. Behind her, she heard a collective *whoosh* of exhalations.

Let the letdown begin.

"No, it's trapped in the lining." Leonora stuck her hand down inside the blazer's pocket and fished around. A moment later, she came up with the kind of small cassette tape that might fit in a mini tape recorder. She stared at it blankly for a moment.

"I felt her . . . I felt her . . . and then I felt *this.*" Leonora clenched her fist around it. "It threw me off."

Nicky could tell from her mother's expression that if there hadn't been strangers and cameras present, she would have given vent to a few choice swear words.

"Here, give it to me." Nicky stepped forward hurriedly and removed the distracting object from her mother's hand. Leonora glared at the tape and then, as Nicky retreated, sticking the offending object in her own blazer pocket, she took a deep breath and closed her eyes again. She ran her hands over the blazer. . . .

"She was surprised. Taken by surprise. He came out of the dark and took her by surprise." Leonora grabbed the left side of her head near her temple. "I feel a pain in the side of my head. He hit her in the head. Then . . . then . . ."

Suddenly, she froze. Her eyes flew open, and she stared fixedly in front of her.

The room suddenly felt cold.

Knowing the signs, Nicky froze, too—except for one frantic sideways glance to make sure that the cameras were running. They were.

"It's all right, we're here to help you." Leonora seemed to be speaking to someone none of the rest of them could see.

"It's Karen," she said in an aside to Nicky. Her voice was tense with suppressed excitement. Nicky felt her heart lurch. She, too, stared at the spot where Leonora seemed to be looking, but saw nothing. The thought that her mother was seeing Karen made her breathing quicken. Only three weeks ago, Karen would have been in this room with them, *alive.* "She's here. I can see her." Then, switching her attention back to the invisible visitor, Leonora nodded sympathetically, then said, "Yes, I know. You have every right to be angry." She fell silent, cocking her head a little to one side, seeming to listen. "Can you tell us who killed you?" She cocked her head again. "Listen, she says. Listen. He's evil? She saying he's evil. Who's evil, Karen? Who? All she's saying now is 'He's evil,' over and over again. Wait. Karen, wait. Oh, she's fading. Karen, come back. . . . Please come back. . . . She's gone."

Leonora seemed to slump a little. Nicky let out her breath. Behind her, she heard another collective *whoosh* that meant everybody else was doing the same.

Nicky stepped forward, microphone in hand, on for the audience at home. "Can you tell us what just happened, Leonora?"

Leonora looked at her. Her eyes were still a little cloudy, as they usually were when she was coming off an encounter of the otherworldly kind. It took a minute for them to sharpen, focus.

"Karen was here," she said. "She's very angry about being dead. She said she wants her life back, she was only twenty-three and she wasn't ready to die. She said we should listen, that the man who killed her is evil. She kept repeating it: evil, evil, evil. And then she just faded away." Leonora paused, then added excusingly, "She hasn't been dead long. It takes a while for them to learn to really focus their energy. She's actually doing very well for such a new spirit."

After that, it was over. Everyone sensed it: All the energy had left the room. After a few more fruitless tries at making contact, they gave up and retreated to the kitchen for restorative coffee—all except for Isabelle, that is, who went outside on the porch to answer a call on her cell phone.

"I hope you're not expecting much out of me tonight," Leonora muttered to Nicky in an aside that only the two of them could hear.

"Whatever you get will be fine. No matter what happens, I've got enough material to carry an hour," Nicky said. "Anyway, that thing just now with Karen was great. You actually saw her. You're getting over the block, Mama."

"I did see her, didn't I?" Leonora seemed to perk up a little. "Maybe I *am* getting better. I certainly hope so."

"Excuse me, Nicky, but Mr. Levin wants to talk to you." Isabelle stuck her head in the back door and frantically beckoned Nicky. Nicky was standing at the counter beside Leonora, who had just finished refilling her cup. Everyone else was sitting around the table. Nicky went out the door to take the call. Even as she said hello, she realized that just three weeks ago, a call from *Twenty-four Hours Investigates*'s Head Honcho would have set her heart to knocking and filled her stomach with butterflies. Today, the fact that he was calling her didn't even really matter. Too much water—too many lives, too many deaths, too many confrontations with the things that were truly important in life—had passed under the bridge to make a mere TV show seem quite as important as it had before.

"I just wanted to tell you that there's a write-up in *Entertainment Weekly* about the show in the issue hitting the stands next week. The story calls *Twenty-four Hours Investigates* the best surprise of the season. It says your segments about the Lazarus Killer are must-see TV and"—there was a pause, as if he meant to let tension build (which, let's be honest, it was)—"it says you are one of the best new television personalities of the year."

Okay, strike her earlier thought about a mere TV show being unimportant. As far as the whole scheme-of-life thing was concerned, it probably wasn't. But for her, personally, it was a biggie. Nicky felt a flood of warmth hit her veins that was as potent as any chemically induced high. She might not have been grinning like an idiot on the outside—she had some dignity, after all—but she was definitely grinning like an idiot on the inside.

"That's good news," she said, trying to project total cool, as though she got news like that all the time. "Thank you for calling to tell me."

"Yeah, well, I'm looking forward to watching the wrap-up tonight. You got four hours until you're on live. You gonna stay there at your mother's house until then?"

"No, I've been staying somewhere else. I'll probably go back there and go over some of the things I'm hoping to use on tonight's show."

He chuckled. "There you go, that's why you're having this kind of success: You're a dedicated reporter. I made the right choice sending you back there. I just want you to know, everybody here is proud of you."

Nicky was still floating—although not, she hoped, in any outwardly visible way—when she left Twybee Cottage fifteen minutes later. Not even the rain was enough to dampen her spirits. It came down in sheets, pelting the ground so hard that it bounced off, making it hard to see where she was going. Luckily, she could have driven this route blindfolded by now. Behind her, Andy Cohen's headlights in her rearview mirror told her that he was right on her tail.

After parking out in front of Joe's house, Nicky exited the car umbrella-first and sprinted for the front door. By the time she got inside, everything except her head and the upper third of her body was wet, and her shoes made small, muddy puddles on Joe's floor.

If she'd been choosing, this kind of weather was not what she would have picked for her last show. The house was as dark as if it were night outside.

"One of the best new television personalities of the year" (and never mind that she'd been on the air since college). It felt good—really, really good.

"This keeps up, we're going to have some major flooding," Cohen grunted as he rushed into the house behind her. Since he was wearing a police-issue poncho, he was a lot dryer than she was as soon as he took it off. Joe's floor, however, suffered a major assault. Nicky went to get a towel and wiped the mess up while Cohen did a quick walk-through of the house.

"So, what's the plan?" he asked, plopping down on the couch and reaching for the remote.

"I need to be over at the Old Taylor Place by eight." That's when they had all agreed to reconvene; that hour before they went on the air should give everybody plenty of time to do what needed to be done. "Until then, I'm going to take a shower and do some work. You"—she grinned at him—"get to watch TV."

"Hell of a job," he said, and settled in comfortably.

Nicky took a shower and put on jeans and a T-shirt. Then she headed for the kitchen. Before she did anything else, she needed a snack.

Engaged as she was in mentally reviewing the contents of Joe's refrigerator, she was half a dozen steps into the dark-except-for-the-TV living room before she noticed anything.

Cohen was lying at an almost unnatural angle against a corner of the couch, which seemed to be turning black around him. His left hand, the only one that she could see, was flapping against a cushion like a small wounded bird. His eyes were closed, his mouth open.

There was a huge black gap, like a grotesque second smile, across his throat. Liquid, shiny like oil, poured from it.

A hot, meaty, slaughterhouse kind of smell hung in the air.

It was the smell that connected the dots for her.

Cohen had just had his throat slit.

23

SOMETHING SLAMMED HARD into the side of Nicky's head. Crying out, she saw stars and stumbled sideways against the orange rocker, barely managing to catch herself before she crashed to the floor. Instinctively, she glanced around.

What? Who?

Her ears were ringing. Her heart gave a great leap like a thoroughbred late out of the starting gate, trying to catch up with the field. Bright splotches of color whirled in front of her eyes. Even as her stunned brain tried to make sense of what was happening, she knew it was bad, knew that her life was in danger, knew that whomever this was who was rushing toward her through the gloomy living room had just murdered Cohen. A scream ripped out of her throat, followed by another and another. Pushing away from the chair, she tried to run, tried to escape, while her heart pounded and adrenaline shot through her veins and her knees threatened to give way. Instead of running, she was staggering, staggering forward, and everything was revolving around her and she couldn't focus and anyway, it was too late: The attacker was *right there*. Out of the corner of her eye, she caught a blurry glimpse of something arcing through the gloom toward her head just in time for her to throw up an arm and duck.

Whatever it was glanced off the back of her head with a sound like a melon hitting the pavement. The blow sent a tinny taste flying into her mouth: blood. Nicky fell to her knees, mewling rather than screaming now, and then the attacker was upon her, straddling her back, an arm shooting around her neck in a chokehold.

She couldn't breathe.

"Please, no—" The words were cut off as the arm instantly tightened.

Gasping for air, so dizzy that the room whirled like a merry-go-round in front of her eyes, she fought for the ability to breathe, clawing at the arm that was crushing her windpipe.

Long sleeves, he's wearing long sleeves . . . and gloves . . .

A cold, sharp prick below her ear sent terror coursing like ice water through her veins.

God, help me. He's going to cut my throat. . . .

"Quit fighting." It was a man's voice, accompanied by another savage tightening of the arm around her neck. Nicky choked, gagging, clawing at the arm. "I said quit *fighting.*"

The blade felt icy cold against her skin. He was pressing harder. . . .

That warm little trickle down the side of her throat was blood—*her blood.*

She froze. Her stomach cramped and tied itself into a knot. Her chest heaved as she fought to breathe.

I don't want to die. . . .

"I want the tape. Where's the tape?"

Familiar. Voice.

But her ears were ringing and everything was swirling, and the lack of oxygen combined with fear had turned her bones to jelly and she couldn't quite tell, didn't quite know *who.*

His grip on her throat eased. She gasped, coughed, and sucked in air.

"I want the tape."

"The . . . the tape?" The choked-out question earned her a punch to the temple that made her see stars again. Tears were leaking from her eyes, running down her cheeks. They were warm against her icy skin. She couldn't think, couldn't see, couldn't hear. Cold sweat washed over her in waves.

"The *tape. I want the tape. The one from Karen Wise's coat. Where is it?*"

The tape from Karen's blazer. All of a sudden Nicky remembered Leonora repeating what she had heard Karen say: "Listen. He's evil." Karen had appeared to Leonora right after the tape had been found. Had she meant listen to the tape?

"*Where's the damned tape?*"

He hit her again, viciously, with the hand clutching the knife so that the handle smashed into her temple. Her teeth slammed together. Pain made her cry out.

"In . . . in the kitchen," she gasped.

It was a lie, a desperate lie, the best her poor fogged brain could come up with. The kitchen seemed a better bet as a place to stage a fight for her life in than the bedroom. To begin with, it had an outside door. . . .

"Show me where."

Keeping his arm tight around her neck and the knife at her throat, he hauled her to her feet.

"*Where?*" He roared in her ear.

Her heart slammed painfully in her chest. Her hand, as she lifted it to point toward the kitchen, was shaking, she saw. She was shivering, trembling from head to toe, so frightened that she was nauseated with it. As he pushed her in the direction she had indicated, she saw, from the corner of her eye, that Cohen's fluttering hand had stilled.

He was dead. She mourned him, mourned Karen and Marsha Browning, mourned her own fate.

I don't want to die. . . .

He was strong, stocky, at least several inches taller than she. She could smell him—a sickening combination of sweat and blood and man—and feel the warm bulk of him all around her, but so far, she hadn't seen his face.

But his voice was familiar. . . .

From somewhere, faint but unmistakable, she heard a phone ring. Her cell phone. It was in the bedroom with her discarded clothes—and the tape. He stopped pushing her for an instant, seeming to hesitate, as if the phone worried him.

Please, God. Someone would grow alarmed when she didn't answer and come looking for her. *Please, God, don't make it too late.*

"I'll get the tape for you," she whimpered. "Just don't hurt me."

That seemed to do the trick. Cursing in a vicious, guttural undertone that told her he was starting to feel pressure, that the ringing phone had spooked him, that time—her time—might be running out, he shoved her through the archway into the kitchen.

"*Get it now.*"

A plan, a plan, she needed a plan, she thought desperately. The kitchen was gloomy, dark. No friendly ghosts in sight. No boiling pots of coffee. Only a small, black pig looking through the partly open mini-blinds that covered the back door. *A plan.* Her phone had stopped ringing. Would anyone come looking for her? *There was no time.* . . .

Nicky pointed. "In there."

"Get it."

He never slackened his grip, and the tip of the knife never left the hollow beneath her ear as she edged across the kitchen with him as close against her as a backpack, matching her step for step. Her mouth was so dry that she couldn't even swallow. Her heart thundered. Her pulse raced. Her breathing came fast and erratic. She was light-headed with fear, woozy with it.

What she planned to do was probably going to get her killed—but if she didn't do it, he was certainly going to kill her anyway. If she had any hope at all of surviving, this was her only chance.

"*Now.*" His tone was savage.

Okay, she told herself. *Take a deep breath.* Here she was, wedged against the cabinets with him so close against her that she could feel the buttons on his shirt hard against her back, one of his meaty arms around her throat, and a knife just below her ear, getting ready to pull open the drawer where she had indicated the tape was stashed. She was going to have to be fast, she was going to have to be vicious. . . .

In the shiny silver knob of the upper cabinet closest to her, she saw a reflection of his face. The kitchen was full of shadows, and the knob distorted his features, but there was no mistaking who it was.

"Sid," she gasped.

He went still. Then he, too, saw the knob. She knew, because their eyes met in it.

"Hello, sweetie pie." His tone was as repellent as the slimy, wet underside of a slug.

"Ohmigod, *why?*" It was the merest breath of sound.

She could feel the sudden jerk of his chest against her back as he gave a grunt of laughter.

"You can take all the credit. You gave me the idea. You and your psycho mother. "Let's scare up the dead victims of a serial killer,' " he mimicked in a savage falsetto. "Helped me out a lot, actually. I was already working on a way to get rid of that bitch Karen Wise. You handed it to me on a platter. I made it look good, didn't I? Even to cutting off some of her hair. To make it stick, though, I had to follow through on the whole serial-killer bit. How'd you like those e-mails? Made for good TV, didn't they? You should thank me: I gave your career a hell of a boost."

Considering the fact that he was about to kill her, she personally didn't feel thanks were in order.

"But why Marsha Browning? And Livvy? And me?" Her pulse was pounding so hard that she could hardly hear over the thudding in her ears. Her one thought was to keep him talking as long as possible.

"Why not?" His tone was the equivalent of a shrug. "I had to kill two more women, and that local reporter was easy. She called me about a possible job. I told her I'd come talk to her about it next time I was in the area"—he chuckled horribly—"and I did. I most certainly did. As for your sister, she was easy, too. Always going in and out. And I thought doing her would add some real emotion to your reporting. I was right about that, too. It did. As for you, I never wanted to kill you. You could have had a real career with us. But twice now you just plain got unlucky. First, you come walking down the driveway right after I finished doing the bitch, and I thought you saw me. Later, I figured out you didn't, but I didn't know that then, so you almost bought it that night. Then today you found the tape. I've been looking all over the place for that. That bitch was using it to blackmail me."

"Karen?" Nicky gasped. Something—her shocked tone or her wide eyes reflected in the knob or his own realization of time passing—caused his face to contort. In the instant before his arm tightened punishingly around her throat, Nicky knew that her little reprieve was over. She choked, gasped, and grabbed at his arm as it cut off her air.

"Enough conversation. *Get the goddamned tape.*"

Nicky managed to nod.

His arm loosened fractionally. Nicky wheezed, sucked in air—and opened the silverware drawer, grabbed a steak knife, and plunged it into the arm that was locked around her neck with every bit of strength she had left.

He screamed and let go. Terror gave wings to her feet as she leaped for the door. Time seemed to freeze. Outside, thunder rolled. Lightning lit up the sky. Rain came down in sheets. Cleo danced on her little pig feet, a silent witness to the nightmare inside. Nicky could see it all through the mini-blinds, see escape so tantalizingly close . . .

"I'm going to kill you, bitch," Sid howled, and threw himself after her.

Her flailing fingers just brushed the knob as he leaped on her back and brought her down.

Shrieking like a train whistle, twisting even as she fell, Nicky smashed into the floor on her side and rolled onto her back, the impact jarring and painful but nothing compared to her abject fear, her horror at what was getting ready to happen. Sid was on top of her, straddling her, outweighing her by maybe a hundred pounds, still with a death grip on his knife, and she shrieked again despairingly as she lifted her hands in a futile attempt to ward him off. Blood spurted from his arm, wet and warm as it hit her skin; his face was twisted and ugly and, yes, *evil.* . . .

From the other room, the living room, she heard sounds, faint sounds as if there was someone at the front door. Sucking in air, she screamed like a siren even as, from the change in his expression, she realized that Sid had heard the sounds, too.

Then she realized exactly what those sounds meant: not succor, but a faster death. He wanted the tape. He would have kept her alive until she gave it to him. But now, with someone at the door, time was up.

She knew who he was.

It was as clear to her as if it were written in the air for her to read: *She had to die.*

As she bucked and writhed and fought with all her strength to win free, he lifted the knife high, and it slashed downward, glinting gold as a flash of lightning was caught on its blade. Nicky screamed and lifted her hands in an instinctive gesture of self-protection and slewed violently to one side.

Cleo crashed hard against the glass, startling them both, attracting Sid's attention, deflecting his aim. Nicky felt a shock of burning pain as the knife sliced through her upper arm. Grabbing for his wrist, she fought to hold on as he cursed and punched her and tried to yank free and Cleo crashed into the glass again and there was a flurry of movement in the living room.

"Police! Freeze!" Joe roared, leaping through the kitchen door, gun drawn. "Drop the knife!"

Behind him thundered what seemed like half of the police force.

Having just yanked his wrist free, Sid froze in the act of rearing up again with the knife in hand.

"Freeze!" Joe screamed again. "Get your hands in the air!"

Sid's face twisted furiously. And then he dropped the knife. It hit the floor beside Nicky's head with a clatter as his hands rose in the air.

Someone scooped up the knife. Someone else hauled Sid to his feet, slapped cuffs on him, and started reading him his rights.

"Nicky? Oh, God, Nicky." Joe crouched down beside her, his face absolutely white, his eyes black with fear as they collided with hers, then moved frantically over her as she lay panting on the floor. She was, she realized, covered with blood—Sid's and her own.

"It's okay," she managed, although her voice was raspy and she was trembling from head to toe with reaction. "I'm okay."

Then, as he reached for her, Nicky sat up and melted into his arms.

HAVING HIS LIFE PASS before his eyes was not an experience he enjoyed, Joe reflected. He had discovered that when he had arrived on his own front stoop and heard Nicky screaming through the locked door. His already-pounding heart had threatened to go into cardiac arrest as he struggled to get the key in the lock and the door open in the near-darkness and pouring rain while a flotilla of backup cars with squealing brakes slammed into park in front of his house and Nicky shrieked like a banshee inside. By the time he'd gotten the damned door open, he was sweating buckets and cursing a blue streak and suffering the closest thing to a near-death experience that he'd had in two years. Then, when he and a contingent of Pawleys Island's finest had burst into the living room, they'd found Cohen bleeding out on the couch. Despite the fact that Cohen was one of his men and a good guy and a friend, Joe hadn't even slowed down as he had hurtled toward the kitchen and the source of the screams.

When he'd seen Sid Levin on the floor, crouched over Nicky, he'd gone half-crazy at the idea that maybe he'd been that half second too late.

That was a little more than an hour ago. Now he had recovered his equilibrium to some degree, and she was sitting in the kitchen, giving her formal statement to Dave, because Joe simply wasn't up to hearing the hair-raising tale for a second time. Just thinking about how close she'd come to getting killed still had the power to make him break into a cold sweat. One missed connection, a couple extra minutes before his good buddy had gotten back to him, and the outcome would have been very different.

Nicky would have been dead. And for him, the light would have gone out of the world for good.

His house was now officially a crime scene. It was crawling with cops, his own men and the better part of at least three other departments, too, all turned out because the murder of a cop is, to other cops, as bad as it gets. They were working with grim determination, getting photographs, bagging evidence, taking statements. The media contingent that had been hanging out on the courthouse lawn was starting to arrive as word trickled out that the Lazarus Killer had been caught. There was a satellite truck on the street, and reporters had started pestering people as they exited or entered the house. The neighbors were out in force, drawn no doubt by the shrieking sirens and stroboscopic lights. Fortunately, the crime-scene tape set up around the perimeter of his yard kept everybody who wasn't supposed to be there at a little distance. Unfortunately, the rain had dried up until it was no more than a gentle drizzle. If the earlier downpour had continued unabated, maybe they would have been spared some of the circus.

Or maybe not.

"How you doing?" he asked Nicky, who was sitting at the kitchen table with Dave across from her.

"I'm okay." She glanced up at him, smiled, and at the warmth in her eyes for him, his heart gave a little lurch. Having her look at him like that made him feel like the man who, after wandering cold and hungry and lost through the wilderness, unexpectedly comes across a cabin complete with welcoming hosts, food, and a fire: a little disbelieving of his own good fortune, a little luckier than hell. A temporary bandage was wrapped around her upper arm, where the knife had sliced through skin and some fatty tissue but done no permanent damage. She had two good-sized bumps on the head where the bastard had hit her, and a bruise was just beginning to darken on her cheek. A visit to the island clinic was definitely on the night's agenda, but the paramedic who had treated her had said that none of her injuries required urgent care, and Nicky didn't want to go without Joe, which suited him fine. As far as he was concerned, she was never getting out of his sight again for the rest of his life.

"I was just telling Dave that Cleo was a hero. Uh, heroine. She saw what was happening and tried to get in and made enough noise to distract Sid at the crucial moment. She—and you guys—saved my life."

Okay, pig, Joe thought with a glance at the door where Cleo still stood looking in, *consider yourself in bacon and bologna for the rest of your life.*

"So, did he talk at all?" Dave asked him. Joe knew he was referring to Sid, who had just been taken away by a contingent of state police. With the murder of Andy Cohen, emotions were running too high in the Pawleys Island Police Department for them to keep custody. Joe knew how these things worked, and under the circumstances, he didn't want to take responsibility for the prisoner's life.

"Not to us." Joe sat down, and George Locke, who was in the kitchen, too, poured him a cup of coffee and handed it to him. Nicky and Dave, he saw, already had coffee in front of them. He nodded his thanks to George and took a sip. The brew was strong and hot, and welcome. He needed caffeine in the worst way. "But since we caught him in the act, and he already shot off his mouth to Nicky"—who had told him everything within minutes of being wrapped up in his arms—"it doesn't matter. This is your basic textbook open-and-shut case." He looked at Nicky. "The window in the spare bedroom is broken. He must have smashed the glass, unlatched the window, and come in that way. I'm betting he was already in the house when you and Cohen got here." Joe took a swallow of coffee to mask the pain he felt when he thought about Cohen. "He wanted the tape, which at that time, you had in your pocket, right?" Nicky nodded. She'd already told him that. "My question is, how did he know you were coming here?"

"I told him. When I spoke to him on the phone. He asked me if I was going to stay at my mother's, and I said no, I was coming over here. I . . . thought he was in Chicago." The idea that Sid had been right there in Pawleys Island, plotting her murder at the time, made her skin crawl.

Joe nodded. "He counted on that. See, he could call people on his cell phone and they would think he was still in Chicago. Which is what he did to Karen Wise on the night of her murder. It was his call that lured her from the house. He called her and pretended there was static on the phone, and told her to go outside so she'd have better reception. He was out there waiting, and he killed her." Joe gave a grim little smile of satisfaction. "See, that's the thing about cell phones. The signal bounces off a tower in the area where the call is made. That's what tripped Sid up. I started thinking that it had to be somebody connected with your TV show, and Sid was the last incoming call on Karen Wise's cell phone. I had a buddy check it out, and bingo—that call bounced off the tower here. His alibi was that he was in Chicago at the time of the murder, and that blew it straight to hell: He was lying. Which made him Suspect Number One."

"Sid said Karen was using the tape to blackmail him," Nicky said.

Joe nodded. "She had the goods on him, too. I just got done listening to that tape, and it's all on there. Really raunchy stuff. Apparently, she was threatening to file a multimillion-dollar sexual-harassment suit against him if he didn't pay her big bucks in hush money. From the time she started working for Santee Productions in August, Sid came on to her, made lewd suggestions to her. Then, when she didn't give him what he wanted, he threatened her with the loss of her job. She got it all on tape and turned the tables on him. She had him sweating bullets. He would have been fired, at the very least. His career would have been irreparably damaged, and he would have had to pay her no telling how much money."

"So he killed her."

Joe nodded. "Yep. And after that, it was basically like a snowball rolling downhill, picking up momentum as it went. He's a pilot, has his own plane. We found records in his wallet showing that he's been flying into Charleston. The dates all fit. He's our guy."

"So I was totally off base with the whole Tara Mitchell's father being involved in something unsavory thing." Nicky sounded a little disappointed, and Joe remembered that they'd been having their own private investigative war. He'd definitely won, any way you looked at it—because Nicky was alive.

For the first time since he'd started trying to reach her on her cell phone and she hadn't answered, Joe relaxed enough to smile.

"Not necessarily off base. For all we know, something like that may have been the reason Tara Mitchell was killed. But it didn't have anything to do with the Lazarus Killer. That was strictly Sid trying to disguise his murder of Karen Wise by playing the copycat game."

"So it's over." Nicky let out a *whoosh* of relief. "I can't believe it."

"All except for the wrap-up."

"THE WRAP-UP! Oh my God!" Nicky's eyes widened and her mouth dropped open as she suddenly remembered that she was supposed to be live on the air at nine P.M., wrapping up the Lazarus Killer case. The good news was: Did she have a ratings-grabbing ending or what? The bad news was that the ending was that the show's executive producer had just been arrested for multiple homicide. In that case, did the old showbiz maxim of "the show must go on" apply? "What time is it?"

"Seven-thirty-five." Dave glanced at his watch.

"*O-kay.* Excuse me. I've got to make a phone call." Pushing back her chair, Nicky jumped to her feet. Bad move. She went a little light-headed and had to grab the back of the chair for support. Then there was the small fact that her legs felt about as solid beneath her as limp noodles, and grabbing the chair had sent a sharp stab of pain through her wounded arm, but other than that, she was good to go.

Live at nine.

"Wait. Whoa. What are you doing?" Joe stood, too, looking at her as though he thought she'd lost her mind. "You're on the injured list, remember? Sit down."

"I will, if you go get my cell phone for me. It's on the nightstand in your bedroom."

His lips compressed, but he left the room, presumably to do as she'd requested, and she sat down again. He was back a minute later, handing it to her.

"Something I should know?" he asked.

She reminded him about the show, and he shook his head at her as she dialed Sarah Greenberg's number.

"No way," he said. "You can't. You—."

Then she waved him to silence as Sarah answered.

By the time she finished explaining the situation to Sarah, who was floored over Sid's involvement but increasingly professional as the news sank in, Dave had discreetly left the room and Joe was looking grim.

What Sarah said, basically, was what Nicky had known all along: The time slot between nine and ten was *Twenty-four Hours Investigates*'s to fill. They could rerun an existing taped show, of course, or Nicky could do a live update on the investigation, turning it into a news piece announcing Sid's involvement and wrapping up the case.

That, they both agreed, would really be must-see TV.

They could still use the taped segments that she had planned to air, Nicky calculated, including the one they'd filmed that afternoon of her mother finding the tape, which was, of course, the catalyst to the case. How great would that be? They'd captured it live—well, live-on-tape.

"That's what we'll do, then," Nicky said to Sarah, and disconnected.

"So?" Joe was looking at her out of narrowed eyes.

"So I've got to go. We're on the air at nine." Nicky stood up again. This time the room didn't spin. Adrenaline had kicked in, and she knew she could do this. Everyone would already be on their way to the Old Taylor Place, she calculated. There was no time to arrange another venue. Anyway, that one would work. She could do everything she'd planned, then keep fifteen minutes or so at the end to describe the events of the afternoon—and announce the identity of the Lazarus Killer.

Yes.

"You're actually going through with this program?" He sounded incredulous. "Nicky, honey, you've been beaten and stabbed and nearly murdered. Get a grip. The only place you need to go is to the clinic and then to bed."

"This is my job, and I'm going to do it." She headed toward the door to the living room—and, incidentally, toward Joe, who stood between her and said door—as she spoke. He stepped into her path and caught her by the shoulders. Her brows snapped together, and she scowled up at him. "Look, I'm in a hurry here. Drop the overprotective thing, okay?"

Dave walked back into the room.

"The mayor's here," he said to Joe. "He's walking up from the street right now. Thought I'd give you a heads-up."

"Shit." Joe said, then met Nicky's gaze and sighed. "Fine. You're going to do this, I can see. You go out the front, though, and you're going to have the media all over you like ants on a picnic. Let's go out the back."

"Let's?" she asked over her shoulder, having already turned around to head for the back door. What he said made sense.

"Think I'm going to let you out of my sight? I'll drive you." He sounded resigned.

"Don't you have things to do here?"

"Lots. Nothing more important than that."

Nicky paused with her hand on the knob as the sense of that seeped into her brain. Despite the rush she was in, her heart gave a little flutter. She smiled at him.

"That's romantic," she said.

"I'm a romantic guy," he said sourly, and reached around her to open the door.

"Joe." Dave sounded alarmed. "What do I tell Vince?"

"Tell him I'll be back."

With that, Joe opened the door and they stepped out into the night. Nicky paused to bestow a quick pat on Cleo, whose velvety snout snuffling at her hand and arm seemed positively loving now, and then she and Joe slipped out the gate in the corner of the yard, did a wide circle around the crowd out front, and managed to make it to his car unseen. Only when he started the engine and turned on the lights did they attract any notice, but by then it was too late: He was pulling away down the street.

As they slowed down at the stop sign at the corner, a man came jogging out of the shadows toward them, waving at them to wait. For a moment, Nicky felt a frisson of fear, and then she remembered that the nightmare was over: The Lazarus Killer had been caught. This was a cop, she saw, as Joe got near enough so that she could identify the uniform. How safe was that?

"Bill Milton," Joe identified him to her, and rolled down his window,

"Hey, Chief, can I catch a ride?" Milton was panting with the effort of catching up to them. He leaned in the window, glancing across at Nicky, talking to Joe. "My car's blocked in back there, and I need to get to the police station. Dave said you're heading to the Old Taylor Place, and it's on the way."

"Hop in," Joe said.

Milton complied. He was still breathing hard when Joe slowed to a stop at the next intersection.

Then, without any warning at all, he slammed the butt of his gun into the back of Joe's head. Nicky was still processing the unexpected blur of action and the sharp *thunk* when Joe slumped against the wheel.

24

———

Nicky was still gaping at Joe, dumbfounded, when Milton grabbed a handful of her hair. The sudden sharp pain made her cry out. Her eyes watered.

"Put the transmission in park," Milton growled. Her eyes automatically cut toward him. She felt the cold nudge of a gun against her neck and froze. With Joe limp and, presumably, no longer putting weight on the brakes, the cruiser was just beginning to roll forward.

"Put the transmission in park," Milton screamed.

Nicky complied. The cruiser jolted to a halt.

Then something slammed hard into the back of her head and she knew no more.

A jolt of some kind of icy liquid in the face brought Joe instantly around. He blinked, coughed, and opened his eyes.

Milton was standing over him with an empty McDonald's large-sized drink cup in his hand. The contents, presumably not water because of the sweet smell and sticky feel, were running down Joe's face and neck and wetting the collar of his white dress shirt. *Sprite*, he thought, tasting the citrusy tang on his tongue.

He could live with that. Or, he thought, as the situation he was in became clearer, maybe not.

"What the *hell?*" he said to Milton in amazement as an abortive movement brought him the unwelcome news that his hands were cuffed behind his back. He was, he discovered, lying on his side on a hard, cold floor. It felt like old stone, uneven and slightly damp. He was in some kind of weird room, a basement maybe, with a wet earthen smell and uneven walls. As far as he could tell, there were no windows, and the only light came from a camp lantern dangling from a hook in the ceiling. His jacket was missing, along with, he discovered with a quick downward glance, the Glock from his shoulder holster. A yellow-and-green bungee cord was wrapped tightly around his ankles, which explained the weird tingling he was starting to become aware of in his feet.

He wasn't quite sure what was going on, but he was sure about this: It was definitely not a good thing.

"You want I should just go ahead and waste him?" Milton said over his shoulder.

"Nah. Let's see if he won't tell me where my money is first. I bet he will if we ask him real nice."

Joe knew the speaker was Vince even before the mayor stepped into the light. As Joe goggled at him, his brain had already processed the fact that this was major bad news.

"What the hell?" he said, to Vince this time.

Vince was looming over him, his shadow falling across Joe's body and the floor. Joe registered that he was dressed in the same coat-and-tie rig that he'd been wearing all day. The only difference was that now Vince was holding a gun in his hand. His arm was down at his side and the gun was pointed at the floor, but it was unmistakably there.

One more bad sign.

"I want my money, Joe," Vince said.

Joe took a breath and tried to make sense of the whole situation. It made no sense at all—except for the fact that if he didn't get out of it, he was probably going to die.

"I don't know what the hell you're talking about." His words carried the ring of truth because, hey, they were true.

"My five hundred thousand dollars," Vince explained patiently. "That you ripped off from that drug deal where you got shot. I want it back."

Joe stared at him. Something was definitely awry here.

"Wait," he said. "You were involved with that drug deal?"

"I was buying that coke, me and my organization, to bring down here and distribute. It was my money. It got confiscated, of course, along with the coke, when the bust went down. Only problem is, I found out from some of my people later that only four million, five hundred thousand dollars was logged in by the feds. *What happened to the other half mill?* I asked myself. Then I asked around. And the word came back: Right before the bust went down, a vice cop named Joe Franconi put the shakedown on my guys for ten percent of the pie. The four and a half million's gone, and I accept that as the price of doing business. But that half million you took? Uh-uh. No way. I fucking want it back."

Vince's voice hardened at the end. Joe, busy absorbing a whole bunch of information that was new to him, simply stared at him for a moment. Vince—*Vince?*—had been the money guy on that deal? Of course, the word on the street had been that the drugs were slated for the South.

And Vince was a businessman, pure and simple. He lived for making money. Fixer-upper housing, hotel complexes, drugs: They were all the same in that they were moneymakers. And where there was money to be made, there was corruption. Joe's eyes widened fractionally as it belatedly occurred to him that one of his own officers, Bill Milton, was apparently working for Vince. A dirty cop. And if there was one, there would be more. Vince, as a former vice cop himself, would know all about dirty cops.

Joe's heart began to beat faster.

"I never took your money." Joe said each word slowly and distinctly. He kept his gaze fixed on Vince, and at the same time tried to use his peripheral vision to assess his surroundings. He couldn't quite work out where he was, but he had little doubt that it was somewhere on Pawleys Island. Pawleys Island, as he saw quite clearly now, had become Vince's little fiefdom.

"I'm gonna refresh your memory one more time," Vince said, and reached into his pocket. "This look familiar?"

When Vince withdrew his hand, there was something in it. He leaned over Joe, holding the object out. It was, Joe saw, a silver cigarette lighter. Joe's eyes began to widen. . . .

"See the engraving?" Vince pointed with a stubby forefinger to the script carved into the lighter's side. "It don't say Mickey Mouse."

In fact, it said "To Joe Franconi with love from Holly Alden." Despite the iffy lighting, which made the inscription almost impossible to read, he knew, because it was his lighter, a gift from a former girlfriend.

"Just so we got things clear between us," Vince said, "I'm gonna tell you that you dropped it when you shook my boys down, and it eventually got handed back to me. So why don't you make this easy on both of us and quit with the bullshit? Tell me where my money is."

The last time he had seen the lighter was when it was being tossed up and down in Brian's hand the day before the bust went down. Suddenly, a light-bulb went on in Joe's head and everything, *everything*, fell into place. *That* was why Brian had sold him out to Martinez: to cover up the fact that Brian, probably with the use of Joe's badge and ID, had shaken down Martinez's business partners for half a million dollars. If things had worked out the way Brian had intended, by the time Martinez found out about the shakedown, Joe, the supposed perpetrator, would have been dead.

Offed by Martinez for being a fed.

And Brian would have been half a million dollars richer, with no one the wiser.

You son of a bitch, Joe said internally to Brian, not without a certain amount of admiration for the sheer ingenuity of the plan. It was simple, and *almost* brilliant—except for the fact that it had gotten Brian killed, and it looked like Joe was going to be next.

"Vince." Having by now fully internalized the fact that he was in a shit-load of trouble here, Joe got busy, mentally reviewing and discarding various options for dealing with the situation. "I never shook your guys down, I never took your half a million, I never did any of that. You got some bad information from somebody. The guy that did it was named Brian Sawyer. He must have convinced your guys he was me."

Vince looked at him. Joe could see the tightening of the other man's face, the slight flexing of the shoulders and the hands, including the one holding the gun, and accepted the fact that Vince was now his enemy and, equally important, firmly set on the course he had embarked on. Even if Joe managed to persuade Vince that he was telling the truth about not taking his money— and it *was* the truth—he was still going to die.

Unless he could manage to do something to prevent it.

"I brought you down here to the island so I could watch you," Vince said. "Didn't it ever occur to you that with your reputation, you should never have been able to get a job with another police department as long as you lived? You thought some old friends were pulling strings for you, didn't you?" He laughed. "You don't got friends that good, let me tell you. It was me wanting you that brought you here. I thought you'd go for the money sooner or later, and then we'd know where it was, and I would get it back. But you've been smart about that, I have to give you credit. Haven't touched a dime of it so far as I've been able to tell."

"That's because I don't have it. I'm telling you, you've got the wrong guy."

"What I didn't know at the time was that you were working for the DEA," Vince said, and Joe barely managed to stop himself from grimacing. Having Vince aware of that was not a positive thing. Drug dealers hated honest cops. They hated *and feared* the DEA. "Had I known it, I would have done things different, like had you whacked back in Jersey. But here you are, and here I am, and now I got no choice but to deal with the situation like it is."

Vince turned, making a sharp beckoning motion to somebody in the shadows. Joe took advantage of Vince's moment of inattention to slide his fingers down inside the right back pocket of his pants. If he was lucky . . .

He was. The last time he'd seen his handcuffs, they'd been on Sid Levin's wrists. But the key was there in his pocket. Joe had just touched it when Milton and George Locke—*Et tu, George,* he thought bitterly—lugged something out of the shadows and dumped it on the floor in the middle of the circle of light.

Nicky, eyes closed, limp as a bag of garbage, hands bound behind her back, bungee cord around her ankles, duct tape covering her mouth.

Joe broke out in a cold sweat.

SOMETHING WET and freezing cold smacked her in the face, and Nicky woke up slowly, a little groggily but enough to be aware that her head hurt and her arms ached—oh, wait, that was because they were tied behind her back. Also, her feet were asleep—ah, her ankles were bound—and there was something—duct tape?—over her mouth.

"She's got nothing to do with this," she heard Joe say in a sharp, hard tone. "This is between you and me. Let her go."

That made her open her eyes. Her face was wet, she realized, with little rivulets of liquid dripping from it onto the floor. She was cold, shivering even. The room seemed to heave for a moment as if she were lying on the deck of a ship on the high seas instead of a mildewy-smelling floor, but then her vision settled down enough that she could see that she was in some kind of old cellar or basement or something with a low ceiling, curving walls, and weird lighting. Joe was lying on his side on the floor about six feet in front of her, facing her, looking at her, his face tight with worry, his eyes dark with it. She gave him a little instinctive smile, because she was glad to see him even under the circumstances, or, as she thought about it, *especially* under the circumstances. Then she realized that she couldn't smile because of the duct tape and grimaced instead, which didn't work, either. Then she followed Joe's gaze up to discover the mayor and a couple cops, Milton and one she didn't immediately recognize, standing over her, all focused on Joe. The mayor was holding a gun, and the cop who wasn't Milton—Locke, she thought his name was; he'd followed her around a time or two and she'd thought he was a nice guy—had a pocketknife in his hand. An open pocketknife with a shining silver blade.

It wasn't a very big knife, but it was big enough to make her skin crawl. She was starting to develop a real phobia of knives.

The mayor snorted. "The hell it doesn't have anything to do with her. She's been poking her nose into stuff that doesn't concern her, stirring things up, getting all kinds of people back in Jersey upset because she and her friends just can't leave things alone. Business is up and things are going good and everything's quiet, and that's how we want it to stay. Little Miss Reporter here is making people nervous with the questions she's been asking. Now that she's found the trail, you think she's just going to let it rest? Particularly if you disappear. She'll be asking questions all over the place. Nobody wants that. Not good for business."

"If *she* disappears, people will ask all kinds of questions." Joe's voice was faintly hoarse. He sounded afraid, and the idea that Joe was afraid scared Nicky worse than anything else. "Maybe nobody much will look for me, but *her*—you're making a mistake with her. She's got family, friends, a whole damned TV audience of probably millions who will be looking for her."

"They won't have to look for her." The mayor gave Joe a smug-looking grin. "They'll find her. And you, too. Tomorrow, maybe, or in a couple of days. See, lots of people—probably even some reporters—saw you two leave your house together in your cruiser, which is what gave me the idea to do it tonight. *Carpe diem*, right? At this moment, that cruiser is sinking to the bottom of Salt Marsh Creek. You two had a tragic accident, ran right off the road, and drowned before you could get out of the car. Your bodies were washed away, and when they turn up, you'll be so decomposed, nobody will know for sure what the hell happened to you."

Nicky realized that the thudding sound she heard was the hammering of her heart.

"It won't work," Joe said. But she could tell from his tone that he thought it might. His face was hard and set, paler than she had ever seen it. He was almost on his back now, looking up at the mayor out of narrowed eyes.

"Oh, yeah," the mayor said with cool confidence. "It will. In fact, it couldn't have played out any better. I've been trying to figure out the best way to do this since Miss Reporter here started stirring the pot up in Jersey. Then tonight you gave it to me on a platter. With all the excitement because the Lazarus Killer's been caught, you two will be just a tragic footnote to a bigger story. 'Police chief and reporter killed in accident after unmasking killer.' I can almost see the headlines." He poked Nicky in the back with his foot. "Sounds like your kind of story, doesn't it?"

Nicky flinched instinctively, and as she did, her eyes fell on something small and pink and sparkling wedged in a crack in the floor. A woman's ring . . . It was so out of place that it made her frown, and then she realized that she was frowning because it niggled something deep in the recesses of her memory.

Without warning, the mayor reached down and ripped the duct tape from her mouth. The force of it yanked her head inches off the floor. The sudden sharp pain made her cry out. Joe started cursing, and made an abortive movement that was instantly stilled as the mayor pointed his gun at him.

"Goddamn you, Vince, if you hurt her . . ." Joe's voice was thick and guttural with anger.

"That's gonna be up to you." He looked at Locke and held out his hand, and the cop put the pocketknife in it. Apparently, this was a common enough practice with them that it didn't require words. Then, knife in hand, Vince shoved his gun around his back somewhere out of sight and knelt by Nicky's side.

She sucked in air. Her gaze shot to Joe. She could see sweat beading on his upper lip now. He was as helpless as she was. Her stomach twisted, cramped.

And still that ring sparkled, sparkled, worming itself into her mind. . . .

"See, here's how it's going to go down," Vince said to Joe. "I'm going to start cutting her face, and I'm going to keep cutting her face until either she has no face left or you tell me what I want to know."

"Look here," Nicky began desperately, forcing the words out through her dry, cramped throat, not sure where she was going with it but not about to just lie there in silence while she was carved up like a Thanksgiving turkey. "If all this is over just half a million dollars, maybe I can—"

Then she broke off as the memory of where she had seen that ring before struck her like a two-by-four over the head. In the picture of Lauren Schultz that was clipped to the front of her file, the teen was wearing that ring. She had just gotten it the day she disappeared, as a birthday gift from her parents.

Lauren Schultz's ring, Tara Mitchell's face cut to ribbons, Tara Mitchell's father murdered the year after she had been . . .

"Oh my God," Nicky gasped as she looked up at Vince. "You killed those girls. You killed Tara Mitchell, and Lauren Schultz, and Becky Iverson."

For a moment, Vince simply stared back at her. Then a slow smile twisted his face.

"She's smart," he said in an approving tone, glancing at Joe. "Real smart. Yeah, the Mitchell girl's dad ripped me off, too. I had to send a message. The other girls—well, they were there in the house. They weren't part of the message, so we brought them down here."

So many years, so much loss, so much pain—that he could dismiss those bright, young lives snuffed out, the anguish to the parents, the years spent searching, with little more than a shrug sent flames of fury shooting through Nicky's veins. Before she thought, she spat in his face.

For a moment, the world seemed to stop. Everything, time itself, seemed to freeze. The spittle had only reached his chin, and Vince stared down at her with widening eyes as he seemed to register its presence. Then realization hit and his face contorted. With a roar of rage, he reared back . . .

And a gun exploded, loud as a bomb in that enclosed space.

Vince shrieked and fell back.

"Roll against the wall, Nicky," Joe screamed, and in the split second it took her to hear and obey, she saw that he was lying on his stomach, unbound hands stretched out before him clutching a pistol, taking two-handed aim . . .

As she rolled, more bullets exploded as the bad guys started shooting back.

Then she was against the wall, huddled as tight against the cold, hard stone as she could get, screaming, eyes closed, ears ringing, nostrils filling with the acrid smell of gunfire as bullets smacked into rock all around her and then ricocheted around the walls like deadly pinballs with whistling screams that echoed her own. Joe, somehow totally free now, crouched over her, snapping off shots.

A man yelled, "Shut the door! Leave 'em!" and she thought it was Vince, but she was too scared to look around to make sure, and then there was the clang of metal on metal and, finally, silence.

Eerie, echoing silence.

"Are you okay?" Joe asked after a moment, sounding breathless. He was moving, doing something with her handcuffs. Even as she nodded yes, she heard a tiny metallic click and then her hands were free.

That caused her eyes to pop open.

"How?" she asked, daring to move, sitting up and chafing her wrists and staring at Joe, who was now unfastening the cord around her ankles.

"I had a handcuff key in my pocket." He grinned at her as the cord came off, and it struck her that he was looking all cocky and sure of himself and full of himself—in a totally sexy, charming way, of course, because this was Joe, and sexy and charming was what he did. She could tell that he was giving himself a big mental "Attaboy," and that made her smile because it was clear that at heart, her big, bad cop was still just a little kid.

"The gun?" she asked.

His grin broadened. "I always keep a spare for emergencies." Then he pulled up his trouser leg to show her the holster strapped around his ankle. "Just thank your lucky stars nobody ever taught these guys the right way to do a pat-down."

Nicky had to admit it: She was impressed.

"Wow," she said.

"You can thank me properly later." He met her eyes with a glint in his that left her in no doubt about what he had in mind. Then he stood, pulled her up and said, "Let's get out of here."

Oh, yeah.

Only they couldn't, as they discovered within minutes. Six running steps in the opposite direction from which Vince and company had taken, and they were in a passage, a narrow, cavelike passage. A passage that was closed off with an iron door. An iron door with a mesh peephole the size of a schoolkid's notebook near the top of it. As they approached the door, water started gushing through the peephole, spilling down the door like a waterfall, splashing on the floor. Puddling on the floor. Pooling on the floor.

"Shit," Joe said, staring at it.

Nicky tugged at his hand. "Let's try the other way."

They retraced their steps, racing through the chamber that widened off the passage like the bulge of prey in a snake's belly, only to narrow again into another passage—that ended in another door. A door without a peephole. A locked iron door. A locked iron door with the lock on the other side.

"Shit," Joe said again, bestowing one final kick on it as all efforts to open it proved futile.

Nicky was starting to think that that was the understatement of the century.

She turned and looked back the way they had come as the rushing sound of water filled her ears.

That was when she faced the awful truth: They were locked in an underground passage that was rapidly filling with water.

Only dignity and a total wish not to humiliate herself in front of Joe kept her from clapping both hands to her cheeks and screaming "We're all gonna die!"

But she didn't. She took a deep breath and tried to think.

"There has to be some way out of here," he said. His face was grim. Clearly, his thought processes had more or less mirrored her own. He was looking at the ceiling, feeling the walls. . . .

She could hear the water hissing and splattering as it poured in through the peephole. Soon it would reach them. . . .

Cold, dark water. The stuff of her worst nightmare.

Her heart was beating in sharp little slamming strokes against her breastbone. Her breathing was fast, erratic. Her hands were cold and clammy, and panic, pure panic, was shutting down her brain.

Please, God, please, God, please, God . . .

Suddenly, it hit her.

"I think I know where we are," she said. He looked at her questioningly. She clasped her freezing hands together in sudden excitement. "I always heard stories about this place, but as far as I know no one—except Vince and his crew, obviously—really thought it existed. It's a tunnel that was once part of the Underground Railroad. It's supposed to run from Salt Marsh Creek under some of the old houses. Harry's a Civil War buff, you know, and I've heard him talk about it." Her voice faltered. "If it's underground, and its entrance is somewhere on the bank of Salt Marsh Creek, I bet it floods when the tide rises."

"Great." Joe looked a whole lot less excited than she felt. "That leaves just one question: How the hell do we get out of here?"

Nicky's bubble burst as it occurred to her that just because she had figured out where they were, that didn't necessarily mean they were saved.

"I don't know," she confessed. "But there's got to be a way."

The door was clearly impassable. Even shooting the lock off was impossible because, as Joe pointed out when she suggested this to him, it was on the other side. Meanwhile, trickles of water were starting to run past their feet.

"There's got to be some kind of ventilation shaft," Joe muttered as Nicky fought back panic. "It's too dry down here for there not to be." He grabbed her hand. "Come on."

She ran with him back into the snake's-belly-bulge chamber, which was now ankle deep with cold water that just kept spilling in through the door.

"Look up," Joe yelled, and she did. The ceiling was in bad shape, with roots poking through the stone in places and dirt only in other places, where the stones were missing. She was so busy looking up, in fact, that she would have missed the stone in the wall with the writing on it if a strand of her hair hadn't snagged on a jagged corner of it. She glanced around to free herself and saw the primitive letters carved deep into the rock: JOSIAH TAYLOR, 1863.

For a moment, she simply stared at it as the water rose around her calves and all kinds of thoughts—from *Please, God, don't let me die this way* to *Ohmigod, that was written by somebody standing right where I am almost a hundred and fifty years ago during the Civil War*—ran through her brain.

Then the surname Taylor registered, and, at the same time, she saw the little brass tube protruding from the crumbled mortar above the stone. It had a wad of filthy cloth wedged in it. She pulled the cloth out and stuck her fingers in the tube. It led both up toward the driveway and sideways, parallel with the passage. Even as she realized that, several things became clear simultaneously: One, they had to be under, or near, the Old Taylor Place, because this passage almost certainly had to end in its cellar; and, two, the shape of the tunnel, at least as far as she could tell, closely followed the driveway; and, three, that being the case, and given that Karen had been walking down the driveway when she had been attacked, it was probable that this tube, which Nicky recognized as a speaking tube, had carried Karen's screams inside the house, where they had provided the ghostly finale for Leonora's first appearance on *Twenty-four Hours Investigates.*

The corollary thoughts came lightning-fast: There would be people inside the Old Taylor Place tonight—her crew—waiting for her, probably frantically trying to locate her by now, as they prepared to film the live-at-nine version of the show.

Water was rushing in faster, swirling around Nicky's knees, rising. Her feet and calves were already numb, her jeans were soaked to the crotch, and she was freezing. She glanced down at the dark surface of the water. Terror made her dizzy. Her heart pounded. Her breath rattled in her throat like a dying man's.

"Help!" she screamed into the tube, praying that she was right, that somebody could hear. A few feet away, Joe let loose with a startled "What the hell?" which was apparently provoked by her sudden screech, but that didn't even slow her down. "It's Nicky! Joe and I are trapped in a tunnel under the driveway! It's flooding! There's a door in the cellar! Come and let us out!"

"What are you doing?" Joe was beside her now, looking at her as if he feared that she had lost her mind.

"I'm pretty sure it's a speaking tube," she told him urgently. "People used them to communicate with their servants and whoever a long time ago. I think you can hear it inside the Old Taylor Place, and I think that explains the screams that we heard the night Karen was murdered: It must have an outlet up near the pine trees, probably so whoever was helping the escaping slaves could talk to them through it." A thought occurred to her. "Do you think the mayor and his friends are still hanging around?"

The possibility that the bad guys might hear their cries and come back made every tiny hair on her body leap to prickling life.

"They should be long gone," Joe said. "Vince was scheduled to be at a press conference to announce the capture of the Lazarus Killer at nine." He glanced at his watch. "It's eight-thirty-five now."

Live at nine, she thought, registering that *Twenty-four Hours Investigates* was scheduled to start in twenty-five minutes and she wasn't there. Then came the newsflash from her overburdened brain: As far as live TV was concerned, "dead reporter" was worse than "dead air."

"Here, let me do that, my voice is stronger than yours," Joe said, and moved her aside to put his mouth to the tube. He, too, started to yell.

Meanwhile, the water kept rising faster and faster.

"We can't stay here," Joe said as it finally swirled up past Nicky's waist. She knew he was right, but she hated to abandon the speaking tube, which seemed to her like their only hope. But the passage sloped upward, and the door without the peephole was on higher ground. Clutching Joe's hand, and almost losing her footing several times in the swirling water, Nicky sloshed with him toward the passageway.

By the time they got to the door, the water was only knee-deep.

"Oh, God," Nicky said, staring back in dread at the filling chamber behind them. "How long do you think it'll take to reach us?"

The answer was, obviously, not long. The water, which had been knee-deep minutes before, was already creeping up her thighs.

Joe was doing his best to kick the door down. It didn't even budge.

As the water rose, fear was replaced by horror. The thing she had always feared the most was going to kill her. She was going to drown—in cold, dark water. . . .

And Joe, too. She could hardly stand that. Knowing that he was going to drown with her made it ten times worse.

He was right beside her, leaning against the door, panting, resting as he paused from throwing his weight against it. It was a futile effort, she knew, but she honored him for making it, for trying to save them. . . .

The look on her face must have been a study in fear and sorrow, because he reached out and pulled her into his arms. With the freezing water swirling around her waist, she wrapped her arms around his neck and buried her face against his shoulder. She could feel his mouth against her hair.

"I love you," she said fiercely, because she wanted him to know before they died. "Love you, love you, love you."

"I love you, too," she thought she heard him say, but she couldn't be sure because his voice was drowned out by the clang of metal on metal. Nicky straightened with excitement as it became clear that the bolt was being drawn on the other side of the door.

Then the door opened, and she and Joe, along with a tremendous surge of water that almost knocked them off their feet, went through it.

"Sorry it took so long," Gordon gasped, "but we couldn't find the door in the cellar."

Nicky looked past him to see Bob, Tina, Cassandra, Mario, Isabelle, Dave, her mother, and a whole crowd of other people clogging the passage.

Then they ran to escape the still-rising water.

"Nicky," Isabelle said urgently over the cacophony of voices as they made it up a set of steps and into the safety of the Old Taylor Place's cellar, "we've got six minutes until you're supposed to be on the air."

This time, Nicky reflected as the door was slammed behind them and she paused to lean against the nearest wall and pant for air, she was just thankful to have the chance to *be* live at nine.

"Okay," she said, straightening. "Let's do it."

EPILOGUE

———

A WEEK LATER, it was one more beautiful day in paradise. The sun was shining, the birds were singing, and the locals were out in force. It was just after nine A.M., and Joe stood at the curb in front of his house with Nicky beside him, waving, as Dave pulled away from the curb in a candy-red convertible Corvette with Cleo sitting in the passenger seat beside him. The two of them had come to say good-bye because this was Joe's last day as a permanent resident of the island. Two weeks from now, he would be back in Jersey—Newark, to be precise—in his new job as an agent for the DEA.

It was funny how much respect busting the biggest drug ring on the East Coast got you.

It worked for Dave, too. He was the new Police Chief. The town was still searching for a new mayor.

In fact, it was good news all around. According to Nicky, Leonora had her groove back. Now that the danger to her daughters was past, she was seeing spirits right and left. Livvy was on a roll, too. She was happily divorcing her cheating husband and planning to embrace life as a single mother. She was also planning to work as a hostess in Ham's restaurant, which would have its grand opening the following month.

Joe and Nicky would be back for that.

Oh, yeah, and that was the other thing. He and Nicky were definitely in a relationship. In fact, they were traveling north together. Driving. Making a vacation out of it. See, she was moving to New York City, because she'd been offered the job she wanted. *Live in the Morning* had called the morning following her last *Twenty-four Hours Investigates* broadcast to offer her the job. They had, they said, been impressed.

New Jersey and New York were only separated by a river. And he and Nicky both had to apartment-hunt when they got there. Who knew how that would work out?

"I think we're ready," Nicky said to him, when Dave and Cleo were out of sight. They had been loading their car, a rented Lincoln, with the last of the stuff from his house, and were standing beside the trunk at that moment.

"Good enough." He looked at her, at the glorious red hair shining in the sun and the beautiful face and figure and, most of all, the warmth in her eyes as she smiled at him, and he thought, *Oh, yeah, this is definitely a woman to keep.* "I love you, you know."

Her smile widened into a grin.

"Careful," she said. "You never know. I might just read a commitment into that."

Okay, he could handle it.

Just to prove it, he bent his head and kissed her. Then he went inside, walking quickly through the house.

And there, in the kitchen, he encountered Brian, leaning against a counter, big as life.

Or not.

Joe stopped and glared at him. "Well, look who it is. Long time no see. My guardian fucking angel."

"Hey," Brian said. "I saved your life."

"Saved my life? I already knew you shot me, you asshole. What I didn't know was that you ripped off half a million dollars, then set me up to take the fall."

"Notice you're alive?" Brian crossed his arms over his chest. "Notice I'm dead? Looks to me like it worked out for you. Anyway, the reason you're not dead is I deliberately didn't kill you. It was all part of the plan."

"*What?*"

"Yeah," Brian said. "Okay, I ran a little scam and set you up to take the heat. But half a million dollars, Joe! Jesus, who could resist? I admit, I sold you out to Martinez. But, see, I knew all along he'd tell me to whack you, because that was the way he operated. Whoever brought you in took you out if the need arose. So I was prepared. I just eased those bullets alongside your head, nothing fatal at all. I knew he'd tell me to get rid of the body, too, so I figured I'd haul you out of there in one of those big garbage cans, and then we'd ease on down the road with half a million dollars to split when you recovered."

Joe narrowed his eyes. "You expect me to believe that?"

Brian held up his hand. "Hey, it's God's honest truth. You ever known a guardian angel to lie?"

Okay, so Brian had him there.

"Anyway, I'm outta here." Brian straightened away from the counter. "I'm through with the guardian-angel bit. You won't be seeing me again." He seemed to reflect. "At least, as long as you're alive."

"Wait a minute. Where's the half a million dollars?"

Brian grinned at him. "Remember that cave in the woods behind the cottage where I used to hide my stash?"

Joe nodded. "Yeah."

"It's in there. Use it in good health. Have a nice life, pal."

And then, just like that, he was gone—vanished into thin air.

Not that Joe considered it any big loss.

He heard the impatient honking of a horn outside. Time to go.

"Have a nice life," Brian had said. As he let himself out the door for the last time, Joe reflected that that was just exactly what he intended to do.

For him, a nice life could be summed up in three words: Nicky. Marriage. Kids.

As for the half a million dollars? He was going to go look in the cave, and if it was there, he was going to do the right thing and turn it in.

Probably.

Grinning to himself, Joe walked across the yard and got in the Lincoln beside Nicky. Then he started the car and pulled away from the curb.

Good-bye, paradise; hello, Jersey.

It definitely worked for him.